The Withered Realm: Inheritance

Brittany M. York

For Brian

Thank you for being the best husband and father,
for never saying no to my wild ideas,
and for believing in me.
I couldn't have done this without your support.

Contents

Chapter 1

Arine anxiously drummed her fingers against the tree limb, eyes shifting between the gap in the foliage and the sun sliding toward the horizon. Maybe she'd been rash. Maybe she'd gambled too much. But she couldn't afford to think that now, not when every wasted minute could be her father's last.

His sunken cheeks and trembling hands flashed unbidden in her mind. She clenched her teeth and shook her head, forcing the image away as she steadied her breathing. She scooted a little lower on the branch for a better view, making sure to move quietly, just as she'd been taught.

There was a bite to the air, but the tree's dense canopy still held its leaves, giving her plenty of cover to watch the stranger below. He set up camp, spreading his bedroll and tending the fire—nothing out of the ordinary. It felt odd to spy on him, but meeting another person during this absurd Pillar test was almost never heard of. Killian Forest was vast enough that few ever crossed paths by chance, so curiosity kept her rooted to her spot.

Her throat tightened. Had she veered off course? She shook the thought away, gripping the rough bark beneath her fingers, clinging to the certainty that she still knew which way led back to the Capital. She needed to pass this test.

Arine remembered the overseeing professor and his dismissive attitude when she had opted into the survival trial without taking any classes. He had clearly thought she would be dead within a few days. He had inspected her possessions, and then dumped her, hands and feet bound, in a remote part of the Forest to fend for herself until she either made it back alive...or didn't. That was the entirety of the test the King had devised to determine whether someone deserved a future in his Kingdom. A real future, at least. Not the life of a bent-backed peasant clawing for scraps.

She could still feel the terror from that first night. The sun had gone down while she was still trussed up in the overseer's extra-tight knots, her wrists rubbed raw from struggling. Hours bled away before she finally wriggled free, heart pounding with every sound in the dark. Four weeks had passed since then—or was it more? Time blurred together. Hunger gnawed at her so often she barely registered the ache anymore. But hunger was only part of it. She shivered at the memory of scrambling through treetops in the dark to escape a pack of Timber wolves, nearly falling more than once as they howled and snapped below.

She pushed the thoughts away, refocusing on the stranger. The angle of the sun was casting even longer shadows across his camp as he went about his business with a practiced ease. His light red-brown hair and stubble-marked face showed him to only be a few years older than her. His age and clothes made her more inclined to assume that he was here for the same test as herself. If he was hiding out or in league with criminals, she would think he would have looked more worn down. Teaming up with him would make life easier—they could share watches and take turns hunting, and generally have a little less stress overall...if she could trust him.

She studied the stranger's movements for any sign of illness or reason he might have been cast out, but nothing seemed unusual. He arranged his bedroll on top of a pile of gathered leaves and all of a sudden, the sharp scent of singed feathers hit her. Arine's stomach clenched at the smell of fresh pheasant, and her fingers twitched against the tree. It had been days since she'd eaten anything more filling than berries and stringy roots.

He had even selected a nice site for his camp. It was protected on one side by a ravine, with a sheer drop. Large rocks lined the edge, the sun glinting off their surfaces. She squinted as she surveyed the small cluster of pines to the side that gave him shelter from the wind, their needles whispering in the fading light.

Arine's chest tensed as she realized how low the sun had fallen. She'd watched him far longer than she'd meant to—too long, since she hadn't even found her own campsite yet. She sighed, knowing she'd have to find her own place to hide. Her gaze lingered on his tidy, sheltered spot, imagining how much easier the night would be there.

The thought of it made her lean forward towards the man again. What if they could team up? She didn't recognize him, but that wasn't surprising. She hadn't known any of the participants; she'd opted not to waste time in preparation classes. Arine wasn't like some of the others—she didn't have time to waste, and her father had already taught her more skills than any bored, old teacher could. Besides, the overseers looked like they were there against their will anyway. Probably punishment for failing to please the King in some way.

His clothes weren't anything special, but they were warmer than hers. He could be from one of the wealthy families who already had enough 'status' for a good life. They forced their children to participate just for bragging rights, already secure with medicine and the higher occupations the test provided.

Arine tensed, ready to call out, but her breath caught. She could still feel the guards' hands shoving her aside, the weight of their sneering glances pressing her into the cobblestones as they threatened imprisonment for just asking to buy medicine. No. Not again. Trust was too dangerous.

Even though the man didn't seem to radiate any kind of evil tendencies, in the end she just couldn't take the risk. For all she knew, this could be one of those flesh traders she'd heard rumors of in the city, spewing honeyed words in the daylight, a knife in the dark. She wasn't going to be that easy to catch. At least she only had animals to worry about right now. Plus, she had to be close to getting out any day now, and she'd do it on her own.

Decision made, Arine shimmied backwards out of her hiding place as the man tossed a couple more sticks on his fire, the crackling masking her move-ment. She gathered up the rest of her belongings and took off quietly South, needing to put some distance between her and the stranger before night descended.

Once at a safe distance, she jogged to make up for the wasted time, though this part of the forest was tangled with roots and underbrush. At least the fallen leaves lying in thick, damp piles helped muffle her footsteps. The crisp scent of autumn filled the air, smelling earthy and rich as she ran.

Hopefully, seeing the stranger meant she was right in thinking she was close to the edge of the forest. They couldn't both be going the wrong way and she needed to get out quickly to check on her father and make sure he hadn't gotten worse. The habitable land shrinking was one thing, but at least there were tangible things to do to combat it. The deadly illness that slowly turned you into a husk of yourself was something else entirely. There was no fighting it, no clear enemy to strike down. It crept through villages like an invisible specter, draining the life from its victims bit by bit until they were nothing more than shadows of themselves.

Arine had seen it firsthand. Just over a year ago, her father fell ill and no longer responded to the village herbs. Desperate, she had journeyed to the capital of Calasis to buy medicine. Her jaw clenched at the memory: despite begging and offering every coin she owned, every doctor in Draske still turned her away. The King had passed a law, sending healers to their deaths for providing medicine to patients who didn't have a certain status by birth, title, or decree.

The message was clear. Only status determined your value.

Arine used the bitterness from the memories to fuel her tired limbs as she pushed through the underbrush, searching for a place to camp. Every step sent a flurry of leaves scattering, the reds and oranges swirling around her like embers from a dying fire. As she ran, her mind circled back to the stranger...had she made the right decision avoiding him? Should she worry about others being nearby? What did it mean? The uncertainty gnawed at her, an uncomfortable weight pressing in on her chest. She hated not knowing if she had chosen wisely.

Her thoughts continued to swirl inside her, distracting her from seeing the loose pine needles until her boot crushed them. She tried to catch herself, but it was too late—before she could even call out, she tumbled into a dark pit, hidden under the carefully arranged needles and leaves.

Her arms pinwheeled as she scrabbled at the wall, trying to grab anything to break her fall. Her fingers closed on a thick vine, burning her hand and straining her arms. But her grip wasn't strong enough, and her fingers slipped through. Arine hit the ground with a large thud, her pack smashing beneath her. She lay on the ground, chest heaving and breath burning, as she tried to wrap her mind around what had just happened.

When her lungs finally obeyed her again, she gingerly flexed her limbs. Dull aches ran along her spine and neck, but nothing was broken. The vine must have caught enough of her weight to save her from worse. As she got her bearings, she realized how deep the pit truly was.. Fear coursed through her as she realized it was about fifteen feet wide, and the edge was well above her. She could barely see the darkening sky above. It was clearly meant to trap a large predator, perhaps a thornback bear.

Her pulse thundered in her ears. Arine forced herself to stand, to move, to *do* something, before the panic sealed her in place. Her palms scraped along the pit walls, desperate for anything that would hold her weight. She found roots nestled in the dirt wall from surrounding trees and she pulled at them, feeling their strength. Most were fairly thick and didn't break when she tested her full weight, so she started to pull herself up.

She made it a few feet, now level with where her head had been, before the vine she was holding snapped. She fell back down to the earthen floor, the wind knocked out of her once again. When she could breathe again, she didn't even give herself time to think about failing; she started climbing again. Every time she fell, she edged left to try a new path, hoping one would lead to the top. She ground her teeth and shoved any whispering doubts aside. She would not even allow a hint of failure to creep into her thoughts.

After the fifth fall, sweat stung her eyes and slicked her grip. Her arms trembled from the effort, her chest tight with panic she didn't dare name. Every fiber of her body screamed at her to stop—but she wouldn't. She removed her pack, tied a rope around it, and secured it to her waist. She prayed the lighter weight would help the vines hold her. After wiping the sweat off her palms, she started again.

When Arine was halfway up, she let herself hope. The removal of her pack was working; she slowly made more progress than she had before. She edged closer and closer to the top, not daring to think of all the broken bones she'd endure if she ended up falling again. Every time she tested out a new vine, determining which would balance her weight, her heart practically beat out of her chest.

Finally, she was just barely out of reach of the ledge. Two more good vines and she would be able to put her chest over. She took a deep breath and grabbed the largest one she could find. She pulled herself upwards, grunting as she reached for the vine right below the edge, the final leverage needed for the remaining inches. She tried to hoist herself up, pulling herself closer and closer, but as soon as her fingers closed on it, the vine snapped. Arine was weightless for a moment, falling backward towards the bottom of the pit, her fingers unable to find anything solid to grab. She closed her eyes to brace for the impact when her arm suddenly jerked hard and she slammed into the side of the wall.

She gasped, snapping her eyes open and saw the man from the clearing holding onto her outstretched hand, straining to keep her from falling. Her arm was almost pulled out of the socket as it supported her weight.

"Grab something," he grunted as he struggled to keep hold of her hand.

Suppressing her surprise, she scrambled for anything to grip with her other arm. Her fingers frantically closed on another vine. She latched onto it and helped pull herself up as he dragged her from his end. His muscles bulged from the exertion as he finally managed to pull her out.

She knelt at the edge, trembling as the adrenaline drained, leaving her lightheaded. It was almost hard for her to believe that she wasn't going to fall back down at any moment.

Once she caught her breath, she glanced over at the man who had just saved her. He looked the same as when she had watched him earlier. His bright green eyes studied her as he patiently waited a few feet away, as if he was intentionally trying to be unthreatening. Realizing she was staring, she managed a rushed 'Thank you' and began pulling her pack up by the attached rope.

"I don't know how you happened to be nearby in time to help me, but I appreciate it. Another fall and I might have been lost in that hole forever." She said as she suppressed a shiver at the thought of lying broken at the bottom, starving in the dark.

But then another thought struck her, how had he known she was here? She'd crept away without a sound. She kept him in her line of sight as she pulled her pack the rest of the way out, not taking any chances.

"Of course. Are you hurt anywhere?" he asked, sounding genuinely concerned. "That pit is no joke. I'm actually surprised you were able to climb most of it yourself."

He spoke with a slightly northern accent she couldn't quite place, but that wasn't surprising since people came to the Pillar from all over Calasis. He didn't seem dangerous, but she did notice he ignored her question of his timing.

He continued to keep his distance while she finished packing her rope away. His stance was easy, but her eyes caught the glint of steel. He had a bow slung over his back, a sword at his hip, knives criss-crossed over his chest. But he had no pack or supplies. Her stomach tightened. Was he expecting something, or had he known she was there all along?

She kept her tone calm and friendly. There was no use in alerting him to her suspicions. "No, luckily there were no stakes and no broken bones. Just a little pain to my pride for missing the trap in the first place, I guess. How did you know I was in there anyway? There is likely not another person within miles of us."

"A mountain lion has been sniffing around my camp for a couple nights. I found this pit and hung some bait above before stopping for the night." He motioned to the canopy above and Arine's eyes followed to see a dead pheasant hanging down. She had to swallow another hit to her pride at not seeing the obvious lure. "I heard some noise so I came to investigate and that's when I found you."

Heat crept up her neck, and her fingers fumbled nervously with her pack straps. How had she been so oblivious? She wanted nothing more than to hurry away before he could see how flustered she felt.

"Well, thank you again, but I need to get going," she said with one last quick glance at him.

She quickly skirted the edge of the pit, mind spinning with what she needed to do. She had wasted even more precious time from her foolish misstep and now had to find a spot far from the bear pit and this mountain lion, for that matter too. The fading light barely pierced through the foliage now. It cast long, twisting shadows making it even harder to see.

"Wait!" The man yelled just as she was about to disappear into the trees.

She honestly didn't know why she stopped.She knew she should put as much space between them as she could, and she knew she couldn't trust anyone. Still, something in his voice made her pause. She turned back to where he was standing, waiting to see what he would do.

"Where will you go?" he asked, taking a step toward her as if knowing she might run away at any moment. "You clearly haven't made camp for the night, and it's dark. You can join mine—it's not far." He gestured back in the direction of where Arine had first stumbled upon him.

She told herself she should keep going—that nothing had changed, and all the same reasons still applied. But a small, weary part of her ached for him to be what he seemed. Just once, she wanted to rest without watching her back.

"I have some leftover pheasant from this afternoon. I don't mind sharing," he said, watching her weigh her options.

The memory of the cooked meat nearly made her mouth water again. She tried to keep her expression even, but he must have noticed.

"I've had plenty of luck hunting lately, so I won't miss it. If you'd rather starve, that's fine too. But wandering in the dark seems far more dangerous. There's the mountain lion, for one. And other traps you might not see until it's too late."

"Ah yes, so my choice should obviously be to go to your camp where your mountain lion will be expecting you so we can both become its next meal then?"

she replied finally, half-joking. She glanced back into the forest, trying not to imagine any of its other foul beasts lurking just out of sight.

"I didn't take you for someone afraid of cats," he called and her eyes flicked back to him at the jibe.

Arine saw the hint of a smile touch his mouth before he masked it. She couldn't help but lower a part of her guard at the joke. Besides, he hadn't so much as flinched toward a weapon.

Making a split decision, she wheeled around. "Okay, if you insist, I will. Lead the way," she said, motioning him forward and surprising even herself with the change of heart.

They walked in silence along a path that ran parallel to the one she'd taken a few hours earlier. Arine watched him out of the corner of her eye as he moved, his every step measured. His eyes scanned the trees encircling them, always alert, as if expecting the cat to emerge from the dark at any moment.

She could feel the weight of the night settling in around them, and a sudden shiver ran down her spine. She reminded herself that if that cat hadn't attacked when he was alone, it was unlikely to do so now with them together. She was suddenly very glad he had found her in time to help her out of the hole. She would have been easy prey even with all her bones intact.

Once they got back to his camp, he handed her the leftover pheasant, as promised. She realized just how hungry she was when she devoured it, only able to mumble a thank you around a mouthful.

As she ate, he unstrapped his weapons on the other side of the fire. He didn't pay her much mind at all, and as time wore on, she relaxed. She realized she was probably treating him unfairly, even if she had every right to be suspicious. He had saved her from that pit and now fed her when neither had been expected of him.

He was a bit of a puzzle, really. People didn't help without a price. At least, not the ones she'd known. The memory of cold refusals and slammed doors flickered behind her ribs. She had seen the worst of humanity as the land withered and food, medicine, and other necessities grew scarce. The new laws the King had passed didn't help either, further widening the gap between the poor and the royal class. She had been raised in a small town outside the Capital, so she hadn't thought much about the King or his policies before. There had been no need when her father was well. Besides, Tyvin had always warned her of the dangers of Draske and its people.

So the fact that a complete stranger—maybe even someone of the upper class—was helping her was something she couldn't make sense of. She definitely wasn't going to give away anything about herself that could be used against her until she figured out his motives. She could, she supposed though, be civil. So when he shifted his bedroll to make room for hers on the other side of the fire, she cleared her throat.

"Thank you again," she said. "I appreciate your help, and if I'm able to repay it in the future, I will. For now, I don't mind taking a longer watch and keeping an eye out for your friend, so you can get some rest."

He was silent for a few moments before responding. "Splitting the watch will be useful, so I'll gladly take that as repayment. The cat usually comes sniffing around just before midnight, so keep a sharp eye then. My name's Ciran, by the way."

He came over and held out his hand. Arine forced down her initial reaction to move further away and instead held out her own hand to shake his.

"Mine's Arine. I will wake you if I hear anything, but you should get some rest while you can. You know the sooner we get out of this forest, the better. I'm sure you have reasons to finish this test just like I do."

He nodded and returned to his bedroll, promptly rolling over and falling asleep. She envied how quickly his breathing evened out. He seemed utterly unconcerned that she might murder him in his sleep.

She settled back against the tree, her eyes heavy but fixed on the darkened forest. Moonlight filtered through swaying branches, and the cool air carried the faint scent of pine. The trees loomed around her, their limbs creaking in the wind. A pair of squirrels skittered across the branches, tails flicking as they chattered in sharp, quick bursts. Silence stretched between those sounds, broken only by a rustle of leaves or the distant hoot of an owl.

She stayed awake well past midnight, while Ciran slept peacefully. When he rolled over a few hours into her watch, she finally had the chance to study him without fear of being caught.

She had to admit he had a strong face. His hair was cut short, which was the fashion right now, and he had a small scar on his right cheek. His plain, sturdy clothes hadn't frayed the way hers had. Even his pack was well-made and reinforced, speaking of someone who hadn't gone without.

His family must have sent him here to make a name for themselves. Her father, Tyvin, had told her the King kept the royals in constant rivalry, each vying for influence and clawing for ways to stand out. The better for the King to control them. The continuous need to watch your back and ruthlessness were one of the big reasons he had always told her to stay away from Draske. She wondered if once he got better, he would be mad that she had disobeyed him.

After all, when she returned and claimed the title of Graduate, she would rub shoulders with the people he had always warned her against. Once her name was entered in the official record, she would immediately gain the higher level 'status'. That status would not only let her finally obtain the medicine her father needed, but also open doors: high-level scribe, merchant's apprentice, even an officer in the royal army. She would have proven her ability to survive in brutal conditions—the only trait the King valued.

Maybe Ciran hadn't been raised in Draske. Maybe he'd spent more time beyond its suffocating walls. Or maybe he was simply better at hiding it, she thought, her wariness returning. She continued to ponder it until she finally roused him, long after midnight, so she could grab a few hours of sleep herself before dawn, never having seen a sign of any big cats lurking.

Chapter 2

S he woke to the soft rustling of Ciran packing up his supplies, the crisp scent of dry leaves drifting through the cool morning air. Soft rays of golden light filtered through the trees, casting dappled patterns across the forest floor. She stretched, sat up, and rubbed the sleep from her eyes as the forest stirred around them.

"Good morning," Ciran called cheerfully when he noticed she was awake.

"Morning," she replied and started to pack up her things.

"There's a small stream nearby where we can fill our waterskins before heading out. With two of us, one can lead while the other watches for game," he said as they got ready to go.

Arine nodded, already picturing their next hot meal together, even if it was built only on a single night of trust. She buckled on her weapons and followed him to the stream. Once she had her waterskin filled and hair tied back, they started off retracing the path from the night before. She took the lead pushing through the underbrush while Ciran diligently scanned the vast sea of towering trees around them for any sign of small animals.

When they passed the bear pit where Arine had fallen, she paused. In daylight, it seemed even deeper, its edges lined with loose soil and torn roots. She wasn't sure how she had survived the first fall without serious injury. As it was, she could already feel the nasty bruises forming on her back and side.

The foliage became denser around mid-morning, forcing her and Ciran to cut through it in some places. When she was clearing away a particularly thick set of bushes that were growing between a group of cedar trees, she saw the leaves on one side were starting to turn. Her breath caught and she pushed through roughly to get closer. It wasn't just a trick of the light or typical fall color changes; the leaves on the tree were turning gray.

The rot had reached this area of Killian Forest. It was spreading more than anyone realized. The gray leaves trembled in the breeze, already flaking at the edges. In a year, she knew, this place would be dust, another territory claimed by the Decayed Lands. She pressed a hand to the bark as if she could keep it alive a little longer.

Arine's face must have betrayed her thoughts because Ciran paused his own hacking and came up beside her. His eyes were drawn to the same spot of wrongness and he started to examine the tree.

"Have you seen this in other parts of the forest?" he asked uneasily, looking around as if the trees might crumble at any moment.

"No. As far as I am aware this is as far east as it's ever been. Do you think we are in danger of contracting the sickness?"

Arine immediately began assessing herself. She was tired and hungry, but otherwise felt the same. She shoved down the worry and squared her shoulders. She wasn't sick, she couldn't get sick. Her father was counting on her.

Ciran shook his head. "That's not how it works. If that were the case, we would all get sick from our proximity to those already afflicted. I think the loss of magic is compounded every moment that it remains severed from the land, making it get worse, faster and faster. But the way it affects us and the land won't change."

He plucked the leaf from the tree and rolled it between his fingers, watching it disintegrate. She studied the remnants left in his palm. It wasn't the same as when the leaves turned in the fall. That was life and death as it should be. This was death as it should not be, a premature end to life that will never come back again. This was the slow extinction of everything. She knew it in her core.

"Do you remember what it was like before?" she asked, the words slipping out before she could stop herself. She knew better than most how sensitive the subject of the Severing could be.

"No," he said slowly. "I was too young. My father told me about it, but it's hard to imagine."

"A world where wielders made artifacts, no one starved, and the land itself wasn't trying to kill you. Yeah, definitely hard to imagine," she replied bitterly.

Ciran raised an eyebrow at her words, his expression turning guarded. "From what I hear, it wasn't all sunshine and rainbows. The Wielders War took many lives."

Arine immediately regretted her impulsiveness. "I'm sorry, I shouldn't have said that...or asked about the past. I wasn't thinking." Her words tumbled out in a rush.

She didn't know why she had done that. She barely knew him, and no one had escaped the Severing unscathed—herself included. All because of one man's greed. Vanin, the rebel leader, had gathered wielders who saw themselves as nature's chosen, superior to non-wielders, and rose against the King. It was strange to think of the King fighting on the right side, but she supposed even he had his moments.

They said Vanin was winning until someone—no one knew who—made the decision to sever magic from the world. Whoever it was hadn't saved the world. They'd only broken it in a different way, cutting off anyone who had been able to wield magic. It killed the most powerful wielders—or drove them mad—when their connection to magic was severed.

Arine had just been a baby when the severing happened, and so many had died. She had lost her own mother, Nadyia, during the aftermath. Her father said it was in the chaos of magic being ripped from the world that she was killed. He had found her cut down, with Arine, only two years old, lying unconscious beside her.

The memory of that story deepened her shame for treating the subject so lightly. Not knowing what she could say to recover from her foolishness, Arine carefully stepped away from the tree and motioned to the south.

"We should probably get going. With the rot this far and winter coming, food will become scarce. We need to get out of this forest and back to Draske," she said, unable to meet his eyes.

"Is your family in Draske?" Ciran asked instead of moving, surprising her since she had been sure he wouldn't want to converse with her anymore after her foolishness.

Normally she would have kept her answers vague, but after her own prying questions, she figured she owed him honesty. And truthfully, she was glad for the reprieve.

"No, I just meant so we could check back in at the Pillar. I grew up in a small village northeast of Draske called Toumre. My father is there." She picked at another leaf mottled with rot. "He's sick. I need to be officially listed with status so I can get him better medicine."

"You are out here just to get access to medicine?" Ciran asked in disbelief, face twisted in confusion.

Arine scoffed, taken aback by his shock. Clearly, she was right about him being wealthy if he thought this was the craziest thing someone could do to try to obtain simple care.

"Yeah, the King's healer was all out when I asked for some," she said defensively.

He stiffened, face hardening, and she wondered if her sarcasm had offended him.

"Do you work in the palace?" He asked, almost accusatorily.

She paused, trying to decide whether he was joking or genuinely thought she had been serious. Either way, he seemed out of touch, thinking she shouldn't have to go to extremes for medicine. As if someone like her hadn't worked for every small comfort. She had been fed well enough growing up, but only because her father took on job after job as a tracker to keep food on the table and a roof overhead.

"Of course I don't know the King or anyone in the palace for that matter," she said, crossing her arms. "It was a joke. You must not have heard about the new law he passed."

She didn't like feeling like she was doing something stupid when this had been her last option aside from thievery.

Ciran's jaw tightened. "I—sorry, that came out wrong," he said quickly, a faint catch in his voice before it smoothed. "I wasn't questioning you, just asking." He shifted his weight, then softened. "I know what it's like to try anything to save family. My mother died when I was a boy, and nothing I did mattered. I wouldn't wish that on anyone."

Arine barely managed to hide her shock and pity, not wanting to make him uncomfortable for sharing. The admission softened her irritation at his earlier questions, and she let it go. At least she wasn't the only one causing awkward conversation.

She nodded to the path, lightening her tone for a fresh start. "How about we get going? We must be close to the edge, I can feel it."

He nodded, seemingly glad for the change of subject as well. "All right, I can take the lead—"

A woman's scream split the air, cutting him off mid-sentence. Arine whirled to the southwest, where it had come from. Nothing looked out of the ordinary.

"Have you seen any others nearby?" she asked urgently.

Ciran didn't hear her; his head was cocked to the side as he tried to pinpoint where the sound had come from.

Just as suddenly as the first, a second scream rang through the air. It was more muffled this time, as if the woman was moving further away. Before she could stop him, Ciran took off toward the sound, crashing through the underbrush as if the thick foliage were nothing more than a nuisance.

It took Arine a few seconds to recover from the shock of him leaving before she gritted her teeth to follow in his wake. She didn't know what was happening, but she knew she couldn't leave some woman to whatever fate was causing those screams. She could only imagine what type of animal this person could have run afoul of. At least it was somewhat in a southerly direction anyway.

She followed as fast as she could, weaving through the trees and clawing her way through the thick underbrush when it blocked her path. The screams fell silent, but Ciran's trail was easy to follow through the torn leaves and thorny bushes.

A final scream rang out, then cut off. In the silence that followed, she caught the muffled sounds of a struggle. She was concentrating so hard on the sounds that she almost ran into Ciran, who had stopped suddenly. He motioned for her to stay quiet. She held her breath as he slowly parted the leaves of a thick bush to peer through. She crept up beside him but couldn't see anything from her angle. Still, she could hear the harsh voices of at least two or three men.

It sounded like they were taunting someone—so something worse than an animal had gotten whoever had screamed. Slavers most likely. Despicable. The lands across the ocean—like Yuak—still dealt in the human labor market and Calasis was barely able to feed itself now, let alone protect its people. A handful even left willingly, indenturing themselves in exchange for food. Die of hunger here, or live and work there. The slavers didn't just take people who were willing though. They would grab anyone who couldn't defend themselves, and no one ever came back.

Arine lowered herself to the ground and crawled forward, careful to stay quiet over the sounds of the scuffle ahead. When she glanced over, Ciran was doing the same—surprisingly, he moved as quietly as she did. His face was grim but determined, and she was sure he'd already reached the same conclusion about the group.

She inched forward until movement came into view. At the edge of the thick brush, she stopped, keeping herself partially hidden. Three men stood ahead. The woman's body lay on the ground, unconscious, her arms and legs bound. Blood trickled from a gash by her ear, matting her auburn hair. Scrapes covered her arms and legs, but her chest rose and fell—she was breathing, at least.

The men spoke in a guttural language she didn't understand, but their gestures told her enough. One was clearly the leader, he had leathery tan skin and jet black hair tied back in a long ponytail knotted at different intervals. The others had the same yellow-tan skin, but their hair was cropped short and tied into thin tails at the nape of their necks.

The leader yelled at one of the others and motioned toward a knife lying on the ground a few feet from the unconscious woman. When he walked over to pick it up, he moved with a slight limp, and blood dripped down his right leg. Arine had no idea how long the woman had been captive—whether this was an escape attempt or they had only just found her. She hoped for the latter.

From the way the men carried themselves, it looked like they knew how to fight. Overpowering the trio wouldn't be easy, but with one injured and the element of surprise, they had a chance. The tricky part would be doing so before they decided to cut their losses and kill the woman for their troubles. She glanced at Ciran. His eyes reflected the anger she felt, signaling his intent; there was no question they would help.

She nodded in silent agreement and mouthed for him to go left and be ready. She had a bow, a short sword, and one knife, but their swords were longer and gave them greater reach. She'd only have time for one arrow before they rushed her. She had to drop one from here, and Ciran needed to be in position to stop the others before they killed the prisoner out of spite.

She counted twenty slow beats after he disappeared, using the time to knock an arrow. Once she was confident he'd had enough time, she drew a deep breath and stood smoothly. She brought the bow up, took aim, and fired. Her shot rang true and one of the men crumpled to the ground. Now came the hard part.

On cue, Ciran swept from the trees to her left. The uninjured man drew his sword just in time to block Ciran's killing blow. Before his companion could intervene and turn the fight, Arine drew her knife and hurled it at him. She didn't want to fight the man in close combat, so she tried to keep her distance.

He dodged the knife easily, even with the slice on his leg from their earlier fight. It whizzed past, thudding into a tree behind him. He drew his sword and advanced on Arine, apparently thinking her the easier target. She would make sure he didn't underestimate a woman again. She pulled out her own sword and faced him. Even though she was disadvantaged by her size, she was light on her feet and speed would give her the upper hand due to his injury.

She darted in, her blade cutting his arm. He hissed, but kept pressing closer, trying to force her into his reach. Arine kept shuffling like her father had taught her. Move and attack, move and attack, in quick succession.

She lunged again, expecting him to guard his injured side, but he pivoted quicker than she'd thought possible. The feint allowed him to cut her on her left arm. She sucked in a quick breath at the pain, but luckily it was a shallow slice. She breathed through the ache and kept moving. He hadn't disabled her, but he was proving more formidable than she'd expected.

She backed away a few steps and glanced toward Ciran. He and the other man were locked in combat, their precise swings and parries betraying long years of training. Watching him fight, she realized just how easily he could have overpowered her—if he'd ever wanted to.

She refocused and saw her opponent favoring his leg more heavily now. His lunge earlier must have cost him more than he intended. She just had to keep going a little more and he would slip up. She darted in, slicing again. He staggered as blood dripped down his side. A couple more minutes and he'd be finished. But—realization dawned on him at the same time and his eyes flicked to the bound woman on the ground.

Panic flared in Arine. He was closer to the unconscious woman than she was, and she wouldn't have time to stop him. He smiled and pivoted, lunging towards the woman with his sword. Arine screamed and hurled herself toward her despite the risk, and knowing she wouldn't reach her in time.

The slaver was a single step from the woman—then suddenly Ciran was there. He caught the man's sword on his own blade and twisted it free, sending it clattering to the ground inches from the woman. Ciran drove the hilt into the man's head, dropping him unconscious and ending the fight in seconds.

Arine nodded her thanks, breathing hard as she hurried to the woman, who was beginning to stir. She crouched beside her and helped her sit up. The woman blinked but didn't fully wake. Arine caught her head as she slumped back down.

"What's wrong with her?" Ciran asked anxiously, finishing the survivor's bindings before rushing over to join Arine.

Blood streaked Ciran's face, but he looked to be uninjured.

"I'm not sure. Maybe there's bleeding inside we can't see?" She replied.

Arine began examining the woman to see what could be wrong. She wore light brown trousers belted at the waist and a billowy, beige shirt. No cloak which was odd in this weather so the slavers must have taken it. The gash on her head wasn't deep—not enough to explain the unconsciousness.

When Arine brushed the hair back and touched her forehead, she realized the problem: the woman was burning up. Then she noticed a tear mid-thigh. Pulling the fabric aside revealed a half-healed knife wound. It wasn't healing properly, angry red lines spread out in every direction from it. Infection. No wonder she couldn't wake. An infection this bad was nearly a death sentence even with the best healers—let alone here, in the middle of nowhere with little to treat it.

She explained the problem to Ciran and dug through her bag for herbs she'd found throughout the forest. She only had coriander, wormwood, and mint. The mint wouldn't help at this point, but the coriander would aid the fever and the wormwood the pain. Arine grabbed a curved piece of bark and ground the herbs with some water to make a paste.

"Help me sit her up a little so I can see if she can get this down."

Ciran's face tightened with a mix of grief and concern as he gently propped the woman against his side. Arine felt the same sorrow looking at her, wondering what horrors she had endured. She slowly spooned the mixture into the woman's mouth. At first it seemed like she wouldn't be able to get it down, but then finally when Arine tilted her head up a little more, she swallowed with a slight cough.

Her eyes fluttered open again, and this time she stayed conscious—though barely. She stared at Arine and then Ciran with a half-aware gaze.

"You're very sick. If you take a little more of this, we'll try to get you to a healer before the infection worsens." Arine kept her tone calm and slow. The woman gave no sign of understanding, but at least she didn't resist when Arine brought the next spoonful to her lips

She finished the medicine with a few sips of water before slipping back into unconsciousness. Her head lolled against Ciran's shoulder, and he caught her weight. Arine found herself watching Ciran—the care with which he lifted the woman's head, the way his jaw clenched when she moaned in pain. People in her village would have done the same, but only for their own. Ciran had no reason to care. Maybe that was what confused her most.

Shame pricked her for ever thinking of him as a spoiled noble. Whether he was nobility or a wealthy merchant, he had shown her nothing but kindness since they met.

He lowered the woman gently to the ground again and looked up at Arine. "We have to get her to a healer," he said, his voice tight with agitation.

She drew in a breath, thinking quickly. Even if they were near the forest's edge, neither of them could carry the woman alone. They needed something to spread her weight between them.

"We need to make a litter so we can get her to a healer in time. I don't have a rope long enough—do you?" she asked.

Ciran nodded, rummaging through his pack and handed Arine a thick bundle of rope. He left in search of something to use for handles while Arine zigzagged the rope across the ground until it was long enough to hold the woman. She worked as quickly as she could, but weaving the knots still took time. By the time she had finished tying the clove hitches, Ciran returned with two sturdy maple poles slim enough to slide through the loops. Together, they threaded the poles into place to make handles.

"Where did you learn to make a litter like this?" he asked as they finished.

"My father. He was a tracker and made sure to teach me too." She slid the litter beside the woman, readying to lift her. "One time, he made me tear one apart three times before I got the knots right," she muttered with a half-smile. "I thought he was the cruelest father alive that day."

"Well, I for one am thankful for it. I don't think I could've endured two more rebuilds," Ciran said wryly, his tension easing now that they had a plan.

"Ha. Ha," she replied dryly, though she was secretly relieved it had only taken one try too.

Ciran crouched beside the woman and slipped his hands beneath her shoulders. "But really—this will help us move her much faster."

Just as they went to lift the woman, the Yuakan slaver stirred. Arine glanced over to see him blinking groggily, trying to push himself upright.

"What do we do with him?" she asked.

Ciran studied the man for several heartbeats, his expression hardening. When he spoke, his voice was low and cold. "We can't take him and still move quickly. We'll have to leave him here and let nature decide. Seems like a fair trade." His eyes met hers. "He's got a better chance at survival than he gave her. That makes him lucky—if he survives at all."

Arine had no better answer. The only other choice was killing him while he lay bound and helpless. Even though they'd cut down his companions in battle, this felt different—execution, not survival. And dragging him along would destroy any chance of saving the woman. He would slow them down and they would never be able to lower their guard.

But she knew she couldn't bring herself to kill him like this. They had to be better than the slavers, or nothing they fought for mattered. She held Ciran's gaze and nodded.

"We'd better move quickly," she said. "His companions will draw predators soon enough."

When she looked back, the man was fully awake, thrashing against his bonds. But she had seen Ciran's knots and knew they would hold for hours since there were no sharp rocks nearby to help him. The weapons had already been stripped from the corpses and tossed far out of reach.

They gathered their weapons in silence while the bound slaver watched with wary eyes. Ciran handed Arine two extra knives he had scavenged; she accepted them with a brief nod. When they moved to the ends of the litter, the man seemed to realize their plan.

He shouted in the guttural tongue Arine had heard earlier. When they didn't react, he hesitated, then forced out in their language, "Bring me, please."

Ciran strode over and crouched until they were eye to eye. His gaze flicked to the unconscious woman, then back to the man—his meaning clear. Color drained from the Yuakan's face, and Arine held her breath. She wouldn't stop Ciran if he chose to end the man's life, but killing someone bound and helpless would stain any conscience.

At last, Ciran shook his head. "If you live, take it as a sign and never return to this land. If not..." He shrugged.

Rage twisted the man's features. As Ciran stood, the slaver leaned back and spat, the glob striking his cloak. Ciran walked on without a glance, as if the man were already dead.

Together, he and Arine lifted the woman onto the litter and secured their packs at her feet. The two of them set off, the sound of the slaver's futile struggles fading behind them.

Arine had never met anyone from Yuak before, and she wondered if they treated their own people as cruelly as they treated those of Calasis—or if they were simply another nation convinced of its own superiority.

After a while, Ciran glanced at the litter stretched between them. "Your father would be proud. Hopefully you can tell him about it when we get back."

Her grip tightened on the handle. "Yes. I will."

$$\cdot\!\gg\!\cdot\cdot\blacklozenge\cdot\cdot\ll\!\cdot$$

Chapter 3

As the day wore on, they staggered beneath the woman's weight, sweat soaking their collars despite the cool air. Arine's shoulders burned, her legs trembling with every step. Breaks grew more frequent, yet still they pressed on—one dragging step at a time. The woman didn't wake again.

When they stopped, Arine spoon-fed her what she could of the herb paste and water. The woman's breathing stayed ragged but steady, her eyelids fluttering with fever dreams. Her skin was still pale, yet Arine clung to the tiny hope that the herbs were holding the worst at bay.

They had a small reprieve when Ciran returned from washing with two rabbits, caught at a den near their campsite. At least dinner came without the cost of a long hunt. Arine tried to get some tiny pieces into the woman, but failed spectacularly at that. She thought she heard Ciran snickering when the last one just slid down the side of the woman's cheek but when she glanced over, he was suspiciously looking at the fire and not her. She glared at him anyway before laying down.

"You can take the first shift tonight," she muttered, rolling over, too exhausted for anything more.

Every muscle throbbed from carrying the litter, new aches settling deep into her bones. Exhaustion pulled at her, but still sleep didn't come easily. Her mind wandered between her father and the fevered woman. Could she finish this wretched test in time to save them both? Or had she made a fatal mistake leaving her father to suffer alone for so long?

She had told herself it was simple: graduate, earn the status, buy the medicine. That was the plan. But each delay gnawed at her, and her father's hollow cough echoed in her mind, louder with every step she took away from him.

What if, by the time she earned the status, it was already too late? What if she should have tried to steal the medicine instead? No—she'd fought that battle in her mind before. If she'd been caught stealing, there would have been no one left to save him. This was the only way. She had to push through and get out, not just for her father's sake now, but for her newest companion as well. What a difference two days makes, she thought ruefully. She had not just one additional traveling partner, but two.

Her mind drifted to Ciran, and she cracked her eyes open. He was sitting against a tree a little ways off. With the fire dying low, she could just make out his expression. His shoulders were squared, his gaze scanning the tree line every few seconds as if nothing else mattered. Every so often, he rose to check on the woman—adjusting her blanket, making sure her fever hadn't worsened.

Arine's thoughts circled the same unanswered questions. He clearly had formal training—making the trap for the mountain lion, fighting with a practiced hand that spoke of years under a master. He had to have been born wealthy, but he didn't carry the cruelty she had come to expect from them.

She mulled it over until the edges of thought grew heavy. In the end, she supposed it didn't matter. All that mattered was how he treated her now, and so far, he seemed decent. She let her breathing slow, and for the first time in a long while, sleep came easier knowing someone was there to watch her back.

A few hours later, Ciran woke her for her watch. The woman was worse—tossing fitfully, the leaves around her bedding disturbed.

"How long has she been like this?" Arine asked, rubbing the sleep from her eyes.

"About an hour. I tried coaxing more herbs down, but she wouldn't take them." His voice was strained, his eyes fixed on the woman. "I don't know how long she has if we can't get her real medicine."

Arine watched the woman's face contort in pain, then smooth out again. A knot pulled tight in her chest.

"We'll have to break camp early and cut down on breaks tomorrow. We have to be close to the southern edge by now. By my calculations, I should've reached it a couple days ago—I couldn't have miscounted by more than a few days."

Ciran nodded. "Then tomorrow we'll find a town and get her to a healer. All towns have at least an herbalist."

There was no challenge in his tone, no doubt in his eyes. The quiet weight of his trust settled in Arine's chest, warm and unfamiliar. Were they becoming friends, even after only a few days? She didn't know what would happen once the test ended, but if he stayed near the Capital, maybe he would be one of the few status-holders she could stand to speak to. It would be nice to trust someone.

She scooted closer to the woman and pressed her hand to her forehead. No surprise—the fever was burning hotter than before. Arine pulled out her canteen and dampened a scrap of cloth, dabbing gently at the woman's brow for whatever small relief it might bring. Then she tried coaxing in some of the herb paste. Like Ciran had said, it was harder now; most dribbled uselessly to the ground, though she managed to get a little down. She wrapped the woman snugly to keep her from thrashing and then settled into a spot with the best view of the treeline, watching for any prowling shapes in the dark.

The hours crawled by, broken only by the distant howls of wolves. At last dawn crept in, gold edging the sky, dew glittering on the grass like stars. The forest looked calm, though her thoughts were anything but. When the sun gave off just enough light to see clearly, she woke Ciran. Exhaustion and worry lingered in his expression as he blinked the sleep from his eyes.

"I found some cranberries while I was walking around to stay awake," Arine said, handing him a small handful she had saved.

"With how resourceful you are, I'm shocked you managed to fall in that pit the other night," Ciran said, eyeing the berries appreciatively.

"I'd just run into someone in the middle of this forest," she shot back wryly.

"So you were spying on me!" Ciran exclaimed, feigning outrage.

Arine huffed. "Not for very long."

"I must have looked pretty intimidating if you were so scared of me that you ran right into a bear pit."

"That's not exactly how it happened," Arine muttered, rolling her eyes. "You were just too boring, really. Laying out your things, making a fire..."

He smiled and opened his mouth to respond, but the woman's loud cry cut him off. Both of them turned at once. Arine pressed a hand to her forehead—it was like touching fire. She thrashed and moaned as if her body itself was trying to drive out the sickness.

Arine tried to coax another dose of herbs into her while Ciran held her steady, but it was worse than it had been only hours ago. Nothing seemed to help. Concern etched Ciran's face as clearly as she felt it herself. Without a healer, the woman wouldn't last. Neither of them said it aloud, but both knew. They packed up quickly and pressed forward again.

By mid-day the endless trees blurred together, oppressive and unchanging. Sweat dampened their collars despite the cool air, muscles burning from the double weight of the litter and the undergrowth they had to force through. Arine thought she saw the brush thinning but kept silent, afraid to jinx it—or worse, to be wrong and draw Ciran's attention to their lack of progress. His mood was darkening with each passing mile.

An hour later, she could no longer deny it. The trees were spreading, the brush less dense. Her arms hung like dead weights, the woman's convulsions making it harder to keep the litter balanced between them, but they had to be close, so she forced herself to push through.

Then, suddenly, she was blinking up at the open sky.

Arine gasped, a wild laugh escaping her as sunlight hit her face. She turned to Ciran, grinning, heart pounding with disbelief—they'd made it out. She had survived Killian Forest. Weeks of isolation, hunger, and fear—behind her.

For a single heartbeat, it felt like freedom.

Then the woman on the litter convulsed, nearly slipping from their grasp. The sound of her strangled cry shattered the moment, and Arine's elation vanished. They weren't finished yet.

They paused to rest and get their bearings. The hillside ahead was choked with weeds and tall grass, the blades already turning brown, but it was still far easier ground than the forest had been. Arine exhaled slowly. A town couldn't be far. For the first time in weeks, the tightness in her chest eased. Maybe—just maybe—she could still pull this off.

When she turned to scan the horizon, her breath caught. A plume of smoke curled into the sky just beyond the next hill. Even better—they wouldn't have to wander to find a settlement.

Ciran's brow furrowed the instant he saw it. "Do you remember a town being this close? That's a lot of smoke for travelers or an outpost. And there wasn't a settlement here, not the last time I checked a map."

Arine's mind scrambled through everything she knew of the area, but nothing surfaced. "Maybe it's a group relocating from the rot?"

Whole towns had been forced to uproot as the decay spread, pushing desperate families toward the Capital in hopes of survival. It wouldn't be strange for a large caravan to set up camp, and if that was the case, they'd almost certainly have a healer among them. Surely she and Ciran could work something out, find a way to barter for medicine.

Ciran continued to study the smoke as it lazily curled up into the blue sky without saying anything. When he finally looked back, his face was unreadable. He looked from Arine to the woman, who as if on cue, began thrashing again. His face softened slightly as the movement, betraying the worry he felt.

"What can it hurt to see if they can help? It's not against the rules of the test or anything," Arine pressed.

Another violent fit nearly sent the woman tumbling off the litter. Ciran exhaled through his nose, jaw tight, before nodding. "You're right. It's probably not an issue. Just... stay together once we meet them."

She agreed, and they trudged on.

At the crest of the hill, the camp came into view. Arine froze.

This wasn't a ragged caravan of refugees—it was some kind of fortified encampment. Large canvas tents stood at the center, arranged in neat rows, with guards in polished armor, some with horses, forming a perimeter around them.

Nobles were the only one who could fund such an expedition but she couldn't fathom why anyone, but especially high status holders, would camp out here. What she did for survival, perhaps they considered sport. Still, no wealthy traveler went far without a healer. If luck held, they might not be turned away.

Arine stepped forward, hopeful, but stopped when she noticed Ciran hadn't moved.

"What's wrong now? Do you think they'll refuse to help her?"

He didn't answer. His eyes narrowed, fixed on the distant group. The sun behind them made the details hard to see, but something about the set of his shoulders made Arine's stomach clench. Did he recognize them? Were they here for him?

She was about to ask when Ciran suddenly spun, trying to wrench the litter back the way they had come. With Arine still holding her side, the sudden movement nearly sent the woman sliding off.

Arine steadied her, heart racing, and looked back at Ciran. His face was pale, knuckles white on the handle, eyes darting between her and the camp. Urgent. Sharp. And almost...afraid.

"We need to go before they see us," Ciran said roughly, pulling her back toward the far side of the hill where the camp's lookouts couldn't spot them.

"What? Why?" Arine struggled to keep pace as he all but towed her along.

"Did you notice the sigil on the flag?" he asked.

She blinked—she hadn't even seen a flag, let alone recognized a sigil. "No. Who are they? The woman needs help now, every minute could be her last!"

Ciran ignored her, continuing to rush her further away.

Her voice dropped instinctively, as though someone might overhear. "Whats going on? Are you... wanted for something?"

The idea seemed absurd. He had gone out of his way time and again for strangers—hardly the behavior of an outlaw. But Ciran didn't answer; he was too focused on finding cover.

They were nearly out of sight when a cry rang out across the hilltop. Arine's stomach sank. They'd been spotted. Ciran only glanced back and quickened his pace, but she pulled back on the litter, jerking him to a stop. She didn't know what was going on, but these people were the best shot of the woman getting help and she knew they couldn't outrun horses. They needed to compose themselves though so they at least didn't look like fugitives.

"Ciran, stop!" she snapped as he tried to pull the litter forward again. Panic edged her voice. If he really was some outlaw, the last thing she wanted was to be dragged into a chase.

He stopped reluctantly, turning to face her. His expression was a storm of emotions—worry, frustration, fear. Arine planted her feet, refusing to budge until she had answers.

"You know we can't escape them," she said firmly. "Not like this. They have horses, and we're carrying an unconscious woman. Who are they, Ciran? And why are you so afraid of them?"

Ciran ignored her questions, his gaze fixed on the riders drawing closer. A minute, maybe less, was probably all they had before they arrived. When he finally looked at her, his face was tight with distrust, and the sudden shift made her chest tighten with confusion.

"I can understand not knowing every noble house, especially if you didn't grow up privileged," he said at last, glancing between her and the approaching group. "But I am surprised you don't recognize the lion-headed sigil of the royal family.

She whipped her head back to the approaching group as her stomach dropped. "Wait, you're saying the King is with them? That makes no sense. Why would he be out here?"

The idea was absurd. She couldn't remember a single time she'd ever heard of the King leaving his castle. And Ciran's tone—like she should've recognized the guard immediately—scraped at her raw nerves. She'd never even set foot in the Capital until the Pillar, and after weeks half-starved and exhausted, he expected her to recall noble crests? Stars above, what did he expect...that she'd memorized every noble family crest between scavenging for food and carrying dying strangers?

She clenched her jaw against the rising frustration, not letting it boil to the surface. It was more pressing to figure out what the King's presence meant. She doubted he would spare one of his private healers for a stranger on the edge of death. But surely he wouldn't detain them either. They were just doing the survival test he himself demanded.

Ciran's suspicion seemed to ease, though only slightly. "I don't know why he's here," he admitted. "But his guards are notoriously protective. To find us in a place this remote, with an unconscious woman and no explanation? They'll be suspicious. Some might even think we planned it—to get close to the King."

He set the litter down and moved between them and the approaching men. Arine noticed he didn't unsheathe his sword, but he positioned himself to be ready to move quickly, as if he anticipated an attack.

"Our names will be on the entry list," Arine said, stepping up beside Ciran and mirroring his stance. "We can clear any misunderstanding if it comes to that."

"We can hope for the best," Ciran murmured, eyes never leaving the horizon. "But prepare for the worst. Let me do the talking. With luck, they won't detain us."

Arine rolled her eyes. Of course he thought he should handle the talking. Still, she bit back a retort—he probably knew how to speak to the King's men better than she ever could. And surely the King had more pressing concerns than two Pillar attendees dragging an injured woman through the wilderness.

The riders crested the hill a moment later. Seven in total—six guards and one officer. Their uniforms were unmistakable: stiff blue coats embroidered with the white lion's head over the breast, black buttons running down the front, white bands ringing their cuffs to mark rank. That much Arine knew.

If you joined the army without attending the Pillar, you started with one band. Survive the test, and you entered immediately with four—enough rank to keep you well-fed and away from the worst infantry details. Not glorious, but better than starving.

Her eyes caught on the man leading them. Seven bands. Impressive, though not surprising if he rode in the King's company. The formation tightened as they approached, surrounding her and Ciran with practiced efficiency.

"State your name and business," the one with seven bands commanded, his tone making it apparent he was not someone used to being refused.

Ciran stepped forward, responding to the man. "We found this woman injured and are trying to get her some help. If you have a healer in your group, she needs to be seen immediately."

He matched the guards authoritative tone and didn't take his eyes off him, clearly marking him as a threat. Arine couldn't see the guards face very well with his helmet's silver face plate obscuring half of it, but his rigid posture and the slow shift of his hand to his sword made his displeasure plain.

"Why are you in this area? How did she come to be injured?" the guard demanded coldly. "Answer directly and immediately when addressed by the royal guard."

Arine bit back a groan. Just what they needed—two men puffing their chests while the unconscious woman worsened with every passing moment. Arine opened her mouth to intervene to try to de-escalate things when she noticed another soldier riding up to the group. In seconds, he made his way to the front.

This one was different. He wore no uniform—just plain trousers and a stiff jacket—but the authority in his bearing was unmistakable. He had no helmet, dark hair cropped close, blue eyes keen and unflinching. Though his shirt looked simple at first glance, Arine noticed the detail that gave him away: a row of tiny lion heads embroidered into the cuffs, stitching fine enough to cost a fortune.

The officer who had been interrogating them stiffened at once. Then, with rigid formality, he bowed low in the saddle.

"Prince," the officer said, "Welcome. We were just questioning these two about their purpose here. I hadn't realized you were joining us, or I would have sent Gabe and Hasin back to escort you."

So much for Arine's plan of avoiding the royalty. She tried to remain calm, not letting the impact of the Prince's presence affect her

"No need Gerin," the newcomer said easily. "I felt like a bit of fresh air and noticed we had visitors."

The Prince's gaze swept over their group with casual precision. His eyes flicked from Ciran's face to the hand resting just above his scabbard. The smile curving his mouth was almost lazy, but his eyes were sharp, calculating. He took in everything—Ciran's sword, Arine's calloused hands, the unconscious woman. Nothing escaped his notice.

"Besides," he added, smirk tugging wider as he met Ciran's eyes, "this small group is no threat to me."

Needling Ciran was effortless for him. Arine nearly groaned as she saw Ciran's fingers twitch toward his hilt, though thankfully he checked himself. She hadn't feared the guards overly much, but she hadn't counted on a royal himself coming out here to scrutinize them.

Rumors about the King's family had reached even her small town. Ruthless, they said—though always cloaked in the excuse of maintaining order. Arine wasn't sure how much of that was truth and how much was simply their desire to rule with an iron fist, barricaded in their ivory tower while villages starved a day's ride away.

With the Prince's arrival, the guards seemed to tighten like bowstrings. Several hands gripped hilts, horses pawed and shifted against the packed earth as if sensing their riders' unease. Arine's throat constricted, palms slick. She dug her nails into her skin, focusing on the sting to steady her expression. What were the odds they all died here if she didn't diffuse things? She doubted the Prince would tolerate much impudence.

Before Ciran could do anything that incited the Prince, she grabbed Ciran's arm, angling herself in front of him. "Your Highness, please excuse the intrusion," she said carefully. "We didn't know this was your group. We're students of the Pillar, taking part in the final test. Along the way, we found this woman—her leg wound is badly infected. We were only trying to get her to a healer. If you have one in your company, we'd be grateful for their help. Then we'll continue on to the Pillar and stay out of your way."

She had never met anyone of royalty, and she didn't know the protocol, so she hoped even if he refused to help the woman, he would at least let them move on themselves. She also figured not going into detail on the run-in with the slavers from Yuak might be best. She knew that the slavers deserved what they got, but who knows what the Prince would think.

Even with her caution, her words drew his full attention. The Prince swung down from his horse in one smooth motion, boots striking the earth. His eyes fixed on her as he closed the distance, unreadable. Gerin and two others dismounted instantly, flanking him and shoving Ciran aside.

Arine sucked in a sharp breath, forcing herself not to recoil as the Prince stopped before her. Her knees locked to keep her from stumbling back. Behind her, Ciran struggled, his voice raised in protest, but the guards pinned him easily.

She stood her ground, though her fingers twitched toward her knife. The Prince's gaze raked over her with unnerving precision, as though weighing her worth in silence. Arine's heart pounded. How ironic she thought, one wrong move and they would be dead because of her. She supposed she should have let Ciran do the talking like he suggested.

"You were taking the final test? What did you say your name was?" the Prince asked quietly, but forcefully.

He stared at her so intensely that she involuntarily swallowed. Something in the back of her mind caught on to the fact that he too had ignored her request for the healer. Irritation reared up suddenly. The fact that he, or any of them, showed no signs that they even realized a woman was dying on the ground beside them gave her the anger she needed to stand tall and not cower. In fact, the lack of empathy from all of them was starting to really infuriate her. They were wasting precious time this woman may not have...time her father did not have.

"My name is Arine Duskraine," she said, her voice clipped, almost defiant. "Now, if you would kindly direct us to a healer—or to the nearest town—we'll be out of your way... Your Highness."

His eyes narrowed. "Arine? Your father is Tyvin?"

Chapter 4

For a heartbeat, Arine couldn't grasp the words. Had he really said her father's name? Shock slammed through her, leaving her unsteady. Was he here to inform her of his death? She tried to step back, away from the stink of sweat and leather and the press of watching eyes, but the Prince moved with her. His hand shot out, steadying her before she stumbled over the unconscious woman. But he didn't let go.

"Is he... is he dead?" she asked, barely above a whisper.

"No. Your father is still alive," the prince said.

His grip tightened, and her skin prickled—a cold rush of instinct urging her to pull away. Out of the corner of her eye, she saw Ciran. He'd stopped struggling against the guards, his gaze fixed on her with sharp, unreadable focus.

They must already know about the slavers and were here to arrest them. But how? Did the one they left behind escape and beat them here?

Her muscles coiled, ready to bolt—but where? Her gaze darted to Ciran, the tree line, the wall of guards hemming her in. Too many. Too far. And she couldn't abandon the unconscious woman. The thought pinned her in place, even as her body screamed to run.

The Prince watched her as if he could read the panic rushing through her. He shook his head slightly and murmured so only she could hear, "Now, we wouldn't want to do anything rash, would we?"

Then, louder for the others, his grip still iron on her arm: "Is your father Tyvin?"

His eyes searched her face, hunting for the smallest flicker of truth. She scrambled for a lie, some escape—but the shock smothered every thought.

When she stayed silent, the Prince's voice softened into something almost cordial—though the words cut like steel. "We had no idea Tyvin was still alive until recently. He's been moved into the palace, cared for by our healers. I wouldn't want anything... unfortunate to happen to him."

He emphasized the word *cared* in a way that told Arine everything she needed to know. He had her father. Her heart sank. How could she even think of escape if Tyvin was at their mercy? The memories of him—barely conscious, unable to speak—gnawed at her. Still, hearing he was alive sparked the faintest flicker of hope...if the Prince wasn't lying.

He didn't release her arm. Instead, he stepped directly in front of her, forcing her gaze up to his sharp blue eyes.

"You are Tyvin's daughter, aren't you?" he pressed.

Her mind clawed for a plan, any path that might keep her father safe, but confusion tangled every thought. The Prince shifted impatiently, and she knew silence would only cause her more problems.

"Yes," she forced out at last. "Tyvin is my father."

Without another word, he spun and dragged her with him, his grip unyielding as he barked orders.

"Gerin! Have some of your men dismount. Two of you, take this woman"—he gestured carelessly at the unconscious figure on the ground—"and as many as needed to escort her companion."

The Prince turned back to her. "You and your friend will continue to our camp and remain under our *protection* for the time being."

That word—*protection*—landed heavy, as though it meant anything but safety. His face stayed composed, as his sharp eyes assessed her with the ease of someone used to sizing prey.

Ciran thrashed harder against the guards, but with three holding him, he was hopelessly outmatched. When brute force failed, he switched tactics, glaring at the Prince with open hostility. The Prince either didn't notice or didn't care because he plowed on, unaffected.

"Oh, and don't worry. We have an Official from the Pillar with us. They'll ensure your test is marked complete and that you're issued the rest of the paperwork."

His gaze lingered on Ciran for a moment, skepticism flickering at the edges of his expression. Did he recognize him—or was he simply toying with him? Every word the Prince spoke stirred more questions in Arine's mind. Why allow them to finish the Pillar's paperwork if he was taking them prisoner?

When neither she nor Ciran answered, the Prince went on. "We can discuss the details once you're cleaned up...assuming your friend won't cause any trouble." His chin tipped toward Ciran, whose low, coiled stance and rigid jaw said everything Arine already knew. He would indeed be trouble.

"Thank you for the offer of hospitality, but I will make sure our injured companion is taken care of and then I will be on my way." Ciran snapped before she could respond.

"Ah but I insist you stay until we are safely back in Draske. The country-side is not safe." The Prince responded, meeting Ciran's stare, unflinchingly.

Hatred flashed in Ciran's eyes, raw and sharp, as he strained against the guards. The Prince flicked his eyes away and nodded at the soldiers. They immediately began to drag him down the hill towards their camp.

Arine's stomach turned over. Her voice broke out before she could stop it.

"Where are you taking him?"

The Prince turned back, looking her up and down again. "To our camp. Don't try anything or I will be forced to tie you up. As much fun as that would be, we are in a hurry."

He smiled at her, his eyes cold, and every fiber within her wanted to fight back. But, she had never heard one story of the royal family being kind. So, despite how much it hurt her pride, she didn't argue or pull away when the head guard, Gerin, brought his horse over and all but threw her into the saddle.

He tied her pack behind it while the Prince waited, fingers drumming on the pommel of his saddle. She sat as still as she could as he buckled the last strap, taking comfort in the fact that they didn't unarm her at least. She didn't know if that was an oversight or if they truly felt like it was of no consequence if she was armed or not. She probably didn't want to know the answer.

When Gerin finished, he gave the Prince a curt nod and fell back to march with the others escorting Ciran. The Prince moved his own horse beside hers, his remaining men closing in as the group set off toward camp.

"When we arrive, you'll be given time to clean yourself up," he said smoothly. "Then we can talk over dinner. As long as you behave and don't try any-thing...ridiculous"—his eyes flicked pointedly to her bow—"no harm will come to you or your family."

"I will behave," she replied curtly. "But my father has nothing to do with this. Could you please let him go?"

The Prince's masklike face barely shifted. "And how would we ensure your cooperation then?"

Hatred flared so hot in her chest she almost choked on it. Never had she despised someone so thoroughly. To use an ailing man as leverage—what kind of monster did that?

Some of that loathing must have shown in her eyes, because the Prince chuckled. "Yes. I think having him as a guest was good foresight on my uncle's part."

With one last disdainful look, the Prince maneuvered his horse ahead to speak with one of his men. Arine watched him warily, her thoughts knotting tighter with every step. If this was about the slavers, how had they known to seize her father? Why promise her food and a bath if she was going to be arrested? Why leave her weapons untouched, her hands unbound, as if this were some casual ride?

She searched for answers, but when none came, her mind drifted to the simplest fact of all: she was finally out of the infernal forest, surrounded by people again. And he had said she could bathe. The thought stirred a rush of longing. Streams had only rinsed the worst of the dirt; weeks of grime still clung to her skin. She finger-combed her dark, thick hair each morning, but there was only so much detangling she could do without a proper brush. Even her hands felt foreign under their layer of grit. The idea of real cleanliness almost made her ache.

Mid daydream, the Prince turned back, his sharp gaze cutting through her reverie. He nodded toward Ciran.

"How long have you and your companion been together? The Pillar makes it nearly impossible for participants to find one another."

His words were somehow accusatory, as if they had planned to meet up.

Arine measured her words carefully. If the Prince asked Ciran the same thing later, their stories had to align.

"Actually, we met only a few days ago. He saved me from an embarrassingly foolish misstep in the woods."

She hoped to bait him into focusing on her mistake instead of other details.

His eyes narrowed, suspicion flickering. "How fortunate for you. And what misstep made you so desperate for aid?"

Arine let out a rueful breath. "Well, it's a bit embarrassing...but I stumbled straight into a bear pit." Inside, she was quietly triumphant. He'd taken the bait.

She went on, recounting her clumsy fall into the pit and her multiple failed escape attempts, ending with Ciran arriving just in time. By the time she finished, they were nearly at the Prince's encampment.

"So you see, not my proudest moment," she said, forcing what she hoped was a self-deprecating smile, but it came out more like her teeth bared in a facsimile.

The Prince just kept the same infuriating expression on his face the whole time, so maybe she wasn't successful in distracting him after all.

Arine used the pause in conversation to look back to see how Ciran was faring, but they were too far away to make him out. Since she was apparently allowed to speak freely, she took a chance to ask him for more information. She didn't have anything else to lose and was tired of pretending,

"If you don't mind," she said carefully, "could you explain why we're being detained? I wasn't aware completing the final test had suddenly become illegal."

Her tone was as tactful as she could manage. Her father always admonished her for being too blunt. Perhaps only half-heartedly though, since he had also raised her to be more independent than most women.

The Prince looked at her for a long moment before responding and she refused to look away. She knew she was probably pushing the limits of his self-control but it was her family's life in the balance, not his.

Finally, he deigned to respond. "Did your father never mention knowing my uncle, the King?" he asked.

His words caught her completely off guard. That was the last thing she'd expected.

"My father has never mentioned knowing anyone of royalty in my entire life," she shot back, frowning. "I think you may have the wrong person."

The Prince scoffed. "So he didn't trust you, his own daughter, either. I can't say I'm surprised. He was always that way before meeting your mother, and even she couldn't rid him of the tendency completely." He flicked a hand in dismissal. "No more questions."

Arine's mouth hung open like a hooked trout before she snapped it shut. Her thoughts scattered too wildly for a retort. The mention of her parents left her reeling, her mind scrambling for any memory that might give truth—or lie—to his words.

They rode past the camp's perimeter. Order and discipline radiated from every corner: rows of canvas tents stood in rigid lines, flaps snapping in the cold breeze. Smoke coiled from cooking fires, carrying the scent of roasted meat over the heavier musk of horses and leather. Armor glinted in the early light as guards moved with drilled purpose—sharpening blades, feeding mounts, standing watch.

The royal banner dominated the center, its crest snapping in the wind above the largest tent, a bold reminder of whose presence commanded this place.

Her mind spun. How could a member of the royal family know anything about her father—let alone her mother? Calling him secretive. Her father was private, but she wouldn't call him secretive. It's not like he hid himself away, he traveled all over to complete jobs.

A small worm of doubt wriggled in her chest. Her father had traveled all over, yes—but rarely near Draske. That was why she'd been so lost trying to buy medicine in the Capital. He'd never mentioned it outright, and she'd always assumed trackers weren't needed as much closer to the city. Could it have been intentional? No. She knew her father. He would have told her…wouldn't he?

She was starting to suspect the Prince being here was about something much different than the group of Yuakan slavers in the woods.

As they neared one of the larger tents in the camp's center, the Prince guided his horse closer to hers. "You may use this tent to get cleaned up. The guards will find you clothes, and everything else you require should be inside. You'll remain here until you are summoned."

As he spoke, a small man hurried forward, ink-stained fingers clutching a satchel of scrolls. A scribe, not a soldier. The Prince didn't spare him more than a flick of his hand.

"This man is from the Pillar. He carries the official lists at my request. He will see to your records so there is no need to stop there on our return."

The Pillar officiant bowed deeply and stepped aside to wait for her. Arine only stared, dumbstruck.

Having at first thought she might be escorted to a prison cell, she certainly hadn't expected a tent and fresh clothes to be brought to her. The Prince didn't give her the chance to question it. He turned without another word and rode on.

Arine watched him disappear around a tent and sniffed at his retreating back in her own small gesture of defiance.

A boy stepped forward to take her horse. She dismounted, passing him the reins, and kept her head low while her eyes flicked across the camp's layout. Tents snapped in the wind, steel caught the morning light, guards moved with clockwork precision.

In the corner nearest her, a sparring ring rang with the clash of practice blades. Nearby, a roped-off space held several guards bent over cookpots, stirring with long wooden paddles. The air carried the heady mix of meat and spice, and her mouth watered at the memory of what real food—seasoned food—tasted like.

Someone cleared their throat, cutting through her thoughts. She turned to find the Pillar scribe waiting, his foot tapping with impatience. He unrolled the scroll on a nearby crate, his nose wrinkling as though the very idea of handling official business in a camp offended him.

Arine recognized the document instantly: the ledger where each name was signed with a thumbprint at entry and again at return, proof no imposter could take someone's place. She pressed her thumb into the ink, then the parchment, scrawling her signature as well. The scribe muttered something about *never in his life* under his breath, too low for her to catch. She noticed a few other return signatures already recorded, but he snatched the scroll away before she could read them. With a stiff bow, he turned on his heel and marched off.

Arine let out a quiet snort of amusement, only to find someone else stepping into place before her.

"Excuse me, my lady."

The speaker was a woman, a year or two younger than Arine. She wore a plain blue frock marking her as a maid. She stood several inches shorter, light brown hair pulled into a tight bun, but there was nothing harsh in her manner. She held her chin high, her tone polite but steady.

"I came to let you know they'll be bringing the bathwater in shortly. I also have some clothes for you to look through." The maid motioned toward the tent.

"Oh—thank you. My name is Arine," she offered as she followed her inside.

The maid dipped a quick curtsy. "I'm Opal. I've laid out the selections on the bed. Choose whichever you like—you may keep them."

Arine's breath caught as she stepped further in. The tent was more lavish than any inn she'd ever stayed at. A wide bed dominated one side, a folding screen shielding a full iron tub—unthinkable to haul into the wilderness. An empty trunk stood beside a polished wash basin. Even the rug under her boots was thick enough to rival the grass outside.

This was no cell, no punishment. It was comfort—extravagant comfort. And it made no sense. Why would the Prince offer *this* to a prisoner?

She turned back to Opal. "There must be some mistake. Surely this tent isn't meant for me. Isn't there one more..." She gestured awkwardly at herself. "...appropriate?"

Opal blinked, expression unreadable. "If this does not meet your standards, my lady, I can send a runner to the nearest town to fetch whatever you prefer."

Her tone was even, polite—yet carried no trace of irony. As though they really would hunt down whatever extravagant item she could think up.

"What? No—I mean this is too much. I couldn't afford any of this."

Opal dipped her head slightly. "Oh, don't worry, my lady. All of this belongs to the Prince. He gave specific orders for this tent to be prepared for you. Of course, I can send someone to confirm, if you wish?"

The faint pinch at her mouth made it clear that was the last thing she wanted to do. Arine swallowed her protest. The Prince's temper wasn't something she wanted this maid to suffer on her behalf.

"No, no need. If you're sure, then I'll use it. But please—call me Arine. I'm not a lady."

She cast another dubious look around the tent. This was what he provided for someone he'd effectively arrested on sight? The cost of the rugs alone could have fed her entire village for a season. How many lives could be saved if this excess were put to use for his people instead of decorating a traveling cage? It was a slap in the face after every humiliation she'd endured just to scrape together medicine. But what did she expect? The King had never spared compassion for the common folk, and clearly the Prince was no different.

The tent flap stirred and another maid entered, bowing quickly. "Good day, my lady. Your bathwater is ready."

The new aid gestured outside. Two pairs of broad-shouldered men carried in steaming barrels and carefully poured them into the iron tub. The heat fogged the air, the rich scent of clean water almost intoxicating after weeks of filth.

When they finished, the men and both maids prepared to leave. Opal lingered only long enough to curtsy again. "Please let me know if there is anything else you require, my lady Arine. Two guards are posted outside and can send word. I will return to fetch you for dinner in a few hours."

With that, the flap closed, and Arine was left alone.

She stared at the tub, half-convinced it was some ploy by the Prince—a trick to lure her into lowering her guard so he could humiliate her when she was most vulnerable. But her eyes kept flicking back to the rising steam, no matter how hard she tried to resist. At last, the water itself made the decision for her. She wasn't going to waste a hot bath, not after weeks in the forest, even if it was a trap.

She stripped off her grimy clothes and slid into the tub. A groan escaped her as her head lolled back, the heat seeping into her sore muscles and easing the stiffness from days of carrying the litter. She scrubbed the dirt from her skin, staying long after the water cooled, only climbing out once the chill set her teeth on edge.

Her eyes lingered on the discarded rags she'd been living in. There was no going back to those now. Reluctantly, she turned to the neat piles of clothing laid out for her. All of them were far finer than anything she'd ever owned, with fabrics soft beneath her fingers. She pushed aside the embroidered gowns and tight riding dresses—pretty, but restrictive—and settled on a plain tunic and trousers. They still felt too fine for her, but at least they wouldn't slow her down. She tied a strip of fabric at her waist for a belt and moved on.

Her hair was another battle. It reached nearly to her waist now, wild from neglect. Someone had left combs and brushes, so she sat and worked through the knots until it lay smooth again, pulling it back from her face in a simple twist.

When she caught her reflection in the small mirror by the washbasin, she froze. A clean face stared back at her—whole, almost unrecognizable. For a heartbeat she didn't know if she was looking at herself or a stranger.

She turned away quickly, unsettled, and dumped her bag out onto the bed. Settling down comfortably, she began to sort through her things with practiced hands, forcing her mind back to something familiar and under her control.

Chapter 5

Arine jolted upright, disoriented for a moment before the past few days came flooding back. She grimaced at the scattered contents of her pack. She must have dozed off while rummaging.

She splashed water from the basin onto her face, then pulled back the tent flap to gauge the time. The sun still hung in the sky, but it was already sinking toward the western edge. There was only about an hour or so until nightfall, she had been asleep for a few hours at least.

Her stomach rumbled, reminding her she hadn't eaten in nearly a day. Ducking back inside, she strapped on a few knives, hiding them on her thigh. She had just fastened the last when Opal called from outside and the small woman peeked into the tent.

"My lady, I was just coming to see if you were ready for dinner. The Prince has ordered your immediate presence."

Arine's mouth twitched before she could stop it, and Opal's raised brow told her she had been caught. She would rather starve than be ordered around, but she forced a deep breath. Refusing would end badly—for her and her father—so she nodded. And maybe dinner would give her the chance to pry answers from the Prince since she hadn't had time to process any of his earlier comments.

"Thank you, Opal. I appreciate the *offer* and am ready to go now." Arine stressed the word, but Opal either missed it—or chose to ignore it.

"Of course, my lady. Please follow me."

"Just Arine, please."

Opal didn't respond and two guards fell in step behind them, lest she forget she was here involuntarily

They stopped at a tent taller than the rest, its heavy flap weighing in her hand as Arine braced herself. She had to keep her guard up—no foolish slips here. The luxury so far left her with a faint hope she might still smooth this over and get back to her father. Easier said than done, but at the very least, she could try to control herself and wrangle her face into submission.

However, the breath caught in her throat the instant she stepped inside. If her own tent had seemed extravagant, it was nothing compared to this one. Cross-beams stretched high overhead, and a long table dominated the center, wide enough to seat eight. Sconces lined the walls just far enough from the canvas to avoid disaster, their steady light pooling across thick layered rugs. A divider split the back half of the tent from view. Guards and servants lined the walls in disciplined silence.

The nearest guard gave her a cool once-over but didn't pat her down. With the stripes on his sleeve marking high rank, she didn't volunteer her hidden blades either.

A servant stepped forward and gestured to a chair near the head of the table. Only two places were set. Just her and the Prince, then. She wasn't sure if she should be relieved there wouldn't be an audience—or unsettled that she'd have his undivided attention.

She had just finished her sweep of the room when the Prince, himself, stepped through the divider. The space seemed to constrict around him. Arine forced her expression flat, fighting to keep the glare from creeping back into her countenance at the sight of him.

"Ah Arine, I'm glad you could make it," he said, as if he hadn't summoned her there himself.

She bit back the urge to snap at him and settled for a small nod, keeping her mouth shut before her real feelings slipped out.

His arrogance was plain as he strode to the head of the table and dropped into his seat, waving the servants on before she'd even reached hers. Heat crept up her neck, prickling under her skin as she stiffly crossed the room

Once seated, she expected him to speak, but he said nothing. Maybe it was some weird court custom to stay silent until food was served. Questions about Ciran, the woman, and everything else burned at the edge of her tongue, but she pressed her lips thin and waited.

Finally, after the servants set the food down, he spoke—but not to her. "Excuse us."

He said it quietly, yet the tent cleared as if he'd shouted. Only the one guard with the most bands lingered, casting the Prince a meaningful look before slipping out as well.

The prince swirled the wine in his glass around as he waited for the final guard to depart. Arine took a deep breath, steadying herself against whatever was to come next.

Only once the flap was firmly closed behind did he speak to her.

"How much of your parents' history do you know?" He asked quietly.

"What about them?" She hedged, not wanting to give away anything too soon.

"Well I assume you know you have a mother and father" he stated, disdain dripping from each word. "What all has your father shared with you about your mother?"

"Why are you asking about my mother and father?" She countered again.

His face was annoyingly devoid of any emotion as he spoke except a small arrogant set to his mouth.

"Ah" he replied, ignoring her question. "He hasn't told you anything, has he?"

A rush of indignation surged through her, tangled with disbelief. Her jaw tightened, and she forced herself not to rise to the bait.

He continued as though she wasn't fuming across the table. "Since your father left you woefully ignorant, let me fill you in. I already said he and my father were well acquainted during the war. What you don't know is that he commanded the King's Select Regiment."

He studied her closely, but Arine couldn't tell whether the revelation should shock or impress her.

"It's not surprising he never mentioned it—roles like his aren't public knowledge. But the King had a vested interest in the regiment's movements. That's how he knows your father, and how your father had the skills to keep you both hidden...until now."

Arine struggled to make sense of it. Her father had never once mentioned the royal family besides vague references. She knew he'd served in the war, but only as a tracker, a job far removed from the King himself.

The Prince lifted his fork and prodded at the heap of steamed vegetables on his plate. Arine knew she should focus on his words, but her eyes lingered on the food—perfectly fresh, untouched by rot. A world away from what most of the kingdom lived with every day.

She stayed silent, refusing to admit she had no idea what he was talking about. After a few deliberate bites, he continued as though discussing the weather, not a past life of her father's that she had never known about.

"Another thing you might be wondering is, given this new information, why *did* you live your life so removed from the court?"

Arine hadn't gotten that far, but clearly the answer was because the Prince was confusing them with someone else. She tried to think of how best to tell a member of the royal family that they were insane without getting her head chopped off, but in the end her anger at his tone and complete tactlessness got the better of her.

"With all due respect, I think you are confusing my father and me with some-one else," she said tightly. "If any of this were true, my father would have told me. And as for putting food on the table—something you've clearly never had to worry about"—she jabbed a hand at the lavish dishes between them—"my father earned it through skill and hard work."

She was gripping the fork and knife so hard her knuckles were turning white, so she loosened her hold before he could call a guard in and have her executed for threatening him with the cutlery. That is if she didn't actually end up stabbing him.

His eyes flicked to her hands, but he made no move to call for anyone. He just raised an eyebrow at her and his annoying smirk got even bigger, which Arine hadn't thought was possible.

"I am quite sure we are talking about the right people. Besides, you greatly resemble your mother, aside from her hair color."

The remark was tossed out so casually she almost missed it.

"You know what my mother looked like?" The words slipped out before she could stop them.

He nodded. "I was eight during the war, so I wasn't often near the front lines. But I remember seeing both of your parents in the war tent when I visited mine. Hard to forget—a common woman being allowed in there. The image stuck with me."

A tightness seized her chest. He carried a memory she would never have. All the drawings of her mother had burned in a fire after the Severing, leaving Arine without even a picture to hold on to.

She knew she had inherited her mother's tan skin, though her own hair was a shade lighter—dark brown instead of jet black. Beyond that, her father rarely spoke of her. His silence had always seemed too heavy, and since her mother wasn't from their village, no one else could tell her what she'd looked like either.

The Prince's sharp gaze held hers as he went on. "I'm not the only one who remembers her. You were recognized a few months ago, when you slipped into a healer's shop in the Garden District."

Another denial died on her lips. How could he know about that? She'd only been in the district for a few hours, sneaking in and out as quickly as she could.

The Prince answered her question without her having to ask. "One of the soldiers who had reported to your father eighteen years ago, who now heads the Select Regiment himself, recognized you. He brought the news to the King who immediately called for a search of the District. It wasn't until a few weeks later that we thought to check the enrollment lists and..." he snapped his fingers, "there you were. But of course, we found out that you decided to go for the final test immediately. Which by the way is almost never heard of, so that led us on this merry chase to find you here."

Twisting her features into what she hoped was a semblance of contrition. "Is this about me being in the Garden district without approval? I was trying to find medicine for my father. I didn't take anything, so if something is missing it wasn't me-" He waved his hand, cutting her off.

"That's all taken care of. Your family would have been in the upper Districts already, if your father hadn't hidden you away."

"What? And again he didn't *secret* me away. We traveled all over together," she replied tersely.

"Just not the Capital, right?" he shot back.

She wanted to slap the insolence right off his face. His strong jaw and blue eyes were unable to compensate for his appalling character. Clearly finding joy in her bewilderment, he paused to take a large gulp of wine, somehow managing to drink it just as smugly while the shadows from the sconces danced along the side of the tent behind him.

"It surprises me you know so little of your own heritage," he went on. "Your father was highly regarded, or he wouldn't have held his position. But your mother..." He let the pause hang. "She was a wielder. One of the strongest of her time. A great asset in the war."

Arine froze, words failing her. Of all the revelations she had braced herself for, that had never crossed her mind. Her father had never once hinted her mother had wielded magic. In fact, he had specifically told her she died *after* the Severing. Either the Prince was lying or....could it be that her father had indeed kept so much from her for twenty years? She was starting to feel like she had no idea who her father was. She couldn't fathom why he would lie to her.

She picked up her water glass and took a drink but it did nothing to help calm her. She quickly set it down before her hands started to shake. For the first time, she wondered if he might be telling the truth—if he somehow knew her parents better than she did.

Across the table, the Prince sighed and ran a hand through his hair, as if *he* were the one who had been deceived all his life. Of course he'd twist it, acting as though he was the one suffering. He muttered something under his breath but all she caught was "in the dark".

She could surmise he was talking about her father again and she was at her breaking point. She had spent weeks clawing through a forest to survive—fighting slavers, dragging a dying woman to safety—only to be kidnapped and forced to listen to a spoiled Prince tear her father down. She was done playing his games.

"Look, Prince," she snapped. "I don't know what sick game this is for you, but I won't sit here and listen to you tear down my father, who is dying because of you. Throw me in jail if you want, but I'm done with this."

She shoved her chair back to stand, not really knowing what her next move would be with all the guards out front. But she knew she couldn't sit here with this annoying man pretending as if they were having a normal conversation over dinner any longer.

The Prince didn't make any move to stop her, he just leaned back in his chair, watching.

"I wouldn't do that if I were you," he called out before she'd taken two steps.

She looked back—he lounged in his chair as if watching a play. Her jaw ached from grinding her teeth. Against her better judgment, she whirled back around.

"Or what? Another threat? More of your obnoxious stories? Surely you have better ways to waste your time."

He watched her for a few seconds, his tone deadly quiet when he finally replied. "Listening to stories, as you call it, with me is a far better way to pass the time than it would be if Gerin thought you were insubordinate. Believe me, I know."

Something about the way he said the last part made her pause. Had he witnessed that guard's punishments? But then if he had and stood by, he was just as bad.

"Your father's life is on the line, remember?"

"Because you kidnapped him! And me for that matter" Arine spat back, voice rising. "And you drag me in here, telling me these things that explain nothing!"

"I wouldn't have to explain a damn thing if Tyvin had told you himself! Don't blame me for your father's choices!" He countered angrily. It was the first real emotion she'd seen in him.

"You know nothing and you're already in over your head. Think about how you've been treated during this 'kidnapping' as you call it. I don't have to tell you anything. I could drag you along blind, entirely at my mercy. Say the word, and I'll make it so. Consider, for even a moment, that there are far greater stakes here than your small world."

He snapped his mouth shut, and she almost flinched at the force behind it. He glared at her as if she were the fool. As much as she wanted to walk out and never see him again, a sliver of doubt crept in. Why was he telling her this? She could accept perhaps that even though he was a cruel man and had taken her and her father against their wills, maybe there was something she was missing that gave her some modicum of power. Why else would he deign to even engage with her? A flicker of something, maybe hope, maybe desperation, caught in her chest. If he was still talking, she still had some leverage.

"Fine," she snapped, "I'll listen. But let me remind you—I only need to survive this because you, a stranger whose name I don't even know, kidnapped me and my father."

Her chest heaved with quick, uneven breaths, pulse hammering in her ears, but she forced herself to stand tall, arms crossed. The Prince inhaled, gesturing for her to sit again. She raised her brows, waiting.

She could have sworn he rolled his eyes before continuing. "This didn't start with me. It began eighteen years ago with your mother. So it was only a matter of time before it reached you. Please, Arine. Sit. We still have much to discuss."

Even though she despised the Prince and the position he put her in, she had to know what was going on to make a plan. Slowly, begrudgingly, she walked back over and sat down.

The Prince poured himself more wine, shoulders slumping before he straightened again. The arrogant mask slid back into place, but dulled, as if even he lacked the energy to keep arguing with her.

"My name is Derik," he said casually, not meeting her gaze. "Call me what you like in private, but in front of anyone else it must be 'Your Highness.' My uncle doesn't find impropriety amusing, and he won't hesitate to punish you—or anyone you care about—to make a point."

She understood the meaning, her father would be the one punished. How despicable they were, to harm someone incapable of defending themself.

"I honestly didn't expect Tyvin to have kept everything from you so I wasn't sure if you were lying or not. But yes, your mother could wield and like I mentioned before, she was the most powerful wielder Calasis had ever seen. If she hadn't defected to our side, who knows what would have happened in the war."

"Wait, defected?" Arine blurted. That couldn't be right. Aligning with Vanin, even at first, would mean siding with a tyrant.

"Yes," Derik replied evenly.

"That's not possible, why would she do that?" she exclaimed.

Why would her mother have ever followed Vanin? He was a monster who wanted wielders to rule over nonwielders, believing them inferior and unworthy of being treated as equals. And why would her father hide all of this and make them live the way they did if he was close with the King? Was he embarrassed because of her mother's past?

He shook his head. "I won't pretend to know what changed your mother's mind back then, but I presume it had to do with meeting your father. They were inseparable afterwards. She was able to provide the intelligence that helped win several key battles in the early stages of Vanin's assaults." He paused and something passed behind his eyes...pity? She straightened involuntarily, bracing for whatever came next. How could it get worse?

"Now, as you know the war ended with the Severing. The destruction caused that day was catastrophic to everyone, involved or not. Your mother was a casualty, but she was also the only one strong enough to have caused it."

Arine sucked in a breath. "Wait, what are you saying?"

"I'm saying that your mother, Nadyia, was the one who severed magic eighteen years ago."

Chapter 6

"That is impossible!" Arine sputtered. "My father would never love someone who could do that."

Her stomach flipped. No—this couldn't be true. Her mother, the reason people were dying? Her chest tightened, her throat raw around the words. Tyvin had spent his life helping those afflicted by the rot. He would never have loved someone capable of such destruction.

And yet...could the secrets be guilt? She shoved the thought away. She refused to believe it.

Prince Derik pressed on, oblivious to her turmoil. "My uncle believes Vanin kidnapped you the day of the Severing, forcing your mother to give chase. He must have done something to make her believe the only way to save you was to sever magic. She likely had no idea of the repercussions—all the lives lost that day, and her own of course."

Her stomach twisted even more. Each word tightened around her like a noose. How could her mother be the cause of so much death? The air pressed heavy in her lungs. She needed out of this tent, away from the Prince's words.

She shoved back from the table, too clumsy in her rush. The chair caught on the thick rug and she stumbled sideways. Derik's hand shot out, catching her arm—again.

Her palm slammed down on the edge of the table, the wood biting into her skin. She gripped hard, forcing herself to breathe, to anchor against the spinning in her head

He nudged her wine glass closer. "Here, take a drink, it will help calm you."

She'd ignored the wine all evening, but now she needed something—anything—to cut the edge. She took a long drink and set the glass down with an unsteady hand. It was smoother than expected, but it did little to settle her nerves. Still, it gave her something to cling to besides the knot of unease tightening inside.

"It could be someone else, though, right?" She asked, her fingers locked around the glass like it was an anchor. "You can't know for sure?"

"Her body was found in the cave where the Severing took place," he said, tone flat enough to crush her hopes. "And no one else was that strong. She was the only one of her kind."

"But where was my father? Wouldn't he know if I'd been kidnapped? He would've had to know if my mother...was...was the one to sever magic."

The Prince shrugged. "I can't say what he knew, only that he was on the other side of the battlefield. Vanin's army staged a massive surprise attack, likely to keep Nadyia from receiving aid. It's said Vanin took her betrayal personally, so his retaliation was not surprising."

Her thoughts spun, colliding with everything she thought she knew. Still—why her? Why now, eighteen years later?

"Fine. Let's say my mother did cause this. Why are you here, then? To put me and my father on trial in her place?" She released the wine glass and slid her hands into her lap, gauging the distance to the entrance. How fast could she draw a knife?

"Please remain calm and do not bring out your knife," Prince Derik said, swirling his wine as though bored.

Damn it. How did he know? Her fingers still closed on the knife hilt in her boot, but she froze. Her thoughts leapt to Ciran and the unconscious woman. If she ran, could she even find them again? And if Ciran learned the truth about her family—would he even still help her?

"If you make too much noise," the Prince warned, sharper now, "the guards will come in—and things will turn ugly fast."

Arine tuned him out, mind racing for a way to keep them all safe. Nothing came.

When she still didn't move, Derik exhaled, exasperated. "Do you really think that little knife against my sword would do you any good? You would be dead in seconds."

Gods, she hated this arrogant man.

"Leave the knife. I'm not here to arrest you—I need you."

Her head snapped up. "Need me? For what?"

"To undo the Severing. To stop the land from dying. You're the only one who can undo what your mother did."

Arine gaped at him. "That's impossible. I have no magic. No one does."

Derik drummed his fingers on the glass. "I knew this wouldn't be simple—and your father keeping you in the dark only makes it harder. You at least know how magic used to work, don't you?"

Reluctantly, she nodded. Everyone knew. Wielders had been born with different levels of power, able to pour that strength into objects. Imbued artifacts could heal, protect, or destroy depending on the magic placed within. But the stronger the artifact, the more it drained the wielder—sometimes leaving them weak for days.

The craft of wielding used to shape every corner of life. In war, they were prized for charging stones that, once launched from catapults, exploded on impact. Others crafted healing artifacts, but the process required precision—each one could only mend a single kind of wound. That meant healers were constantly needed to create new artifacts for every fresh injury or illness.

Arine had read that the process drew energy from the wielder and bound it to a single purpose in the object. To her, wielders seemed born with a sense others lacked—like a baker's knack for bread or a blacksmith's skill at forging steel. Each had their specialty: those gifted in healing rarely excelled at making weapons, and vice versa. Their talents kept them in high demand, and usually among the wealthy.

She lifted her chin and recited what she knew.

"Yes. And you know that if someone tried to pour too much power into an artifact, it could kill them?" he asked, once she was done.

She nodded, though she still didn't see how this had anything to do with her.

"And have you heard of blood binding?" he asked casually.

She froze. Blood binding? She searched her memory, but none of the books she'd read had ever mentioned it.

Seeing her confusion, he explained.

"My uncle said blood binding was discovered late in the war. A powerful wielder would first craft an artifact meant to bind. Using that, they could then create another artifact tied to their own blood—usable only by them, unlike normal artifacts anyone could wield."

"The process of making the first binding artifact and then the second blood-bound artifact drained a wielder for days, even weeks. Few outside the front lines knew of them before the Severing. But my uncle believes your mother used one when she severed magic. That's why no one's been able to undo it, no matter how many have tried. And that's why we need you. Her blood runs in you—we believe you are the only one who can undo it."

The soft glow of the sconces continued to flicker on the fabric walls of the tent, casting shifting shadows that seemed to echo her confusion as she turned his words over in her mind. Logically it made sense, seeing as she had always wondered why someone couldn't fix the Severing if a person had caused it in the first place, but the fact that it could be her was...absurd.

"You think I can fix everything?" she asked incredulously.

"Yes," he replied simply.

She searched for any trace of mockery, but it was gone. He was serious—too serious. Outside, muffled voices drifted through the tent walls, but the silence between them pressed heavier than anything beyond.

"Why do you think my mother used a blood bind?" she pressed, hunting for a flaw in his story—proof this was just some elaborate game.

"Well, firstly—my uncle found a knife in the cave where your mother died that matched the type used in blood binds. And second, the fact that no one has been able to undo the Severing after nearly two decades speaks for itself."

With every response, her uncertainty grew. She would know if she could do that...wouldn't she? Arine's gaze remained fixed on the Prince as his words hung between them, heavy and persistent.

"If I could actually do all of this"—she waved a hand at him—"why wouldn't I have done it already? I would have saved my father in a heartbeat if I had the power. Never once have I felt a spark of magic, let alone the strength to undo the Severing. And why would my father keep that from me?"

His gaze was steady as he replied, still unfazed by her questions. "You couldn't have before. It has to be done in the cave at Mt. Farna—where the Severing happened—and with the binding knife your mother used."

"You didn't answer my last question. Why would my father have hidden this from me if it was true?" she pressed, because this was the hardest to understand. "I know him, regardless of what you think, and I know he would want to stop the suffering if he could."

He sighed—she was starting to realize it was his favorite habit. A flicker crossed his eyes, maybe pity. "I'm not sure. There's a chance your mother never told him about blood binding. And maybe he just wanted to escape, to live quietly where no one knew him after she was gone."

Arine thought back to childhood. Her father almost never spoke of her mother, as if even her name was too painful. And if blood binding was so rare, maybe he hadn't realized the knife's importance when he found them—taking Arine and leaving—otherwise he would have taken it himself. Still, unease gnawed at her. She took another swig of wine, weighing what to believe.

"So, let me get this straight." She set the glass down. "You're saying if I go to the cave where magic was severed, I'll somehow be able to fix everything just by...existing?"

"Close," the Prince said, almost civil. "But there's more. When you get to the cave, you'll have to slice yourself—just enough to draw blood." He added quickly when she twisted her face in disgust. "Then you should be able to release it. So yes, almost by existing. And then, once magic is restored, new artifacts can be made, and your father can be cured."

In the back of her mind, she knew he dangled her father's cure as bait, but she couldn't stop the surge of hope that rose in her chest. With all the new information he had piled on her, she hadn't made that connection until now. Not only would hunger end with farmland restored, but her father—and countless others—could be healed.

Her eyes narrowed on his too casual posture now. "What's the catch then? What happens to me afterwards? Will my father and I be free to go?"

"Having magic restored benefits everyone. No one wants to rule a dying land. If you succeed, you and your father will no longer be detained." He replied smoothly.

Her thoughts flicked to Ciran and the unconscious woman, and she wondered if she could trust him.

"You'll let Ciran go and have a healer tend to the woman we found as well. They have nothing to do with this, and it will show me I can trust your word," she said, mimicking his tone of command from earlier.

He considered her request for a moment, and she made sure to meet his eyes unflinchingly. She wasn't sure what she'd do if he refused, but he didn't know that.

"Done," he said finally, shrugging as if it was of no real concern to him.

Relieved, she gave a small nod to seal the agreement. But as quickly as the relief came, a weight settled over her, sinking into her chest with the finality of what she'd just agreed to. Doubt crept in, sharp and persistent. She dropped her gaze to her hands, half-expecting to feel something. Maybe some spark or dormant pull toward the magic she was supposedly tied to. But there was nothing. She felt exactly as she always had. If there was a part of her capable of fixing all this, it remained as hidden from her as ever.

Prince Derik stood, straightening his already immaculate jacket. "With that settled, we leave tomorrow. But first, we must detour to the palace. The King won't allow the knife out of his sight unless he's certain you are Nadyia's daughter. If it were lost, there would be no way to restore magic. He'll require a meeting, so I suggest you show more restraint than you've shown here. And not only with him. His men will seize on any excuse to earn favor by reporting dissent. Remember—you're under my protection, and impropriety reflects on me."

She bristled at his accusations. He and his uncle were the ones forcing this, after all. But, she kept her mouth firmly shut so as not to play right into his words. If he noticed her reaction, he wisely chose to ignore it before he continued on.

"I don't suppose you've had any reason to travel to the Decayed Lands," he said, almost offhand, "but it's worse now than it's ever been. The ground is treacherous past a certain point, horses won't make it. We'll have to resupply before we leave."

She hadn't been near the Decayed Lands in years, but the stories stuck with her; air thick like ash, patches of ground that sank beneath your feet, animals with twisted limbs and hollow eyes. A cold ripple traced her spine. She'd understood what Derik meant, that she would need to return to the place where the Severing began, but somehow, she hadn't let her mind follow that thought far enough to realize it meant crossing miles of dying, dangerous land to get there.

At least she would get to see her father before they left. She needed to see for herself how he was being cared for.

She stood, meeting the Prince's eyes. "I will be ready in the morning then."

❧ · ✦ · ☙

Chapter 7

The Prince clapped his hands. "Excellent. One last thing. I'd think it obvious, but to be clear—under no circumstances do you tell anyone what we're doing. We can't risk anything before you restore magic. This will be a long shot, but if anyone asks, you are a cousin to the throne from my mother's side."

He gave her a once-over, slow and deliberate, the insult barely concealed. She couldn't help but retort in the sweetest tone she could muster, "Yes, I'm sure everyone would be expecting a cousin of yours to be someone horrid, wouldn't they?"

"Remember that, and just maybe you will survive everything that is to come."

She rolled her eyes and stepped around him before pausing. "Am I allowed to see my...travel companions?"

"Can you refrain from speaking about what we just discussed?" he asked.

She turned, startled he'd even consider it. His closeness caught her off guard, her breath hitching at how little space was left between them.

"Of course," she said coolly, forcing herself not to step back.

"What will you tell him?" he pressed, utterly unfazed by how close they stood. "I doubt you pretended to be my cousin during your travels."

She had told Ciran she'd never met the royal family, so this would be tricky to explain, but she wasn't about to let him know that.

Before she could think of a lie, he continued, "You can visit the woman. From my men's reports, she's still unconscious—but not Ciran. If you have some sort of attachment to him, you may write him a letter, as long as I can read it before it's given to him."

"That's not...we just met in the woods," she sputtered.

Heat flared in her cheeks as she fumbled for words, while the Prince only cocked his head, her scrambling amusing him.

"Ugh, just let me go see the woman," she grumbled, taking the opportunity to finally step away from him. She probably wouldn't come up with a convincing story in time anyway.

He smiled at her reaction and she almost pulled her knife. She walked toward the entrance, back stiff as she hid her face from view, sure it was bright red at this point. He wisely refrained from needling her any further, instead calling out for one of the guards.

"Lian!"

The high-ranking guard who had paused earlier re-entered. "Yes, Your Highness?"

"Escort Arine to the healer's tent and then her own. We will leave for home in the morning."

"Of course, Your Highness. But first—one matter to discuss."

Lian gave Derik a meaningful look, then motioned Arine toward the flap. She stepped into the night, the cool air a stark contrast to the stifling tent. Only then did she notice how late it was—well past dark. She drew in the air, trying to clear her head, but her thoughts still reeled.

She drifted further down the tent line and the guards kept their distance, just glancing briefly in her direction every so often. After a moment, muffled words from inside reached her. Her stomach tightened as she weighed the risk. Then, feigning aimlessness, she edged closer, straining to catch Lian's raised voice.

"...A little while ago there was a fire near the picket line, and when some of the guards came back, they found tracks by the side of your tent." She assumed he gestured somewhere. "There's no way whoever it was could have been there long, but they may have overheard something. I apologize for the laxness, but the horses were nearly breaking their lines. It was chaotic."

"I'm sure whoever it was couldn't have heard much," Derik replied. His words cut off as another soldier walked by, then resumed, muffled. "...new guest's friend, where was he at the time?"

"Already gone, Your Highness. He was sent in the opposite direction not long before. Very unlikely it was him, but we can send a runner after him if you think it best?"

She sucked in a breath. Were they talking about Ciran? The Prince had already let him go? Why wouldn't he have just said that? For a moment, confusion warred with relief. Of course he had nothing to do with this. But still...Ciran had left without even so much as a goodbye? The sting of it surprised her.

Silence stretched, then Derik spoke again. "Do it. Even with witnesses, he could have doubled back. Bring him to me if you find him—and keep it quiet, especially from Gerin. Put everyone on high alert and give the order to ride for the palace at first light. We need to be ready for anything."

"Yes sir."

Arine shuffled further down the tent to disguise her eavesdropping just as the flap rustled. Lian stepped out, helmet tucked under his arm, a few streaks of gray in his dark hair catching the torchlight. He looked younger than her father but worn from years of service. His eyes skimmed her, appraising, before joining her. She wondered how much he knew—if anything—about why she was really here.

"The healer's tent is this way," he said, gesturing for her to follow. "One of my men brought word not long ago that your friend was still alive. Nasty cut she had—how did you say she got it again?" His tone was more casual than when he spoke to the Prince.

She recognized the prying for what it was and stuck to the story.

"I don't know. We just found her."

"Interesting that it is so rare for those taking the final test to see anyone, let alone two others."

Since it wasn't phrased as a question, Arine chose silence, knowing it was her best defense. Thankfully, he let it drop.

As they walked, she turned over what she had learned—and overheard. With this many guards, who would be desperate enough to try anything? Then again, food and medicine were so scarce she had recently contemplated stealing herself. She smirked faintly at the thought of someone pulling one over on the Prince.

They passed rows of orderly tents, guards tense and alert. Armor gleamed in the firelight, every path illuminated so no shadows lingered. Smoke still curled from the east side of camp where the picket line must have been. The animals had calmed, but Lian inspected every soldier they passed, his face grim.

"Were there this many fires earlier? Seems like you'd go through a lot of wood," she asked casually, keeping her eyes forward. She watched him from the corner of her vision, gauging his reaction.

"Just being extra cautious, ma'am. There are bandits and slavers all over these days and the Prince would be tempting to ransom."

So a skilled liar then. Noted.

"Am I able to see my friend who was—" she paused, searching for something softer than *taken prisoner*—"detained earlier, after the healer's tent?

His eyes flicked to her for a moment, but that was his only reaction.

"No, ma'am. He chose to depart a while ago. Unfortunately, he left no farewells."

At least he'd escaped this madness—even if he had left her to fend for herself. Not wanting to risk drawing suspicion to her earlier eavesdropping, she let it drop, and they continued in silence until they reached another tent with two guards at its entrance. Both saluted, and one pulled back the flap while Lian motioned her inside.

Unlike her own or the Prince's, this tent held no finery. Tables crowded the space, jars and tinctures stacked in uneven piles. Each bore a slip of parchment marking its use. A larger table nearby was covered with half-filled bottles where herbs and liquids were being combined. She wrinkled her nose at the sharp odors—each breath carried a different smell from the variety of plants.

All she could see, though, was how much medicine was hoarded here. No group this size could possibly need so much. Another reminder of the King's and the Prince's callousness: while people died from the rot's sickness, these supplies sat idle, reserved for the Prince's comfort should he suffer so much as a scratch.

Lian's guarded look told her she hadn't hidden her disgust well.

"Is something wrong?" he asked, his tone too neutral.

"Of course not," she replied tightly, biting back anything sharper. "Where is she?"

He gestured to the back, where a curtain had been hung for privacy. A small woman stepped out as they spoke.

Arine's first thought was that she was young for a healer, and striking besides. Her skin was deep as midnight, and her black hair was pulled back in braids wrapping around her head like a crown. Her skin almost glowed in the light from the candles that were set haphazardly around the room.

"You must be here to see my newest patient!" the woman said cheerfully, her bright tone jarring after hours of the Prince's cold superiority.

She was probably five years older than Arine, but still young to have her own healing practice. Most healers apprentice for much longer before they are allowed to go on their own; the smallest mistake could take a life rather than save it.

"I'm Shian. Please, come see her. The fever has just started to break. I was afraid it was too late with how far the infection had spread, but I think she may yet recover."

Arine moved over behind the curtain and saw the red headed woman laying under a thick blanket. She grabbed her hand. It was clammy still but when she touched her brow it was markedly less hot. That plus the fact the woman wasn't thrashing in her sleep anymore, had her agreeing with the healer's assessment. Even so, Arine held her hand for a moment longer, looking over her features now that she had been cleaned up.

Her red hair was brushed and hanging in loose curls along her face, which Arine noticed was actually quite pretty. She had sharp features that were balanced with freckles across her nose. Her skin was still pale and she noticed thick muscles on her arms, rare for a woman to have. Not for the first time Arine wondered who she was and how she had been kidnapped. From the shape she was in, it seemed like she would have been able to hold her own.

She regretted not questioning the man they'd left in the woods, but they had been in such a hurry it hadn't crossed her mind. She would have to wait until the woman woke.

As if reading her thoughts, the healer moved closer. "Can you tell me how she got the knife wound, or if she had other injuries not visible?" she asked softly.

Arine brushed the woman's hair from her face as she weighed her answer. Even if no one would blame her for killing slavers, she wasn't about to risk it.

"No. We found her like this. Slavers had taken her. We freed her and carried her back. I don't know how they captured her or what they did to her."

Shian gave an understanding nod and adjusted a bandage on one of the smaller cuts. "Well, my name is Shian; I'll send a runner if her condition changes." She started back toward her herbs, then turned. "She's lucky you risked yourself. Most wouldn't."

Arine watched her as she started mixing another cocktail of herbs and put it in a crate already loaded with medicine. Her kindness struck Arine, but it did little to ease the anger simmering as she took in shelf after shelf of hoarded medicine, untouched while people outside starved and died.

Her jaw clenched. She spun on her heel, stiffly walking out before she said something she'd regret. She couldn't stand being in the tent with such a hypocrite. How could a healer of all people think that was right?

She gulped fresh air, her pulse still thundering in her ears, as if she were drowning despite the open sky above. She should have stayed, asked more about the woman's condition, but everything was unraveling too fast to grasp. Her father's secrets, the half-truths, the gaping holes in what she thought she knew—all of it pressed in on her at once. Who were her parents, truly? Who was *she*? And if so much of her life had been a lie... what truth was left to stand on?

Lian lingered behind with Shian, but Arine decided she didn't need his watchful eye either. She wasn't under arrest, and the King needed her. She would be damned if she let them treat her as a prisoner.

She stormed off toward her tent, fists clenched, finally letting the emotions she'd been suppressing surge to the surface. What was the point of restoring magic if these were the people who would profit? Did they even deserve her effort?

Mind spinning, it took a few wrong turns before she finally recognized the area of camp where her tent had been. The cooks were gone now and all of the freshly washed pots were stacked. She didn't see any guards either—the lack of activity giving the whole area an eerie stillness. The flickering torchlight cast long, wavering shadows across the empty cooking stations, and even the soft crunch of her boots on the packed earth sounded too loud in the stillness.

She looked up, drawing in one last breath of crisp night air. She knew she had every right to be angry with these people, but they did not make up the majority of people like her friends from back home. They deserved a chance to live and she needed to remember that's why she would try to restore magic, no matter how far-fetched it was. For them.

Her shoulders slumped, and the tightness in her chest slowly eased as the realization settled over her. Her father, her friends, the people who had been treated cruelly for no reason, they mattered. She reached for the tent flap, as shouts erupted behind her, sharp and urgent, yanking her back to the present. She spun around instinctively, heart leaping to her throat.

At first she just heard running and clanking from the handful of soldiers who had still been awake. She squinted, struggling to see from where she stood. Boots pounded against the hardened earth, the clatter of weapons mixing with the barked orders from guards scrambling to respond.

Suddenly, a tent went up in flames, illuminating the sky and spreading rapidly. More soldiers were waking up and it was mayhem in a section on the other end of the camp. Then the unmistakable sounds of fighting reached Arine's ears, along with the call for water. Her pulse raced but she was rooted to her spot. What should she do? She cursed herself for leaving Lian behind.

A deafening boom rattled the ground, jolting her out of her stupor. She spun toward her tent, desperate to grab her bow and sword. Just as she reached for the flap, she caught a flicker of movement inside. Her hand froze mid-air.

Ciran? No—he'd been seen leaving.

Her hesitation gave her away. A man burst out, sword flashing. Instinct took over—she threw herself sideways as the blade carved the air where she had stood.

She hit the ground hard, rolled, and scrambled backward, yanking free one of her three knives. With no time to aim, she hurled it at the advancing man, cursing her own carelessness in leaving the rest of her weapons behind.

He ducked aside, giving her the moment she needed to stand and draw her second knife. His short sword still outmatched her blades, so she kept backing away, careful to stay on the lantern-lit path where she could avoid tent ropes and stakes.

She cried out for help, but only the distant clamor answered. No one was coming.

The man stalked forward, face hidden behind black cloth. Only his eyes showed through, and they glittered with malice. Her ears rang with the rush of blood. Hopefully he assumed she had more knives than she actually did and was wary that she would throw more—that was her only protection against him rushing her.

As if on cue, he lunged. She flung her second knife and he dodged, but it slowed him enough for her to retreat toward a crate of wooden utensils. Useless. Still, she kicked them over, sending them sprawling across the path, trying anything she could to slow him.

Running out of options, a reckless plan took shape. She gripped her last knife and hurled it. Without waiting to see if it struck, she dashed down the row of tents towards the ones with the large cookpots. There were no fires or lanterns lit near these tents so she was unable to make out anything specific, but she hoped they would have what she needed.

Her feet pounded across the packed dirt and she heard the man swear. Hope mixed with her adrenaline that she had actually gotten a good hit on him. She didn't slow and seconds later she heard his footsteps sounding after her again. Now it was her turn to curse.

She lunged for the jumble of pots, hands fumbling through the shadows. She'd seen the long hooks earlier by the fires, but now, in the dim light and with panic clawing at her, she couldn't find them. Seconds bled away.

Despair threatened to overwhelm her until a glint of metal caught her eye, and she dashed forward, hope surging. She wrenched it up only to find it was just the metal chains they used to hoist the pots over the fire. A curse escaped her lips, but with nothing to lose, she grabbed the chain in both hands and turned to meet him.

She swung the chain as she turned, not knowing exactly how far away or where he was, just trying to frantically sling something at him. The chain crashed into the dirt, sparks of grit scattering, but the surprise forced him to dodge aside.

He recovered fast and his sword sliced at her ribs. She scrambled away, but pain seared across her side, hot and sharp, driving the chain from her grip. Blood ran down her body, and she knew even though the cut wasn't deep enough to hit an organ, she still wasn't going to be able to defend herself for much longer.

Her only option now was to twist around the pot, using it as a shield against his next swing. Its iron belly rang under the next blow as she kept trying to scuttle around it, reaching for anything behind her.

Her fingers closed on a mallet. Useless again. She hurled it anyway. He didn't flinch, stepping aside with cruel ease. His eyes locked on hers through the mask, steady and unhurried. He knew she was running out of weapons. And so did she. Arine could almost imagine him grinning underneath his mask.

That knowledge—that he was enjoying this—lit a spark of fury in her chest. She would not cower. If she was going to die, she'd at least go down with a fight.

Her hands scraped the ground again until they closed on the chain. Weak as she was, she hauled it up and swung. By sheer luck, the man stepped right into it. The links wrapped around his leg, yanking him off balance. He grabbed for the cook pot, but his sword snagged on the handle and tore free of his grip as he toppled.

Arine dove, her momentum carrying her over him as they both seized the weapon. She clung with everything she had, twisting to land on her uninjured side. Even so, pain ripped through her ribs, stealing her breath, but she refused to let go.

She gasped for air, her eyes fixed on him, searching for any hint of his next move, but he was utterly still. Slowly, she edged closer. He lay still, staring at the sky, a dark gash cut across his midsection. The sword must have caught him as she tumbled over. She stared, numb. Dumb luck was all that had saved her.

Her hand pressed to the hot sting at her side as boots thundered toward her. Metal clanked, voices shouted. She turned her head just as Lian appeared, guards fanned out behind him. Her body refused to move, her arms trembling as she kept the bloodied sword lifted toward them.

Lian halted, calling the others back. His voice was steady, almost gentle. "It's me, Lian. There are no more Syarans here. You're safe now."

Syarans? The word echoed in her head. They were nowhere near that border. Why would they be here?

Her thoughts crawled, sluggish and slow. Lian approached, eyes flicking from her face to the corpse. He reached for her hand—deliberate, unhurried—then twisted the sword from her grasp in one clean motion. She didn't resist. Her arm dropped, pressing again to the wound at her ribs, her gaze still locked on the lifeless man at her feet.

Arine remained frozen as Lian's men pulled the mask from her attacker. Pale eyes stared sightlessly, blond hair clotted with dirt or coal in a crude attempt at disguise. He was just a man, no different from dozens she'd passed in the streets. Ordinary, yet he'd waited in her tent with the intent to kill her.

Nausea overwhelmed her, and she retched violently, the meal from earlier burning her throat.

Lian stayed by her side, silent, until the spasms eased. When she finally straightened, the wound in her side tore with fresh pain and she swayed on her feet. Adrenaline still buzzed through her veins, making the world feel like it belonged to someone else. She thought of the slavers she'd fought with

Ciran—those deaths had been necessary to save the injured woman. This felt different, personal.

Guilt cut deeper than her wound. She never should have ditched Lian; she'd blundered through the camp like a child who didn't know the risk of her situation. She could already picture the Prince's look of judgement when he found out.

Lian spoke again, jarring her out of her thoughts. "Are you okay? Were you injured anywhere besides your side?" he asked.

"I don't think so," she said quietly.

"Then let's get you to Shian's tent." He motioned to his men, sending one to fetch the Prince while the others closed in around them, weapons ready.

Arine glanced at Lian as they walked. His coat was streaked with blood, so heavy it nearly obscured the buttons. "Are you injured?" she asked in turn, only a little breathless.

"No, it's not my blood," he said.

"Oh," was all she could think to respond with.

Above them, the night sky glittered calm and unbothered, a cruel contrast to the chaos tearing her world apart.

Chapter 8

Arine glanced at Lian as they walked. "Do you know who that man was? Was he after me...or someone else?" The words snagged despite her effort to sound casual.

Part of her still wanted to believe it was all a mistake. No one would purposefully try to kill her, it was absurd. But another part of her already knew what his answer would be, because if he hadn't been after her, he would have gone after whoever else once he realized he had the wrong person.

"His clothes and face mark him as a Syaran; several groups of them have been terrorizing towns in the area."

So she hadn't misheard him earlier.

"Why would Syarans be this far from the border? And why come after me?" she asked, confusion clawing at her. They threaded through the tents as guards streamed past, the smoke thinning where the fires had burned.

"The rot has only made them worse," Lian said. "As our land withers, their fanaticism grows. They believe their god spared Syar—that purging their wielders kept the rot away. They have spread that poison inside their borders for years. And their farmland, small as it is, still feeds their people. Ours doesn't. It emboldens them. In recent months, they have started to attack randomly across

Calasis in the hopes that our people find us too weak and convert. And famine," he added grimly, "makes even the wisest desperate."

Arine listened as Lian spoke, surprised he was sharing so much yet grateful for the scraps he offered. Still, relief quickly gave way to unease—none of it explained why the man had been waiting in her tent.

Even so, what he had revealed was still shocking. Especially since Syar's beliefs about women were nearly as harsh as their views on wielders; they claimed magic passed through the mother's line, not the father's. That alone could make her a target, but Lian said the Syarans had been attacking for months. And Derik had only just found her. How could they possibly know who she was? She regretted not having asked the Prince for more details about the secrecy earlier. Did anyone else know?

"Well, that explains why they're here," she said carefully, "but I still don't understand why they would come after me. I'm sure Derik has many cousins."

If Lian knew her "cousin" cover story was a lie, he gave no sign. He only shrugged, slipping back into silence. "The Prince will meet us at the healer's tent. He may have more to say."

Guess he met the quota for words, she thought irritatedly. Arine held in a huff of annoyance and kept walking, clutching her side to blunt the pain of each step.

When they reached Shian's tent, it was transformed. The vials of medicine were stowed away, trunks stacked in the corner to clear space for the wounded. Four new cots lined the interior, each occupied by soldiers in varying states of injury.

Shian had just finished tending to the wounded soldiers, most of them unconscious on their cots. She looked up from her notes at a small desk. The moment her gaze landed on Arine, her expression hardened into a thin line.

"Those animals have to be stopped," she snapped at Lian, her friendly tone from earlier gone.

Shian motioned Arine over to a bench next to a table laden with bandages. Lian didn't respond, he just took up a position at the front of the tent with the remaining guards outside. The familiarity of the outburst surprised Arine, given the Prince's stern warnings on propriety, but Lian didn't strike her as someone who would report her.

Shian began working without preamble, cutting away fabric to reach the wound. Her hands were precise, efficient, and almost unnervingly clean—more than enough proof of how she'd earned her place here so young.

While Shian was preparing her needle to stitch the gash, movement at the door drew Arine's gaze. Lian saluted as Prince Derik pushed into the tent along with the guard from the morning, Gerin, she thought was his name. Was that really just this morning? It felt like a lifetime ago.

Gerin turned first to Lian, demanding an update in a low, clipped voice. Arine couldn't make out their words. But from their grim expressions—and the frequent glances cast her way—she knew they weren't pleased with how things had unfolded.

Without his helmet, Gerin looked younger than she'd expected, no older than Derik himself. His brown hair was matted to one side with blood, and grime streaked his face.

She wondered how he had risen to his position so young, but it explained the hotheadedness he'd shown earlier with Ciran. The thought of Ciran brought a pang of worry. She hoped he was far enough away before the Syarans attacked. He was skilled, yes, but judging by the number of bloodied soldiers here, there had been far more than just a handful of attackers. He would've been hard pressed to escape alone.

As Lian finished his rundown, Prince Derik and Gerin crossed to her. Shian's brow was furrowed in concentration as she stitched Arine's wound, so focused she didn't seem to notice Derik's presence. That suited Arine just fine—being stuck with a needle was painful enough without having to bow or perform pleasantries for the Prince at the same time.

Anger flickered in Derik's eyes before he smothered it, his tone clipped and controlled as he addressed her. "Lian told us what happened. From now on, you'll be assigned a guard at all times. Lian has volunteered, and he'll appoint another to alternate with. You will not be unaccompanied again on our journey."

He kept his expression smooth, but his voice betrayed the strain of temper barely under control. A part of Arine bristled, wanting to refuse the idea of a constant babysitter. But she forced herself to nod, the practical part of her knowing the demand wasn't negotiable.

"Do you know why or how they were in my tent?" she asked. Her gaze flicked around, hesitant about what could be said in front of so many.

Both Gerin and Lian stiffened. She looked between them, wondering what had happened—surely she hadn't given anything away from that?

Derik's sneer was sharp as he replied. "Your Highness is the proper address. I know you've been away from court for most of your life, cousin, but you would do well to remember it. Only those with sufficient rank are privy to briefings."

He turned from her to Lian just as Shian tied off the last stitch. "Escort my cousin to her tent. She's had an eventful evening, and rest will do her good."

Bitterness washed over Arine at the Prince's words. She hadn't expected him to tell her everything, but treating her as if she were out of line for asking why was absurd when she had almost been killed.

Arine opened her mouth to demand answers, but the younger guard's stance made her hesitate—almost like he was waiting for her to do just that. Before she could place the look, Lian's hand closed lightly around her arm, guiding her toward the exit. His gaze was intent, almost pleading with her not to fight him.

Her fingers twitched at her side, the question burning on her tongue, but something in Lian's tense grip held her back. She couldn't afford to err right now, so she let Lian pull her forward through the tent's opening. She refused to look back and risk meeting their gaze as she stiffly walked out, the pain in her side only slightly dulled from Shian's administration.

As soon as they were out of the tent, Lian dropped her arm and motioned for her to keep going. Not until they were far enough away to be out of ear shot, did he finally speak.

"Some advice, since we will be closely acquainted for the time being. If you want to avoid punishment, keep your head down and don't draw attention to yourself. After years of famine and disease, only strict governess keeps order. Remember that."

His tone wasn't cruel, just blunt. Arine didn't answer, though she knew he was right. She needed to play by their rules if she wanted to keep her father safe.

Then his words struck her, and she stopped, turning to face him.

"Are you going to be punished for this?" she asked.

Lian turned toward her, something unreadable flickering in his eyes. Hurt? Guilt? Anger?

"No. Another has taken the punishment since I wasn't officially assigned as your guard until now. But in the future...yes."

Arine blinked. "Why? It's not your fault—or anyone's. Why would the Prince punish his own men for being attacked by an enemy? That's not something you could control."

"The King doesn't care about fault and his word is law. He cares that we were caught unprepared. He doesn't abide failure. So before we leave, the highest-ranking man will deliver lashings to whoever bears responsibility for the laxness."

Disgust twisted through her. "Men died and the Prince will spend time tomorrow injuring another man for nothing more than an absurd rule meant to instill fear. Why follow him?"

He looked at her for a long moment. "Do not ask such questions aloud. Spies can be anyone, even me. And I would not be so quick to cast judgment without having been in someone's position yourself. In times of crisis, it's better to have strict laws and order rather than lawlessness."

He started forward again, and after a beat she hurried to catch up, every step jarring her side. A knot tightened in her stomach—revulsion tangled with reluctant understanding. She hated the cruelty of it, but he wasn't wrong about what fear of chaos could do.

Still, she knew where the true blame lay. Not with the soldiers, not even with the King's harshness, but with Vanin—the rebel who had started the war, and if the Prince was right, forced her mother to make the ultimate sacrifice to stop him. He was the root of all of this, the source of every loss and every wound that still bled through the land.

Chapter 9

They made it back to her tent without any further incident, but everything was starting to wear on Arine. Her body felt like it weighed double, each movement heavy as Lian opened her flap and inspected every inch of her tent. Once he was satisfied no other assassin was hiding to kill her, he gave her a brief nod and closed the panel without another word.

As soon as he was gone, she loosed a breath and tried to calm her racing heart. The image of the assassin waiting here for her still clung to her mind, sour and suffocating. She forced herself to steady her breathing the way her father had taught her after sparring, counting each inhale and exhale until her pulse slowed.

She laid her knives within easy reach and stripped off her bloodstained clothes, replacing them with a set of leathers from the trunk. The silk nightgowns tucked inside might as well have belonged to someone else; she had no intention of sleeping in anything that left her unprepared.

When there was nothing left to do, she blew out the candle and sank onto the bed, one knife gripped tightly in her hand. She lay rigid, ears straining for the scrape of boots or the hiss of steel, sleep hovering just out of reach.

At some point, exhaustion dragged her under, but it felt like mere moments later when she stirred to Opal's gentle hand on her shoulder. Arine's eyes burned, her head throbbed, and her limbs were heavy as stone.

The early morning blurred past her, her exhaustion dulling every detail of the camp's rush to depart. Theo, her new guard, had taken over from Lian sometime in the night, but she barely noted the change. She went through the motions automatically, her body moving where directed though her mind lagged behind. At least she hadn't been forced to witness whatever punishment the Prince had doled out for her lapse in protection.

Barely two hours after waking, they were already on the road to the capital. The day droned on, her injury a constant, dull ache as she rode. Exhaustion became its own strange comfort, narrowing her focus to the simple act of staying upright in the saddle. It left little room for her mind to replay the Prince's words or the assassin's attack.

When her thoughts inevitably drifted to what she had learned, a sharp sting of pain coursed through her. If even part of it was true, her father had lied to her. Maybe he didn't know everything, but he knew enough and he hadn't trusted her with the truth. Still, until he could explain it himself, she wasn't ready to accept that there was no good reason for his silence. She shoved the feelings deep down, boxing the feelings up. Nothing good would come of the thoughts until she had more answers.

The temperature had dropped several degrees while she slept, and a cold wind whipped through the group as they traveled. The sky was a marbled gray, heavy with the promise of rain. As they made their way back toward Draske, she noticed the emptiness in the countryside. The land here was far enough from the Decayed Lands to remain fertile, but the laborers moved sluggishly, drained of strength, as they brought in the final harvest before winter.

Two-and three-band soldiers were stationed at intervals, keeping watch over the crops so the harvest could be distributed however the royal family decreed. Despondency hung over everything—gaunt faces, shuffling steps—a stark contrast to the gleaming royal party surrounding Arine. It was a jarring reminder that even if the Prince claimed he wanted her to restore magic to spare his people, there was surely more he could be doing to ease their hardship now.

Thinking of the Prince, she didn't see him at all during the ride, not even when they stopped for lunch. Dried meat and cheese were passed around, and

Lian took back over for Theo, bringing a salve from Shian. He told her the healer had sent word that the red-haired woman's fever had broken that morning, though she was still mostly unconscious. Finally, a piece of good news, even though Arine couldn't see her while they traveled.

It was dusk when they finally reached the new "Outer District" of Draske, which was really just the slang for where all the commoners who couldn't afford to live in one of the original districts resided.

The people who lived here had built their houses on the outside of the gate, hence the name. If you could even call them houses. It was really just a mishmash of small one or two room ramshackle buildings, precariously stacked side by side. Unofficial roads snaked through the buildings as the number of inhabitants grew and more and more buildings were haphazardly added, making it more of a maze than a true thoroughfare. You could get turned around very easily and find yourself in one of the ever-feuding gangs territories, so it was never safe to wander in the Outer District alone.

Day workers were finishing their shifts, trudging home to families or stopping at inns to dull the weight of their reality. Wives called out to their husbands, and a handful of children darted through the streets, their shouts and laughter filling the air with more energy than anything else could. The sight of them, even so few, sparked a small flicker of happiness in her chest.

As their group moved down the road through row after row of buildings, Arine realized just how long she had been gone from real civilization and how much she missed the bustle of activity and life.

She eyed the crowds, looking for any signs of trouble, but everything seemed normal...until they passed one group of three men standing in a small alleyway, their muscles bulging around the weapons they held. The men didn't shrink back or avert their eyes, instead they openly assessed the group. The waning light and shadows from the shacks made it too hard to make out any specific details, but Arine could have sworn one of the men's eyes lingered on her as they passed.

A shiver ran down her spine. She tried to watch them from the corner of her eye, body tense for any sign of trouble, but the Prince's guards around her didn't seem concerned. The man never broke his gaze before leaning over and whispering to another, who slinked off behind the building. Arine braced herself for an attack that never came. When her group moved past without incident, she finally let her hand fall from her sword and realized it was trembling, memories of the previous night rushing back. She shook her head, scolding herself for seeing threats in every shadow.

By the time they emerged from the gate house into the Garden District, a light drizzle had begun to fall. Within minutes it turned into a downpour. Arine pulled her hood up and urged her horse forward. Whatever the circumstances, she would welcome a roof and a real bed tonight.

Through the curtain of rain, the castle loomed in the distance, its dark spires rising against the gray sky, stark and foreboding. Mist curled around its towers, and Arine couldn't stop herself from wondering which window hid her father. Was he worse? Would she ever hear him speak again, or share some small piece of wisdom with her? She forced the thought down. If the King and Prince were holding him as leverage, they had to be caring for him... she hoped.

They passed through the Garden District and into the Elite District without issue. The Garden District lived up to its name—multicolored houses with flower gardens filling every spare patch of dirt, even climbing walls and roofs. Though it was fall, a few bright colors still peeked through.

Her father had once told her this section was originally a vast park, built by an early king for his wife who loved nature. But as the Capital's population grew, space within the Outer Wall became scarce. To preserve the district's intent, residents covered their homes with flowers and vines, each display more elaborate than the last. Now, as she tried to glimpse the beauty through the rain, the memory of his story was soured by questions of how Tyvin had known the information himself. Why hadn't she ever questioned him on his deep knowledge of the Capital? She fought down the bitterness rising in her chest, wondering what other stories were founded on lies too. The weather seemed to match her mood as she rode on through the dreary rain.

Another gatehouse marked the border into the Elite District, and they passed through as quickly as before. Unlike the chaotic beauty of the Garden District, the Elite District was orderly and intentional. Brick roads spread in a precise pattern, and houses sat far apart—space enough for two or three times the population, if the wealthy hadn't claimed it all for themselves.

There were fewer people milling about, likely due to the downpour. They made it through the Elite District quickly and were soon at the gates for the Royal District. More guards stood watch here and it took several long minutes for their party to be verified before they were finally admitted.

Arine had only ever snuck into the Garden District, so she hadn't seen any of the others. She had to admit, the Royal District was breathtaking. Smaller castle-like manors dotted the avenues, each with grand archways and tree-lined paths leading to massive doors. Yet all of them paled beside the towering castle at the center. Six spires pierced the sky, its white stone gleaming through the rain. An inner wall surrounded the palace, more ornament than defense—any army that had made it past three gates would hardly be stopped here. Behind it, the Northreach River flowed, rain streaking its surface and turning the current into a sheet of silver that glimmered against the looming silhouette of the palace.

They wound around a giant sculpture of some long-dead ruler, past a sprawling shrub maze and orchard where a stream wound through lantern-lit trees. Guards peeled away in twos and threes to return to regular duty until the remaining escort brought her to a smaller, though still imposing, side door. Servants rushed forward, helping her dismount and leading the horses toward an immense stable.

Her legs ached and her wound throbbed as she climbed the steps, doing her best to mask the pain. Despite her exhaustion, the sight of the palace sent her pulse racing. There was no going back now. Once she crossed this threshold, everything would change.

Inside, it took her a moment to adjust to the bright lights, but she quickly recognized the decor—the palace was a gaudier reflection of the Prince's tent. Marble floors stretched beneath her, etched with golden patterns, while a black carpet lined the hall. Paintings, vases, and glass figurines adorned the walls, and servants stood at perfect attention along the edges, waiting to be summoned.

Most of the guards dispersed until only Lian, the Prince, and two others remained. A servant slipped off Arine's dripping cloak while Derik barked orders to an elderly man, who bowed sharply and scurried away. He issued a few more hushed instructions to the guards, then dismissed them as well.

That left her standing awkwardly to the side, damp and exhausted, waiting for someone to tell her where to go. She fought a shiver as Derik finally turned.

"Lian will show you to your room. I'll meet with the King. I expect he'll summon you tomorrow." His tone was clipped, and he surveyed her for a moment before adding, "Remember the advice you were given whenever you are among others."

Before she could ask about her father, he strode down the hall without a backward glance.

Arine muttered under her breath as Lian gestured for her to follow. They wound through corridor after corridor and up staircases until she gave up on memorizing the route. The palace was a maze—she would never find her way out on her own in such a short time. And she still had no idea where her father was being kept.

At last, they stopped. Lian glanced around, then nodded her inside. The chamber was more modest than the splendor she'd glimpsed elsewhere, though still far finer than anywhere she'd stayed. A four-poster bed dominated the space, with a washbasin and small privy to one side. Heavy curtains framed a balcony door, rain drumming steadily beyond it.

Part of her wanted to storm off and find her father—or even the Prince—and demand answers, anything to feel less helpless. But she knew it would be foolish and likely pointless. Instead, she forced herself to save her strength for tomorrow. She dabbed more of the healing salve onto her side, then crawled under the soft covers. The warmth was a small mercy, but it did nothing to soften the storm of questions waiting for her when she woke.

Chapter 10

Light streamed in through the cracks in the curtains the next morning as Arine blinked her eyes open. Groggily, she wondered where she was until the memories crashed back into her. She sat up, scanning the room, but everything was just as she'd left it. She pushed out of bed and stretched, toes sinking into the thick rug, then crossed to the window and pulled the thick drapes wide.

Sunlight spilled across the room, sharper than she expected after the storm. Judging by its angle, it had to be late morning. She hadn't expected to sleep at all, much less so deeply, but thankfully the rest left her mind clearer.

After washing up, she opened a massive armoire carved with curling vines only to find nothing but dresses. Suppressing a sigh, she chose the plainest option—a dark gray dress with white buttons up the front that would be easy to fasten herself.

She rebandaged her wound, relieved to see it was healing cleanly. The ache was still there, but dulled. After twisting back her hair, she slipped two knives into hidden folds of the dress, then studied her reflection. The circles under her eyes had faded, and her gaze looked sharper, but her cheekbones were still gaunt from her days in the woods.

First, she'd find her father's room and get word from the healer. After that she would worry about food.

Theo greeted her warmly in the hall. Without his helmet, she could see his sandy brown hair and guessed he was a year or so younger than her. He had an earnest, almost boyish charm that many would probably find attractive.

"Good morning," she said. "I was hoping to visit my father before grabbing some lunch. Would you be able to direct me to his room?"

"Sure, my lady. Right this way," he replied, surprising her.

They took off down the hall Arine had traveled the previous night. Theo bounced with energy as they walked, his open demeanor at odds with the cold decor around them. After only a few turns and one staircase, he led her into a secluded hallway with muted colors instead of the intense grandeur of the prior wings.

He stopped at a door and Arine could hear murmured voices inside. When she stepped in, she found two men speaking quietly beside her father's bed. Her eyes flew to Tyvin, bracing for the worst, but miraculously, he looked almost unchanged. Tears of joy stung her eyes. Against all odds, he looked stable and well cared for.

He lay asleep, his breathing steady. His mostly gray hair was combed short, only slightly mussed from sleep. A neatly trimmed beard covered his strong features—not quite how he'd once worn it, but close enough that she could almost believe he'd done it himself.

Before she could reach the bed, the two men turned. The older one stepped forward, blocking her path.

"This room is private," he said curtly.

He had a severe face, with thin streaks of gray above his ears framing an otherwise bald scalp. The other man looked to be in his middle years, black hair shot with gray and a hooked nose dominating his features.

Arine ignored them, striding to the far side of the bed. "This is my father. I am allowed to see him," she said firmly, holding the older man's stare. He had to be the head healer.

"Well, no one informed me there would be visitors," he spluttered and eyed her suspiciously. "Havel, go double check."

The hooked-nose man hurried out. Arine ignored the older man's indignant looks as she grabbed her father's hand and waited. His skin was warm, his pulse steady. Relief surged through her.

The old healer harrumphed, bending back over his work, unwilling to risk throwing her out until her status was confirmed. Arine's gaze flicked to a nearly empty bowl of broth and a cup of water on the side table—he must have just been fed. She absently wondered where Shian was.

After a few minutes of the head healer mumbling under his breath and Arine pointedly ignoring him, the younger man stepped back into the room. "She has permission," he told the older man.

She fought to keep her satisfaction from showing, though a faint smile tugged at her mouth. The head healer only scowled deeper and turned back to his patient, speaking to Havel as though Arine wasn't in the room.

"Next time, make sure you keep the visitor list updated, Havel. I don't want to be caught off guard again."

"Yes, sir," the man replied, gathering the dirty dishes.

Arine waited until the silence stretched, then asked, "Can you tell me what his condition has been? Has he improved at all?"

The healer adjusted his spectacles, his voice even. "He was in dire condition when he arrived months ago—frequent seizures, unable to keep down water, dangerously dehydrated. Under my care, he's improved. The seizures have stopped, and he can eat when fed. He wakes at times, though without awareness of his surroundings. Some regain it... some never do."

He delivered the words without emotion, though not unkindly.

Shock tightened Arine's chest at how far her father had declined, but at least he'd been brought here in time to survive. If being a pawn kept him alive, she would take it, however bitter the bargain.

Despite his gruffness, it was clear the healer was taking good care of her father. Arine thanked him before murmuring that she'd return later and moving towards the door. He muttered something about proper visiting hours and turned away.

Her hand was on the latch when guilt struck—she had forgotten about the woman they'd rescued. She turned back.

"There was a red-haired woman brought in last night. She is my friend as well. Which room is hers?"

The healer looked up, expression dark. "You mean the she-devil?"

Confused, Arine described her.

"Yes, she's here and being treated—against my advice after her behavior."

"What behavior?" Arine pressed, but he waved her off angrily.

"No, you were given permission to see your father and you have done that. I don't have time to take you along to all of my patients or for you to disrupt their healing. Be gone."

With that, he shoo'd her out the door and closed it behind him firmly.

"Come, Havel," he snapped, practically hauling the other man down the hall.

Arine watched them go, unsettled. Still, if the woman was well enough to cause trouble, that had to mean she was strong enough to recover. For the first time in days, a flicker of hope stirred. Her father was alive and the woman was healing. She didn't know where Ciran had ended up, but she trusted he was still out there. He was a survivor.

She forced herself to hang onto the positive thoughts, pushing aside any dread about the journey ahead. Letting the flicker of optimism guide her, she turned to Theo. "Let's find something to eat."

The dining hall was nearly deserted when they arrived, the long tables mostly cleared. They ate quickly in the hush of the off-hours, and by the time they stepped back into the corridor, the emptiness had started to feel unsettling. She passed only a handful of servants, no courtiers at all. She had expected a steady parade of nobles, given the competitive atmosphere the King fostered.

When they returned to her room, Lian and Opal were waiting inside. Some of the tension drained from her shoulders at the sight of familiar faces. She hadn't realized how oppressive the quiet halls were becoming.

"Good afternoon, my lady," Opal greeted as Lian left the room to join Theo in the hall for his report.

"Not 'my lady,'" Arine corrected again.

Once Opal closed the door she responded. "I will respect your wishes in private, but where others are present, I must address you as required."

Arine winced. Of course—she was foolish to ask Opal to risk punishment just because she felt uncomfortable.

"I'm sorry. Address me as you must. I didn't mean to put you in a difficult position."

"Thank you." A faint blush colored Opal's cheeks as she held out a folded piece of parchment. "I came with a message from the Prince."

Surprise coursed through Arine. She hadn't expected to hear from him until it was time for her meeting with the King. She took the note and saw that the Prince offered her a tour of the grounds if she would like or she could remain in her rooms to rest until dinner.

She deliberated his offer, somewhat shocked he had given her a choice. She would love to get more familiar with the palace—relying on the Prince's staff to navigate the fortress was an uncomfortable feeling and would leave her ill prepared. And if she were being honest with herself, she knew there would be few other opportunities to see something so grand, even if it meant having to be in the Prince's company for longer than necessary. She appeased herself with the thought that she'd be doing reconnaissance the entire time anyway.

After she gave her answer, Opal quickly swept Arine's hair into a more polished style suitable for the Prince's company, ignoring her attempts to wave her off.

While Opal worked, Arine seized the opportunity to ask about the lack of courtiers.

"Ah yes, this is the royal wing. Only the King, Prince, and their guests stay here. On your tour I'm sure you'll see more of the lords and ladies around." She paused, then added, "If I may, you'll need to stay guarded in front of them."

Arine looked up at her in the mirror. "Why do you say that?"

Opal placed the last pin and then met her eyes. "I don't mean any disrespect, but for a cousin of the Prince's, you seem to be unfamiliar with a lot of the customs here. You may become a target to try to get closer to the royal family."

Arine couldn't help but laugh at Opal's words. "Yes, Opal, you are correct in that assessment and don't worry, you won't offend me. I would appreciate any help I can get at the moment."

Opal smiled genuinely at her response and Arine wondered how someone as nice as her survived this place.

"Well, just know every woman here will see you as competition the moment they realize you have a private audience with the Prince. Nearly every eligible lady in Calasis—and a few who aren't—are vying for his attention. After all, he is in line for the throne."

Arine twisted her mouth in disgust. "Well no concerns there, I have no desire for his favor. What about the King? He is unmarried, do they not vie for his affections as well?"

"Some did at first, but after years of refusals, they accepted that he would not take another wife after the death of Her Majesty, Lissa."

Arine could understand that. Her own father had been the same way. "Thank you for the warning. I guess we should be off so that we don't need to try the Prince's patience right before I will have to spend some time with him."

"You're welcome. I'll be waiting when you return to help you dress for dinner."

Opal began tidying, and after one last glance in the mirror, Arine joined Lian in the hall. After several turns through the gilded passages, he guided her beneath a high archway into a courtyard of towering trees. She stopped, struck by the sight.

The branches blazed with autumn color—red, orange, and deep violet—each leaf catching the sunlight until the canopy seemed to glow.

She let her gaze wander until it found the Prince, standing to one side with a finely dressed older gentleman. As she and Lian approached, she realized the courtyard was filled with nobles—just as Opal had warned.

"Good afternoon, Your Highness," she said brightly.

The Prince narrowed his eyes slightly but did not show any other outward reaction at her pleasant demeanor.

The older man turned to her, curiosity in his gaze. "And to whom do we have the pleasure of being introduced?" he asked, glancing between her and the Prince.

"Lord Berowyn, this is my cousin, Arine," the Prince said smoothly, cutting in before she could speak. "Her father is gravely ill, and the King has graciously agreed to see to his care here. With no other family to turn to, she has come to stay as well."

"On your mother's side, I presume?" Lord Berowyn asked, his tone polite but probing. "How interesting. I would very much like to learn more about your family...Arine."

Before she could respond, Prince Derik interjected again, voice laced with easy charm. "Of course, though perhaps another time. Lady Arine arrived only last night and her poor mind tires easily. We wouldn't want to overwhelm her."

The Prince grabbed her arm and patted her congenially on the shoulder as if she was a simpleton. Arine could only grind her teeth in annoyance at the implication without risking calling the Prince an outright liar. She forced herself to smile pleasantly back at the Lord, trying to mask the irritation she felt as best she could. The older man seemed mollified with the knowledge that Arine was apparently an idiot and withdrew, bowing as he threatened a future luncheon with his wife and daughter once she was 'well enough for company'.

As soon as they were out of earshot, she jerked her arm free. "Wouldn't want to overwhelm my poor mind?" she hissed.

"Trust me, you don't want his attention fixed on you," the Prince replied, his smirk irritatingly smug. "I did you a favor."

Then remind me never to ask you for a real one," she muttered. "I'd probably end up drooling in a corner, unable to read or write." The bite in her words lacked real vehemence though.

He grabbed her hand and placed it back on his arm. "Appearances, remember."

She clenched her jaw, silencing a retort that would surely make the Prince rescind his offer to show her the grounds. After a few moments, she steadied herself and asked about the courtyard—if only to needle him with questions as payback.

"How old is this place?" she asked, her genuine curiosity softening her tone.

The courtyard stretched wide, trees lining either side with space enough to walk comfortably beneath them. A few small groups strolled along the paths while others clustered in threes or fives, murmuring quietly as if this were their main amusement for the day. Perhaps it was—servants handled the real work while they displayed themselves like peacocks. She did notice everyone eyed them as they walked, whether that was from curiosity or envy, she couldn't tell, as no one dared approach them.

"Centuries," Derik replied as they wound along the path. "The founding King had this planted in his old age, when he could no longer hunt. He wanted a reminder of the forest he loved."

Along the path, small groups bowed and stepped aside to let them pass. Derik acknowledged each with a nod but didn't linger. Lian shadowed them silently, ever watchful.

For the next couple of hours they kept a steady rhythm, pausing only for brief, guarded exchanges with those bold enough to approach. Against her will, Arine found herself absorbed—the history unfolding with every new room and artifact sparking a genuine curiosity and a welcome distraction from the heavy weight of her thoughts.

She noticed how easily Derik shifted with each encounter. He was distant yet unfailingly polite, an ease born from a lifetime in this world. Arine envied that confidence. Even without royal blood, she suspected he would have found a way to rise.

Though the bubble-like atmosphere of the palace didn't escape her notice. Outside the gates of the three Districts, the less fortunate died in droves while those within simpered and pretended all was well. Arine was proud she kept her disgust hidden, though inside she battled with whom to truly blame. Vanin was nowhere to be found, yet the Prince and King were right here doing nothing.

Her anger sharpened the reminder of why she was here—and that the Prince still hadn't told her anything more of what to expect. They walked a massive hall with old paintings lining each wall that seemed to stare down imperiously, even in death. Once they were out of earshot of other guests, she turned to him.

"How was your conversation with the King last night?" She asked suddenly, trying to keep the annoyance from her tone. "Is there anything specific he'll be looking for from me—or anything else you can tell me about the upcoming journey?"

His eyes snapped to hers. "It's impossible to guess what the King will do. Just answer his questions and hide your emotions. As long as you are who you say you are, there will be no issues."

The audacity of the suggestion that she could be lying hit like a slap. "What?!" She seethed. "You are the ones saying I'm who you're looking for. I didn't ask for any of this." Arine gestured sharply around them, angry that he wasn't even trying to help prepare her. "You dragged me here and are holding my father hostage, remember."

Ignoring her outburst, Derik went on, tone flat. "So long as you don't offend him, we'll be gone tomorrow. And remember—'your highness' belongs at the beginning, middle, or end of your words. Maybe if you practice, you'll manage it at least once."

He raised an eyebrow at her, challenging her to continue and show that she would end up offending the King. Insufferable man. She clicked her jaw shut and quickened her strides even though she had no idea which way to go. Luckily the Prince didn't press the topic further, matching her pace and continuing to guide their way through the maze of rooms. She looked back over and gave him her fakest smile.

"Your majesty, would you please tell me what I should prepare for, your majesty?" she asked, and she could have sworn she heard Lian snort before masking it with a cough.

The Prince gave her a smug look. "Almost. Remember—it's 'your highness' with me, and 'your majesty' with the King. I suggest you flush out any nonsense before your audience with *his majesty*. Even though you're used to my laid-back personality, the King won't hesitate to teach you the importance of obedience however he deems necessary."

The reminder of the punishments he and his uncle dealt to their own subjects made her stomach turn. She could only imagine how many had suffered lashings for nothing more than failing to smile on cue.

Before she could stop herself, she spun back around to him. "Should I expect the same lashings you gave your own man yesterday? Or do women get something even more special?"

That finally broke his composure. He stopped, astonishment flashing across his face—and something else...wariness?

His head snapped toward Lian, anger blazing. "I thought you, of all people, would know what should and shouldn't be shared."

"Lian didn't do anything wrong—he was warning me," Arine cut in quickly, heart lurching as his fury turned on the guard.

Panic shot through her. Would her outburst do exactly what she was criticizing the Prince for and cause Lian to end up on the receiving end next?

"I apologize, your highness. I was only instructing her generally on potential outcomes that are broadly known," Lian interjected, stressing the last words.

Something unspoken passed between them before Prince Derik slowly turned back to Arine. His tone was clipped, as if he were discussing the weather, not punishments.

"Any number of penalties might be chosen. The King likes to be creative. Pray you never earn one—or worse, cause someone else to suffer one in your place."

The Prince looked at both her and Lian as if to discern whether they would heed his words or not. Arine took a protective step in between them to shield Lian from any repercussions.

Prince Derik's facial expression was indecipherable but he didn't address either of them on the comment again.

"I think that concludes our tour," he said and then turned and walked away, the muscles stiff against his back.

Chapter 11

Arine followed Lian back to the royal wing, neither of them speaking about the incident. She still didn't know what to make of the Prince. He shifted between so many personalities that she could hardly keep track of them. At times, he was the hard-hearted heir, quick to mete out punishment. Other times, he played the aloof yet charismatic court politician. And then there was something else—something in his dealings with Lian, and occasionally with her, that contrasted sharply with both. The mutual respect he and Lian showed each other didn't line up with his other personas.

Another puzzle for another day though, she told herself, forcing her thoughts back to the looming meeting with the King

Opal was waiting when Arine reached her room, a steaming bath already drawn in the corner. Relief nearly stole her breath at the thought of easing her aching side. She had no idea how Opal managed the timing so perfectly, but she reminded herself not to underestimate the maid.

As she bathed, Opal asked about her afternoon. Arine offered only distracted, half-hearted answers until Opal let the subject drop and helped her prepare with quiet efficiency. The hot water eased her muscles, but by the time the maid finished arranging her hair, the knot of nerves in her stomach had returned in full force.

Arine stood before the mirror, studying Opal's handiwork. Her dark hair was twisted into smooth waves that wrapped into a braided wreath around her head, perfectly suited to the high-necked gown chosen for her. The black fabric knotted neatly at her waist before flowing to the floor in clean lines—simple compared to other court fashions, but elegant all the same.

Opal smiled at her handiwork before wishing her goodnight. She promised to return early to wake her, leaving Arine alone with her restless thoughts. Anxiety coiled as her mind circled back to the uncertainties ahead. Derik had said the King only needed to confirm she was Nadyia's daughter, which made it sound as if her task was merely to look the part. Yet a little guidance would have eased the weight pressing on her chest.

She knew she'd partly pushed the Prince away earlier, and now all she could do was steady her nerves and hope the meeting would be as simple as he made it sound. To distract herself, she tried to find a way to strap one of her knives onto the foolish gown, which offered nowhere to hide them, when a knock at the door finally came. Taking a deep breath, she smoothed away the wrinkles and opened the door.

Expecting Derik, she was surprised to find Gerin instead. She masked her shock quickly, not wanting to give the prickly man cause for offense, before stepping into the hall with him.

He didn't speak. Simply motioned for her and Lian to follow, then strode off without a backward glance. The silence set her teeth on edge. Remembering Derik's warning from the night before, she kept her questions to herself, though the tension in Lian's shoulders made her uneasy. She hurried behind the young guard, wondering if their last conversation angered the Prince so severely that he had sent him just to punish her.

They traveled through the winding halls in silence until they stopped in front of two large wooden doors with intricate carvings of vines winding across it. The King's private dining room, Arine assumed, as she waited for the two guards posted outside to open the doors and allow her to enter.

Just as they swung the heavy doors outward, hurried footsteps echoed from the hall Arine had just walked. They all turned to see Derik round the corner, face flushed. He had discarded his normal casual attire for a formal set of coat, waistcoat, and breeches. The deep blue and gold colors set off his eyes and fit his lean body while also accentuating the hard lines of muscles beneath. Without explanation, he closed the distance, his expression unreadable.

Lian bowed, confusion flickering across his face. Gerin dipped just enough to avoid insolence, his smirk firmly in place.

"Your presence is not required here," the Prince said evenly, though a muscle in his jaw twitched—the only sign of anger bubbling beneath his calm tone.

"Not yet," Gerin replied, his smirk widening.

Arine's brows almost jumped off her face before she could stop herself. What in the world was going on between these two? No one offered an explanation. Instead, Derik stepped forward and pulled her into the room. She stole a glance at his face, but his face might as well have been hewn from stone.

Gerin and Lian stayed behind with the other guards, the heavy door shutting firmly and leaving another mystery for a later time.

She composed herself as best she could while Derik dragged her into the dining room. Her gaze swept ahead, landing on the man already seated at the end of the large table. The King's attire mirrored the Prince's, though it was more gaudy—brocade gleaming with gold thread, jewels winking at his cuffs and collar, as if he needed his wealth to speak before he did.

There was probably room for at least twenty people to dine comfortably, but only three places had been set, the King's and one on either side of him. Thick velvet drapes the color of bruised wine hung heavy over the windows, muffling the outside world and casting the room in deeper shadows than the early evening light would normally provide.

The air was heavy with the sweetness of spiced meats and exotic flowers, cloying enough to remind Arine of fruit gone just past ripe. She forced her face into a neutral expression and took in the massive candelabras lining the table, their flames barely stirring in the still air. Along the walls, portraits of kings and queens stared, eyes glinting with a lifelike sheen that made it hard to tell whether they were painted or watching from beyond the grave.

She kept pace with the Prince as he walked down the length of the table towards the solitary figure at its head. The King's hair was darker than Derik's, his frame shorter and thicker, but he carried the same haughty bearing, the same sharp twist to his mouth. His gaze snapped to her at once, and the sheer force of it nearly stopped her in place.

Those eyes, dark and unyielding in the firelight, seemed to strip her bare. Her steps faltered before she forced her feet forward until she was within a few feet of the King. The Prince bowed, and Arine hastily did her best impression of a curtsy.

"Your Majesty. I present Arine Duskraine, the only descendant of Nadyia Duskraine—formerly Tarshek," the Prince said formally.

Tarshek. Her father had never spoken her mother's maiden name. The sound of it rang unfamiliar, unsettling. Arine clenched her dress to still her hands, dread prickling. What if she wasn't who they thought? Would she be punished? Would her father?

The King's impenetrable gaze lingered on her a moment longer, giving nothing away.

"So, Nadyia's daughter in the flesh. I see why you were recognized so easily." The King paused. "Perhaps you can tell me why Tyvin kept you hidden for so long?"

His tone was calm, almost flat, but there was a dangerous edge in his gaze. Arine chose her words carefully, relieved when her voice came out steady.

"I don't know, Your Majesty. Before meeting your nephew, I knew nothing of my parents' history—nor my own."

"Let's hope you are successful then, so that I might ask Tyvin myself."

The King's eyes never left hers as his mouth curved into a slow smile. Arine's jaw clenched at the implication that her father had done something wrong. She prepared a response in his defense, but Derik cut in before she could.

"Forgive the interruption, Your Majesty. There is still the matter of the prisoners from the raid. The highest ranking is in critical condition. If we want to question them, we don't have much time."

The King's eyes flashed as they flicked to the Prince's. "Kill them all." He said without hesitation. "Stake their bodies outside the city limits as a reminder to the vermin if they dare come this close again."

Derik's voice tightened. "But, Your Majesty, shouldn't we try to learn how they knew where to strike?"

"I don't need to know how. Your men's negligence is why. Thank you for reminding me." His gaze sharpened. "Choose five to be whipped in the morning."

Arine's stomach dropped. The ease with which he condemned both enemy and soldier alike turned her blood cold. She forced her legs to move when he added, "Sit. Dinner is ready."

She walked stiffly to her chair, disgust twisting in her chest, and kept her eyes locked on the Prince across the table, fighting to control her rising anger.

He lifted his wine, eyes flicking briefly to the goblet as he raised it. Arine, desperate to steady herself, mimicked the gesture. The cool glass felt unfamiliar in her hand as she pressed the rim to her lips, the bitter taste of the wine doing little to calm the storm brewing inside her. Still, she kept her gaze steady, refusing to let her frustration slip into her expression further.

"Let us discuss your journey after we've eaten, shall we?" the King said, not waiting for a reply before signaling the servers.

As the attendants moved about, Arine recalled how Derik had held his tongue before his own men, so the King's restraint came as no surprise. At least it bought her a reprieve, giving her time to shove her loathing deep down. The dishes were delicious—seared duck in sauce, roasted vegetables—yet no flavor could erase the King's complete disregard for his own men.

During dinner, she was excluded entirely from the conversation, though no one seemed to care she was listening. So with every bite she focused on their words, determined to glean what she could. She stabbed a carrot—Derik updated the King on winter food storage. She speared a piece of meat—she listened to the projected crop yields. Each detail made her stomach sink further. From what she overheard, Syar might outlast Calasis by a handful of years, while her own country had perhaps ten bleak years left at best.

When she grew bored, she spent some of her time counting the gold plated dishes and ornaments around the room. She even noticed every finger of the King's was covered in gold rings streaked with different colors. Of course he would flaunt his wealth while others starved. If she thought she could get away with it, she would have tried to swipe some of the silverware to give to some of the needy families on the way out, but she was too worried some poor servant would get the blame once they were gone.

What she didn't expect was how formal the King and the Prince were, even in this intimate setting. Were they never simply uncle and nephew or were they behaving differently because of her presence? She watched Derik report on the state of the countryside, his shoulders straight and tense, and she wondered about his childhood. It was widely known that his parents had both died when he was young. His mother from the Severing and his father soon after. She hoped their stiffness was only for her sake. No matter who it was, she wouldn't want him to have gone through life with no close family bonds.

Finally, once everyone had finished and the servants cleared away the last plates, the King dismissed them with a flick of his hand, leaving the room in a heavy, expectant silence. Arine braced herself, heart thudding, for whatever came next.

The King turned, his gaze settling on her like a weight. He studied her in a way that made her want to squirm, his eyes trailing slowly over her features as if he could somehow carve her mother out of her himself.

"Seeing you in person is like seeing a ghost. You really do look exactly like her."

Disgust flooded through her at the familiarity of his words. Not trusting herself to not betray her revulsion, she remained silent, dipping her head in acknowledgement. He fiddled with one of his rings, the only one that was pure gold, as he continued to study her. His eyes bored into her.

"Do you know anything about how to wield?"

"No, your majesty," she replied.

He nodded, as though he had expected the answer. "Derik will instruct you as best he can, but it will only ever be guesswork. You must be prepared for anything."

Slowly, he reached under his coat and drew a dagger that seized her attention at once. Long and slender, it gleamed with intricate gold vines winding along the hilt, a deep blue sapphire embedded at its center. The jewel shimmered so vividly it felt as though it were trying to pull her into its depths.

"This is the dagger Nadyia used to sever magic," the King said, breaking her trance. "My nephew and a small group of soldiers will escort you to the cave where you will restore it. After hearing of the..." he shot Derik a pointed glance, "...disappointing attack on your return, I've concluded speed and stealth will still serve you best should the Syarans—or others—attempt to interfere."

He passed the dagger to Derik, who accepted it almost reverently. "Thank you," Derik said, voice formal. "You honor me with your trust."

Arine schooled her expression, fighting the urge to roll her eyes.

The King rose, the Prince following an instant later. With a curt nod, he dismissed them. Startled by the abrupt end, Arine pushed back her chair and stood, the legs scraping against the marble floor. She had barely taken two steps when the King moved, blocking her path. His presence loomed over her, heavy and deliberate—close enough for her to catch the faint scent of cloves and wine on his breath.

He extended his hand and she stared at it before realizing he meant her to shake it. Slowly she reached out and grasped it, her fingers stiff at first before she forced herself to relax them.

Arine gave a small smile and nod before moving to pull away, but his fingers clamped down, holding her fast. He leaned in, eyes glinting in the candlelight, his breath sour and hot against her cheek.

"The healers tell me Tyvin will not recover on his own." His smile never reached his eyes. "You will have to return here to heal him—because of course, you will want to be present for it."

Arine forced herself not to rip her hand away, at the deliberate reminder of the leash he held on her.

"Now, I'll excuse you so you can get some rest. Be ready to leave at dawn."

As his hand slipped away, one of his rings raked her finger, tearing the skin and drawing a sharp breath from her. She curled her fist, blood already welling from the shallow cut.

The King paused, glancing back. "Something the matter?" The challenge in his voice was unmistakable.

"No, your majesty," she forced herself to say. She bent into a curtsy, using it as an excuse to avert her gaze.

"You are dismissed. Derik, a word."

She heard his slow measured steps as he moved away.

Arine turned on her heel and walked out as quickly as she dared without drawing more attention. In the hall, neither guard spoke, but she felt their curious eyes tracking her every move. She forced her expression into something neutral and hurried over to Lian.

"Please take me to my father," she whispered, only a little breathless. She needed to see him one last time before she left—and somewhere quiet to collect herself.

It took only minutes to reach the healers' corner, where she found Tyvin sleeping peacefully. She sat at his side until the candles guttered low, unable to bring herself to leave. The King's words replayed in her mind, bitter and heavy. Had he purposely tried to hurt her, to show her what he could do to her father? Why hadn't Tyvin told her about any of this? Why hadn't he prepared her for what was to come?

Doubt pressed in as he lay unmoving. What would it take to fix this? What if she couldn't do it—if she failed and doomed everyone? She wished she could hear his voice again, offering one final piece of advice before she set out. His chest rose and fell with a quiet rhythm, almost as if he were napping—not lost in a haze of unconsciousness. It was at odds with the memory of the man who had raised her.

She remembered him teaching her to swim in the pond when she was five, patient even as she clung to the shallows in terror. Or later, when she scared off every deer on her first hunt with her chatter, he had only laughed and kept bringing her back.

Her heart had ached to know her mother only when she saw other children with theirs, wondering what that bond might have felt like. Tyvin had been enough though. He had filled the absence of a mother in every way he knew how.

Her resolve hardened as she wiped her tears. Just as he would do anything for her, she would do anything to bring him back. And if she succeeded—if she unsevered magic—then so help her God, if the King ever touched a hair on his head, she would return with a vengeance. King or not.

A knock at the door shattered her thoughts. Arine's head jerked up, her jaw tight, and she wiped the last trace of tears from her face.

"Come in," she called, assuming it was Lian come to fetch her. "I'll say my goodbyes."

After folding her father's hands and tucking in the blanket, she turned—only to startle at the sight of Prince Derik standing silently in the doorway. The low light carved deep shadows across the sharp planes of his face.

"I apologize for the intrusion," he said quietly. "I went by your room to update you on tomorrow's plans, but you weren't there, so I thought I'd find you here."

She steadied herself, determined not to show him anything he could use later.

"It's fine—you just startled me. Ever since the attack, I'm a little more jumpy than usual. Although I may be more shocked at your desire to share any information with me. I thought I wasn't allowed to know anything," she said mockingly as she walked over to him.

He sighed, and for a moment the mask slipped, revealing exhaustion in his eyes. "I was angry my men had been killed. And there are people who would twist any scrap of information to their advantage. If I'd given you more details, someone would have noticed, and eventually gossip would have spread about you being...special. Or worse, it could have been used against me. I admit, I may have erred too far on the side of caution."

She paused, unsettled. Was he drunk? Admitting he was wrong was the last thing she had expected. Why was he acting so...normal?

In the dim light, she studied him. He leaned against the wall, arms crossed in feigned indifference, yet his shifting feet betrayed a restless energy. His gaze flicked toward her and away again, as if he couldn't quite bring himself to hold her eyes.

She turned his words over in her mind. Was he truly forced to live in constant suspicion, always fearing betrayal for someone else's gain? After witnessing his cold distance from the King earlier, she couldn't quite stomach treating him the same—even if he was unbearable most of the time.

"If that's what you want to call it." She said, giving him a pointed look, but choosing not to continue to fight over it.

Her eyes drifted to a few vials cluttering the windowsill, and Shian came to mind. "Why haven't I seen the healer from the camp since I've been here? Doesn't she live in the palace too?"

A flicker of relief softened his expression at the change of subject. "She was granted a few days' leave after the journey. But if you're looking for her, you likely won't find her before we depart. She spends most of her time in the Outer District."

"The Outer District?" Arine asked, surprised. "Does she have family there?"

"No. She spends her free hours and her own coin making remedies for the needy. You must have noticed her stores of supplies when she treated you."

She wondered if he knew, if he could read her that easily to know how her first thought was of Shian being selfish to hoard so much medicine. Now that she knew the full story, shame pricked at Arine.

"Oh, I hadn't realized," she replied softly. "How is she able to do that when the King has his strict laws on the matter. I couldn't find a single person willing to sell me anything for the rotting sickness, not without status."

"She doesn't distribute the regulated medicine. She is always working on new mixtures of other herbs. That's why she pushed so hard to travel with us, she wanted the opportunity to restock from the countryside."

Arine's cheeks flushed with embarrassment, and she ruefully regretted bringing up the subject at all—especially since it was obvious he and Shian were close. Not wanting to admit her misjudgment in front of him, she scrambled for something, anything, to say instead.

"Why are you so guarded with everyone? Surely the King would believe you over others, given that you're his nephew?"

His eyes flicked to her, as if to say he knew exactly what she was doing. Instead of calling her out though, he answered.

"No. The only thing you can be sure of is that the King trusts no one implicitly. He does trust some more than others to ferret out information and report it back to him, of course."

"But what does it matter? Why does the King need to resort to such tactics?"

"Because he's never sure whom he can trust. He stamps out rumors quickly, but the Syarans aren't his only problem. A group of rebels plague him as well."

Arine was stunned. She had never heard of anyone trying to dethrone the King. And a darker thought struck her: before the past few days, would she have supported them?

Suspicion edged into her voice. "Why are you telling me this?"

"So that you understand there is more to everything than you see and there are more dangers awaiting us. You need to be prepared."

He opened his mouth as if he was going to say more but must have thought better of it because instead, he turned to open the door. He paused with his hand on the knob.

"I don't know what Gerin said when he beat me to your rooms to escort you to dinner, but you must have noticed he's young for his station, yes?"

Arine nodded, keeping to herself that Gerin hadn't spoken a single word to her.

"He is one of the King's top informants. Hardly anything escapes his notice; he uses any information or misstep he can to sway the King against me."

Arine thought about Lian and Derik's reactions to Gerin so far and that lined up. She also would guess that Lian and Derik were much closer than they let on, but she didn't mention that.

"But why target you specifically? It's not as though he could ever be named heir, or that you'd work against the throne you're meant to inherit."

"No, ruling isn't something he desires. He never was one to want to be in the spotlight, but he has his own perception of things that is hard to change."

"What do you mean?" she asked.

"We grew up together before…" He trailed off and cleared his throat, tone changing to the more flippant style she was used to, though it lacked the previous vitriol. "It's not important. I was able to select the six men joining us tomorrow and he was not one of them, so we won't have to guard our backs on the journey. And with that reminder, let me escort you to your rooms so you can get some rest."

He opened the door, ending the conversation.

Arine wished she could have asked more questions, but she knew he'd locked himself behind his mask again. The scraps of information weren't enough to change her opinion of him. She could admit though, that even if he'd never worried about food or money, growing up without family and constantly fearing betrayal was no childhood she'd envy.

As they walked, Derik told her the names of the guards who would join them and outlined their route through the Decayed Lands. The safer path around Lake Katuna and through Raville had been considered, but it would add weeks to the journey without reducing their time in the Decayed Lands. Instead, they would cut straight toward Mt. Furna—where her mother had died—passing between Lake Katuna and the fringes of Killian Forest.

Once, that land had been breathtaking: sandy beaches along the sparkling lake water spilling into flower-strewn meadows where the wealthy spent their summers. Now, with the rot spreading, those fields and sands had sunk into the boggy wetland that had recently been dubbed Katillan Swamp. Since the Decayed Lands offered no food and horses would founder in the marsh, they would be on foot after the Trader's Outpost. Arine didn't relish slogging through swampland, but after hearing of raiders and Syarans, she understood the need for stealth and speed.

Still, something nagged at her. It was like the puzzle was not quite lining up and she couldn't figure out what she was missing or even what part of the puzzle was not quite right to dig into. She was grateful Derik no longer treated her as a puppet, but she couldn't shake the sense that he still kept things from her. Secrets were one thing—but not when they involved her. She could only hope his omissions wouldn't return to haunt them.

They reached her chambers a few hours before midnight, leaving just enough time to get a decent night's rest before morning. Arine checked her weapons, laid out the sturdier clothes from the new bundle, and was relieved to see no dresses among them. With her gear ready, she stretched out on the bed. Her thoughts churned restlessly—of what waited in the days ahead—until at last her body gave in to fatigue.

Chapter 12

In the morning, Opal came bearing gifts. She brought her a new, fur lined cloak, plus three sets of supple leather outfits that would allow her to move more freely than any of the clothing she had chosen the night before. The cloak was a reminder that they were not only undertaking a dangerous journey, but they were also doing it as fall was nearing end. She hurriedly put on one of the outfits and then packed the spares. They fit perfectly and even had more loops and pockets for weapons than she had knives for.

"Thank you, Opal. I didn't realize how much I was dreading traveling in the other clothes until now," she said.

"I only gave the seamstress your sizes, the Prince ordered the clothing." Opal replied distractedly as she finished braiding back Arine's long hair for her.

Arine stood to face her. "Well, regardless, you've been kind to me, and I appreciate it. I hope to see you again soon."

Opal looked briefly surprised, then recovered with a curtsy. "And I you, my lady."

Arine smiled as she fastened the cloak. With her gear belted on, she shouldered her bow and pack, then strode into the hallway. Theo was waiting, similarly outfitted in the candlelight.

"Shall we?" she asked with a small smile, anticipation for the journey edging out her wariness.

Arine gave Opal a final wave before hurrying after Theo, whose long strides forced her to quicken her pace. They made good time and reached the west tower just as Derik and Lian arrived from the opposite direction. The three other guards Derik had mentioned were nowhere in sight.

Derik scanned the area, his expression tightening before he exchanged a dark glance with Lian. Footsteps echoed from the corridor behind them, and Arine turned to see Gerin approaching with two unfamiliar guards in tow. Were these supposed to be the missing three? Confusion pricked at her—Derik had made it clear last night Gerin wouldn't be coming. One look at Derik's flashing eyes told her the change was no accident.

The young guard stopped before the Prince and dipped into another of his insolent bows.

"Your highness, it seems the other three guards were unfortunately injured in the confusion last night and will be unable to accompany you. With the heightened security concerns, his majesty thought it prudent that I and two of my best guards take their place to ensure no further...mistakes."

Derik's face hardened to stone. "I'm curious," he said slowly, "how could they have been injured when the barracks are on the opposite side of the palace from the healer's quarters?

The healer's quarters? Arine's stomach lurched. She shoved past Theo before she could stop herself. "Wait, what? Is my father okay?"

Lian caught her arm and pulled her aside before she could reach the two men facing off. He kept his voice low, careful not to draw attention.

"Your father is fine. The girl escaped in the night."

Arine's pulse slowed in relief—her father was safe. But his words sank in with a jolt. The woman escaped?

"What happened?" she whispered. "Did something happen to her?"

"No. We don't know how she slipped free. She was supposed to be drugged to keep her docile for the King's questioning today. Somehow she avoided it—knocking out a guard and stealing a horse from the private stable before vanishing."

"Oh." It was all Arine could manage. She wished she had learned who the woman was, but at least she was beyond the King's reach now. Arine shuddered to think what his "questioning" would have entailed.

When she turned back, Derik and Gerin were still locked in a silent glare.

"Feel free to interview the guards yourselves to confirm their stories," Gerin said, gesturing casually behind him. "But we won't wait for you to return. His Majesty was most insistent there be no delay."

His tone was bored, but Arine caught the glint of satisfaction in his eyes—he relished making Derik squirm.

"I have no doubt their injuries and stories will match yours," the Prince replied, voice low and seething. "Join us if you must, but remember—I lead this expedition, by the King's command. You and your men will obey my orders. Any hint of disobedience, and I'll see the offender strung up."

Gerin let a thin smile curl his lips as he and the two soldiers moved to stand with Arine's group. "Of course. We're all loyal men here."

Arine felt the weight of the divide—three against three—and wondered what it would mean when danger pressed them.

"Enough," the Prince said coldly. "We'll take the districts on foot to keep from drawing eyes. Our horses will be waiting outside the gates." His command snapped the group forward, unwilling or not.

Arine fastened her new cloak tight against the morning chill and followed as the group wound through the empty streets. The sun was only just peeking over the eastern rooftops. Most buildings lay in shadow, yet already she could see more than when they'd first arrived through the rain. The structures were old and stately, and she let herself imagine what their interiors might hold as they passed.

Few townsfolk were out this early, and those who were kept their heads down, giving no trouble. A couple of miles past the last house in the Outer District, the Prince veered toward a copse of trees where a stable master and two hands stood waiting with seven saddled horses, packs bulging with food and provisions.

After handing over a bag of silver, the Prince brought Arine a white mare before mounting his own paint horse, the same one she had first seen him on.

They set off westward, wide fields stretching out on either side. No one spoke except to call directions. Derik led, with Lian, Arine, and Theo following, while the newcomers trailed at the rear. The air was cool, the breeze mercifully light—lucky, Arine thought, for this time of year often brought sharp gales that could cut straight through to the bone.

They made good time, not pushing the horses too hard. After a few hours, they stopped for a quick meal of cold meat and cheese beside a stream that seemed a common waypoint for travelers. A few large boulders lay loosely arranged like chairs, which Arine gladly made use of.

Once they were done eating, Derik asked Arine if her water was low, motioning her to join him by the stream, away from the others.

"We will have to keep the lessons brief so the others don't overhear," he said as he filled his waterskin.

"Wait—they don't know what we're doing?" she asked, glancing back at the group. "Why not?"

"You can never be too safe."

She gave a short laugh, but his steady expression made her falter. For a moment, she almost felt guilty; it struck her how alone he must be. "Fine, but you realize they're going to question it sooner or later?"

"Fear of the King's wrath keeps curiosity in check. If they do wonder, it won't be anytime soon." A trace of bitterness edged his words before he smoothed it over. Then he shifted to instruction. "Wielders once described magic as a part of themselves. For some, it was like a second skin. For others, a muscle they could train. Either way, you should feel the power within you once magic is unsevered."

Derik paused, scanning the group. Gerin was eyeing them suspiciously, but after a moment he went back to sharpening his sword. The Prince continued. "I know you say you've never felt it, but maybe you just don't recognize it. Right now it's like a paralyzed limb—still there, but useless. As we ride, try to take inventory of yourself. See if you can sense something that doesn't quite belong, something that just...is."

"Look for something inside me that exists, but doesn't exist?" Arine repeated flatly. "You hear how that sounds, right?"

"Do nothing then," he snapped, his voice tight with frustration. "I'm trying to help you."

Arine bit back another retort, watching him glance nervously at the guards again. "Look, I'm sorry. I just don't know anything about this, and it doesn't make sense to me."

"It's fine. We need to get going anyway." He twisted away, leaving her crouched by the stream alone.

She muttered a string of curses at his retreating figure before capping her waterskin and rejoining the group. If this was the training he meant to give her, it was going to be a long journey. Still, she spent the rest of the day trying to feel within herself for anything strange, but she might as well have been trying to feel the sky for all the good it did. Derik, the coward, made sure to be nowhere near her as they rode.

By evening, Arine's legs ached from the saddle. Her one day of riding earlier hadn't prepared her for hours on horseback, yet thankfully her wound seemed to be healing—she hadn't felt a twinge from it all day.

That night, the divide in their camp was unmistakable. The Prince, Lian, and Theo settled on one side of the fire while Gerin and the newcomers—Jove and Matthew—took the other, leaving Arine awkwardly in the middle. They ate roasted rabbit in near silence, the fire crackling as the men glared past her.

The rift was almost comical. They spoke to each other only long enough to decide watches, scouts, and chores. Once that was done, they ignored the opposite side entirely, as if sharing words might be contagious. The two new guards weren't especially awful—just overeager to win Gerin's favor. Otherwise, they were typical Kingsmen with bad jokes, inflated egos, and not a thought to include Arine in the planning. She found it all too familiar.

Theo and Lian included her in small talk, but they never assigned her to watch duties or other tasks. The Prince spoke to her the least of course. Though he barely spoke to anyone. He never seemed relaxed; his eyes swept the campfire's edge and the darkness beyond, as if he expected danger from within as readily as from without.

No one was openly hostile to where they could be called out directly on it, Gerin though took every opportunity to give patronizing orders to Theo and Lian when they were "off babysitting duty" and to find as many ways as possible to insinuate that Derik was ill suited for whatever task he happened to be doing. It became glaringly obvious that according to Gerin, the Prince could do nothing properly.

She had no idea what had transpired between the two, but Gerin hated Derik with a passion that could become deadly. Not because he was stupid enough to try to harm him outright, but because he was pigheaded enough to have to argue with any decision, which could end up costing more lives than just the Prince's, if it was the wrong decision at the wrong time.

And as if on cue, the group's first big argument came the next day. They had left the main road since it angled slightly southwest while they needed to go more north. The new 'road' they were following was more of a hybrid between a well-worn path and a game trail in most places, and in some it disappeared altogether.

The Prince had been in the lead and must have misread the signs because they found themselves at the edge of a steep ravine with no discernible safe route down and no reprieve as far as they could see. Derik turned the horses to continue traveling north, saying they must not have gone far enough to pass it, while Gerin argued he had missed something and they needed to go back south.

At last, after a heated argument, Gerin took the lead, turning them back south since Derik had no proof he hadn't missed the path earlier.

Arine could tell Derik didn't want to give in but was also trying to keep peace and in the end the need for a united group must have won out. Another few hours going south with no way to cross ended up proving the Prince right, but to what end. They had cost themselves half a day's ride between the two of them, their only accomplishment showing that neither of them knew where they were going.

Once they turned back north, trying to make up time, Arine leaned over her horse to whisper to Lian beside her. "Has anyone been this way before?"

Lian shook his head, keeping his voice low. "Not recently. Harrick knew the land—he grew up here—but he was one of the three Gerin replaced with Jove and Matthew."

"Excellent," Arine said sarcastically. "So we're just winging it then?"

"I know Gerin is trying his best to make the Prince look like he doesn't know what he is doing, but he has been this way on several occasions when he was younger." He looked over at the antagonistic guard and then added begrudgingly, "And though his methods are not preferable, Gerin is truly one of the top swordsmen in the guard and has brought two of his top pupils. They may be frustrating, but they do make up for it with their skill."

Arine nodded, conceding the point. As long as they eventually reached their destination, the presence of skilled fighters was some small comfort.

The next morning they found the trail again and continued without incident, easing the tension from the day before. Still, Arine couldn't shake the sense that too much was missing. Derik offered no further guidance on wielding, leaving her unprepared for what lay ahead—or for what was happening across the land at all.

The world seemed darker somehow, as though it had soured even further during her time trapped in Killian Forest. The guards kept their distance, leaving her few chances to ask questions. Perhaps their ignorance of the mission made them cautious, but she was determined to learn what she could.

Theo seemed the best target. He was talkative when not on watch duty—he took that very seriously. Maybe it was his youth, but his open demeanor and lack of political scheming made him seem refreshingly straightforward.

She found a moment when it was just the two of them; the others were already mounted, planning the day's route. She carried a saddle over, and unlike the others, he didn't try to take it from her and do it for her. Emboldened by his ability to see her as an equal, she pressed on with her plan to pry for information.

As they worked together to ready the white mare, she realized she'd spent four days with the horse without asking her name. Deciding it was as good an entry point as any, she asked casually, "Theo, do you know her name? I'm embarrassed to admit I never asked until now."

"Aye, my lady," he said, brushing sandy hair from his eyes. It had grown too long to stay neat but too short to tie back. "Her name is Cloud. She comes from the Prince's own stable."

"Cloud," Arine said to the horse, who fixed her with a wide brown eye—almost as if reproaching her for taking so long to ask. The name fit; her coat was bright and white, like sunlight on clouds. Arine patted her nose and murmured a quiet apology.

"Thank you, Theo. Have you lived in Draske your whole life?" she asked, keeping her tone light.

"Aye, my lady. My father is mid-rank in the army, which earned me the chance to apply for the guard. That way I could stay in Draske and look after my mother."

"Does she have the rotting sickness as well?" Arine asked sympathetically. "Who is watching after her now?"

"No, my lady, nothing so bad as that. Years ago she broke her leg in a fall, and the infection left it poorly healed, so she struggles to get around. The Prince arranged for my father to take paid leave until I return." He finished the last buckle and smiled up at her, freckles flashing. "I wager he'll gain twenty pounds with nothing to do but take after momma for a month or more."

Arine laughed. "Well, I'm sure they'll both appreciate the rest."

"Aye, that's true. My father hasn't had more than a day or two off in years, not with all the trouble the Syarans have caused."

"Oh, that's terrible. I grew up in Toumre, a day's ride north of Draske, and we've been fortunate not to see any problems."

"It is, my lady—you are fortunate. Likely your closeness to Draske spared you. My father has told me of worse. A few months ago, near Folse, he found a village burned to ash. Bodies filled the streets—women, children, and men alike—and many more were missing."

Arine gasped. "Why would the Syarans do that? They're zealots, sure, but I didn't think they killed innocents."

Arine's stomach turned at the news. Were they no longer trying to convert people to their fanaticism and were forcing them to it instead?

Theo came over, his boyish features tight with worry. "I'm sorry, I shouldn't have told you that. It's not something that is widely known and I certainly shouldn't burden a lady like yourself with such worries. Please forgive me."

"No, it's fine, Theo. I'd rather be prepared than ignorant. I hadn't realized how bad it was."

He said nothing as she mounted; his shifting stance betrayed his agitation. She waited, giving him space, until at last he stepped closer, voice low, eyes flicking toward the others.

"Please, my lady—don't tell anyone I said that. My father isn't supposed to speak of such things. If word got back, it could ruin his standing in the army, and we rely on that. We could lose everything." His tone was pleading, and Arine was struck by just how young he was.

"Of course I won't say anything. I promise," she said quickly, leaning down to grip his shoulder. "We've not known each other long, but I trust you. And I hope you can trust me to keep this secret."

He held her gaze a moment, then nodded. "Aye, my lady. Thank you."

He mounted quickly, as if afraid she might press him further. She didn't. Still, unease lingered. If his words were true, the pattern was troubling: slavers in the woods, Syarans striking at royals, an assassin in her tent—all the very night the Prince found her. Could it all be connected?

She looked around at the small group and for the first time wondered if Derik's heightened concern wasn't just because of the King's normal paranoia. What if more people had found out about her when she was recognized trying to buy medicine in Draske all those months ago? But even so, she couldn't think of a reason why anyone would not want magic unsevered. The Syarans could preach their lies but they would still die, just like everyone else.

Arine mounted her horse, still trying in vain to make sense of it. The rest of the group busied themselves with assigning roles, blind to her concerns, and eventually she had to set her thoughts aside when no answers came. Jove took the lead as the first scout, ranging around the party and watching for signs of pursuit or trouble.

Over the last day, the terrain had shifted into dense shrubland, forcing them to travel much slower than when they'd crossed the fertile farmlands that still fed most of Calasis. The ground was choked with growth, from thorny bushes barely knee-high to thick clusters of fir trees they had to detour around.

The smaller plants let them push straight through, but they were treacherous for the horses, often hiding rocks or holes, so the group was forced into a cautious crawl. The weather had turned colder too. It wasn't freezing during the day, but it took at least an hour before Arine felt the chilliness in her bones from the night start to dissipate. She huddled deeper into her fur cloak, sending another silent thank you to Opal.

The slow pace was more convenient for her to listen in on the sparse conversations the men were having, hopeful they would let slip information, but at mid-morning she still hadn't heard anything useful except that apparently Matthew had a younger sister that was causing problems with more than a few suitors at the palace.

Matthew and Jove were beginning to warm to the others, but Gerin stayed as aloof as ever. Derik, meanwhile, seemed barely to speak at all, issuing only clipped orders. He was clearly on edge, though she couldn't tell why. He hadn't seemed this uneasy when they'd spoken in her father's room, so something else must have unsettled him. Or perhaps it was simply Gerin, whose daily mission seemed to be making him uncomfortable.

As they picked their way through a dense patch of brush, a noise sounded from behind.

Gerin, riding at the rear, wheeled his horse around, Lian following a step behind—both already drawing their bows. Theo shifted back to block Arine from sight while Derik edged to her other side, bracing in case an attack came.

Arine yanked her sword free, pulse thundering, images of Theo's massacre tale flashing back as she braced for the worst. The pounding of hooves grew louder until Jove burst through the brush, his horse crashing heedlessly through thorns and undergrowth.

He hauled his mount to a skidding stop, eyes darting between Gerin and Derik as precious seconds bled away. Arine nearly cursed—their foolish feud would get them all killed in the end. Finally, Jove turned toward the Prince.

"Your highness, two riders are following us, only a few hours behind. At first I thought it a coincidence, but after watching them—it's clear. They're tracking us."

Derik's gaze sharpened on the trail behind him. "Did you recognize either of them—or their clothing?"

"No, sir. They wore plain cloaks and had their hoods up. I couldn't see their faces. I didn't dare get closer and risk them spotting me before I could warn you."

"No, that was wise." The Prince turned to Gerin. "Are you expecting anyone else you haven't mentioned?"

"No," Gerin answered tersely, without his usual goading. "We should assume they mean to ambush us, likely with reinforcements nearby. There's a rock outcropping not far back—ideal for a defensive position. If we double back, we might surprise them before they choose the terrain. With luck, we can also keep them separated from the rest of their group."

Derik nodded. "Agreed. Let's move quickly. As long as Jove wasn't seen, we should be able to handle two riders. But remember—the goal is to take them alive so we can question them."

He scanned the others to be sure they'd heard, then set off. Retracing their steps was easier; the worn trail let them cover ground faster. Soon the outcropping came into view, and Derik raised his hand, bringing the group to a halt.

He beckoned Lian and Arine forward. "Stay back here where there's enough cover to hide. If those riders spotted Jove, they might have called for others, and I don't want all of us caught together if that's the case."

Arine gritted her teeth. She hated being left behind, but she couldn't deny the sense in it. If things went wrong, better to minimize their risk than see the entire party captured. Meeting Derik's eyes, she gave a reluctant nod.

His hand drifted toward his cloak, where she guessed the dagger was hidden. But after glancing at Gerin, he let it fall without offering it to her.

He met her eyes briefly before turning his horse back. The meaning was clear. The threat wasn't big enough for him to trust his companions with the dagger. She wondered how much they knew—and how deep the distrust ran.

The five others rode to the outcropping, taking positions to watch the path behind them. It was too far for Arine to see clearly, and she didn't have a direct line of sight to the trail either. She and Lian had to sit blindly, waiting. Thirty minutes passed, then an hour, and Arine began to grow impatient. Jove had said they were only a few hours behind—if they were tracking, they should have appeared by now, unless they'd noticed his extra tracks.

She was about to ask how long they'd wait when a flash of metal caught the light. Squinting through the brush, she saw nothing at first. Just as she was ready to dismiss it as a trick of the sun, a group of riders broke from the outcropping and rode toward them. They weren't in a rush, but she counted seven of them.

As they drew closer, she saw two newcomers slumped at odd angles, their hands bound and rough cloths tied over their eyes. Their horses were led by Jove and Matthew, while the others scanned the trees for more assailants.

Arine frowned—how had they captured them without any sounds reaching her and Lian? If there was a possibility of a trap, why lead them straight here? She was about to ask Lian when her gaze fell on the larger of the two prisoners, and she gasped. Lian tensed as Arine spurred her horse forward without a second thought, rushing to meet the group.

"Ciran?" she shouted as she rode up to the group.

Derik quickly intercepted her before she could get close enough to remove the blindfold. She tried in vain to get around him before settling for throwing a glare his way as Lian caught up to her on the other side, further blocking her.

"Arine?" Ciran's voice came from behind the cloth, tinged with relief. He turned his head toward her voice.

Beside him rode the redheaded woman they had rescued. Arine's mind reeled. What were the two of them doing together—and why were they following them?

Derik's composure cracked, fury twisting his features. "Not a word from anyone until we make camp and I've decided what to do with these two." His blazing eyes locked on her. "That includes you. Lian, keep her back a good distance. For her safety, of course."

He held her gaze for another moment before turning to bark orders at the others. The column pressed forward, leading the captives in silence. Neither Ciran nor the woman resisted.

Derik took up a position in the middle himself as if he didn't trust her not to try to break past Lian to reach them. He didn't realize she was too confused to even know what to do. And as she slowly followed, she begrudgingly admitted he was right to be cautious. She really didn't know them. She trusted Ciran to an extent and she was glad to see he hadn't been harmed by any of the roaming Syarans, but she was leery of the circumstances of his arrival here and how he came to be traveling with the redheaded woman.

It was late afternoon when they found a large clearing, mostly free of prickly plants. The sun had just begun its descent as Derik ordered Ciran and the woman to be set aside while the others cleared an area for the fire pit and bedrolls.

On the way, he had locked down his outward anger. Even so, Arine could see he was still seething as he stood over them, arms crossed. His gaze flicked to her often, as though he half-expected her to bolt over and cut them loose. However, it was Gerin who broached the subject of their prisoners once everything was settled.

He strode to Derik. "We should kill them and keep moving. If there are others around, we don't want to be slowed down dragging these two. And if there aren't..." He shrugged. "Well, they won't be missed."

Arine gasped, the words escaping before she could stop them. "You can't kill them!"

She looked at Derik, but he only gave Gerin an insufferable look before turning back to the group, voice slipping into one of his crueler tones. "No one is killing them until we find out what they know." He met Arine's eyes and shook his head slightly. Understanding dawned on her—it was an act, meant to rattle the captives.

She studied Ciran and the redhead, both still blindfolded. Neither flinched at the threat. In fact, they looked like they could have just been sitting down to a picnic. It made her wonder again what they were doing there and why they didn't seem too worried about their safety. It was going to be an interesting interrogation.

Derik ignored them, instead, he quietly directed Jove, Matthew, and Theo to guard the camp's edges while sending Lian to watch the trail they had come by. When finished, he stood before the prisoners. Arine leaned against a bare tree where she could see every face clearly, without being in the middle of the confrontation.

Gerin tugged the cloth from their eyes and moved behind them, looming overhead. Ciran blinked against the sudden light, scanning the camp until his gaze landed on Arine. Calm and steady as ever, he gave nothing away, though she saw him quickly take stock of everyone before turning back to Derik.

Arine turned to the girl, curious to see her awake at last. Without even saying a word, the woman somehow seemed to possess the complete opposite personality as Ciran. She whipped her head around with a smirk, studying the guards like they were little more than insects. She twisted to survey Gerin from head to toe, then pivoted her back on him in blatant dismissal. She managed to exude a certain haughtiness even while bound, that Arine found admirable for a woman.

Gerin's face flushed, exactly the reaction the woman must have wanted, and Arine nearly laughed. The redhead settled back with her spine straight and chin high, as though the camp existed at her command. Arine had to fight to keep her grin hidden.

Derik, for his part, kept his expression carefully neutral, but Arine would have bet good silver he paused only to smother a laugh at Gerin's obvious discomfort before the interrogation began.

He cleared his throat and fixed Ciran with a hard stare. "Where should we start? Why are you following us? What is it you want—gold, medicine? You're outnumbered. You couldn't possibly think to ambush us."

Derik rested his hand on his sword, ready to draw at a moment's notice, and Arine fought the urge to roll her eyes.

"What a tactician," the redheaded woman muttered, echoing Arine's thoughts—until Ciran cut her off.

"We are here to protect Arine," he said, his gaze hard on Derik.

Arine straightened, confusion knotting in her chest.

Derik's eyes narrowed. "You barely know Arine."

Ciran looked to her as he answered. "I know she helped me save Cilia"—he nodded toward the redhead—"and that you kidnapped her. Cilia owes her a debt. We can repay it by keeping Arine safe from you." He spat the last word like a curse.

"Interesting," Derik said quietly, his expression unreadable at Ciran's accusation. "But if that's true, you've given no reason for your presence—only hers." He tipped his head toward Cilia. "And how did the two of you come to travel together at all? From Arine's account, your companion was half-conscious. How could she possibly have remembered you, let alone sought you out for this 'grand quest'?" He arched a mocking brow.

Ciran flicked a look at Arine before answering, something in his expression putting her on guard. Cilia, meanwhile, stared at Derik with undisguised boredom; if her hands were free, Arine suspected she'd be picking her nails.

"You forget I was there when you found Arine," Ciran said. "I know you kidnapped her, and after what she did for Cilia, I couldn't just leave her to whatever fate. Cilia is my half-sister, which means I owe Arine for her life as well."

Arine sucked in a breath. Half-sister? That couldn't be possible. They had traveled together for days, carrying the woman in turns—how could she be his sister? And worse—how had she ended up in slavers' hands so near where he was taking the Pillar's test?

But no—she sifted through their time together, memory after memory surfacing. He had never actually said he was there for the test—she had only assumed, and he'd never corrected her. He had charged the Yuakans recklessly, as if he already knew their strength. His fierce determination to protect the woman made more sense now too. Could it be true?

He had the decency to look ashamed under her stare, but it didn't stop the wave of betrayal that surged through her. Another person who hadn't trusted her. He had lied to her for days while she blindly helped him. Why did he feel the need to keep the truth from her? And when—if ever—would she be worthy of honesty from anyone?

Her fists clenched, nails biting into her palms as she forced her face into stillness. She couldn't afford to be naïve any longer. Ciran's glances brushed over her, but she refused to meet his eyes again or betray anything on her face. He had left her in the dark regarding his presence in the forest and she was ashamed to have let down her guard so easily. A mixture of embarrassment and anger churned inside her as Derik continued to press him.

"We will need more information than that," Derik said evenly. "Let's start with why were you in Killian Forest in the first place, and how did Cilia become injured?"

"Cilia has a habit of ignoring common sense and finding trouble." Ciran replied as he shot Cilia with an admonishing look.

Cilia tensed at his words, a faint flush spreading across her cheeks.

"Cilia and I were searching for a safer place after the rot overran our home." Ciran continued, his voice sharp but laced with concern. "We stumbled on a band of slavers, and instead of avoiding them, Cilia had the brilliant idea she could handle them herself. She snuck off during her watch and by the time I woke, they had hours on me. I found one dead at camp and the rest gone, with no sign of her. They were skilled, using a stream to hide their trail, and it took me days to find them again. The next day, I found Arine in the bear pit. With slavers so close, I couldn't let her travel alone. Her path and mine aligned, so I stayed with her."

He made it all sound so straightforward, as if he hadn't spent days lying to her face while she thought she could trust him.

"I would have had no issue with the scum if that mountain lion hadn't yowled behind me, alerting half the continent," Cilia muttered.

So the cat was real. Arine's eyes flicked to Ciran, a smile half forming at the memory of the story she had called a lie—before she caught herself and forced her gaze past him, fixing on Cilia instead.

It was bold, thinking she could best four Yuakan flesh traders alone. Either she had an inflated ego, or more likely, the same training as Ciran—the kind of experience Arine had already seen firsthand. It wasn't abnormal since they grew up together, but it was still rare for women to be as well trained as the men in Calasis.

"How did you each escape and find each other?" Derik asked. He paused, his gaze cutting to Gerin before continuing. "And why, Cilia, were you on the other side of the palace in the barracks the night of your escape?"

Gerin stiffened.

"First of all," Cilia replied, "a child could have slipped out of that infirmary. That old man is a terrible liar. He thought I wouldn't notice the weirwood root he ground up with the hydriscus stems to knock me out until your King"—she spat the title—"could torture me. I only pretended to drink it, then walked out. Child's play."

She must have caught the shift in the air between Derik and Gerin, because her eyes flicked to the guard before she went on. "I found a storage room with servant's clothing, and within ten minutes I strolled out the front door. Whatever happened in the barracks was someone else's doing... but it seems you already knew that." She finished sweetly, smirking at the Prince.

Silence followed. Derik and Gerin stared each other down, unmoving, while Theo, Matthew, and Jove shifted uneasily. At last, Gerin broke the silence with a shrug.

"Obviously, she's lying," Gerin said, locking eyes with Derik in a silent challenge.

Derik held his gaze, then smiled slowly. "Of course."

Gerin looked away first, wisely choosing not to push his luck. Cilia, however, smiled wide, clearly savoring the tension.

"Silly me. I must have forgotten my stop at the barracks. Tell me how many men I injured, and I'll be sure to remember it next time." She winked at Gerin.

His answering smile was sharp. "It must be hard to keep track of all the men you visit."

Ciran stiffened at the obvious insult but Cilia just laughed even more. "Sounds like you're just jealous you don't have as many women visiting you."

Color crept up Gerin's neck as Jove let slip a chuckle before smothering it with a cough, suddenly fascinated by the ropes around Cilia's wrists.

Ciran seized the chance, cutting in with a glare at his half-sister. "As for how we're traveling together, I followed your group back and was preparing to find Cilia when I saw a maid with red hair stroll out of the palace. It took us the rest of the day to regroup and figure out what you were doing with Arine. We followed as soon as we could and caught up when you lost half a day backtracking." He offered Derik a tight smile. "Thanks for that."

Derik looked at Gerin again, but refrained from commenting on his involvement in that mishap.

"So you expect us to believe that you two took the trouble to not only ferret out when we left, but also voluntarily followed us out here towards the rot infested lands to fulfill a debt of what? Arine helping to carry you?" He arched his eyebrows in his annoyingly arrogant manner. "And mind you," he continued, "this is after each of you took *somewhat* great pains to escape our custody in the first place."

He looked between them, expectant.

"My brother already told you about my wanton disregard for rules," Cilia said flippantly. "And frankly, from what he described after leaving the forest, even if I didn't owe Arine a debt, I'd still want to see what this was all about. You're questioning us like we're the suspicious ones—yet I haven't heard a single reason why the six of you are marching her this way. Unless I'm mistaken, you only met Arine a few days ago—in a field, yourself."

She met the Prince's gaze with arrogant defiance, but it was Gerin who cut in from behind her.

"I think she might be dense. She clearly doesn't realize that she's the one tied up with six soldiers surrounding her."

Cilia tilted her head. "If my tied hands are all that stop you from answering, then what about now?"

With a flick, the ropes slid free. Before anyone could react, she rolled toward Matthew, hooked his legs with her own, and toppled him. In one fluid motion she locked him with her thighs and produced a small dagger that had escaped notice, the blade pressing to his throat as she smiled.

Gerin instantly seized Ciran, putting a knife to his neck, but Ciran made no move to resist—his stillness as deliberate as her movements were wild. Jove and Theo edged closer, ready, but none dared intervene for fear Cilia would cut deeper.

Derik crossed his arms and surveyed the group. After a few tense seconds, he stepped forward between the two pairs. Arine shifted to the side for a better angle and saw Matthew's eyes darted with panic, but Cilia looked utterly unfazed, as though she had all the time in the world.

Derik met the newcomers' eyes before speaking.

"I'll make a deal with you. You swear to me now that you will follow my orders until this mission is over and surrender *all* of your weapons and we will let you continue with us."

"What?!" Gerin barked. "You can't be serious. We can't trust them."

"It's that or kill them now," Derik replied. Arine's shoulders tensed, her body half-poised to leap in.

Gerin's gaze darted from Cilia to Ciran, weighing it as Derik pressed on.

"Twice now, they've shown restraint. Earlier, they never even reached for their weapons. And just now, she had Matthew at her mercy and didn't harm him. Her brother didn't move against you either. Besides—" his eyes flicked toward Arine "—slitting her friends' throats won't exactly keep her cooperative."

Damn straight, Arine thought.

"She's outnumbered, and he's tied up," Gerin snapped. "Of course they didn't try anything more."

Derik's mouth curved faintly. "I think you'll find his ropes are no longer tied."

Gerin yanked at the cord binding Ciran and swore as the cut ends dangled loose.

"Who tied this?" he demanded, eyes blazing as he raised the knife closer to Ciran's throat.

Ciran only shrugged, unflinching. Arine's pulse leapt—she couldn't let Gerin slit his throat out of pride.

Derik's voice cut the tension. "If you won't give me your word, and let my men search you again, then I'll order your deaths. I'm giving you this chance because of Arine and because you've shown restraint. But if that changes, nothing will stop us from continuing. Decide. Now."

"I accept," Cilia said smoothly, chin high.

Ciran made a strangled sound, the blade pressed too close for him to speak.

"Gerin," Derik said, his voice low and sharp. "Stand down. That's an order."

For a long, dangerous moment, Gerin's arm trembled with defiance. Then, finally, he withdrew the knife and shoved Ciran back with a sneer.

"Fine, but don't expect me to intervene when one of them tries to put a knife in your back."

Derik ignored him. His gaze locked on Ciran. "Well?"

Ciran cleared his throat, then gave his answer. "I accept."

❧ ·─·◆·─· ❧

Chapter 13

Cilia released Matthew and withdrew two more knives she'd hidden during the first search, flashing Gerin a sly smile as she revealed them. He stomped off, muttering curses and something about *traveling with morons* that Arine couldn't quite catch. From his reaction, it was clear he'd been the one to search her the first time—and Arine would have bet a horse Cilia hadn't surrendered every weapon even now.

Ciran handed over three knives of his own, plus a small blade Derik uncovered, sewn into the back of his pants. Only then did Arine realize how he'd sliced through the ropes unnoticed. It only worked one time since he had had to cut through the secret pocket, but one time was enough.

When the camp finally quieted, Arine busied herself with lighting the fire and tending to her horse. Each glance toward Ciran tightened her chest, a pressure she couldn't shake. She longed to talk to someone, but aside from Lian, who was still out on patrol, the guards felt like strangers. With no one else to confide in, she found herself drifting closer to Derik despite their rough lesson on wielding.

After confiscating the newcomers' weapons, Derik had led his mare a short distance from the others. Arine seized the moment to walk over and help rub his horse down, hoping it would make it clear that she meant no trouble. Her boots crunched against the dry ground with every step, giving him plenty of warning of her approach.

He didn't speak as she stopped beside him, only held out a grooming brush in silent invitation as if he already knew why she was there. She accepted it and for a while they worked in quiet rhythm, the mare flicking her tail at flies, until Arine finally found the words she'd been searching for.

"Thank you for intervening earlier and letting Ciran and Cilia live. But, I have to ask, why did you? Gerin was right, it would have been easier to just kill them. Now you will have to watch them all the time."

Derik kept brushing, silent long enough for Arine to scold herself for thinking the person he was the night before they left was anything but a ruse to put her at ease. She patted the mare once more and had started to turn away when he finally spoke.

"Whatever you may think of us, when it came down to it, neither Gerin nor I would have killed them. But now they think one of us might—and they think another might be an ally, at least somewhat." His voice betrayed more weariness than he probably intended.

Arine let the quiet stretch, giving him a taste of his own medicine. She understood his reasoning; he couldn't simply allow two strangers to join them without a challenge. She just wished she was a part of something, anything, instead of always being the one who had to learn the plan afterwards.

Derik came around to her side of the horse and took the brush from her hand, his fingers warm against hers. "And if Gerin had actually killed them," he added dryly, "we'd have had to tie you up and drag you to the cave. Your insults alone might have driven us mad before we arrived."

She arched a brow at his attempt at humor, unsure whether to be annoyed or amused.

"Hmm." Arine tilted her head. "Careful, or someone might start to think you actually have a heart. I can't believe you would consider your men's feelings like that."

"Ah, but you're missing the part where I'd still tie you up and drag you there anyway."

The image flickered in her mind. "I'll stick with my version," she said, forcing a gruffness she didn't quite feel.

Derik shook his head in mock disappointment and stepped back around the horse, but she caught the faint smile as he turned away. She put a mark in her corner for once. Emboldened by his lighter mood, she circled to the other side after him.

"Do you believe them?" she asked.

"Who?" He kept brushing the mare's flank.

"Don't be an ass," she snapped, surprised by the heat in her own voice.

He looked up, blue eyes locking on hers. She braced for a royal reprimand, a reminder to show proper respect.

"No—but I also don't think they're here to harm you or any of us," he said instead, catching her off guard.

"Why?"

"Call it Princely intuition," he said arrogantly before smiling at her suddenly. This time, it took her a second to realize he was joking.

She scoffed, scooping a handful of dry needles from the ground and tossing them at him. "You really think you're something, don't you?"

He swatted the needles aside with lazy precision and arched an eyebrow. "You know assaulting a royal is punishable by death, right?"

Arine winked at Derik. "I'll bank on you not wanting to admit a girl armed with pine needles got the better of you."

Feeling lighter despite the unfinished business with Ciran and Cilia, she turned back toward the group. Jove was stirring a small stew as she joined the others and Lian and Gerin had returned.

Gerin's new tactic was pretending the newcomers didn't exist, which oddly comforted Arine; for once, she wasn't the only outsider at camp. She chose a seat on a log a ways away from everyone, despite the chill. It was obvious she was avoiding Ciran, but she didn't care. A conversation would come eventually, but forgiveness would take longer.

Conflicted thoughts swirled as she ate. On one hand, he had done more for her by coming after her to make sure she was okay than she had done for either of them. Sure, she had helped him get Cilia to safety, but after that she had basically left them to their own devices. While they had put aside their own goals, whatever those were, to traipse off into the middle of nowhere after her.

Of course, there was still the question of if they knew more than they were saying. Even if they did though, what could they hope to do? They may have been able to take out several of the guards by surprise, but gauging by everyone's skill level, there was no way they would best all six now that they were on full alert and why would they want to? Surely they would have no reason to stop her from healing the rot and trying to save more people from starving and dying. They had said themselves that their food source had run out, forcing them to migrate, so they knew firsthand how bad everything was.

Arine ate slowly, pretending interest in her food while sneaking glances at the newcomers. They chatted with easy confidence for having forced their way into the group only mere hours ago. Ciran even managed to draw Theo—who sat nearest—into conversation. At first Theo was guarded, but after enough praise for his stew he began sharing stories freely. Arine felt a twinge of jealousy at how quickly they won him over.

Ciran was far more talkative than he'd ever been during their time alone, but she supposed that was because he was trying to ingratiate himself with the group. Cilia was the opposite of cautious, tossing remarks at anyone who caught her eye and laughing loudly at every joke, even when others tried to leave her out. The two siblings had completely different styles of interacting, but they complimented each other. Arine couldn't help noticing that, at this rate, they would befriend the others sooner than she had. Still, she was grateful they didn't try to force her into their awkward conversations, despite the occasional glance in her direction.

When the meal ended, Cilia sprang up and challenged everyone to a game of runes. Derik and Lian declined, and Gerin ignored her completely, but Theo, Jove, and Matthew caved after only a little coaxing. Cilia set out the ten six-sided cubes, each etched with symbols whose meaning changed depending on how they fell. Players could only roll three at a time, up to twice per turn so you had to be intentional on what you hoped to roll based on what rune was 'set' for that round. The mix of luck and quick calculation allowed for sudden upsets, though a skilled player could tilt the odds in their favor.

Arine couldn't hear how much Cilia was trying to wager, but after a few moments they must have settled on an amount because she saw them put some coins in a pile to the side and begin playing. Arine didn't have much money to waste on gambling, but she enjoyed watching them play and cajole each other, trying to lure one another to roll unnecessarily or stop too soon.

Matthew seemed to be the one off to an early start—he rolled with a steady calm, unfazed by the manipulation tactics. Arine didn't realize how intensely she was watching them play until the log beneath her shifted as someone sat down beside her. She turned, startled to find Ciran.

For an instant she thought of standing, but she squared her shoulders instead. She wasn't the one who had lied. Out of the corner of her eye she saw him fidget before speaking.

"I can leave if you aren't ready to talk—well, not leave, but leave you alone at least," he said awkwardly, looking down.

Arine stayed silent, anger still tangled with the memory of their easy companionship. Though they'd known each other only a short time, she had almost considered him a friend.

"I'm sorry I didn't tell you Cilia was my sister," he began at last, when it became clear she wasn't going to make it easy for him.

"And didn't correct me when I assumed you were enrolled at the Pillar," Arine interjected. She supposed she did have something to say after all. "Essentially you didn't trust me with any information about yourself. Was anything you told me true or did you just make up stories for the fun of it?"

She glared at him, annoyed that he wasn't even grasping the crux of the issue. She hadn't wanted to talk yet because of this very reason. She had wanted time to calm down so she wouldn't reveal just how much it hurt to be lied to and not trusted.

"I get it," Ciran said placatively, and he did seem to genuinely care that she was upset. "But to be fair, I never lied to you. Yes, I withheld information about myself and Cilia but that was because I didn't know you and there was the possibility *you* were lying to *me* about why you were there. Slavers employ many tactics to lure unsuspecting travelers into their grasp. And honestly, how do I know the truth even now? I mean, the Prince was waiting for you and now you are traveling with him and five other royal guards. One of which is high ranking. What you told me about yourself doesn't really line up either, does it? Can you really blame me for being cautious? What would you have done in my place?"

Arine grudgingly saw his point, though her anger still smoldered. Sensible or not, it still hurt. She'd trusted him easily, asked too few questions, and now every interaction they had felt like a lie. Foolishness burned in her chest, and she blinked back the tears that threatened to form before he could see how much it hurt.

Arine took a small breath and forced her thoughts to what she could do now. She wasn't going to be that naive again. If he was going to claim that he hadn't ever lied to her then he could start proving it right now by answering some hard questions, honestly.

"So why are you here then?" she asked.

"What I told the Prince was true—I came to make sure you were safe. When I last saw you, there was no love lost between you and him, and I assumed he had thrown you into a cage like the one where he kept me. That night I searched for you but couldn't find you anywhere. I wasn't able to get Cilia away because I wasted too much time trying to figure out where you were, so I had to make the decision to leave and try again the next night. I meant to hide nearby and follow the group, but the Syarans attacked and I had to avoid them for several hours. Some of them noticed my tracks and started following me. It took me almost the entire next day to lose them and when I got back to the camp, you were gone."

He paused, giving Arine a chance to speak. She stayed silent, sifting through his words for any hint of another half truth. When she offered nothing, he continued, voice steady but earnest.

"The rest you know. I went to the palace to find Cilia and learn what happened to you, only to discover you'd already left. Cilia overheard the healer being asked to prepare spare herbs for a journey and insisted we follow. She's too stubborn for her own good on her best day, but I didn't need very much convincing this time anyway, so we set out immediately."

Arine weighed his explanation. Everything fit and her experience with him so farn didn't indicate a need to fear his motives...yet caution still held her back.

"And what of your original purpose—finding a better home for your family?" she asked.

Concern flickered across his face before he dipped his head. "Every day we delay is another day our friends and family may not survive. Others are searching too, so perhaps they'll find something. But I would never forgive myself if I just left you."

There was a sincerity to his voice that she couldn't help but notice, a steady familiarity woven beneath the words that she didn't have with the others. It made her want to relent, but she also knew having them here would put them in danger. She couldn't let his friends and family suffer more because of her, especially since her mother's actions were the reason they needed to find more suitable land in the first place.

"Well, I appreciate you coming," she said, forcing a bright tone. "Really. But I'm fine. There's nothing to worry about. You should be helping your family, not babysitting me."

"Are you fine?" he asked, his voice sharpening.

He studied her face, then glanced at the guards and finally at Derik. When his gaze returned, his green eyes almost glowed in the firelight. She hesitated, unsure how to answer, and he pressed again. "Tell me this, could you leave if you wanted to?"

She opened her mouth to brush it off, but his question was hard to answer. She technically couldn't leave if she wanted to but, she also knew deep down she wouldn't leave if given the chance.

"No," she said softly. "I can't leave, but it's not for the reasons you think."

She stopped herself from telling him about her mother. She could lie to herself and say it was because of Derik's warnings and the attacks, but the reality was she was afraid of what he would think of her if he knew she was the daughter of someone who had caused so much pain and destruction.

"So I was right—you are in trouble," he said flatly, glaring again toward Derik and the others. When he faced her once more, his gaze burned with new intensity. "You have no idea who these people really are. With three of us and only six of them, we can catch them by surprise and get you out. I'm sure of it."

She shook her head as he finished. "No. Even though the circumstances of this trip are not ideal, believe me when I say that I don't want to leave. If we succeed here then we have a real chance at helping everyone, including your family."

"What are you talking about?" he asked, confusion tightening his brow.

She only shook her head again, catching the brief flash of hurt in his eyes before he masked it. "I'm sorry, but I can't tell you. It's safer if you go back. I'll find you in the city when this is over," she offered, hoping they truly could remain friends when she returned.

He studied her in silence, his gaze hard. "I take it the Prince, or more likely the King, came up with whatever it is you are doing? How can you trust them? How do you know what they've told you about your role in whatever this is," he gestured angrily at the group sitting across the camp, "is actually true? The King and his lackeys are not kind. What if you are willingly walking to your death?"

"You're right, I don't know that everything anyone says is the truth," Arine said defensively, angry at him pointing out her own fears. "You act like you are some saint and no one else can be trusted when you are the only one who has lied to me so far."

He opened his mouth, but she cut him off with a raised hand. "No, listen. I may not know everything. In fact, I'm sure of it. But I know enough. I know that if there's a chance to save even one person, I'm going to try it. Wouldn't you? I am telling you that I want to be here, and if you can't take my word for it, you would be no better than what you are accusing them of doing. Don't try to force me away."

Ciran stiffened, staring at the fire while the others played and talked. Now and then someone glanced their way but quickly looked back, granting them privacy.

When he finally spoke, his voice was steadier, though something unspoken lingered beneath it.

"Fine. But at least let us protect you. My family can manage for a while, and if you're truly helping people, making sure you succeed can't be a bad thing. And it can't hurt having people here only on your side—not a part of their politics."

Arine could see how determined he was and she couldn't lie to herself and say she didn't want him here. She wouldn't mind having traveling companions that would actually speak to her. But, even though they appeared to be genuine in their intentions, this time she wouldn't let her guard down so quickly.

"Fine," she said and smiled at him, giving in. "But, don't lie to me again."

Ciran grinned and rose. As he walked away, Cilia paused mid-throw in her runes game to glance between them. Whatever she read in her brother's face made her flash Arine a quick smile before turning back to the game.

Arine felt lighter, relieved to be on civil terms with Ciran again.

Chapter 14

An air of distrust still lingered in the morning that even the runes game hadn't been able to dispel. The quiet tension carried through breakfast and breaking camp—everyone moving around the two newcomers with careful, sidelong glances. One small benefit of their arrival was that Matthew and Jove no longer kept as much distance from Theo and Lian. Now they felt more like one group against Cilia and Ciran, and any shift toward unity was still progress, Arine supposed.

After a quick breakfast, Derik gave orders for Theo to range and the rest of the group mounted up to follow at a slower pace. Gerin took the lead of the group this time with Matthew and Jove behind him. Despite the unsettled mood, the promise of reaching the Trader's Post within a day or two—and the thought of a real bed and meal—quickly lifted everyone's spirits.

With Derik and Lian positioned at the rear, Arine found herself next to Cilia in the middle. The redhead offered her an easy smile and immediately struck up conversation.

"Ciran thanked you yesterday, but I wanted to say it myself—thank you for saving my life. What he told you is true, and I'll help you however I can to repay the debt."

Cilia cast a quick, meaningful glance at the guards surrounding them; Arine only hoped Ciran had passed along her firm refusal of his earlier escape proposal. Regardless, she returned Cilia's smile, glad for the woman's refreshing company.

"It was nothing anyone else wouldn't have done," Arine said. "And like I told Ciran yesterday, I appreciate your concern—but I'm exactly where I choose to be, even if it looks otherwise."

"He said you'd said that, even if it doesn't seem like it," she replied with a trace of doubt, then shrugged. "Still, this is far more interesting than searching for better farmland."

Cilia glanced up at Gerin, who was scanning the path for rough spots. She turned back and winked. "Very interesting," she said and smiled again.

Arine nearly choked at the implication. Gerin? His arrogant attitude aside, hadn't he been arguing to kill her and Ciran less than a day ago?

"So I take it you aren't with anyone back home then?" Arine asked, once she managed to control her shock.

"No, I prefer to stay unattached. Why let a man tell me what I can or can't do? Until I meet someone who can match my drinking, beat me in a sword fight, and look striking while doing it, I'm fine on my own." She flashed a grin as she listed her terms.

"Well, I can't argue with that logic," Arine said.

"So I take it there is no Mr. Arine back home then?"

"Ha, definitely not." She chuckled. "I grew up with only a few others my age in a small town, learning everything together, so they all felt more like siblings than anything else. I could never see any of them that way—though I do miss them."

Cilia asked Arine about her hometown and how she learned to sword fight, also acknowledging it was rare for a woman. Arine told her how her father had insisted she know how to protect herself.

Grateful for the normal conversation, Arine lost herself in the diversion of a normal companion. So it wasn't until they stopped for lunch, that she finally noticed the tension settling over the group as they entered a small copse Gerin had chosen. The trees were jagged and rough looking things that stuck up at odd angles, but at least they broke the sharp wind.

As she dismounted Cloud, Derik pulled Gerin aside to confer in private, which struck her as odd. Meanwhile, Matthew, Lian, and Jove scanned the surrounding terrain instead of taking a break. Ciran and Cilia lingered nearest, so Arine motioned toward the others.

"Do you know what's going on?" she asked.

Ciran nodded, his expression grave. "The younger guard who was supposed to be ranging out hasn't been seen since this morning. His tracks disappeared a while ago."

"Theo is missing?" she asked, chastising herself for not noticing sooner.

Ciran shrugged. "That's all I overheard—they're not exactly sharing details with me."

Arine glanced at Derik and Gerin, still deep in tense discussion. "What do you think happened?" she pressed, hoping Ciran would have some insight.

"Honestly, it could be anything—maybe his horse was injured, maybe he got turned around, or...maybe he ran into trouble."

Arine didn't need to be reminded about what trouble could mean out here. She really hoped it was one of the inconvenient and less threatening scenarios. While they were talking, Derik and Gerin wrapped up their private conversation and walked towards them, motioning for the others to join.

"Theo has been gone longer than usual, and we haven't seen any sign of his passing," Derik said. "We need to send a group to look for him. Hopefully, it's nothing serious, but we have to plan for the worst. No one goes out alone—there could be Syarans or other threats—and we don't have enough people to search quickly unless we split up. Here's the plan: Jove and I will take the eastern side, Lian and Matthew the western. Report back in three hours no matter what, then we'll reassess."

The men nodded and moved toward their horses.

"What about the rest of us?" Ciran asked. "We can help search too."

Gerin cut in before Derik could answer, one hand resting on his sword. "At this point you're suspect number one. If I were you, I wouldn't draw too much attention. Did you bring another group to ambush us?"

"If we were working with someone else, why would we put ourselves at your mercy? We'd just be with them and attack together," Ciran said patronizingly.

Gerin started to retort, but Derik raised a hand and met his eyes, stopping him cold. Gerin clicked his mouth shut and glared, but said nothing more.

Derik addressed them in a tone that left no doubt he expected obedience. "You three will stay here under Gerin's direction and make sure Arine is safe."

"Wait, is he supposed to be our babysitter?" Cilia scoffed. "And I think Arine is more than capable of defending herself from what I heard from Ciran."

"I don't doubt it," Derik replied, his voice hard, "but I won't risk her safety needlessly. And isn't that why you claimed you were here—to protect her? Unless, of course, you were lying..."

"I'm right here, you know," Arine cut in, irritation sharpening her words. "If you need more people to search, let us help. The sooner we find Theo, the sooner we can all move on."

"We can't risk everyone running around blind," Derik said, voice hard. "If Theo manages to continue on, he'll look for this campsite. He needs somewhere to return to instead of wandering while we search." He fixed her with a hard stare. "Not to mention, your safety matters more."

"But, surely finding Theo as quick as possible will mean we are all back together *keeping me safe*." She responded, refusing to just accept his decision that her life was more important than the others.

Cilia voiced her agreement, and Arine saw the tension in Derik's shoulders as their pressure mounted. He clearly wasn't used to being challenged.

"One of these days you'll have to stop treating me like a child," she insisted.

"Refusing to accept wise judgment and the chain of command doesn't make that easy for me to do," Derik shot back. "You put Theo's life at greater risk arguing instead of letting us be on our way. Even the greenest recruits know respect is earned by following orders first."

The words struck like a slap. Heat crept into Arine's cheeks, but she swallowed every retort. Arguing further would only prove his point. All she could do was scowl at him in silent anger.

Derik glared back at her for a few seconds, opening his mouth to respond, but he clamped it shut and strode over to his horse instead.

"Let's go," he snapped without a backward glance, and the mounted group rode off as one, leaving Arine and the others to stew in his decision.

Gerin watched until the riders disappeared, then turned back to their small group, clearly ready to start issuing orders. But when he caught Arine's tense expression, he shifted his attention to Ciran and Cilia instead.

"Pick one weapon each from what we confiscated," he said coolly. "Just in case. But don't get any illusions that the two of you can best me."

Excitement crossed over both their faces followed quickly by annoyance at hearing he felt they were no threat to him. To top it off, Gerin promptly turned away and found himself a seat on a log nearby, dismissing them as if he truly found them completely unthreatening.

Ciran and Cilia exchanged a glance. Ciran gave a small shake of his head, and after a beat Cilia moved to retrieve her bow without a word. Her movements were stiff, but she didn't rise to the bait and respond to Gerin's dig this time. Ciran followed her lead, walking over and grabbing his sword before sitting down to sharpen the edge.

Arine sat down as well, her irritation building. It was infuriating, how they treated her. Here she was just sitting around, no information...nothing. As she thought about it, her perturbation increased, which in turn seemed to make the time pass even slower.

Ciran apparently felt the same way because after sharpening his sword, he mumbled something about spotting grouse. He took a bow and disappeared into the trees. Gerin raised an eyebrow at the extra weapon but said nothing. Cilia had stationed herself at the opposing end of the clearing and was openly glaring at Gerin, while he pretended she didn't exist.

If she hadn't still been irritated with Derik, she might have found it amusing enough to watch them. Unfortunately, as the time crawled by, she reluctantly started to admit to herself that he was partly right—normally you don't question your superior's orders, especially in front of the rest of the group. Her father had told stories of soldiers punished for far less insubordination than she'd shown.

In her defense, she hadn't signed up to be in the guard or the army. She wasn't a soldier to be commanded without a say. This whole journey had been thrust on her; the least he could do was try to understand her perspective. Honestly, at this rate it would be a miracle if he even let her attempt the unsevering without trying to take control of that too.

She knew she was being a little peevish because he was right in the sense that if something were to happen to her, everything was at risk. Still, she wished he'd show even a shred of respect instead of treating her like dead weight.

After an hour or so, when she was utterly bored of sulking, she decided to go find Ciran, who had wandered out of sight in his search for the grouse. She was surprised Gerin hadn't ordered him to remain, but with Cilia present he probably assumed Ciran wouldn't risk her safety. Her guess was confirmed when she told Gerin she planned to find Ciran.

Cilia jumped up to join her, but Gerin called out before she'd taken two steps. "You will remain here."

He didn't even glance at Cilia to see if she obeyed, missing the rude gesture she tossed his way. Cilia flopped back down, edging closer to him than before. As she walked off, she heard Cilia challenge him to a knife-throwing contest. Arine was slightly worried one of them would be seriously injured when she got back, but not worried enough to stay. She needed to move around and distract herself.

She found Ciran further out than she had thought he would be, but true to his word he already had three plump birds at his side. They heard a fast moving stream a little ways away so they walked over to start cleaning them. The trees were green in this area with small patches of grass for them to sit on. The running water was soothing as they worked together in comfortable silence, picking off the feathers. Their quiet camaraderie reminded her of their time escaping the forest and soon they had most of the feathers removed from the birds.

As she picked off the last feather, she held up her bird for Ciran to appreciate. The words died on her lips though when she saw movement within a large group of short, stubby trees about twenty feet behind him. She stared at the foliage hoping it was just a squirrel or some other rodent.

Three men stepped from the brush, swords drawn, the sound of the water having masked their approach. A heartbeat later the threat registered. She sprang up, sword flashing, Ciran spinning to meet them a beat behind her.

She caught only a few details: one wore a battered leather jerkin, the others rough wool tunics in varying states of wear. Two rushed Ciran while the third veered toward her. She struck first, her blade meeting his with a sharp clang. His eyes widened—clearly unprepared for her skill—so she pressed the advantage and attacked again.

He tried to block but was a heartbeat too slow, and her blade cut across his thigh before he could retreat. He swore in a language she didn't know, the sound sparking her memory of the Yuakan slaver she and Ciran had left after freeing Cilia. Another group? The thought chilled her.

A flicker of déjà vu tightened her chest before she forced her focus back to the fight. He lunged again, fast but sloppy, his haste illuminating his next strike. She dodged and sidestepped along the stream, careful not to be driven onto the slick rocks near the water's edge.

He fought with brute force—larger and quicker than her father—forcing her to parry hard to avoid a crippling blow. After several exchanges she realized his cuts aimed to disable, not kill—slashes toward her sword arm or legs, an elbow feint to her head. They wanted her alive. Dead slaves were worthless.

She knew she had to finish it before exhaustion set in, and a risky idea flashed through her mind: if they wanted a captive, she might turn that need against him.

The next time he struck, she gambled it would be for her sword arm rather than her chest or stomach—despite knowing a wrong guess could mean her life. She drew a sharp breath, ducked low, and his blade cut only air. Already inside his guard, she slashed a deep line across his chest.

She stepped aside in case of a last desperate swing, but he only stared down in surprise before collapsing. Arine darted past him toward Ciran, knowing the man wouldn't recover.

Ciran had already felled one attacker and fought the last in a flurry of blows. When Arine joined him, they overpowered the third quickly. They stood for a few seconds, catching their breath. Arine checked her side—her stitches still held—while Ciran scanned the trees for more enemies.

"How many slavers are roaming these lands for us to encounter two groups so close together?" she asked once she could breathe easier.

"I'm not surprised they're here," Ciran said, frowning. "They prey on destitute regions like ours, where the law is weak and resistance scarce. But this far inland is unusual. Normally they stay near the coast for a quick escape."

"We'll have to ask Derik what he thinks when he returns," Arine replied. "We should get back in case there are others."

Ciran's mouth twisted at the mention of Derik, but worry for Cilia outweighed his disdain. They hurried toward camp, little more than half a mile away by Arine's estimate. A cold unease settled in her stomach as they neared—she heard nothing. She was sure Cilia would have been goading Gerin in some way or another.

As soon as Ciran saw their horses were missing he stopped and put his hand up to keep her from going further. He knelt down to examine some markings on the ground as she quietly peered through a gap in the foliage in the fir trees to where the others should have been. She gasped as she made out the unmistakable color of blood next to a body on the ground that she couldn't identify.

Before she could think, she pushed past Ciran into the clearing, heart hammering. She hurried to the fallen figure and exhaled in relief when she saw it was neither Gerin nor Cilia—it was a man dressed like the slavers they had fought by the stream, one side of his head shaved and the other braided. Another prone form lay fifteen feet away amid trampled shrubs.

Still trying to make sense of it, Arine ran toward the second body, calling for Ciran to hurry. He paused to study the disturbed ground. She realized her mistake just as the twang of a bowstring snapped through the air.

She tried to duck, but she was too late—pain seared her left arm and the impact threw her backward. Ciran shouted her name as she rolled into a half-sitting position, but all she could was grasp her arm in agony.

Pain radiated through her body and she had to steel herself before she could glance over at her arm. When she did, she saw an arrow embedded in the flesh. The tip had gone all the way through and the shaft was sticking through the underside of her arm. A couple more inches to the left and it would have been her chest.

Strangely, she noticed she wasn't bleeding much for something that was so painful. She groaned as she tried to reach over to the wound, the pain intensifying to an almost blinding level as she moved. Tears blurred her vision as she fought to stay conscious.

Ciran reached her within seconds, cursing at the sight of the arrow. He dragged her behind a bush for cover, each movement wringing another burst of agony from her arm. One harsh tug tore the flesh further, and she nearly screamed as the hot surge of blood quickened.

Ciran tore a strip from his shirt and tied it tightly above the arrow to slow the bleeding.

"I need to check if they're coming back. Stay here."

Arine nodded, unable to speak. He slipped into the shrubs, leaving her alone with the pain and the pounding of her own heartbeat. Each minute stretched like an hour as she imagined what she'd do if Ciran—or the rest of the group—never returned. How could she remove the arrow herself?

Less than ten minutes later he reappeared, breathless but unhurt.

"They're not coming back for now, but they've taken Cilia and Gerin. I need to get this arrow out so I can bandage you and find a safer spot before I go after them."

Safe. The word almost made her laugh. Wasn't she left behind precisely to be safe? She couldn't wait to see the look on Derik's face when he realized he should've let her go with him. Although with all the injuries she was wracking up, he might just never let her leave his side.

"Arine—stay with me." Ciran's voice cut through her drifting thoughts. He cupped her face, eyes intent. "You're losing blood too fast. This will hurt, but it has to come out so I can stitch it."

He handed her a stick. She clenched it between her teeth and tried to brace herself. The first snap of the arrow's tip sent white-hot pain through her arm. She cried out and jerked despite herself, but Ciran held her steady. Tears streaked her cheeks as she drew shallow breaths, preparing herself for what she knew was coming next.

He inhaled sharply—and then came the sharpest pain she had ever felt. Darkness rushed in before she could scream, swallowing her whole.

✦ ·•◆•· ✦

Chapter 15

Arine woke to the sound of low, angry voices. Her eyelids felt heavy, so she remained still, trying to orient herself.

"Why would I need to wait for you?" one voice demanded.

"Because she's in pain and someone had to make sure she's all right," the other replied—Derik's voice, sharp with the same icy tone that spoke of a rage held just barely in check.

Memory surged back: the fight with the slavers, the empty camp, the arrow in her arm. The ache remained, a deep pulse that felt strangely distant, as if dulled by some herb or salve. Relief washed through her when she realized Derik was safe.

A small groan escaped before she could stop it, and both men turned. In the dim light she saw Derik pivot and stride toward her, dropping to one knee beside her with something like concern in his eyes.

"I told you you should've let me help search," she rasped, unwilling to miss the chance to point out she'd been right.

She could have sworn he almost rolled his eyes at her before he started checking her over. He fussed over her as if he were afraid she was hiding other injuries from him. She actually had to swat him away, and when he finally leaned back on his heels, she caught a flicker of sadness in his gaze she hadn't noticed before.

"What is it?" she asked, bracing for bad news.

"Theo," Derik said quietly. "They ambushed him. He fought hard, but they overwhelmed him."

"No," she whispered and closed her eyes to hold back the sorrow. She hadn't known Theo for long, but she felt the loss even so.

"How did they know where we were?" she asked, "And why attack us like this? I thought slavers, especially those from Yuak, liked easy targets. Between all of us, we have killed way more of them than they have taken as slaves. None of this makes sense."

"That's the question," Derik said, rising to his feet. His gaze shifted to Ciran, hard and suspicious. "You and Cilia arrive, and a day later we're ambushed. Convenient, isn't it?"

"I would never work with Yuakans or any other slavers," Ciran seethed, "Besides, they attacked Cilia. Why would they do that if we were working with them?"

Derik's eyes narrowed. "We'll wait for the others to return before deciding. But understand this—any hint of treachery, and there will be no leniency." His voice snapped like a whip.

Arine kept silent, torn. The timing looked damning, but Ciran had a point—why would the slavers harm Cilia if they were working together? Faking such an attack seemed absurdly elaborate.

"Where are the others?" she asked at last, worry tightening her chest.

"They are seeing where the slavers are camped and getting an estimate of how many and how well armed they are before we plan any rescue attempts." Derik said, though his eyes stayed locked on Ciran.

If she had had to guess, Ciran had wanted to mount a rescue immediately and had been stopped. She couldn't blame him. If it had been someone she loved, she probably would have tried to go chasing after them as fast as possible without thinking too. And she hated to admit it, but Derik's caution was the right choice.

Her stomach tightened as her mind jumped to what the information the others brought would mean. What if they found out there was a large force?

How could they save Cilia and Gerin—or even escape themselves? She couldn't bring herself to voice the question to Derik because deep down she thought she already knew the answer. Apparently, she wasn't the only one with that train of thought because a few tense seconds later, Ciran gave life to the same questions she hadn't voiced.

"And if there are too many? If there's no way to reach them?"

Derik didn't look at either of them and was silent for so long Arine thought he might just end up ignoring the question all together. When he finally did respond, his voice was flat, but Arine could feel the depth of emotion reverberating off him even though he tried to pretend the decision was devoid of feeling.

"Then we leave them."

Ciran stepped forward, fury sharpening his features. "I will never abandon my family or friends to a fate worse than death while there's even a sliver of hope. If you choose to leave them, I hope they haunt your nightmares for the rest of your life and that you suffer an even worse fate."

Derik didn't flinch. He met Ciran's glare with a weary half-smile. "You assume I don't already have worse nightmares. But this mission is larger than two lives, and I won't waste Theo's death on a fight we can't win. Someone has to weigh the bigger picture—you, of all people, should understand that."

Ciran's eyes flicked toward Arine, and she thought he looked embarrassed to be chided in front of her, but before he could reply Derik pressed on.

"You're free to act as you wish, so long as you don't endanger my group—once you're cleared of suspicion. Still, I'd hate to see you captured or killed alongside them. Consider the people depending on your safe return, and whether losing you as well as Cilia would truly serve them."

Ciran glanced at Arine again before he gave a quiet snarl of frustration and stalked to the far side of their hiding place to glare at Derik instead.

They continued to wait in uneasy silence—a relief to Arine, whose fatigue made it hard to follow their heated exchange. The temperature dropped, but they couldn't risk a fire for fear of alerting the Yuakans of their location. Arine huddled into her cloak while the pain in her arm sharpened as the earlier herbs wore off. Derik had told her he had given her a special tincture that Shian had packed, but she declined another dose. She chose to take some of her own herbs she had kept from her time in the woods that wouldn't make her drowsy instead. The ache settled to a manageable throb so long as she avoided sudden movement.

She spotted Cloud standing between a cluster of short trees—someone had retrieved their horses—but the sight brought little comfort. She still couldn't believe Theo was gone. She blinked back tears at the memory of his always smiling face. People died all the time these days, from the rotting sickness or famine, yet she couldn't shake the feeling that his death was her fault. He wouldn't have been here if not for her.

Arine thought of their brief conversations, how he'd been the first to warm to her, and wondered who would care for his mother now. Anger became the only steadying force, and she clung to it. She would do everything in her power to make sure his death wasn't wasted. That meant getting Gerin and Cilia back safe and getting as far from these despicable people as possible.

After what felt like hours, footsteps approached. Lian, Matthew, and Jove slipped into the hiding place. They looked as bad as Arine felt. They were covered in dirt, scrapes, and blood that were hard to tell apart in the darkness.

"Did you see where they took her?" Ciran asked, just as Derik cut in with a sharp, "What did you find?" and shot Ciran a warning look to stay silent.

Lian answered Derik. "We counted twelve left. They're about an hour's ride north—just inside the forest fringe. Gerin and Cilia are tied to a tree in the center of camp. Neither moved while we watched, and the slavers left them alone...for now. We couldn't tell how badly they're hurt, but the Yuakans were bandaging their wounds. Who knows what happens when that's done." He met Derik's gaze with grim meaning.

Derik eyed Ciran as he asked Lian, "What do you think?"

Lian paused, his gaze flicking to Ciran first. "Can't say one way or the other yet. It's in the realm of possibilities that they tied her up for show."

Derik nodded thoughtfully while Arine held her breath, waiting for his decision. At last he spoke. "Tie him up and check him thoroughly this time. Jove, untie the horses so they can graze while we're gone."

Jove and Lian moved at once, Lian showing no sign of surprise at the order. Ciran seethed as the older guard forced him into a sitting position and bound his hands.

"They'll kill them the moment you attack! You'll need me if you want them alive!" he shouted.

"One would think you'd be grateful we're attempting a rescue instead of leaving them to their fate," Derik replied coolly.

"How many times do I have to tell you I am not in league with the slavers. You are seriously mad. And you really would distrust me over him?" he snarled. "If anyone is in league with them, it's him!"

Before Arine could figure out who he was talking about, Derik stepped forward and struck Ciran on the side of the head with the hilt of his sword. Ciran slumped, unconscious but breathing.

"Why would you do that? And who was he talking about?" Arine demanded.

"Gerin, of course, because of his...less than favorable attitude," Derik said nonchalantly, as though knocking a man senseless were routine. "But we can't risk Ciran escaping his ropes again. We still don't know he isn't involved."

He turned away to gather his weapons. Arine longed to press for more answers, but the urgency of rescuing Cilia and Gerin outweighed her questions.

Arine gingerly stood with the others and Derik glanced over at her, holding up a hand for everyone to wait. He strode to the pile of packs they were leaving behind, too burdensome to take on the rescue mission. Digging through his own, he pulled out a shirt, and tore it into strips. Braiding the pieces together, he returned to Arine and slipped the makeshift sling over her shoulder.

She almost saw stars when he cinched it to her side so her left arm couldn't move. He assured her that it would help keep her from accidentally jostling it if she needed to fight, so she carefully gave her sword a few test thrusts and he nodded at her appreciatively when she was able to hold it firmly. The sharp ache left her unsure whether her dizziness came from the pain or the whiplash of his mood swings.

They set out through a tangle of dark brush and short, stumpy trees that turned every step into a fight to avoid being slapped by wet branches. Needles scratched her arms, the damp air bit at her cheeks, and within minutes a cold drizzle began to fall, but Arine grit her teeth and stomped after the others.

For the first hour they pressed on at a steady pace, unconcerned about the noise. As they neared their target, however, Lian slowed the group, and Matthew ranged ahead to watch for lookouts. No signs of the slavers appeared as they crept north toward the forest's edge, until a stand of dense pines loomed ahead. Lian raised a hand for silence, and together they edged forward, peering through the thick needles at what lay beyond.

Arine scanned the tree line, but the darkness revealed nothing. She finally stepped back, finding the others doing the same while Derik glanced at Lian for a signal. Deeming it safe to speak, Lian whispered that the slavers' camp had been just ahead when they scouted earlier. A knot tightened in Arine's stomach. Where had they taken their prisoners now—and could they find them in time?

"They must have realized their camp was too exposed and moved to stronger ground," Derik murmured. "The good news is they probably haven't had time to harm Cilia or Gerin, since they're still on the move. The bad news is we have to track them before they can regroup with a larger force. Lian can follow their trail, but we'll need to move fast and stay unseen."

They set off toward the abandoned camp. The larger trees loomed overhead now that they were on the fringe of the forest. Arine knew all too well the terrors that lurked within and that was in what was considered the safer sections in the east. The further west you traveled, especially with the Decayed Lands encroaching, the more dangerous everything became. She forced down a shiver as they stepped into the Yuakans' former campsite.

Distinct impressions marked where Cilia and Gerin had been tied, but there were no bloodstains—only a few patches where the slavers had likely stitched wounds before moving on. No drag marks marred the soil, a hopeful sign the captives had been able to walk.

They slipped between the towering trees as lightning flared through the sky, illuminating the area. The trees seemed to magnify from its presence and the forest's depths were a mass of shadows and glistening orbs as the flashes reflected off the rain falling throughout. Arine shivered uncontrollably before following the others as they decided the Yuakans probably hadn't had time to lay any elaborate traps.

They moved as quickly as they dared, trusting the slavers had already scared off any predators. About a mile in, a peal of thunder rolled overhead, followed by lightning that silenced the forest for a heartbeat. In that pause, men's voices carried—angry shouts, then a groan, and finally a woman's cry defying them.

Derik glanced back; every face confirmed they'd heard it. He drew his sword and pushed forward, the others following carefully, weapons ready, watching their footing in the thick undergrowth.

Not far ahead, he halted them with a sharp gesture. They huddled close, listening. Through the storm, the voices grew louder.

Arine edged forward until the scene came into view. Beneath the thick canopy of towering trees, a small fire burned low, sheltered from the rain. It cast just enough light to reveal the fight.

Arine was drawn immediately to the figure in the middle of the group. Cilia was fending off a few of the men who were circling her warily while the others yelled what Arine could only guess were obscenities, egging the men on. Arine could see one man was laying near her unmoving and another was clutching his leg and bleeding heavily. That explained their caution—they could overwhelm her if they rushed all at once, but not without paying in blood. None of them seemed eager to be the first.

She hated to see Cilia in danger, but she was relieved that this at least proved her and Ciran weren't in league with the slavers. Which she would admit, if only to herself, she hadn't been sure about until that moment.

Arine couldn't make out what Cilia was using as a weapon and she noticed she wasn't moving from her spot. It was providing the slavers with the opportunity to strike at her when she should have moved to dodge it. She squinted, finally seeing that Cilia was guarding a body laying behind her. It must be Gerin, because he was nowhere else to be seen.

Derik seemed to realize it too. "Let's go," he whispered.

As one, they charged through the trees, rushing into the back of the group while they were still distracted by Cilia. Arine's arm jolted with each step, but she clenched her teeth and ran.

They reached the camp in seconds. Arine targeted a smaller man on the right whose back was turned. He half-turned at the last moment, not quickly enough to stop her blade from cutting across his hip, though he managed to get his sword up for the next blow.

She scanned for attackers while pressing him hard, but the surprise had stripped the slavers of the advantage from their numbers. Though they were still outnumbered, Derik's guards were proving their worth and quickly tipping the fight.

Her arm burned, but adrenaline blunted the pain as she drove her opponent back. Blood slicked his tunic, the slice on his leg slowing him. When he tried to pivot to her weak side, she turned with him, refusing to give him the angle her injured arm couldn't defend.

He lunged for her left shoulder—too slow. She twisted, parried, and the clash of steel sent a fresh jolt through her wounded side. She barely kept her grip, then swung again, driving the strike with the raw grief of Theo's death. The man flinched, throwing up his offhand in a futile shield. Her blade cut through, biting deep across his chest. He staggered once, then collapsed in a heap at her feet.

Breathing hard, she spun to check for more slavers and was relieved to see the others were handling the rest. Taking advantage of the lull, she ran to Cilia. The woman looked even fiercer in the dying firelight—hair wild, face streaked with blood—as she clubbed her last assailant with a pale, jagged branch.

Arine nodded to her and dropped to Gerin's side. His chest rose and fell, but he remained unconscious. A shallow slice cut across his thigh, deep bruises mottled his torso, and a swollen lump stood out on his head. She prayed there was no hidden bleeding, but there was nothing she could do except get him back to camp.

In the seconds it took to assess him, the others dispatched the remaining slavers. Derik shouted "Wait!"—too late. Jove's blade had already struck the final man down.

"Quickly, we have to leave before they return. Someone help me carry him," Cilia called, eyes still wild from the ordeal. She tried to lift Gerin, but Derik stepped in and hoisted him over his shoulder as if he weighed no more than a sack of potatoes.

"Since no one is still alive to question for information, start searching the bodies. See if they carry anything that tells us why they were here," he ordered.

Lian, Jove, and Matthew began rifling through the fallen Yuakans, but Cilia snapped, "No! There's no time—we need to go now!"

Derik continued to ignore her while he watched the others search. Arine caught the terror in Cilia's eyes and scanned the clearing herself, half-expecting another wave of attackers. All she saw though were a pile of bleached white sticks laying on the ground nearby. The damp grass gleamed silver in the firelight, casting the scene in an eerie, dreamlike glow.

Cilia's voice climbed, sharp with panic. "You don't understand—there aren't more Yuakans—"

Derik cut her off, his tone edged with accusation. "If there aren't more slavers, then we need to know why this group was here. Or is there something you're hiding?"

"Shut up, you fool!" Cilia's frantic cry made the hairs on Arine's arms stand on end.

Arine's gaze dropped back to the pale shapes scattered across the ground—and she recoiled. They weren't sticks at all...they were bones. So many bones. They looked to be a mixture of humans and animals and she almost vomited as she noticed a small skull that couldn't have belonged to an adult. What she'd taken for rain-slick leaves strung through the branches was in fact a massive spider web, each strand thick and rope-strong.

The realization struck like a blow. "White Spiders!" she gasped at the same time as Cilia.

⊰⊱ · ✦ · ⊰⊱

Chapter 16

"The Yuakans knew you were following." Cilia snapped, her voice sharp with urgency. "They saw how Gerin and I reacted to the signs of a nest nearby. The leader, who spoke the common tongue, shrugged us off as exaggerating, but gambled that fear would keep you from pursuing." She snatched a fallen sword from one of the dead slavers. "We're fortunate the spider that nests here hasn't returned yet, but that luck won't last. We need to leave—now."

White Spiders were apex predators of the forest, large enough to devour a horse. Humans rarely crossed into their territory, leaving the creatures to feed on deer or any animal careless enough to stray into their traps. The scattered bones around them likely belonged to anyone who had once thought these trees offered refuge.

Their only real weakness was sunlight due to their eyes, and even then they weren't completely powerless. They hunted in near silence, dropping from the canopy too quickly for most warriors to counter. Arine's heart hammered as she scanned the dark branches, certain unseen eyes were already watching, even though she knew an attack would come without warning.

Derik wasted no more time. Supporting Gerin's weight, he hurried back the way they had come, the rest of the group running after him and watching the trees for movement. They had covered only a few hundred feet when the hairs on Arine's neck prickled. Instinct urged her to go faster, but with Derik leading through the dense forest there was no way to move any quicker. Her pulse thudded in her ears, every flicker of shadow tightening the knot in her throat.

For a fleeting moment, Arine almost believed they might escape—until Lian cursed.

"It's in the treetops!" he shouted, and her blood went cold.

Her head swiveled up to the leafy depths above them and she saw the limbs shaking and dipping about thirty feet behind them from a massive body. The spider's ghostly white appendages shone out in stark contrast to the brown and green foliage, each leg longer than a full-grown man. Its body blended in more with the forest, so it was hard to make out its size between glances, but it was easily bigger than the largest cow she had ever seen. It was also much more agile than its size would belie. Even though she couldn't see it, she knew it had massive fangs containing a venom so pungent it would burn you even from the smallest bit of contact.

"Derik, you'll need to pick a spot in less than two minutes or we're all dead," Lian yelled.

"I'm trying!" Derik barked back, breathless under Gerin's weight. If he couldn't find ground that favored them soon, they'd be forced to fight among the trees—where the spider would have every advantage.

Arine's wounded arm throbbed with each jarring step. Sweat slicked her back, half from the exertion, half from raw fear. A bitter thought flickered: if only Derik had made her stay behind this time. But she knew she'd rather face the danger head on than wait helplessly and wonder.

Suddenly Derik veered sharply, leading them into a small clearing. They stumbled after him into open space no wider than forty feet. Here the treetops broke apart, stripping the spider of its perch. Arine glanced up: the rain had stopped, and a few faint stars shone in a calm, indifferent sky—a peaceful contrast to the terror racing through her chest as she imagined the white monster bursting from the shadows to drag them back into the dark at any second.

Derik unceremoniously slung Gerin on the ground towards the far side. He was still out cold which made Arine concerned even more for injuries they couldn't see, but there was no time to check on him.

They formed a quick defensive triangle facing the forest's edge. Lian took point, Matthew and Jove flanking a few steps back. Behind them, Derik stood with Arine and Cilia while Gerin lay shielded at the rear. The bright moon cast their only light, which was thankfully enough to make out their surroundings. Had the night stayed as dark as before, they'd have been blind against the creature bred for darkness. As it was, even with six of them, they might be hard pressed to come out alive.

The spider burst from the lower branches in a blur of motion. Its forelegs speared past the tree line, forcing Lian to pivot aside as one stabbed into the spot he'd just vacated, tearing up the ground. Each of its four front limbs gleamed with hard, scale-like plates and barbed tips strong enough to pierce bark and hold prey fast. Arine shuffled closer to the group, heart hammering, and caught a glimpse of the swollen sac beneath its abdomen—proof it was female.

The spider's head was also covered in hard plates that shielded the sensitive flesh between its many eyes. Its back lacked armor but was covered in a thick, matted hide tough enough to blunt most blades. Only the eyes and the soft belly offered true weaknesses—targets nearly impossible to reach without risking a limb.

Lian lunged for its head, but the creature drew its face tight to its body, presenting nothing but armored plates as it pivoted to track him and Jove with glittering black eyes. The others circled warily, searching for an opening, but without strung bows all they could do was dance around its stabbing forelegs and avoid colliding with one another.

Lian and Jove bore the brunt of the assault as it stalked after them. The spider lashed out with barbed limbs, each strike fast enough to spear a tree. They miraculously managed to dodge each of the spider's killing blows, yet failed to land a fatal hit themselves, either. Arine and Cilia stayed close to Gerin's prone form, guarding against the possibility that the beast might seize him as an easy prize.

Without warning, the creature scuttled backward. Matthew barely dove clear as its bulk surged past, one limb slashing across his leg and leaving a red streak before it withdrew. Derik yanked him out of reach before the spider could drag him away. Deterred for the moment, the monster slipped into the shadowed treeline, the clearing suddenly quiet except for the labored breathing from the group.

Arine could hardly dare to hope that they had actually driven it off. Maybe the spider had thought they were more work than her usual prey and had decided to find easier pickings. It would have plenty to pick from in the nest where they had slain the group of slavers.

Derik used the reprieve to tear some fabric from Matthew's shirt and hastily tie it over the slash on his leg. She was about to go help him when a rustle behind her snapped the clearing back to life. The creature burst from the shadows and landed on Gerin's prone body, fangs snapping at Cilia. Venom splattered inches from her as two hind legs began wrapping Gerin in the thick webbing.

Arine dashed in beside Cilia to stop it from cocooning him. The spider's confined angle slowed it, but Arine was no substitute for Lian or Jove and she couldn't risk the seconds it would take to swap one of them in her place. She slashed and ducked, narrowly evading a barbed limb that whipped past close enough for her to see the stiff hairs along its edge. Only Cilia's quick tug on her cloak kept her from stumbling straight into the strike.

Together they harried the beast, forcing it to abandon its wrapping. With a frustrated screech, it dropped Gerin, leaving only his upper body sticking out of the cocoon. Freed of its burden, the monster lashed out with wider sweeps of its legs, driving her and Cilia back step by step.

Arine braced for another single-leg thrust, but instead the spider swung in a vicious arc while feinting a charge. She and Cilia leapt back, expecting a rush, only for the creature to crouch low and snatch at Gerin again—determined to claim its prize before they could react.

The spider must have decided one prize was better than fending off everyone. Arine knew they had only seconds at best before it leapt up into the upper reaches of the trees, taking Gerin with her. If she wrapped Gerin enough where she could drag him behind her she could easily outrun them and finish the job unhindered.

Understanding dawned on Cilia too that the spider was poised to escape with Gerin. With a raw scream, she hurled herself at the nearest leg, hacking in a frantic arc. Her sword bit between two plated scales, cutting deep enough to make the limb buckle before the creature could steady itself.

The strike bought them a heartbeat, but at a cost. The spider's head snapped toward Cilia, and Arine saw—too late—that she would never outrun the reach of those venomous fangs.

"No!" Arine shouted, hurling herself at the spider's side.

Her sword bit into a rear leg—shallower than Cilia's cut, but enough to drag the monster's attention away. More venom splattered the ground inches from Cilia's boots as the spider swiveled toward Arine.

Fear shot through her as she realized she was now at its mercy instead. She tried to leap clear, but a back leg lashed out too fast. All Arine could do was throw up her arms to try to take the brunt of the blow as it caught her in the chest.

It felt like a horse's kick. Air blasted from her lungs as she slammed into a tree. Her head cracked against the trunk and the world spun black. For a heartbeat she couldn't breathe, her chest locked tight.

She clawed for air until a ragged gulp finally came, sharp pain spiking through her skull. Every nerve screamed; she couldn't tell her arrow wound from the new agony radiating through her ribs. All she could think was she was glad it was a back leg and not a front one or else she would have been gutted.

Her vision swam in a haze of shadow and blunted noise. Shapes blurred and the forest tilted. She fought the urge to sink into darkness, forcing her eyes to focus while the battle raged beyond the ringing in her ears.

Arine forced herself upright, gripping a tree for balance. Fresh blood seeped through the bandage on her arm, the arrow wound pulsing beneath it. She could only hope it would hold until they escaped.

Cilia had retreated beyond the spider's reach. Gerin still lay beneath the creature, its long body hunched protectively over him. The injured leg Cilia had hacked earlier made the spider wary, its movements tighter, but not enough to expose the soft belly where a killing strike might land. For all its effort, Arine couldn't fathom why it hadn't abandoned the fight for easier prey.

Her head cleared by degrees. She saw the spider glance in her direction and she tensed, but it quickly dismissed her to scan the surrounding area. She reclaimed her fallen sword and edged back toward the others. Derik gave a quick nod as she slid in beside him. She doubted she could add much with her battered arm, but at least she could watch for an opening.

The spider swept its head from side to side, dark eyes glinting as its front leg shot toward Jove. He dodged, barely, and the spider's head swiveled back the other way. Arine suddenly understood—fear gripping her chest.

"Oh my god," she breathed.

Derik turned sharply, scanning her for wounds. "What is it?"

"She's waiting for her mate," Arine whispered, urgency breaking into a shout. "We have to get Gerin and get out of here!"

Derik's eyes widened. He whipped back toward the creature, where the female crouched low over Gerin's body, her gaze searching the surrounding forest for signs of her partner.

If the male spider reached them before they could pull Gerin out, none of them would leave the forest alive.

Derik called out to the others and they redoubled their efforts, frantically hacking at the spider trying to get enough of an upper hand to either drive her away or maim her enough to get a killing blow. But, no matter how many small hits they scored between her armor like plates, it wasn't enough to make her budge.

She had chosen her strategy well, somehow knowing they wouldn't leave their friend. If she could just hold out long enough, they would be caught in between her and another deadly beast, fresh and ready to fight.

Lian turned to Derik and said something Arine couldn't hear. Derik shook his head, almost yelling back. "No! I won't leave him."

Arine looked around at the haggard group and could see the exhaustion that she felt written on everyone's face. They truly were chancing fate with every moment they stayed. When she met Derik's eyes, she saw the war inside him—forsake someone he had grown up with, regardless of how complicated their relationship was or potentially jeopardize the entire mission by staying. His gaze dropped. When it lifted again, the decision was made.

"Disengage," he said, barely above a whisper, but everyone heard.

One by one they began to edge back, blades raised. Only Cilia lingered, clearly torn. She had just taken a beating trying to protect him and who knew what had happened while they were captives. After a heartbeat though, she too stepped away. The spider didn't follow. It simply watched, motionless, as though savoring its victory.

Halfway across the clearing, Arine froze. The creature snapped its head south and rose higher on its legs as if in anticipation. A wave of despair ran through Arine at the sight. Not when they were just about to escape.

As if emboldened, the spider abandoned Gerin and crept toward them, each step deliberate, unhurried—as though certain there was no escape now that its mate closed in.

Derik's eyes swept the group and finally found hers. He gave a small, rueful smile and a slight shrug. Arine dipped her head in grim acknowledgment. At least they had tried.

Cilia's voice cut through the tense silence.

"Well, I'll be damned if I don't go down swinging," she said, hefting her stolen sword.

Lian shook out his arms and raised his blade beside her, grim resolve etched into his face. One by one, the others murmured agreement and turned toward the advancing spider. Arine's injured arm throbbed, threatening to buckle her knees. She took a deep breath and lifted her sword anyway, fighting against the pain—she would not give the creature an easy meal.

Gathering the last bit of their strength, they formed up again to try to rush the spider one final time. If they could maim her enough, they would just have her mate to deal with instead of both of them at the same time. Maybe then at least some of them could escape.

They fanned out, closing in. Lian, Jove, and Cilia struck first, their exhaustion burning away in a final surge of fury. Steel rang against the spider's armor; some blows skidded harmlessly off its plates, but others bit deep enough to draw black ichor. The creature reeled, forced to defend from every side.

A sudden lunge brought its fangs inches from Cilia's arm. She screamed as venom splashed across her arm—burning through her sleeve to eat away at her skin. Lian darted in, slicing a middle leg and knocking the monster off balance just in time to save her from worse. Cilia stumbled back, biting off a cry while she scraped at the corrosive fluid with a handful of wet leaves.

Jove seized the opening, driving his sword at the creature's mouth. He couldn't reach the brain, but his blade sheared off a jagged shard of fang.

It skittered backward, and for a heartbeat Arine dared to hope they might finish it—until a pale streak flashed from the trees where they'd seen earlier movement. Her blood turned to ice.

"Look out!" she shouted.

The white shape shot through the branches. Arine braced for the strike—then froze.

Not a leg. An arrow.

The shaft buried itself deep in one of the monster's eyes. A second arrow followed in a blur. For an instant she thought she was imagining it, concussion twisting her vision. But the spider convulsed, its limbs locking before it toppled with a heavy crash that sent Lian sprawling beneath its weight. After a few violent tremors, the legs curled inward and stilled..

Jove turned around looking for the other spider while Lian struggled to his feet.

"What happened?" Jove asked almost in disbelief. "Is it really dead?"

"How?" Matthew sputtered.

Derik positioned himself in front of Arine looking towards the tree line and held up his sword, indicating for the others to stay ready. She clutched her sword tightly, unsure of what they were supposed to be preparing for. Could it be another group of Yuakans who had saved them just to put them into a slaver's pen?

A figure emerged instead. Ciran strode from the shadows, bow in hand, moonlight catching the fierce set of his face. Relief and disbelief crashed through Arine all at once, so intense she felt she might collapse under the weight of it.

Ciran said nothing at first. He crossed to Cilia and steadied her as she struggled to her feet, her body trembling from the venom's burn. Though the fact that she could stand meant it hadn't touched her long enough to cause lasting damage—outside of the painful burns.

"Took you long enough," Cilia said jokingly, but it came out somewhat of a rasp as she tried to keep control of her body.

Ciran's brow tightened in concern, and he kept an arm around her until she shoved him away and pointed toward Gerin.

Matthew was slicing through the sticky webbing while Gerin began to stir. Without a word, Ciran strode over, hefted him across his shoulders, and turned back to the group.

"Should we move before another one shows?" he asked, voice flat.

Derik nodded, face equally unreadable. No one lingered to debate.

They quickly grabbed any discarded weapons and then hurried back the way they had come as fast as their tired limbs would carry them. When they were just outside of the tree line, a piercing screech split the night.

They broke into a run. White spiders rarely left the forest because of the sunlight, but no one wanted to test that rule.

Arine shuddered at the thought of how narrowly they'd escaped. If Ciran had arrived even a minute later, none of them would be alive to hear that scream.

Chapter 17

Dawn hadn't yet broken, but Arine didn't need sunlight to see the group's exhaustion when they finally staggered back into camp. More than one of them collapsed to the ground rather than sat.

Ciran, still the least battered, started tending to Gerin without a word—showing none of the anger Arine suspected he felt at being knocked out and left behind.

Derik and Jove fetched water from the stream and passed skins to the others. Arine drank greedily, then half-crawled to where Ciran was examining Gerin.

Gerin was awake but clearly in rough shape. His nose bent at an unnatural angle; a split lip oozed blood, and a dark bruise already shadowed one eye. Propped against a fallen log, he stared past them with a glassy look. When Ciran tried to unfasten his shirt, Gerin weakly slapped his hand away, muttering about not being an invalid. The words lacked his usual anger though and he eventually stopped fighting.

Arine helped ease the shirt over his shoulders and sucked in a breath. His torso was a patchwork of rising bruises and angry welts. His breathing was shallow and he winced when Ciran pressed along his ribs.

"Two breaks—or at least cracks," Ciran said tersely. "And likely a concussion, though since you're awake now, the danger period has probably passed."

Gerin just nodded and closed his eyes, so Arine helped Ciran clean away the blood and dirt before wrapping his torso. When they finished, Gerin gave them both a faint nod of thanks. He must have been in worse pain than she'd guessed to finally let go of his stubborn pride. His gaze lingered on Ciran for a beat—no words exchanged, but Arine thought she caught the barest flicker of respect. Ironic, considering Gerin had threatened to kill him only hours earlier.

Arine sank beside Gerin, nearly collapsing from sheer exhaustion. Across the camp, Lian was helping Matthew bandage his leg while Cilia rinsed her burns in the stream. With the adrenaline gone, Arine's own wound screamed for attention. She prodded at the bandage as Derik returned with the horses and crouched beside her, eyes sweeping over Ciran and Gerin.

"Well, you look like hell," he said to his former friend without preamble.

"Speak for yourself," Gerin rasped with a grim smile that better showed off his injuries.

Derik might have fared the best out of everyone in their group, but he still had his own collection of cuts and bruises showing through any exposed skin. He had a nasty slice along his jawline that would probably need stitches and whether it would leave a scar would remain to be seen.

His gaze lingered on Gerin, checking Ciran's bandaging until he seemed satisfied the man would live. Their history was a knot Arine still couldn't untangle. Gerin was a complete bastard most of the time, but Derik's reluctance to leave him showed he still cared about the friend he used to be. She doubted this near-death ordeal would be the last reminder of that tension.

The corner of Derik's mouth had twitched with the hint of a smile he usually fought to hide at Gerin's jab, but he let the game of insults drop.

"Tell me what happened," he said instead.

Gerin must have sensed the direction of the conversation because he launched straight into the story.

"After Arine and Ciran left, I was doing my best to avoid the crazy one." He flicked a glance toward the stream where Cilia was apparently trying to remove every scrap of dirt for fear of it containing remnants of the venom, though his look held none of its usual disdain. "We heard rustling in the trees, but with seven on two and the advantage of surprise, we never stood a chance. We managed to take down at least two before they overwhelmed us, I think."

Derik nodded, and Arine recalled the bodies she'd found before the arrow struck her.

"They knocked us out. I woke up tied to a tree, but we didn't stay there long. They forced us deeper into the forest until we reached the white spider's nest. We tried to warn them, but they laughed, and the one who spoke our language called us liars. A few looked uneasy when they saw the bones, but their leader refused to leave. He said if we were truly frightened, then our companions would be too. Unlucky for them, you lot were too dimwitted to avoid it either, eh?"

"Is that your way of thanking us for saving you?" Derik asked, unruffled.

"Maybe," Gerin replied solemnly, without his usual bravado.

She knew from her own experience that coming close to death made you see things differently than you had before, but his attempt at gratitude still surprised her.

"After that, things get hazy," Gerin continued. "They decided to hedge their bets—just in case the white spiders were real—and leave one of us as an offering. I'll let you guess who they picked."

He paused, spitting a clot of blood onto the ground. He flicked a glance toward the stream where Cilia sat with her back to them, and something flickered in his eyes—was it respect?

"She kept them from doing worse," he said quietly. "If not for her, I doubt there would have been anyone to bring back." His eyes slid toward Ciran, a flash of guilt there before he quickly looked away.

Derik studied Gerin for a long moment before turning to Ciran. "I still don't fully trust your motives," he admitted, "but I can acknowledge when I'm wrong."

Ciran offered no reply. He cast Gerin one last look, then walked toward Cilia without a word—not even to Arine. She couldn't blame him; a grudging admission hardly erased being tied up and branded a traitor, and she herself hadn't spoken up for him either.

Arine watched as he settled beside Cilia. They sat in silence at first, then exchanged a few quiet words, their eyes flicking more than once toward Gerin. Arine took the opportunity to give Derik and Gerin some privacy as the former continued to ask for more details of the Yuakan group.

The chill of her damp clothes began to bite, so she dug into her pack for something dry and moved a short distance away to change. Returning to the fire, she eased down and began unwinding the bandage on her arm. The pain throbbed steadily, a harsh reminder of the additional damage from her collision with the tree.

Peeling away the blood-stiffened cloth, she finally saw the wound for herself. A two-inch gash gaped open where several stitches had torn, fresh blood seeping slowly from the wound.

She wondered how badly it would scar, but Theo's face flashed in her mind and guilt pricked her for caring about something so vain when he'd been murdered so callously. Blinking back tears, she forced the thought aside before it consumed her. Lifting her shirt, she checked her side quickly, and seeing it was still healing well, she refocused on her newest injury.

Before she could start to tend to her arm, a weight settled beside her. She looked up to find Derik studying the gash.

He nodded toward it. "Want me to help restitch? I'm no Shian, but I've had plenty of practice. At this point I could rival half the ladies at court with my needlework." His tone tried to sound lighthearted, but the rasp in his voice betrayed his exhaustion.

"Do you spend a lot of time stitching with Shian?" The question slipped out before she could stop it. Heat flooded her face—why had she said that? His eyebrows shot up, and she wished she could rewind the last few seconds. She knew he was going to take this and run with it. Another thing to add to his ego thinking she cared who he was with, when she clearly did not.

"Why ever would you care how much time I spend *stitching* with Shian?" he asked, grinning like an idiot at her and emphasizing the word stitching as if it had an entirely different meaning.

"There is nothing I care less about than what you do or with whom," she shot back, forcing nonchalance. "I just wanted to know if you actually have any sewing skill or if you're about to butcher my arm."

His grin widened. "For the record, Shian and I grew up together. Her parents treated me like family after mine died. She's like a sister to me—so yes, I've spent time with her, but not in the way you were asking." He winked at her and she almost punched him in the face.

"I wasn't asking it in *any* way," she said sharply, eager to end the subject.

Something in her chest loosened at his words, though she couldn't explain why. Why should she care about his relationship with Shian? The realization made her suddenly awkward, trapped between wanting to move away and knowing the cramped camp would only make it obvious. If she could laugh it off, maybe he wouldn't notice.

"Do you take requests for the images you sew," she asked lightly, "or is that up to your discretion?"

Her voice sounded blessedly normal despite how ridiculous she felt.

Derik's eyes twinkled as he held out his hand for her arm but, mercifully, he didn't goad her any further. "Honestly, with how tired I am, I might be over-promising anyway. Everything we just went through has me loopy."

Arine nodded, relieved. Maybe that explained her own strange mood. "Well, I'm not sure that confession inspires confidence in your sewing, but I hate stitching myself. So hurry up and fix it, if you don't mind."

As he scooted closer to get a better angle, she noticed the back of his shirt was torn, allowing her to see angry red marks that striped his shoulder blades. Had the spider cut him? Before he could stop her, she reached over and pulled the fabric aside.

"Why didn't you say you'd been cut? We need to wash those wounds too—"
Her words faltered as more of his back came into view.

It wasn't a single gash but a patchwork of old, healing scars crisscrossing his shoulders. Some were far too old to be from the spider.

"What...what is that from?" she whispered, aghast that he'd been traveling and fighting with wounds still knitting themselves closed.

"It's nothing," he said gruffly, jerking away to hide his back.

"It's not nothing," she shot back, holding his gaze.

He ignored her and resumed stitching, firmly repositioning her arm before cleaning the needle and threading it. She huffed at his refusal to explain, but didn't press—badgering him while he stitched her arm was hardly the right time.

He must have gotten those wounds during the first night's attack. He hadn't shown any pain, but she supposed he was too proud to reveal weakness in front of his men. She braced for the sting of the needle, yet he was surprisingly gentle as he worked.

"I'm collecting quite the set of scars, huh?" she said lightly when he tied off the last stitch.

He paused, eyes flicking up to hers.

"I'm sorry." He said and held her gaze for a moment before dropping his eyes.

The simple admission startled her—shock coursing through her that he would admit fault at all. She almost let it go—accepting the small admission, but a part of her rebelled against the easy forgiveness. All the resentment she had buried for days at being stripped of her choice, even if she would have come here anyway, roared to the surface. She didn't blame him for the injuries but she did blame him for his demeanor and how he had handled everything so far.

"For what exactly? It's not like you wielded the weapon in either scenario," she asked pointedly.

He cleared his throat and picked at a piece of the bandage, buying himself time before finally answering. "That you are..." he gestured at her injuries, "...in harm's way. I thought this journey would be safe, but it's been far more dangerous than I expected."

"Seriously?" she said, her voice edged with disbelief.

She should have known he was too full of himself to truly apologize. After nearly being eaten by a giant spider and shot in the arm, she wasn't about to let him off easy.

"What about apologizing for taking away my choice? For kidnapping my father? For treating me like an imbecile because I'm a woman? For being a royal ass half the time and pretending to be decent the other half?"

She jabbed a finger at him. "You pick and choose when to act decent instead of simply being decent."

She tried to snatch the bandages back from him, but he annoyingly held on to them until she turned away hoping he would just leave her alone. She was stupid to think he wasn't going to be infuriating. He was a Prince after all; he was probably bred that way.

He was silent, making no sign of leaving so she sat there stiffly refusing to be the one that moved first. It almost got to the point where she was going to give in and turn to tell him to go away before he finally spoke.

"I understand why you'd feel bitter about not having a choice—better than most."

The resentment in his tone was the only thing that made her not bite out some other angry retort. She slowly turned back to look at him. He was staring straight up at the sky as it was turning gray around them. His gaze flicked up even higher to the moon that was still visible before he continued.

"People are dying, Arine. In a few years, sickness and famine will consume us if nothing changes. The King didn't know you, and he couldn't risk you refusing to come."

"So you both decided for me," she said coldly. "You took away my ability to choose. That's one step from being a slaver yourself. I may not wear chains, but you imprisoned me all the same."

"I would never do that to anyone," he said, meeting her gaze. "I'm doing the best I can with the situation we've been given. You have a role to play, and so do I. Working within the system doesn't mean I'm not trying to change it when I can."

"Except you get to choose what you do—and what you try to change."

Suddenly she wondered, if he did have a choice, why did he come on this journey? Clearly everyone was risking their lives and you would think the sole heir to the throne could have had someone else go in his place. She knew the knife was important, but Lian or Gerin even could have carried it... so why was he there?

"What *is* your role here exactly? Why did you choose to come?" she asked.

"I think you said it was royal ass, right?"

For a second she didn't register his response and then it was all she could do to try to keep her face straight. She couldn't hold it back and a laugh finally escaped her. After another second Derik was chuckling alongside her. The others shot them puzzled glances before turning back to their tasks. She must have been getting loopy too from the exhaustion to think it was that funny.

When she finally caught her breath, she narrowed her eyes. "I'm serious. Besides being a royal ass—why did you come? Why not send someone else?"

"The King trusts very few," Derik said, plucking a dry leaf from the edge of the bandage roll, as he evaded the question.

"He seriously couldn't have trusted anyone else but his one heir?" she pressed.

"He would risk multiple heirs on this, I think," Derik said, a flicker of bitterness sharpening his tone.

Arine couldn't figure out what she was missing. Something was still off about it all. She studied Derik. "None of this fits," she said at last. "He rules like a tyrant. If he truly cared about saving his people, why not treat them better now?"

Derik kept his eyes on the bandage roll in his hands. "I know he's made mistakes, but a harsh ruler is better than no ruler. And he does sometimes listen—at least to those he favors."

She nearly scoffed. His words echoed what Lian had told her that first night. Was that the line they all repeated to keep their guilt at bay? If they managed to restore magic, could things get better or would they just swap out a tyrant of a dying land for a tyrant of a living one?

"Just because it could be worse is no reason to continue down a bad path instead of trying to look for a better one...that is a coward's way. You even take part by continuing to enforce tyrannical punishments, following in his footsteps instead of standing up for what's right."

Derik's head snapped up, as if she'd struck him. "You think I can just denounce him and ignore the laws?" His voice was sharp, but a trace of sorrow threaded through it. "I've told you—he allows no disobedience, not even the smallest. Doing what you ask would mean my imprisonment—or worse."

He paused, eyes clouding despite his effort to stay composed. "He's also the closest thing to a father I have. I still hope that when this is over"—he touched his chest, where the knife lay hidden, then gestured toward her—"maybe then, I can figure out a way to change things. But, all I can think about right now, is making sure my people have a future to fix...no matter the cost."

He started to rise, but Arine caught his sleeve with her uninjured arm, halting him.

"Wait," she said.

Derik stilled, eyes flicking to her hand before meeting her gaze. For a heartbeat something unguarded flickered there—before he masked it again.

Arine didn't want to fight with him. He was the only one who truly understood this mission, so she forced herself to consider his side. She felt a reluctant empathy. He'd grown up without family, and the King was the closest thing to a father he had. Of course he would want to try to do what he could to influence him to be better as opposed to going against his last living family member.

Yet if the King refused to recognize his own cruelty, Derik would have to take a harder stand before she could believe he truly sought change for anyone beyond the throne.

"I'll say this once to set the record straight," she said, keeping her tone even. "There are other ways to get what you want besides abducting people and forcing them to obey you. You know, even if you hadn't taken my father, I would have come. Some people do the right thing simply because it's right." She met his eyes, unflinching, daring him to deny it.

"I know," he said quietly and a small jolt went through her at his simple acknowledgement.

"Good," she replied.

He shook his head with faint amusement and began to wrap the fresh bandage.

Why did it matter that he knew she would have come willingly? She didn't know why she cared, but for some reason, she did. Maybe his recognition meant he still had the capacity to choose differently—but for now, all she could do was wait and see.

She forced her attention back to the larger threat, pushing aside the swirl of uneasy hope. "Now that that's settled," she said, eyeing the shadowed trees, "what do you think is behind all these slavers? Are they here for us...or for me?"

"I was wondering the same thing." Derik said, switching topics easily. "My uncle keeps most things private. He only tells specific people about certain things so it's easier to keep everyone from knowing too much, but I have an advantage living at the palace. It allows me to hear more than others."

"What?" Arine asked, feigning shock. "Are you telling me, Mr. Do Everything the King Says and Don't Step Out of Line has been eavesdropping?"

He cleared his throat and ignored the jab, though she caught the faintest ghost of a smile beneath his serious tone.

"As I was saying," he continued with mock haughtiness, "I've heard rumors of more Yuakans pouring in from the southwest, but that doesn't explain how—or why—they came here. Why risk traveling toward the Decayed Lands, where even common folk won't tread?"

His brow knit as he stared into the dark trees. "It doesn't seem likely they're here for us. Still, without certainty, we'll need to stay alert. Traveling this late in the season was supposed to be safer—most of the rabble tend to start hunkering down by now."

As if on cue, a sudden gust howled through the trees, driving a chill that made Arine burrow deeper into her cloak.

"I should let you warm up instead of keeping you talking. We can discuss wielding later, after you've rested." Derik said and he stood before she could stop him.

The others glanced over at his movement and he surveyed their sorry state before addressing them all, reverting back to his usual guarded tone.

"Four hours of rest, then we move," Derik ordered. "I don't want to be here if anyone else shows up. I'll take the first watch; Ciran will relieve me in a couple of hours. Everyone else, sleep."

He crossed to a spot with a clear view of the stream and settled in, ignoring the group as he scanned the dark woods. Ciran offered no objection—or surprise to being assigned the second watch, merely returning to his quiet exchange with Cilia.

Arine didn't need to be told twice. She eased onto her good side and scooted as close to the fire as she dared, grateful for the warmth even as fatigue pressed her eyelids heavy. Within moments, the crackle of flames and the muted murmur of voices blurred into the welcome haze of sleep.

Chapter 18

Cilia's gentle shake pulled Arine from sleep. Pain flared in her shoulder at the touch, and she nearly hissed, but she forced herself silent to avoid drawing attention.

"Time to get moving," Cilia murmured before returning to roll up her own blanket.

The morning air stung her face. Frost coated the ground, the brambles and pine needles glinting faintly in the gray dawn—beautiful if not for the bitter cold. Gray clouds smothered the sun, stealing what little warmth the light might have offered. Arine was really starting to regret not traveling in spring, especially after everything that had already gone wrong.

She pushed to her feet and joined the others as they gathered to plan the day. Four hours of rest had done little to mend the bruises and fatigue left by the night before, and Theo's absence weighed heavily over the group. More than one pair of eyes lingered on the few belongings salvaged from his pack.

She hated that his fate had been determined so quickly without any of them being able to help. Arine shoved the thought aside before grief could take hold and focused on Derik's voice.

"We're close to the Outpost," he said. "If nothing else goes awry, we'll reach it by midafternoon. Lian, you and Matthew will range today. We move in pairs from now on—it puts you at higher risk of being seen, but it's safer than being caught alone."

"Yessir," was the only reply before they mounted up and rode out.

Arine stifled a groan as she hauled herself into the saddle, grateful the others were too absorbed in their own aches to notice. She refused to be seen as the weak link. If Cilia could endure kidnapping and the burn of a white spider's venom, Arine could manage her own pain.

Despite everyone moving at a slower pace than usual, they still left the clearing not long after Cilia had woken her. Whatever tension lingered from earlier was gone—washed away by the shared fight or simple exhaustion. Jove and Ciran even discussed the terrain without a trace of distrust. Arine might have smiled if the victory hadn't come at such a high cost.

As the day wore on, the undergrowth thickened and the soil softened. Trees rose with heavier limbs, some roots twisting above the ground in gnarled masses to brace against the damp earth. Ciran told Jove the ground wouldn't turn to true bog until after the Outpost, though the spongy footing suggested they were already close. The previous night's rain only worsened the conditions.

Arine tried to gauge Ciran's mood, but he rode too far behind for conversation. Part of her was relieved; she owed him an apology for not defending him more. Glancing back again, she was struck by Gerin's distant expression. Though every jolt of his horse must have sent pain lancing through his cracked ribs, he gave no sign, lost in thought.

She remembered her own turmoil after the Syarans' attack and wondered what battles raged behind his blank stare. After all, he had come close to being beaten to death from his own account, with only Cilia keeping him from that fate. She knew he was sure to have been in fights or skirmishes before but being beaten while bound was different. Perhaps the experience might finally temper his eagerness to mete out the King's justice on men beneath his rank.

Lian and Matthew returned at midday for a quick lunch, reporting that the Outpost lay only a few hours to the northeast. Derik asked if it seemed like it had seen any trouble, but Lian and Matthew hadn't been able to tell. Even so, he ordered them to stay with the group for the remainder of the journey rather than risk a split so close to safety.

Arine focused on the thought of walls and a bed waiting at the Outpost. Her whole body ached for warmth and a proper meal. Before she could indulge the idea of rest though, she knew she had to make it right with Ciran first. She edged Cloud closer to his horse, ready to speak—then guilt tightened in her chest, and she faltered.

"How is Cilia faring after everything?" she asked instead, wincing at her own deflection.

Ciran held her gaze a heartbeat too long. His calm expression revealed nothing at first, though a deeper intensity simmered underneath. "She's tough," he said at last, looking away. "I doubt she'd complain even if the spider had taken her arm off—except to lament having one less hand to throw knives with. And you? How's your arm?"

The formality in his tone stung, but Arine forced herself to press on. "I'll be fine. More importantly, thank you for saving all of us. I'm sorry it took me so long to say anything. I should have spoken up when others doubted you. Everything happened so fast, and that's no excuse, but it's the only one I have." She hesitated, then added, "I'm glad you didn't just take Cilia and leave the rest of us. After how you've both been treated, I wouldn't have blamed you if you had."

Ciran met her eyes as she finished. She offered a tentative smile, hoping he understood. His jaw tightened, a flicker of something sharper passing through before he glanced toward Derik.

"No," he said at last, a faint smile breaking through, "but I do wish I'd seen Derik spun up in a spider's web like Gerin. Might have knocked him down a peg or two."

Relief loosened the knot in Arine's chest at his wry acceptance, the tension between them finally easing.

"There's always the return trip, right?" Arine joked.

His smile wavered almost imperceptibly at her joke, but Arine caught it and looked away as if she hadn't. He was probably calculating their chances of surviving after everything they'd endured, and she couldn't blame him. Still, she refused to linger on the grim possibilities.

"It's crazy how attacks by Yuakans—or whoever else—have become just another day," she said, forcing lightness into her tone. "I bet you wish you'd left me in that pit by now, huh?"

"And miss out on the cold walks through the rugged brushland while under constant threat of attack? Why would I ever want to miss out on that?" he replied, dry amusement edging his voice before a peel of laughter caught their attention.

They looked over to see Cilia riding beside Gerin, of all people. Both were laughing at some private joke. Ciran's eyes darkened immediately. "I just hope I can keep Cilia from doing something stupid in this wonderland," he muttered.

Arine studied the two of them and watched as Cilia teased Gerin about something and he didn't immediately ride off like he normally would. Instead he seemed to give it back to her in kind which only made Cilia that much more amused.

"I mean, he's never struck me as particularly interesting," she said thoughtfully, "but would he really be the worst choice?"

If nothing else, Gerin was capable and hardworking.

At her words, Ciran turned sharply, visibly bristling that she would even suggest Gerin could be a match for his sister.

Arine didn't fault him. Gerin could be insufferable, and it was hard not to resent anyone tied to the King—but Gerin was trapped by the same system as Derik. Perhaps he was doing the best he could as well. He would never be Arine's choice, yet nothing she'd seen suggested he would treat Cilia badly.

She raised her hands in mock surrender. "Hey, I'm not saying we should hope for a wedding tomorrow—or ever. But she needs someone who can stand up to her, or she'll walk right over them. And maybe with the right person he could learn to be a little less...obnoxious?"

Ciran shot another look at his sister and Gerin. His white-knuckled grip on the reins betrayed how badly he wanted to break up their laughter. When he turned back though, it wasn't Cilia and Gerin that he commented on.

"Could you?" he asked quietly. "Could you forget who kept your father from getting medicine—who enforces the status laws and looks away while the rest suffer?

"What? Of course not. I'd never be interested in Gerin," she said, frowning at the sudden shift.

Ciran's eyes flicked ahead to where Derik was leading them and realization dawned on her. She felt herself flush, despite herself, with embarrassment. Ciran looked back and must have noticed her flustered state. Instead of dropping it, he leaned over his brown mare to speak to her so his words didn't carry.

"Just be careful. People like him spend their lives learning how to twist the truth to their advantage. That's how his uncle keeps power. Don't think for a second the Prince hasn't mastered the same tricks."

Arine wasn't surprised by Ciran's warning; there was truth in his words—thoughts she'd already wrestled with herself. No one could grow up in a palace like Derik's without absorbing some of its habits, whether they meant to or not. Still, Derik had begun to show flashes of something better, even if not at the pace she wanted. Could he simply be telling her what she wished to hear? But why, when she was already following him on this fool's journey?

"Why are you so certain he has no redeeming qualities?" she asked cautiously. "Is there some history between him and your family?"

"My people—my family—have suffered greatly under the King's rule," Ciran said tightly, keeping his voice low.

Arine pretended to study the thinning clouds while scanning for eavesdroppers. The trees were growing denser as they neared the Outpost and the western edge of Killian Forest, forcing the riders closer together. Around them, the others murmured in low tones, none paying undue attention.

"I know he and the King rule with an iron fist, and change must happen," she said, letting her own hopes spill out. "But I think he's willing to push back against the laws—to make life better for ordinary people. Maybe one day we could even live in a nation without status laws, where birth doesn't decide a person's worth."

Ciran gave her a sidelong glance, his expression unreadable but edged with skepticism.

"Do you really think someone born to rule would ever give up that power—and the comfort that comes with it—just to let others take their place?"

"I think some people—people like you and me—want to do what's right. Why can't Derik be one of them? He is here just the same, risking his life as the rest of us."

"Yeah? And what exactly are we risking our lives for?" Ciran's voice carried a bitter edge. "Have I earned enough trust to be filled in yet? Maybe then I'll see him the way you do. I'm not optimistic, but hey—anything's possible."

He was right. They all deserved to know the truth instead of following orders blindly—otherwise she was no better than the King if she expected them all to put their lives on the line for her with no choice in the matter.

"You have," she said firmly. "Tonight I'll ask Derik to explain everything. If he refuses, I'll do it myself."

She'd warn Derik first, but the decision settled like a weight in her chest. After everything they'd endured, these people were her friends now. They deserved answers.

"I'll hold you to it," Ciran replied. "Until I hear more, my opinion of him stands. Especially after what happened with his little sister. If there's one thing the King excels at, it's using leverage."

Arine stiffened. "What do you mean? What about his sister?"

Ciran's tone turned grim. "So I guess he didn't mention that during your conversations about him pushing the King for change? His sister lost the use of her legs three years ago and is now under the King's *care*. Whatever Derik says about pushing for change, do you really think he'd risk her life?"

A sharp ache knifed through Arine's gut. If the King held Derik's sister hostage, every word Derik spoke—every promise—might be chained to that threat. Why hadn't he told her? She had stupidly felt like Derik was actually treating her like an equal, like someone he trusted and wanted to confide in. Thinking that could be a lie too might've hurt even more than being wrong about his desire to change the policies.

"Look I get it." He continued, his voice low but unrelenting. "I want to believe someone can change and be better but the reality is most people don't. Least of all those with the most power. Just be careful and make sure you are getting as much information as possible because if there is one thing I know for sure, it's that he isn't telling any of us everything. His sister's state is one example and won't be the last. There are no limits to the varieties of control people like him and the King employ to ensure everyone else falls in line."

Arine forced her face into a neutral mask, swallowing the storm inside. She refused to give Ciran even a flicker of the confusion or hurt roiling within. Not because she thought he would use it against her or judge her, but because she wanted time to think through everything herself. She was tired of being such an open book while everyone else kept all of their secrets to themselves.

"I appreciate the warning," she said evenly—then broke off as Derik raised a hand, halting his horse.

"We've reached the Outpost," he announced, his words cutting cleanly through the group's low murmur and, mercifully, through the chaos in her thoughts.

Arine craned her neck past the others to take in the settlement ahead. A tall palisade of upright tree trunks enclosed the village—far broader than she'd expected for a mere outpost. The far side all but vanished into the edge of Killian Forest, the wall blending so cleanly with the trees that she couldn't tell where timber ended and wilderness began.

Inside the ring there was space for several buildings, even small homes and livestock should a siege force them to shelter within. It wouldn't withstand a true army, but the defenses were strong enough to serve as a safe haven this deep in the northwest and to guard the trade routes that depended on it.

The wall's trunks remained solid despite years of weathering. Here and there fresh logs replaced older ones, their brighter wood standing out against the gray of the originals—a rare sign of upkeep in a world sliding into decay.

Above the heavy gate a few guards watched their approach, rabbit-fur hats and thick cloaks fending off the cold. Before the group came within earshot, Derik gave quiet instructions.

"You've been kept in the dark on the full purpose of this journey by order of the King himself," Derik said, as Lian and the other guards clustered around him. "That should tell you how uncertain this mission is. Keep a tight guard on what you say. Even the smallest slip could mean something to someone here."

The four men nodded in unison, their expressions tightening before Derik continued. "We keep the story that Arine is my long-lost cousin whose father fell ill, and we're escorting her to the palace. We'll say the Yuakan attack drove us here to regroup before heading to the Capital. If anyone notices the horses we leave behind, we'll be long gone before they investigate."

He turned to the siblings. "Cilia, you were a traveler we rescued—it's close enough to the truth. Ciran, you're a member of the royal guard."

Cilia wrinkled her nose at her alibi. "Don't worry," she muttered, clearly unimpressed with her fictitious part. "Ciran and I don't even know what we're doing out here, so there's nothing for us to spill anyway."

Derik's eyes narrowed at her. "Also, it will look even more suspicious if I am not obeyed with every order as the highest ranking officer. They are familiar here with the King's expectations."

Cilia grumbled under her breath, but still nodded her acceptance along with the others. With the plan settled, they urged their horses forward and covered the last stretch to the Outpost gate.

"Are you selling or buying?" the older man called, his voice carrying across the gate as their group approached.

"Neither," Derik replied, scanning the guards and the shadowed walls behind them. "But Haverson will be expecting me."

"You don't say?" the man rasped with a laugh that broke into a cough. "Well, by all means—come in."

Something in his tone made Arine's skin prickle. Two men swung open the oversized gate and hurried them through. The doors boomed shut behind them the instant they were inside.

Arine edged her horse closer to Lian's. "Who's Haverson?" she whispered.

"For all intents and purposes," Lian murmured back, "think of him as the ruler of this little kingdom."

As they dismounted, Derik asked if there had been trouble lately. One didn't respond and the other just looked at him darkly, as if he had told some joke he didn't think was very funny.

Despite the curt welcome, Arine sensed no immediate danger—only the uncomfortable awareness of eyes tracking their every move. A few townsfolk lingered in doorways or along the muddy paths, mostly men wrapped in worn coats, but none approached. She chalked the tension up to exhaustion and the days of attacks still weighing on her nerves.

Wooden planks lined the soggy ground, but it didn't do much to help and they were all covered in slop up to their knees in the couple of minutes it took to be led through the small town. Because town, it was. There was a tannery, a trading post, a butcher's shop and smokehouse all circling a large inn in the center of the town with a stable attached.

The inn dominated the Outpost skyline, its narrow spire stabbing into the gray morning like a spear. Halfway up, a row of windows overlooked the settlement, and Arine finally understood the source of the prickling at her neck. From that perch someone could track every movement below, and she would have wagered Haverson himself had watched their entire approach.

Most of the people they passed were men, though a few hard-eyed women moved among them with the same brisk precision. No one lingered. Every step, every glance spoke of purpose, as if the entire place beat to a single, disciplined rhythm. There were no idle loiterers, no beggars like those who crowded Draske's Outer District—only workers carrying out unseen orders.

Chapter 19

They left their horses in the stable, Derik slipping the master a few extra coins for feed after the rough journey. Inside, the inn mirrored the settlement's tidy precision. Like everything in the Outpost, it was meticulously kept—the cleanest Arine had ever seen, even compared to the inns she'd visited with her father before his illness.

The tables were plain but spotless, not a single mug ring in sight. Behind the bar, glasses and pitchers gleamed in neat stacks, catching the lamplight. Two grizzled guards leaned against the doorframe, barely glancing at the armed newcomers.

A few patrons were coming in and out for an end of the day drink and meal, but it wasn't packed by any means. There was a table of three rough looking men who seemed to have arrived just before them by the looks of their full drinks. They had fur on almost every piece of their clothes and weather worn faces but didn't seem overly threatening. A couple tables away from them was a man by himself who was easily the heaviest man Arine had ever seen. He sat precariously on his chair, the legs straining under his weight as he sipped on his ale.

The inhabitants seemed to be traders and trappers who had arrived at least a few days before them or lived there. They chatted amongst themselves and between tables calling out to each other gruffly as they went about their meals and drinks. They glanced up at Arine and her group as they entered but quickly returned to their previous conversations after it was clear her group had nothing to sell or trade.

A few eyebrows were raised at their lack of goods, but no one commented on it. In fact, it seemed like they were inclined to act like Arine and her group didn't exist with how fast they dismissed them.

Two serving girls slipped through the tables with practiced ease, topping off mugs and taking orders while batting away wandering hands with quick flicks of their wrists. One was older but still striking; the other looked to be about Derik's age. They laughed off crude jokes without showing a hint of offense.

At the bar, an old man sat on a stool polishing mugs. He rose slowly as Derik approached.

"Good evening," Derik said, his tone polite but steady. "We'd like four rooms for the night, two beds apiece."

He slid a few gold coins across the counter.

The barkeep studied Derik and then the rest of the group, his gaze deliberate. After a long moment, he rasped, "Not accepting reservations at the moment, sir," and returned to his stool, resuming his careful polishing without another glance.

Derik let the coins slide back into his palm and leaned against the bar, masking any reaction behind an easy posture.

"What about drinks?" Cilia called down the counter.

The man just ignored her and continued his polishing. "Well, he certainly is overpaid," she grumbled when it was clear he wasn't going to be persuaded to serve them anything.

Their group clustered near the bar, the tension easing only because Derik appeared unbothered. To pass the time, Arine turned to the notice board on the wall behind her, scanning the collection of faded postings while the barkeep's quiet defiance hung in the air.

Most of the notices were routine: requests for livestock, pelts, herbs, or medicine, each with a price scrawled beneath. One corner of the board, however, was devoted to bounty hunters and the kingdom's most wanted.

Four faces stared back at her—two men and a woman wanted for petty theft, another man with a twenty-gold reward for killing two guards during a jailbreak. But, it was the final posting that made her catch her breath. The reward was staggering: fifty gold pieces. There was no portrait, only a written description and a warning not to approach without alerting authorities.

Apparently this person was wanted for "inciting insurrection". It listed off numerous crimes of murder and theft on a grand scale. The description of the person, however, was too vague to do any real good, except for a brand the man apparently had on his forearm that would distinguish him. At first, Arine couldn't make sense of the shape until her eyes focused and she realized what it was—a broken crown.

Arine's stomach clenched. She knew that emblem—it had flown on Vanin's rebel banners during the war, the very conflict that had driven her mother to sever magic. She read through the last known locations of the mystery man, but they were all over the place, so Arine suspected more than one man was involved. And if that were the case then it most likely meant whoever this person was, he was trying to resurrect the rebel cause that tore the Kingdom apart the first time. The one that had driven her mother to sever magic in the first place.

Anger flared through her. Hadn't the realm suffered enough? Even a small army would drain food and supplies, stealing from farmers who had no choice and no defense. The land was already withering; another uprising would only bleed it faster.

Ciran must have sensed her sudden tension, because he moved beside her and studied the board. His eyes skimmed past the plain sheet at first, then flicked back to the bold reward. His brows climbed as he read the staggering sum.

"That much money and you could live right next to the palace for the rest of your life, if you so chose, of course." Ciran said, reading through the rest.

His eyes narrowed on the illustration and detailed crimes but before he could comment on it the older serving lady strode up, skirts swishing.

"Drinks and food or just drinks?" she asked curtly.

"So we're allowed to eat, at least?" Cilia quipped as Arine and Ciran turned back to the group.

The woman tapped her foot, unimpressed. "No one stays without being vetted, but I'll take your coin in the meantime—unless you'd rather go hungry."

Derik answered before she could leave, sliding several gold pieces across the bar. "Food and drinks for all."

With a brisk nod, the woman guided them to a long table off to the side. Arine followed, grateful for a solid chair after days of horses and hard ground.

Within minutes the woman returned, setting heavy mugs of dark ale before them. A second trip brought platters of roasted meat, potatoes slick with gravy, and a heap of greens, the simple meal smelling better than any feast Arine could remember.

Arine nearly salivated at the sight of the gravy. After weeks of dried meat and the scant fruit or vegetables they'd scrounged this late in the season, the steaming meal felt almost decadent. She took a large bite and savored every taste.

However, before she'd finished her third mouthful, a stocky messenger approached their table and addressed Derik. A short sword hung at his belt, though his ox-like build suggested he rarely needed it.

"Boss will see you now," he said, eyes sweeping over the group and lingering on Cilia and Arine as if weighing their worth before settling back on Derik.

Derik calmly finished the bite he'd been halfway to raising and stood. "Of course. Lead the way."

The man bared what might have been a smile—a toothy grimace more than anything. "Them too." He pointed directly at Arine and Cilia.

Arine looked between Cilia and Derik, baffled by why they were singled out. Their conversation had been mundane—nothing an eavesdropper could have seized on.

Ciran stiffened but remained seated, glaring at Derik. Arine was surprised—and relieved—that he didn't challenge the order and risk their cover.

She set down her utensils and stood, Cilia following a heartbeat later. Their guide led the way up a narrow staircase off the backside of the room. They wound up two floors to where Arine guessed the level she saw earlier was located. There was a plain door off the stairs on the landing where they exited while the stairs continued up into the smaller tower above them. Beside the door sat a heavy chest where the big man gruffly instructed them to place their weapons.

One by one they surrendered their blades. When the guard only stared, Derik met his gaze for a long moment, then patted himself down, pulled the King's dagger from beneath his coat, and dropped it in with the others. Only then did the man step aside to let them pass.

"Forgot it was even there—my mistake," Derik said lightly, but the man ignored him and finally swung the door open, motioning them inside.

Arine was mildly surprised it was Derik this time and not Cilia, but she supposed Cilia was better at hiding her weapons than Derik. She knew there was no way she had removed all of hers.

Derik entered first, moving with easy confidence and offering a courteous smile as the guard deliberately crowded the doorway, forcing them to squeeze past. Arine slipped in behind him, careful not to brush the man's massive frame.

Cilia on the other hand didn't try to be subtle at all, instead she just pushed in murmuring a sarcastic apology about not having seen him. The man smiled at her again, his eyes flashing dangerously and Arine wondered if they would have to make sure Cilia didn't go anywhere alone later.

Once she was in, the door thudded shut behind them. Their escort leaned against it, arms crossed, making it clear they wouldn't be leaving without permission.

At a desk across the stark room sat the man who had to be Haverson. He continued writing, quill scratching across parchment, and didn't look up until he finished. She almost rolled her eyes at the obvious dominance tactic.

Though older than her father by at least fifteen years, he carried a wiry strength beneath the wrinkles and streaked gray hair. A single rug softened the floor, and one extra chair—pushed to the far wall—made it clear guests rarely earned the privilege of sitting.

When he finally set the parchment aside, he lifted his head and gave the three of them a slow, measuring look. His gaze traveled over Derik first, then slid deliberately to Arine. She kept still and forced a mask of calm, matching the careful indifference of her companions.

"Your Highness, I find the lack of notice of your arrival out of character," Haverson said at last, his voice flat. "Your uncle is quite the stickler for propriety, is he not? And you travel with such unusual company. I would hate to think you were engaged in something...nefarious without the King's consent." He tapped the table with long, rhythmic fingers.

Derik answered smoothly, his tone politely edged. "My apologies for the unexpected visit. We recently had word of a long lost cousin in need of assistance when her father fell ill and then we ran into trouble with slavers. It's strange you haven't had any issues with them, because of course if you had, I know you would have informed the King,"

"Indeed," Haverson replied, nodding once, his sharp features betraying no hint of deference. "We've heard rumors from passing traders but nothing worth reporting. Though the whispers I hear speak less of Yuakans than of rebels. Shocking, considering the supposed peace of recent years."

Beside Arine, Cilia stiffened at the mention of rebels. Arine stayed still, grateful that Derik had already warned her, and kept her expression carefully neutral.

"Of course," Haverson continued, tapping his jaw with a bony finger. "I can't help but question your unusual companions. A new guard downstairs, a newly acquired...cousin, and a stray woman who looks ready to leap across the table and attack me." His eyes narrowed on Arine and Cilia. "With such a small and curious party, I'm forced to regard you with suspicion. You know I would never dream of questioning you personally, but in times like these one must be certain nothing is amiss."

He pursed his lips in a thin smile, feigning the air of a harmless official merely following procedure rather than the man who set the rules.

"Your concerns are appreciated, as is your commitment to the throne," Derik replied, only a trace of sarcasm threading his voice. "The King gave me something to show you, so you'll know we travel with his blessing—should you consider detaining us."

The guard by the door tensed, but Haverson waved him off. The ease of the gesture unsettled Arine; that they recognized Derik yet still dared to restrain him hinted at Haverson's own influence.

Derik drew a small object from his pocket. Arine leaned forward and saw a ring shot through with deep purple veins—one of the many she had noticed on the King's hand the night they met. He set it on the desk.

Haverson froze. He didn't pick up the ring; instead his hands retreated to his lap, eyes flicking between it and Derik as if the piece might leap off the table to bite him. Did the ring carry some private meaning for him, or simply confirm Derik's story strongly enough to make him regret the interrogation?

"Ah—apologies, Your Highness," Haverson said at last, his thin smile returning. "But surely you understand my caution in times like these. How long will we have the pleasure of your company?"

Derik ignored the half-hearted apology. "We'll stay only one night and leave in the morning. You already understand the value of discretion, so I trust you'll keep this quiet."

"Of course," Haverson said, lips curling into another tight smile. "No one appreciates discretion more than I—though one must always be careful where and when things are said."

Haverson gave another of his tight smiles and Derik dipped his head in acknowledgment. Watching them, Arine understood why Haverson spoke to the Prince as an equal. The Outpost master clearly held information the King preferred to keep buried. With traders from every corner passing through, he likely collected secrets on more than one powerful figure.

Yet if Derik truly defied royal orders, the King would have warned him. So why this show? Why summon her and Cilia—merely to prove he could?

"Gill," Haverson said to the door guard, "escort the Prince and his friends downstairs and tell Walston they may book rooms."

Derik took the ring from the desk and slipped it into his pocket. Haverson's eyes flicked toward the object for the briefest instant before he forced his gaze away. Derik motioned for Arine and Cilia to follow, but before they reached the threshold Haverson called out.

"It's remarkable how much you resemble your father. Most of my generation has died from one thing—or another," he added, stressing the last word. "I, however, remain fortunate in my health, one of the few old enough to remember your parents' time. When I saw you on the path, the likeness was...striking."

Arine glanced back. Haverson's sharp gaze slid from Derik to her, lingering in silent challenge before moving to Cilia. Derik's face paled before he mastered his expression and motioned for them to move on.

"Thank you for the compliment. I hope to be worthy of any comparison to my father," Derik said evenly.

Haverson didn't acknowledge the reply. He bent over his papers, quill scratching once more as Gill ushered them into the hall and closed the door firmly behind them.

"What was that about?" Cilia hissed as they started down the stairs. Derik only shook his head, a curt gesture for silence.

Gill glanced back with a crooked smile but offered no explanation while he led them through the narrow stairwell and back to the common room.

"You two return to the others while I arrange the rooms," Derik instructed, following Gill toward the bar where the old innkeeper waited.

Arine watched him go, noting the tightness in his shoulders. Haverson's words had unsettled him, and she understood why when he paused so deliberately on her: the man clearly recognized her parents and knew exactly who she was. His comment wasn't a compliment—it was a message. Still, Derik didn't seem alarmed enough to order an early departure, so she could only hope Haverson wouldn't cause them any trouble before morning.

When she turned back she saw Cilia scowling after Derik. She was so intense Arine thought she might pursue him for some reason. She finally turned away when Arine called her name, breaking the spell, and they both hurried back to where the others were waiting with questioning expressions.

She sat down, eyeing her now cold meal with dull resignation. Across the table, Ciran tried more than once to catch Cilia's eye, no doubt eager to ask about the meeting, but Cilia leaned toward Gerin instead, whispering in low tones. When it became clear she had no intention of looking his way, Ciran finally gave up and glanced at Arine, who only shrugged.

Moments later, Derik returned, and this time he brought welcome news.

"Warm beds for everyone tonight; we'll stay a few extra hours in the morning to recover, and then continue our next leg. Rest while you can—we leave four hours past sunup, breakfast included."

Arine smiled across the table at Ciran. After a moment he returned the look, easing the knot in her chest. A full night's sleep without a predawn start felt like pure luxury after days of cold ground and endless travel.

The promise of real rest lifted everyone's spirits. Despite their bruises and fatigue, no one rushed off to bed. Even Derik lingered, laughing at a few of Cilia's wilder stories—though he cut off ale and wine after two cups apiece, a decision Arine welcomed. The last thing she wanted was to wake with a pounding head.

Easy chatter filled the air and after a while, Cilia regaled them with a childhood tale about rescuing what she believed was a wounded dog, only to discover after bringing it home that it was a baby cave bear. She nursed it back to health, and then the bear promptly crashed through their house in a rampage before bolting for the woods. Laughter shook the table as she mimed the chaos, even drawing pained chuckles from Gerin despite his injured ribs.

The mirth ended when Ciran abruptly announced it was time for bed. His tone was light, but Arine noticed the quick glance he shot toward Gerin—still leaning close to Cilia, clearly enchanted by her tale. She wondered if Ciran's sudden curfew had less to do with fatigue and more to do with the unexpected warmth growing between the two.

Ciran stood and fixed Cilia with a steady look until she huffed dramatically and relented.

"He always was jealous of my Fluffy," she teased before sashaying upstairs.

Arine was fairly certain Cilia had snuck another mug, or even two, of ale from the younger serving woman when Derik wasn't watching, warranting Ciran's concern.

She said her good nights as well, glad for the excuse because her eyes had started to feel like weights and her arm was still a painful reminder of how much rest she really did need. She grabbed her pack and headed up to the room she would be sharing with Cilia. Ciran joined her on the walk up, clearly not wanting any bonding time of his own with Gerin.

"I haven't forgotten about my promise," Arine said as they climbed the stairs, keeping her voice low. "I just don't feel safe talking inside the inn with Haverson likely listening."

Ciran nodded, distracted, his gaze lingering on the door to the room her and Cilia would be in.

"She'll either be passed out or trying to sneak another drink. Do me a favor—if it's the latter, don't let her slip back out." He paused, frowning. "Also, why did Haverson ask for both of you to go with Derik? Did anything happen?"

Arine hesitated, unwilling to reveal the full story. "I think he wanted to remind Derik that he knows I'm not really his cousin," she offered, a half-truth at best.

Ciran's eyes narrowed toward the door as though debating whether to confront his sister.

"Is something wrong?" Arine asked.

"No, it's nothing," he said after a beat, shaking his head but staying where he was. "I know she can handle herself—it's just hard to know when to step in."

He leaned back against the wall, his voice dropping. "And... I'm sorry for dumping that business about the Prince's sister on you. I was still angry about last night. I know we chose to come here willingly, but I don't trust them. Things aren't adding up with the Yuakans attacking."

Arine moved to stand beside him. "What do you think it means?"

"I don't know," he admitted, frustration tightening his jaw. "That's the troubling part. The Prince said you were attacked in his camp the first night too. Do you know why?"

His green eyes searched her face, and she hated lying to him after everything.

"Not exactly," she said, voice low. "But it could be because of who I am."

The last words barely escaped a whisper. Her chest tightened—guilt for keeping secrets, fear that once people knew, they'd lay the blame on her. What if Ciran and Cilia couldn't see her the same way again? Maybe she felt drawn to Derik because he already knew and spared her the fear of judgment.

Ciran stayed silent, pain flickering across his face before he softened it with a patient look. "You can trust me, you know that, right?"

The gentle certainty made her guilt sharpen. This was the man who had rescued her and offered his camp without hesitation. She opened her mouth to tell him everything, but boots thudded on the stairs, drawing their eyes as Derik and the others headed for their rooms.

Her gaze met Derik's and she froze. He looked from her to Ciran without a word, but the quiet weight of it felt like a warning. Then he turned away toward his room.

When she turned back to Ciran, his jaw was tight. Whatever else he'd been about to say was gone now, swallowed by the silence Derik had left behind.

"Goodnight, Arine," he said quietly. His eyes met hers for a moment, frustration and something sharper flickering there before he looked away. When she didn't immediately respond, he gave a stiff nod and turned into the room he shared with Lian.

Arine stared at the closed door until her eyes drifted back down the empty hall to Derik's, thoughts tangling in restless knots. She should have told Ciran despite Derik's warnings—Ciran had saved her life twice. Yet doubt crawled through her—the rot's shadow touched everyone in some way.

Despite the larger worries of how her friends would feel about her secret, her gaze refused to leave Derik's door. Frustration tightened her crossed arms. Why did his silent disapproval weigh heavier than everything else? It was ridiculous, really—yet her stomach still tightened as she wondered—did he think her foolish to trust Ciran?

All of a sudden, his door swung open and Derik, himself, stepped into the hall. He stopped short, catching her lingering there, staring like an idiot.

Heat flared in her cheeks. She half-turned toward her own room but stayed rooted, fingers frozen on the cold knob for some reason. She glanced back over at him and waited.

Derik didn't continue on whatever errand had brought him out. Instead he crossed the narrow hallway, each step soundless on the aging boards, until he stood beside her.

"Did you tell him?" His voice was quiet, carefully neutral.

"No," she said, turning toward him. "But I should have."

"Why didn't you?" Derik tilted his head to peer down at her in the waning candlelight.

She sighed, "I don't know."

Derik was silent for a long moment before he finally turned and leaned back against the wall next to her, much like Ciran had, except Derik's shoulder lightly brushed her own.

"For what it's worth, I don't think Ciran has bad intentions—just conflicting priorities...much like all of us, I suppose. But, unless you're certain you can trust him, wait. Anything could happen before we reach the cave." His tone carried a weary resignation.

"And you?" she asked, heart thudding. "Do you have conflicting priorities?"

Would he tell her about his sister?

Derik looked over at him, his frame shifting slightly so that his arm was pressing tighter into her own. His blue eyes held hers, something—guilt?—flashing behind them. He drew a breath to answer, but a creak on the stairs sounded and he jerked away, moving in front of her protectively.

It was only the younger serving girl. She shuffled past them, eyes down as if she were afraid to have intruded in a private moment. Arine wanted to tell her it was nothing like that, but she knew protesting would probably make her sound just as guilty so she kept quiet.

When Derik turned back, his expression was once again unreadable. "You need your rest so your arm can heal. Good night."

Hurt flashed across her face before she schooled her own face to match his. Then he was gone, his footsteps echoing down the stairs, leaving her alone in the quiet hallway. Arine stared after him until she finally nudged open the door to her own room.

She found Cilia was already asleep on her bed. She hadn't even taken her boots off. Arine set her things down and stripped off her thicker garments. After hesitating a moment she walked over and pulled Cilia's boots off for her and set those to the side. The woman never stirred, only gave a faint snore.

The room wasn't anything special, but it was clean and served its purpose. She washed in the small basin of water left for them. Her arm had improved, though a dull ache lingered, so she swallowed a bit more of her herbs to blunt the pain.

Finally she slid beneath the thin blanket. The mattress was narrow and the feathers occasionally poked through, but after days on cold ground it felt like pure luxury. She blew out the candles and drifted into sleep within minutes, hoping answers would come with rest.

Chapter 20

Arine woke to pounding on her door and hurried footsteps racing through the inn. She jerked upright, tangled in the blankets. The hall beyond thudded with running feet. She tried to guess the hour, but the sky outside the window was still black, giving nothing away.

Cilia stirred with a sharp intake of breath, already reaching for her boots. "What's happening?" she asked while lacing them up.

"I don't know," Arine said, crossing the room and cracking the door.

Derik stood on the other side, his hand raised mid-knock, eyes flicking down the corridor toward the other rooms.

"What's going on?" she asked, voice still thick from sleep.

"Hurry—grab your things. The Outpost is under attack."

"More of the Yuakans?" she asked, still groggy.

Depending on their numbers, she wasn't overly alarmed. The slavers had fought like amateurs the last time, and from what she'd seen of the Outpost, its walls looked sturdy enough to repel another untrained band.

"Yes, but it seems this group—and possibly all of them—have allied with Syar," Derik said grimly. "Fifty men or more are trying to breach the walls, and Haverson needs every able fighter to defend them. Can you shoot yet?"

A knot tightened in Arine's stomach. She shook her head. Drawing a bow would only rip her stitches open.

"Bring everything anyway—just in case—and meet downstairs in five minutes." Without waiting for questions, Derik hurried off.

Arine shut the door and started gathering her gear while she explained to Cilia.

"I'm not surprised," Cilia said, slinging her pack over one shoulder. "Syar keeps slaves just like Yuak—they only dress it up as religion. Anyone labeled a 'sinner' is branded Godless and forced into labor ranging from housework to work camps, depending on the so-called sin."

Her lip curled as she tied her hair back. "They tell prisoners if they survive five years, the God Syere might absolve them. No one lasts that long, and anyone who does is framed for new crimes to keep them there. Upset the wrong person, and they'll condemn you out of spite."

Arine's stomach turned. She had known the Syarans were zealots, but not that they preyed on their own. Cilia spoke of Syar and Yuak, yet Arine couldn't ignore the parallels to Calasis—where birth and wealth decided a person's worth. Different rulers, different excuses, but the same cruel hierarchy.

Almost ready, Arine paused to grab the sling Derik had fashioned for her the night before. They would likely be moving fast, and the support had kept her arm from jarring during the previous night's battle. Cilia helped tighten the straps, then they set off. Arine cast one last glance at the bed she'd barely used, sighing as they left for the common room.

It was three hours past midnight, and everyone looked as exhausted as she felt. Lian, Gerin, and Ciran waited near the table where they'd laughed only hours ago, their faces drawn and shadowed. The tense silence was a stark contrast to their previous mood.

Scrawny messenger boys darted in and out, sprinting upstairs toward Haverson's office and back again with fresh orders. Derik and Matthew descended a few minutes later, Jove jogging to catch up. Another runner slipped past him to deliver a message outside.

Derik wasted no time. "Good—you're all here. The enemy force is large enough to be a nuisance, but Haverson's men are well trained. They should hold the walls. Anyone who can shoot will join the defense."

His eyes landed on Arine and Gerin—the only ones unable to handle a bow. "The rest of you will assist at the gate. Only bring your weapons, but keep your packs together in case we need to evacuate."

His meaning was clear, no matter how low he estimated the odds of the attackers succeeding, they would be ready to escape if need be.

They filed out behind Derik, following him up the same muddy path they'd traveled yesterday. Arine's boots squelched in the soft earth as they kept to the edges, letting villagers rush past with crates of arrows, bundles of rope, and sacks of sand. Every able-bodied resident worked with crisp efficiency, as if defending the Outpost were just another part of daily life—evidence either of frequent raids or relentless training.

They reached the wall in short order, stepping into controlled chaos. Guards lined the battlements, loosing arrows at figures clustered beyond the gate. No heavy thuds echoed against the wood—no siege weapons, at least not yet.

Torches blazed along the parapet, throwing the stonework and sentries into sharp relief. The light let defenders spot grappling hooks the moment they landed, but it also made easy targets for archers hidden in the dark. From the rarity of arrows flying by, it seemed like the risk hadn't outweighed the benefit yet.

Derik approached a grizzled man a few years older than Lian, who studied their group with a practiced eye.

"How goes it?" Derik asked.

"Nothing we haven't handled before," the man replied, spitting to the side. "Old Haverson keeps us sharp. We move too fast for 'em to gain a foothold. Not sure why they bother—they don't have near enough men to take the gate from outside. They'll slink off in a few hours."

"Then why even try?" Derik asked as another guard ahead chopped through a dangling rope.

Arine's stomach tightened. She hoped it wasn't just bravado talking.

"Desperation," the man said with a shrug. "They think we're easy pickings this far from the cities, but no raid's come close yet. This lot doesn't even have the stomach for it. Most of 'em hang back, watching a few fools test our walls. But like Haverson says—best be ready." He spat again. "Now stop jawing and find a station."

Lars snapped out orders, pointing each of them to a station and instructing them to give his name on arrival. Lian and Matthew were sent east where the wall met the forest; Ciran and Jove to the west. Derik and Cilia were assigned to reinforce the defenders above the gate. After a quick glance at Arine and Gerin's bandages, he nodded them toward a makeshift infirmary where the wounded were being treated. Gerin muttered about not being too injured to fight, but one look from Lars silenced him and he followed Arine without protest.

Arine glanced back at the wall where her friends were and hoped it was over as quick as Lars seemed to think it would be. Maybe they would even be able to get a little more sleep. A skinny man who looked to be more bones than flesh directed her to fetch clean water while he had Gerin help hand him instruments as he picked out splinters of an arrow from a man's back. The arrow hadn't gone deep, but it had shattered, leaving tiny fragments to pluck free.

The minutes ticked by and Arine's eyes started to droop. The infirmary offered little to hold her attention, but she couldn't really complain about the quiet. Then, as she helped stock bandages, the unmistakable twang of several bows cut through the stillness. Dread filled her as she whipped her head around. Those bows had fired in the kind of unison that only came with hours and hours of practice.

She stared at the black sky for the longest heartbeat before she saw what she was fearful of...thirty or more arrows rained down just inside the walls. Screams filled the air seconds later as numerous men and women were struck down. Her and Ciran were back far enough to not be in the danger zone but she knew Cilia and Derik had been right in the middle of it.

People cried out, running every which way, some even having to crawl. She cast around frantically where she had last seen her friends. Finally she caught a flash of Cilia's red hair in the torchlight—both she and Derik were still standing, unharmed for now.

Derik hauled a wounded fighter away from the parapet while Cilia shielded them with a broad plank, deflecting the arrows that hissed in from below. Muscles straining, he finally dragged the injured youth back—barely fourteen, with an arrow buried in his thigh. Derik hoisted the boy onto his shoulder as a fresh volley of grappling hooks whirred up the wall, forcing him to set him aside and join the defenders hacking the ropes free before the enemy could climb.

The chaos blurred together. Arine stood frozen until Gerin seized her arm and pointed toward the gate. A deep, ominous thud reverberated through the fortifications, and the massive doors shuddered under a heavy ram. Crossbars groaned, sturdy but not invincible.

Gerin yanked her toward the stairway, and they raced upward. The low buzz of the fight had swelled into a deafening mix of shouted orders and agonized cries making it hard for her to figure out what to pay attention to. Torchlight flickered, casting garish shadows over everything and they passed more than one man crumpled over with blood pooling from arrow wounds.

When they reached the top of the wall, the defenders were reeling from the arrow storm. A couple of the attackers had even made it atop the wall. Outpost soldiers clashed with them in brutal, close-quarters combat. Arine watched another defender fall as steel rang against steel and the night burned with firelight and screams.

Another boom shook the wall under their feet and the wood rattled precariously. She resisted the urge to try to look over the edge to see what was being rammed against the wall. At least the interval between the impacts told her the attackers were having to pause to defend themselves.

Gerin waved her toward a cluster of scaling ropes snaking over the parapet. Shoving down her confusion, she crouched low and hacked through one line after another, barely checking whether anyone clung to the far end. On her third cut she rose to strike again—and faced a man instead of a rope.

He clung to the battlement, leather vest creaking as he dodged her first swing, her blade skimming past his neck and glancing off the thick hide. Arrows hissed overhead. Arine ducked, heart pounding, as shafts clattered against the stones.

The climber lunged upward. She bared her teeth and dove forward, driving her sword straight up in a desperate thrust. Pain flared through her injured arm, but she held fast. He tried to twist back, lacking the leverage, and impaled himself, sliding down the blade with a wet, sickening drag.

Too late she realized his falling weight would crush her. She rolled aside, sparing her wounded arm, but his body slammed across her legs. Gasping, she wasted precious moments twisting free before she could wrench her legs and sword loose, the steel slick with gore.

Another grappling hook arced over the wall. She slashed the rope in a single motion and watched the next assailant plunge into the darkness, bones cracking on the frozen ground below. Adrenaline surged, sharp and cold—one heartbeat slower and she would have been the one lifeless on the ground.

She dropped into a crouch, forcing a steady breath as the wall beneath her feet quivered with another dull boom. She gripped the wooden wall until the tremor passed, splinters biting her palm. Down the rampart, Gerin shoved an attacker back into the void—headless—then staggered, one arm clutched across his ribs, before driving forward again.

Another strike rocked the wall as she staggered to her feet, a splintering crack warning that the gate's bars wouldn't hold forever. Gerin had gathered four archers and was snapping orders.

"You two cover! You two target the ram crew!" He spotted her as she moved up behind them and gave a quick nod. "Arine—you're with me. Watch the flank."

She slid into position while the bowmen loosed arrow after arrow, screams rising from the dark below as shafts found their marks. A flash of Cilia's red hair caught her eye further down the battlement, but she barely registered it before a hulking figure charged along the wall.

The man was at least two heads taller, his boots thundering across the planks, a predator's grin flashing in the torchlight. He swung for her head in a brutal overhead cut. Arine braced, meeting the blade with hers. The impact jolted her injured arm, but instead of matching his strength she let his weight drive her sword downward, twisting with the motion and forcing him to overreach in surprise.

His momentum carried him off balance while Arine pivoted, ready to strike again. She ducked under the man's arm and slashed behind her, cutting across his elbow. He grunted but kept his grip on the sword. She pivoted to block again, yet he suddenly halted and gestured over the wall to his comrades. The unexpected motion threw her off. She lunged too far, lost her footing, and reeled back.

She took precious seconds to reorient herself and the big man swung hard. She caught the blow on her blade, but his sheer strength forced her backward, panic coursing through her.

Then Gerin burst from behind, spinning like a deadly tornado as he stabbed at the man from the other side. His ribs slowed him down but it didn't matter. He struck with sharp, efficient thrusts—three rapid exchanges—and the giant crumpled beneath a final stab to the head. Arine quickly stumbled back to her feet, nodding to Gerin in silent thanks, not trusting herself to speak yet.

The rain of arrows had eased, so she risked a glance beyond the battlements. Torchlight revealed the bodies of men who had carried a crude battering ram—a thick log sharpened to a point and lashed with rope handles. The gate beside it sagged inward, splintered from repeated blows.

Gerin's archers had dropped all but two of the carriers; the survivors crouched against the base of the wall, hidden from the defenders' aim. Beyond the killing ground, more corpses littered the mud. A larger force waited in the shadows beneath the trees, one tall figure issuing orders. As Arine started to duck back, the leader gestured towards her section.

Confusion flashed through her face as she looked down to see what he was pointing at. The gate was off to the side and there were no cracks on the wall or anything special of note. She looked back up and froze; he and the others were staring at her, bows raised. But none fired. Even at that distance she thought she saw a faint smile. Heart hammering, she dropped flat against the parapet.

Could they have been pointing at her? How...why?

Before she could make sense of it, Gerin seized her sleeve and pointed toward the healer's tent below. Matthew and Lian stood there, signaling urgently.

"He wants us to disengage," Gerin shouted over the twang of bowstrings and the cries of the wounded.

Arine nodded, unease tightening her stomach. She hadn't seen Ciran or Jove since the first clash, and dread sharpened her fear that this recall meant one of them had fallen.

Gerin gave instructions to the archers to keep holding any reinforcements back and then they hurried down the wall towards the stairs. They were slower than Arine had hoped, having to stop every few yards to either slash through dangling ropes or drive back another attacker who had gained the wall.

When Arine glanced back, Gerin's makeshift group of defenders had grown. Another archer had joined them plus a stout woman who looked like she had just walked out of the kitchen. The woman still had her apron on, flour marks from making the morning bread covered the front side but she held up the spear she had brought with her defiantly and scanned the wall for any threats. Gerin's improvised squad was the only reason the gate still held.

The healing tent below was almost unrecognizable. Dozens of wounded lay on the ground where cots had run out, blood slicking the packed earth. The thin medic from earlier barked orders to a knot of women and boys barely old enough to fight. Groans and hurried footsteps blended into a single, relentless din.

Lian pulled Arine and Gerin aside where Matthew waited, his limp worse but otherwise intact. Arine scanned the chaos, frustration knotting her chest.

"What are we doing here?" she demanded. "Derik and Cilia are still up there—and Ciran and Jove, who knows where—"

A deafening boom reverberated through the air, cutting her off and shaking the very ground they stood on.

Chapter 21

Arine spun toward the gate, bracing for it to collapse—but the massive doors held.

Then a pillar of fire burst along the western wall. Flames leapt skyward, black smoke boiling into the stars. For a heartbeat the battlefield went silent—attackers and defenders alike frozen by the sudden inferno—before the screams began. Men near the blaze shrieked as the fire consumed them.

Terror clenched her chest. Her friends were stationed on that side. Smoke churned through the torchlight, hiding everything she needed to see.

"We need water—anything!" Arine cried, searching for a bucket, a barrel, anything to fight the flames.

Lian's face was pale, his usual calm shattered. "We stay here," he said, voice unsteady. "Derik sent word to bring you to this spot. The messenger said he'd meet us here...but—" His eyes stayed fixed on the wall, words trailing into the roar of the fire.

Arine couldn't simply wait. If Derik and the others were trapped, someone had to reach them. She started to call the others to follow when two figures broke through the haze—Cilia and Ciran, running toward them out of the burning section of the rampart.

Firelight and smoke outlined the two figures as they staggered closer. Relief surged through Arine—if they knew where to go then Derik was still alive to give orders. The feeling faded quickly when he and Jove didn't materialize as well. She squinted into the haze, but the smoke was too dense, billowing into the cold night sky. At least the flames behind it hadn't spread beyond the initial blast; the fire was already losing strength.

Arine almost vibrated with questions as she waited for Ciran and Cilia to reach them. When they finally did, both were panting and streaked with soot. A shallow cut across Cilia's collarbone oozed a thin line of blood, lending a garish cast to her smoke-stained skin. Ciran's injuries were hidden beneath the grime, but he moved well enough. They leaned against the infirmary wall to catch their breath.

"You…guys…look…terrible," Cilia wheezed at last.

"Good to see you too," Arine said, forcing a smile. "What happened—and where are Derik and Jove?"

"Not sure," Cilia rasped. "Derik and I weren't on the section that went up. My guess? Someone got frustrated at failing to scale the wall, so they tried to burn it down instead. Not the worst plan, but Haverson was ready. One of the men said he coated the timbers with a vinegar paste that keeps fire from spreading for long."

Ciran finally stopped coughing long enough to speak. "I lost Jove just before the flames went up—it was chaos. I was trying to find him when Derik and Cilia caught me." His voice rasped with each word. "The smoke hit me hard so Derik told us to meet you here and went after Jove himself."

Arine winced as another cough wracked him, hoping the smoke hadn't done lasting damage. She fixed her eyes on the battlements, tension coiling tighter with every minute Derik and Jove failed to appear. Somewhere near the gate a fresh commotion rose, but she still heard no strike from the battering ram.

Below, Lars's crew worked frantically. They'd hauled away shattered timbers and braced the gate with two fresh logs, buying time until real repairs could be made. The attackers might have withdrawn for now, but the force she'd glimpsed on the wall felt larger than any mere band of slavers.

Her thoughts flicked back to the man who had pointed toward her during the fight. He'd risked exposure to signal the others. Had they truly singled her out—or was it her imagination? Guilt twisted through her at the possibility that this destruction somehow tied back to her.

As more smoke cleared, it was starting to look like the fire had inadvertently done more harm to the enemy versus those within the walls of the Outpost. Due to Haverson's foresight, it hadn't stayed lit long enough to make a gap in the wall, but it had knocked everyone who had been fighting on the walls into chaos. The defenders regrouped faster than the attackers, who struggled to reach the walls while the Outpost fighters moved freely along their own ramparts. Even so, there were still enough injured men to make it hard to say if they could hold if the Yuakans and Syarans rallied for another big push.

At last a figure emerged from the thinning smoke farther down the wall, a smaller man slung across his shoulder. As the pair drew closer, torchlight revealed Derik with Jove draped over him. Relief flooded Arine's chest—they were alive.

When Derik reached them, he didn't pause to explain. He scanned each of them quickly for injuries, then turned down a darkened path toward the center of the Outpost, away from the battle, and motioned for them to follow.

Arine pushed to the front, desperate to check on Jove and get answers. He was breathing, but a burn scorched the left side of his face and body—injuries that would need salve as soon as possible.

"What happened to him? What's going on?" she asked.

Derik's gaze flicked to her as he kept moving. "He was near the flames when they erupted. The blast threw him into a wall—knocked him out—but it saved him from burning like some of the others."

Another bout of concern washed over her. If the explosion had reached this side of the wall, Jove's burns could be severe. She hurried after Derik as they continued to wind their way through the muddy paths. As they passed one building, two small heads peeked out through the window, eyes fearful as they listened to the sounds of the battle in the distance. She didn't want to think about what would happen to them if the men couldn't hold the Yuakans and

Syarans back and she felt another wave of guilt at them going the opposite way instead of helping. She didn't turn around though and neither did anyone else.

"Where are we going?" she asked, trying to keep her voice even, though the guilt sharpened her words.

"Haverson demanded we report to him immediately," Derik replied without slowing.

"Haverson?" Arine frowned. "Why pull us from the defense?"

Derik didn't respond, and Arine's thoughts raced as they neared the inn. Why would Haverson pull them off the wall now? The only explanation she could imagine was blame. If he meant to punish or arrest them—or simply cast them out—she wasn't sure which fate was worse. She grabbed Derik's arm, halting him just short of the door.

"Wait, why are we willingly just delivering ourselves to him?"

"What do you mean?" Ciran asked, pushing forward. "What's going on?"

"Haverson has ordered us to stop aiding his men and return here instead." Arine said. "Why would he keep able bodied men from helping his people? It can't be anything good."

"That's not a good sign," Cilia muttered. A knife slid into her palm as she scanned the shadows. "Prince, is he planning to arrest us...or worse?" She scanned the shadows as if any one of them could be Haverson waiting to leap out.

"For once," Derik snapped, "can you all just listen? If Haverson meant us harm, he could have acted long before now. You'll have to trust me."

"You can't be sure," Ciran shot back. "Your title won't protect you here. If he kills us, he can claim we died in the raid and no one would dispute it."

Derik opened his mouth to reply but the door swung open and Haverson himself strode out. He was outfitted with a wicked looking sword that curved backwards on itself slightly and light, scarred armor strapped over his leathers. Only Gill followed, the door closing behind them. No squad of guards. No angry townsmen demanding recompense.

Arine flicked a glance along the inn's dark sides, half expecting an ambush, then forced herself to breathe. Maybe Derik was right—Haverson wasn't moving against them. But if not that, why summon them away from the fight at all?

Haverson greeted them with disarming calm, a composure that only sharpened Arine's unease.

"Pardon us, Your Highness, for interrupting such a lively debate among your motley group of guards."

He looked at each of them in turn, lingering on her and Cilia again before returning his gaze back to Derik with the hint of a smile on his face. Derik ignored the obvious criticism of the alibi he had given. Instead he nodded at Haverson as if the remarks were sincere rather than a taunt. His haughty court mask adopted smoothly.

"Haverson. How does the battle fare? I'm curious as well, how did they manage to get such a large group here unnoticed?"

"Shouldn't I be asking you that?" Haverson's voice was mild but edged with steel. "We've had years of quiet, and suddenly a full warband arrives—right after you appear."

A runner skidded to a halt behind him and waited silently.

"Let's be frank with each other, eh? It was truly one of the poorest covers I've heard in years." Derik moved to protest, but Haverson held up a hand forestalling him and continued.

"And it strains belief that the Prince and the Captain would travel together for some mysterious family errand."

Derik's mask cracked. "If you intend to detain us, the King will hear of it."

Haverson gave him a flat look as if Derik was acting dense. "I've no desire to keep you. In fact, I suspect the sooner you depart, the sooner the trouble at my gate will end. Gill here is going to direct you to a hidden exit on the northwestern side."

He nodded to Gill who stepped forward to open the inn's door. "Collect your belongings quickly," Haverson added, already turning back toward the night. "I have other matters to attend to."

The runner boy dashed off at Haverson's quiet word. Straightening, Haverson faced them with a bland expression, as though merely waiting to see whether they would obey. No one moved, tension thick in the cold air.

Cilia, closest to the open door, finally leaned forward and peered inside. "Looks empty," she said quietly.

Arine's unease spiked. None of this added up—why would Haverson think the attackers were after them? Before anyone could collect their packs, she stepped forward.

"What do you mean, the sooner we leave, the sooner your troubles end? We had nothing to do with this attack."

Haverson tilted his head, the faintest sigh of annoyance escaping. "I'm only noting the obvious. You arrive with stories of Yuakan raids, and less than a day later—here they are. Until now we've had no trouble. Simple arithmetic: either they're with you, they're following you, or this is all a big coincidence." He ticked the options off on long, deliberate fingers.

"The lowest probability is coincidence. The highest is that you drew them here. So, rather than risk unpleasant decisions later—decisions that might earn the King's wrath—I prefer to speed you on your way and trust my calculations. Your packs are already provisioned. I would not wish anyone to call me an inhospitable host."

"What about our injuries?" Arine asked. "Jove is badly burned. He'll need salves, and we can't forage for those ingredients."

Haverson turned just as the young runner from earlier appeared at the edge of the clearing, a satchel in hand. "Ah—perfect timing," Haverson said with a thin smile. The boy offered a lopsided grin at the praise before jogging back the way he'd come.

"I think this should be enough to keep him from suffering more than my men already are," Haverson added, handing the bag to Arine.

Inside lay a jar of burn salve and a bundle of antibiotic herbs—items worth a small fortune even in the best of times. He was clearly eager for them to leave with as little pushback as possible.

"Lian, Matthew—check inside and make sure we're alone," Derik ordered, easing Jove to the ground.

The two men slipped into the inn and called back moments later, "Only one here is the old barkeep."

She heard indistinct grumbling as she assumed Halston was being maneuvered somewhere besides his usual haunt.

"Get your packs," Derik ordered.

The group moved quickly, eager to leave before any hidden snare could tighten. Haverson murmured to Gill as Arine stepped into the inn with the others. True to his word, someone had replenished her provisions—dried fruit, smoked meat, even a wrapped loaf of fresh bread resting on top.

Before they finished fastening their gear, Gerin approached Derik, shaking his head. His expression was tight with distrust.

"This is too risky," he muttered. "What if Haverson tipped them off? We can't fight a force that size. If they catch us, we're dead—or worse."

Derik paused, eyes flicking to the door before he answered. "I know the risk, but Haverson lives on his reputation. If he's ever caught lying, his trade in secrets collapses—and so far he's done nothing to make me doubt him. Besides, what choice do we have? Fight the entire Outpost? Even if I shouted my identity, it wouldn't matter. We go."

He brushed past Gerin and strode out the door. With no better options, the others followed.

"Keep the horses fed and watered until I return—or the King sends for them," Derik said to Haverson as a way of goodbye, moving past him without waiting for a response. He grabbed Jove again and motioned to Gill to lead the way.

Haverson dipped his chin almost imperceptibly and didn't respond.

Gerin reluctantly fell in behind Derik, the rest trailing close. Arine and Lian brought up the rear. As Arine passed, Haverson's hand shot out and caught her arm.

"Trust no one in your group. Do it alone," he whispered.

A jolt of cold ran through her. She yanked free, but he was already walking away, disappearing between the buildings before she could find words.

Lian slipped beside her, following her gaze into the shadows. "Did he say something?"

Arine hesitated only a moment, pulse hammering. "No—just bumped into me."

His eyes lingered on her, skeptical, but after a beat he turned forward, attention shifting back to the dark streets ahead. Arine quickened her pace, the weight of Haverson's warning pressing harder with every step.

As they slipped between darkened buildings, farther from the clash at the gates, Arine's thoughts churned. Haverson's warning echoed in her mind. It was obvious he knew who she was—his veiled threat to Derik the night before about remembering their parents had made that clear enough. Still, he seemed to know more than he should. He had steered them toward their next destination without being told, and his fear of her companions felt deliberate, not misplaced. Whether it came from uncertainty about Cilia or from something deeper, Arine couldn't tell. Either way, she couldn't reach the end of this alone. Not after everything they'd already endured.

She studied the others as they moved in silence. Every face was pale with fatigue or streaked with soot; no one looked smug or unconcerned. If a traitor hid among them, they masked it well. Cilia seemed the least likely—twice nearly killed by the slavers—but then, why had Haverson insisted she be present in the meeting when they first arrived, unless it was because he was wary of her in some way?

Each theory only spawned new questions, leaving her no closer to the truth. If she'd grown up knowing more of this fractured land and the people in it, maybe she could separate ally from enemy. Instead, a lifetime of seclusion had left her ignorant of the very knowledge she needed most. Her father had taught her how to survive in the wild, but that now felt like only half the battle.

The northern wall loomed above them, manned by only a thin line of sentries. Their grips tightened on spear shafts as their eyes swept between the approaching group and the shadowed treetops beyond. No one spoke. Gill didn't bother with stealth; he strode directly to a cluster of four guards and murmured a few quiet words.

Arine followed his line of sight and noticed a narrow outline worked into the timber. The hidden door was cleverly built—without the watchful men she would have missed it entirely. After a brief exchange, one guard unlocked the panel. It swung open on well-oiled hinges, silent despite its size.

Gill stepped aside, arms crossed, waiting in his usual taciturn manner while the guards kept their wary eyes fixed on the strangers. Derik adjusted Jove's limp weight on his shoulder and motioned for Lian and Matthew to scout ahead. They slipped through the doorway and disappeared into the gloom beyond.

Several tense minutes passed before Lian returned. "I haven't seen signs of anyone passing through this area recently," he reported.

Derik nodded and ducked through, leaving the rest to glance awkwardly at each other and Gill's impassive face before following. Arine trailed last, the cool, night air brushing her face as she stepped into the clearing beyond the wall.

The first hints of dawn lightened the sky, and she stifled a groan. Another night lost to fighting. At this rate, they'd be battered to death long before they ever reached the cave. Just thinking about it made her injured arm throb with each hurried step across the barren stretch toward the forest. Behind them, the clamor of battle faded, and guilt pressed heavy on her chest. If the Outpost fell—and if it truly was because of her—she wasn't sure she'd ever forgive herself.

They pushed on as fast as their aching limbs allowed, keeping to the forest's edge until the last echoes of the Outpost faded and only the hush of the sleeping forest remained. At last Derik halted and gathered them in a tight circle.

"Well," he said, voice low, "we didn't rest as much as I'd hoped, but at least the Syarans and Yuakans are distracted. If they're following us, this is our chance to lose them. We will continue on foot to the Decayed Lands."

Cilia cleared her throat and raised her hand. "Exactly what is the plan in the Decayed Lands? I think I missed that part."

She looked around at everyone expectantly, but no one was immediately forthcoming with any information.

"Are you not telling me because it's some weird suicide pact or something because I really can't think of any other reason to be casually heading into the Decayed Lands."

The others shifted uneasily. Arine caught Ciran watching her and looked away, guilt pressing in. She had promised to make Derik explain their purpose, but Haverson's warning and the attackers' strange appearance left her unsure whom to trust. Was there a traitor among them? If so, and they were in league with even just one of the groups back there, then they had enough men to keep them from making it to the cave. Logic pointed to the siblings, but after everything they'd endured, the thought felt wrong.

"I'd like to know as well," Gerin said quietly. The other guards exchanged wary glances but stayed silent.

Arine lifted her eyes to Derik. He was already watching her. After a moment she dropped her gaze in silent assent to keep the secret.

Derik exhaled as if he'd been waiting for her cue. "If you're still alive when we make it there," he said evenly to the siblings, "I'll tell you. Otherwise, you are free to leave, though I suggest you stay away from the Outpost."

Derik turned to Gerin, voice clipped.

"No one asked you to come here either, and the King himself gave the order for secrecy. Feel free to question him on the decision at your earliest convenience when we return. Until then, follow orders or leave."

Gerin's nostrils flared, his grip tightening on his sword hilt. He shot Matthew a hard look but held his tongue, settling instead for a glare in Derik's direction.

Cilia, on the other hand, would not be silenced.

"Are you serious? Haven't we bled enough to earn an explanation? If you told us what's actually happening, we might be able to fight smarter instead of getting hacked apart step by step. You endanger everyone, but especially Arine, if you continue to keep us in the dark—if we know what's going on, we could help choose a path that keeps her safe."

Derik endured her tirade without a word, staring blankly back at her.

His lack of reaction only fueled Cilia's fury. She stepped toward him, and Arine's breath caught, unsure what would happen next. Ciran was there in an instant, grabbing his sister and murmuring something low in her ear, his own tension unmistakable. A knot formed in Arine's stomach—was he angry at Derik, or at her for helping keep the secret?

Before Cilia could speak again, Derik swept his gaze over the group, eyes cold and commanding.

"Enough. We move. I want more distance between us and our pursuers before we stop to rest."

Without another word, he strode into the shadowed trees, the branches stirring around him and Jove's limp form like restless banners. Lian and Matthew followed at once, but Arine and Gerin lingered. Arine honestly didn't know if Gerin lingered because of his affection for Cilia or his hatred of Derik. Maybe a bit of both.

Arine longed to say something to Ciran and Cilia—a thank-you, an apology, anything—but no words would change the situation, and none came to her.

Sorry I won't tell you what we are doing out here even though you have both almost died multiple times. But there is a tiny part of me that might think you could be betraying us even after everything.

Didn't really seem like something that would help the situation. At the end of the day though, she hadn't asked them to come here, they had chased after her of their own accord.

They stared back at her with a mixture of anger and disappointment as the weight of her silence hung heavy between them. Cilia's face flushed crimson with indignation before she abruptly wheeled away from Arine and Gerin. Ciran's gaze lingered on Arine for a beat, a flicker of something unreadable in his calm eyes, before he, too, turned to follow Cilia.

Arine slowly pivoted to follow Derik. She heard Gerin move after her without saying anything either. She knew he was probably just as conflicted since Cilia had saved his life, but she supposed years of ingrained duty to his King would not be so easily dismissed. Regret pressed against her chest as she trudged forward, glancing back several times despite herself. She wanted them to keep following, even though she knew it was selfish.

Minutes later, a rustle in the brush made her turn. Ciran and Cilia were jogging to catch up. Relief bloomed where guilt had been and she wondered when she had become such a hypocrite.

Chapter 22

The siblings rejoined the group without a word and no one else commented on it either. Arine wanted to say something—thank you...or sorry—but feared angering them and potentially making them reconsider so she stayed silent. She noticed Gerin glancing at Cilia several times, proof she wasn't the only one relieved by their return, or conflicted about it.

They walked on in tense quiet as the forest shifted even more deeply, signaling the swamp's edge. The tall, familiar trees of Killian Forest were gone, replaced by their gnarled, hunched counterparts; their trunks sagging under the influence of the encroaching rot.

Their limbs drooped under their own weight while vines coiled over every bare surface. The rotting vine was either a new species of plant that had developed from the rot or some perverted version of a former plant. It wrapped its tentacles over anything it could reach, sucking the life out of it and taking the sunlight for its own use. Half the trees were already smothered, and she knew the choking growth would soon dominate at the swamp's heart.

She was studying a vine creeping over a low-hanging tree when Jove jolted awake with a cry. Derik had to lay him down before he accidently dropped him from the thrashing.

His eyes were wild as he looked around at the group and their surroundings. He rolled onto his side and vomited, then pushed himself upright with a groan.

"What happened?" he asked, shaking as he tried to examine the burns on the right side of his body.

Arine remembered the medicine Haverson had given them and knelt beside him while Derik offered a brief account of the explosion and their hasty escape from the Outpost.

Jove seemed too dazed to comment, but true to Haverson's word, the medicine worked quickly. After a short rest he was able to rise unsteadily to his feet. He matched the group's slow, injury-hampered pace so they set off again, eager to put distance between themselves and any pursuers.

They marched until the sun stood high and bright, though its light brought no warmth. Cold air gnawed at them until even Derik shivered. The ground grew soggier as they neared Katillan Swamp, and Arine silently thanked the sturdy new boots that kept her feet dry—for now. How they would hold up inside the swamp was another matter.

A few lazy snowflakes drifted down, and Arine hunched deeper into her cloak. From what she'd heard, the Decayed Lands beyond the swamp would be warmer, their air thick and stagnant—a side effect of a poisoned land. It wasn't truly a comfort, but after a night of biting cold and aching muscles, the thought of warmth didn't sound entirely unwelcome.

At last Derik chose a sheltered clearing for their midday rest. "We'll stop here for a few hours," he said. "We're far enough from the Outpost that no one should find us."

The break could not have come soon enough. Arine's muscles burned as she sank gratefully to the ground, the memory of their frantic night still heavy in her limbs. Derik took the first watch again while the others eased down to rewrap bandages, adjust packs, and steal a moment's relief before the next leg of their journey.

Jove sat across the fire, staring into the flames. Arine wanted to ask how he felt, but Cilia dropped beside her first, cutting off the question. Arine tensed, bracing for a scolding.

"I'd say I'm mad at you, but I'm too tired to bother," Cilia huffed, startling her.

Arine turned cautiously. She knew she deserved no forgiveness after refusing to confide in them after everything they had been through, still the need to mend the rift pressed on her.

"I'm sorry," Arine said. "This probably sounds like a poor excuse, but everything keeps unfolding faster than I can make sense of it. I feel like I'm losing my grip—new revelations come every day, and we're attacked at every turn. I barely have time to think, let alone explain. I know that doesn't make it right, and I really do hate that I'm keeping you and Ciran in the dark, but I truly don't know what to do or think half the time, myself, anymore."

She was almost pleading at the end, but she cared about Cilia and Ciran and she wanted them to understand she wasn't keeping them in the dark because she got some sick pleasure from it.

Cilia sighed and leaned against her shoulder in quiet solidarity. "Look, I said I owed you my life, not every secret you hold. Would I like to know why we're crossing the most treacherous land in Valasia? Absolutely. Do I hope you'll trust me enough to share someday? Of course. But you risked yourself to save me without knowing a thing about me, and I'll do the same. No one will say I failed to repay a debt."

She lifted her chin with defiant pride before offering a quick smile. Her words eased the knot in Arine's chest, replacing tension with a fragile sense of comfort...and determination. She would do anything and everything in her power to make sure they weren't all risking their lives for nothing.

"Thank you," Arine murmured. "You're far more understanding than I'd be if our roles were reversed."

"Well, I'll still hold out hope that you'll confide in us—or even just me, screw Ciran," Cilia teased. "Besides, I'm not finished with the serious one yet." She winked, before casting around for Gerin.

Her gaze landed on him as he bent to rewrap his ribs. Her stare was appreciative of the many muscles clearly visible with his shirt off. Gerin must have felt her eyes on him because he glanced up and saw her staring. His face turned the deepest shade of red Arine had ever seen and he quickly turned around so his back was to them.

Cilia looked amused at Gerin's flustered reaction but, for once, didn't tease him. Instead she yawned and announced she was going to sleep, warning the others to wake her if they caught anything worth eating. Within seconds she was snoring, back dangerously close to the fire.

Arine decided to follow her lead. She chewed a bit of dried meat from her pack, then settled beside Cilia. Close to the fire and sheltered from the wind, she could almost pretend to be comfortable. Yet her thoughts refused to quiet.

Could she really do this? She'd avoided the question when the journey felt distant, but now the end loomed closer and the weight of it pressed in. Could she truly restore magic to the world? Since learning her mother's history everything had moved too quickly for reflection, and Derik's scraps of information about magic offered no real guidance. How could the survival of an entire realm rest on her shoulders?

The thought was absurd—and terrifying. Each attack had been more dangerous than the last. What if they were all wrong, despite everything and she couldn't do it? What then? But no answers came, only a tangle of doubts, and she finally drifted into a restless sleep.

A gentle shake woke her. She blinked away the haze, stretching as gray mist clung low to the ground. The sky above was a dull smear of blue behind the tangled canopy, telling her it was already late afternoon.

Cilia crouched beside her and handed over a strip of roasted lizard. Arine eyed it warily; she'd never eaten anything like it. Across the fire Ciran sat beside more sizzling carcasses, calmly chewing his own.

"Never had a bogscale before?" he called, raising his portion.

Arine shook her head, eyeing the charred tail.

"They're surprisingly good," Cilia said, pushing the meat closer. "I've already had two. Ciran found a nest nearby."

Not wanting to offend them anymore than she already had, Arine bit into the tail. The crisp skin gave way to tender flesh with a flavor oddly like chicken, only richer and faintly nutty. She offered a quick smile to the siblings before finishing the rest with unexpected enthusiasm.

Cilia nodded in appreciation and handed Arine another. Only Jove and Derik still slept. Matthew and Gerin stood watch on either side of the small camp, while Lian was nowhere in sight—likely scouting ahead. Arine hoped their escape had bought them at least a single day free of danger. They desperately needed a break from impending death for at least a full twenty-four hours.

After finishing the lizard, she forced herself to stand and stretch her stiff muscles. Once her blood was moving and the chill had eased, she set about changing the bandage on her arm. The stitches had held, and there were no signs of infection. Testing the joint, she found the movement sore but manageable and decided not to strap her arm this time.

Jove stirred, groaning softly. Arine moved to his side and asked how he felt. His answers were brief but coherent—an encouraging sign that there was no bleeding inside his skull. She applied another coat of salve to the burns, the angry red skin already beginning to peel. He flinched but said nothing more, his eyes were distant with shock so she left him to his silence.

With little else to occupy her, Arine tried to rest by the fire, but Cilia and Ciran's lighthearted debate over the best way to cook bogscale kept distracting her from more sleep. Across the clearing, Gerin continued to stand at the base of a tree, quiet and alert. Before she could second-guess herself, Arine found her feet carrying her toward him.

She wasn't entirely sure why at first, only that something pulled her in his direction. He watched her approach, silently acknowledging her as she came to stand beside him. She hadn't planned to come over, not really, but as the silence stretched between them, she realized what she truly wanted to ask. Still, she kept the question to herself, knowing if she came at it too directly, he would likely shut her out. Getting him to talk about his connection to Derik would take more care than that.

"Is it always this...exciting for you guys?" she asked, nodding to where Derik slept.

Gerin looked over at him, eyes lingering on Cilia and Ciran before he swept them back to Arine and replied. "Not in the same manner, but Derik did always somehow find ways to be in the thick of things."

He picked at a seam in his cloak, as though debating whether to say more, but in the end stayed silent.

"Well, if this sort of chaos was normal, I feel foolish for ever envying your easy lives," she replied.

He gave a quiet snort but offered no answer. In his gaze she caught the familiar spark of anger—yet beneath it lay a trace of sorrow. He held her eyes for a beat before lifting his face to the sky as if to find answers in the patchwork of clouds.

"What happened between you two?" she said, deciding to ask bluntly, rather than keep beating around the bush.

Her direct question immediately drew his focus back down to her. His eyes narrowed and she thought he was going to say something nasty to her, maybe tell her to screw off, but surprisingly, he didn't.

"He told you we grew up together, I assume?" he asked, his tone brittle but almost desperate at the same time. As if he had already been thinking about it before she came up.

When she nodded, his lip curled in disgust. "Nothing else though? I suppose he wouldn't want to bandy it around. He wouldn't want his precious image ruined." His pent-up anger slipped into his voice. "We grew up together, me, him, and his younger sister Helena. She is a few years younger than us, and we were like family. I thought of them as my own brother and sister. Helena was like a bright star, impossible to ignore and impossible not to love."

He inhaled sharply, almost startled by his own admission, but continued.

"One day about three years ago, a report came in of a small group of Syarans raiding a town half a day's ride from the palace. This was one of their first attacks on a village so far inside our border so there weren't any soldiers close by. The King ordered some of his guards to take care of it. We are all trained even harder than the army so it wouldn't be anything for us. Derik had requested to go but the King denied him, sending me instead."

"Helena...she'd taken it into her head that she would become a warrior, like the heroines in old tales. She practiced bow and sword every spare moment, and Derik and I humored her, teaching what we could."

He paused as if remembering her, shaking his head in anger. Arine could guess where this was going but not how it would cause such a rift between him and Derik.

"I warned him it was a dangerous game, but he only laughed—said learning to defend herself could do no harm. Before I left, she begged to join my patrol. I told her no, of course, and rode out to follow the King's orders."

Gerin looked toward Derik where he lay sleeping, the fading afternoon light casting a dull sheen across the damp ground. Hatred hardened his features. Around the fire the others spoke in low voices, their quiet conversation mingling with the distant cries of swamp birds, paying little heed to where she and Gerin stood apart.

"Derik didn't like that the King chose me to lead the men instead of him," Gerin said, his voice thick. "He gathered a few of his own soldiers—and took Helena with them. He could never stand not being her favorite, no matter the consequences. They took a more dangerous route and reached the village half an hour before us. When we arrived, the Syarans were already dead...and only a shell of the girl I once knew remained."

He drew a sharp breath. "An arrow struck her spine. Her legs and the entire left side of her body were paralyzed. Gone was the girl who used to run through the halls of the palace laughing as she chased us. Gone was the girl whose smile could dazzle even the surliest guard. All because he couldn't follow the King's orders." A tear slid out of the corner of his eye and he wiped it away angrily. "Her life is reduced to one who has to rely entirely on others for even the basest of needs just because he couldn't put his pride aside and let me lead."

Arine's thoughts reeled. She couldn't decide what shocked her more—the tragedy that had befallen Derik's sister or the raw emotion in Gerin's voice. It was difficult to grasp how anyone could gamble so recklessly with another's life, let alone his own sister's. That kind of arrogance blinded a man to the danger he created for everyone around him. There had to be more to the story, but even so, she couldn't shake the pit that formed in her stomach at Gerin's words—what if Derik was doing the same thing now.

Before she could speak, a new voice came from behind. She turned to find Lian approaching through the trees.

"Helena's fate is terrible," Lian said evenly, "but you lay the blame at the wrong feet."

Gerin's head snapped up, anger rising. "You would know. You went with him—chasing glory instead of duty."

"You fool. You really think Derik cared one bit about what the King thought of dispatching some small group of Syarans? Out of everything you know of him from childhood, when he befriended you, of all people, you truly think he would endanger Helena for something so petty?"

He stepped closer, voice sharp. "No. You were too scared to face the truth, so you hid behind your ignorance all of these years and made his life as difficult as possible to mask your own guilt. Derik didn't gather us to go fight some silly battle. He rushed to us when he found out Helena had slipped away on her own. She was angry that you refused to let her join the mission and set out on her own to prove you wrong. Derik was furious and we raced after her, but when we caught up to her she had already been shot. The Syarans were taunting her when we arrived. Derik cut every one of them down—didn't let a single man escape, even as they begged for mercy."

Arine struggled to absorb the new information, but Gerin looked as if the ground had tilted beneath him. His gaze went distant, eyes narrowing as if he were searching the depths of his memories, then he shook his head violently.

"Then why," he demanded, "did Derik tell the King he organized the raid when we returned?"

"To shield Helena," Lian answered without hesitation. "You know what the King would have done if he'd learned she defied an order." His tone softened. "And—believe it or not—to spare you."

"Me?" Gerin's anger faltered into uncertainty.

"You are still a fool. He didn't want you to blame yourself and go back to that dark place you were in when the King first brought you to Draske. He thought he was doing what was best for both you and Helena."

Gerin flinched as if struck. "That's...no. He wouldn't do that. Why would he let me think that it was his fault this whole time if it wasn't. That doesn't make sense. I hated him for it. He would have brought up the truth at some point." His voice cracked, the years of resentment suddenly stripped of certainty. "He could have told me at any time."

"You know why," Lian said evenly. "It's the same reason he let you lash him instead of me when you demanded punishment after the attack at the camp. He's the same person you knew as a child—you've just been too blinded by anger to see it. He never knew how you'd react, and he wouldn't risk Helena's safety."

"I would never let anything happen to Helena," Gerin choked, his voice raw.

His face tightened, a storm of disbelief and pain flickering across his features. For a moment Arine thought he might strike Lian.

"Then why tell me now?" Gerin demanded. "If I am so untrustworthy and low in his eyes that he would think I would jeopardize Helena, why would you tell me now?"

"I heard you talking and thought that maybe with a little time away from the King and after everything that has happened, you might have more of an open mind." Lian replied, his tone taut.

Gerin opened his mouth, then closed it again as a rustle came from where Derik lay. They turned to see him stirring. Color drained from Gerin's face as if he were seeing a ghost. He stumbled back, then spun and disappeared into the trees.

Arine instinctively stepped to follow, but Lian caught her arm. "Give him space," he said quietly, settling into the watch post Gerin had abandoned.

"Aren't you worried the Syarans or Yuakans might find him alone?" Arine asked, uneasy at the thought of Gerin wandering the wetlands in such turmoil.

"He won't go far," Lian said. "He just needs time to make sense of it."

Across the camp Derik was fully awake now, so Arine retreated to her pack and pretended to rummage through it. The truth about Helena—and about Derik—recast every sharp edge of his character. She had thought whatever happened between them was something silly, not...this. Why Derik refused to leave Gerin behind in the white spider attack and then when he got so angry about Lian talking to her about the punishment was starting to make more sense now. The cold, calculating Prince who seemed to revel in indifference had been shielding the people closest to him all along, whether they knew it or not.

Derik stretched, then strode off to check the horses. He nodded to Jove as he passed but spoke to no one. Arine fought the urge to follow and ask about his sister. He had kept that secret from her for a reason—would he be angry that she knew?

As she was still attempting to order her thoughts, Derik returned, scanning the small clearing until his eyes found hers. She pretended to be very interested in a large rock, hoping he would find something else to do, but to no avail. He moved towards her, giving her about five heartbeats to pull herself together before lowering himself beside her.

She managed a garbled greeting that even to her own ears sounded like nonsense. Cilia shot her a curious look but stayed silent. Arine cleared her throat, scrambling for something—anything—to say.

Derik spared her the effort. He plucked one of the last Bogscales from the fire pit and held it up. "What is this?"

"Bogscale," Arine replied, trying to act normal. "It's actually quite good. Ciran apparently is fairly proficient at hunting them." She smiled at him and pointed to the pile of lizard carcasses nearby.

He looked at her skeptically and she just tried to keep smiling, hoping he would think everything was great. She even went so far as to nudge him to eat it, thinking that if he was busy eating he wouldn't have time to ask her anything and she could get herself together.

He studied the roasted creature, then her, sharp eyes searching for whatever had unsettled her. Finally he took a deliberate bite.

Arine kept her smile fixed, but her thoughts churned. She had once envied the ease of his privileged life, but now she understood the cost. How must it feel to let your best friend believe you'd ruined your sister's future—enduring years of silent blame—just to shield her from the King's punishment? The realization left a tight ache in her chest, a quiet pity she hadn't expected.

Derik looked back over at her, holding up the half eaten piece of lizard, blue eyes flashing with wariness at whatever he saw on her face.

"What? Were you saving it or something?" he asked.

Arine met his gaze—clear, startlingly open—and wondered if she'd judged him too quickly. Maybe he was only doing the best he could with the hand he'd been dealt. Perhaps she could give him a chance to show a different side of himself, if he wanted to.

She reached for the other half of the lizard. "If you're just going to leave it sitting there—"

Before her fingers touched it, he popped the rest into his mouth, eyes gleaming.

"Too slow," he said around a mouthful.

A surprised laugh escaped her and she swatted his arm. "Rude."

"I think you tell me at least once a day that I'm rude, so I just wanted to make sure I live up to expectations." He smiled, a rare, brief flicker before he took a drink from his waterskin to hide it. A few gulps later, he cleared his throat.

"Almost choked. Worth it, though," he said, half coughing.

"Serves you right. Though I'm surprised you haven't heard of them before, I thought you knew everything."

He cocked one eyebrow at her. "That's quite a compliment."

"Ugh. I didn't mean it as a compliment," she grumbled, rolling her eyes.

"Are you sure? It sounds like you think I'm very smart and knowledgeable on all subjects."

He smirked at her and she huffed as she settled back into her cloak. He leaned over the dying fire and threw another log on it. Heat flared across the clearing, and Arine realized how cold she'd grown.

Derik turned toward Ciran with a casual question about the Bogscales, but Ciran's clipped replies made it clear that one polite exchange wouldn't erase the morning's events. A few more of Derik's easy remarks, however, were enough to draw Cilia back into conversation.

"Did you know Bogscales were almost extinct before the Severing?" Cilia asked.

Derik shook his head.

"Their old predators couldn't survive the swamp afterwards," she explained. "Now the lizards are bigger and everywhere. That doesn't mean the swamp is safe—its predators just prefer larger prey." She popped another roasted lizard into her mouth and glanced around the dark trees. "Not that anyone really knows what lives in there. Most sane travelers avoid the place."

Arine suppressed a shudder. The swamp was their best chance to lose pursuers, but she didn't welcome discovering what might stalk them in its depths. What Cilia said wasn't just superstition, it truly was a dangerous path, especially with the Decayed Lands on the other side. That's why they rarely had anyone from Falke, the neighboring country on the northwest side, pass through anymore.

The Decayed Lands extended over the easiest stretch of land that the Calasis and Falke shared. Sharp Mountain peaks and dangerous passes made up the rest of the way on foot. They could take ships down the coast and cut around, but the coast was so far from the Capital that the King's influence no longer stretched that far, allowing pirates to rule most of the waters these days.

Mercifully, Cilia shifted to a lighter topic—how the Bogscales could change color and hibernate for weeks without food. The thought gave Arine a small, strange comfort: even in a world choked by rot, some creatures had found a way to thrive.

Derik listened with polite interest, occasionally glancing at Arine, but she kept her head down. For a heartbeat she thought he might cross to Lian and spare her the coming conversation.

But, when the talk around the fire finally dwindled and Cilia poked idly at the embers, Derik brushed dirt from his hands and stood.

"Come help me collect firewood," he said, far too casually.

Arine's stomach sank. It was a poor excuse, especially given her injured arm, and they both knew it. She swallowed a sigh, cursing her inability to dodge the summons, and followed him toward the deeper trees. *That's what I get for prying,* she thought sullenly as she trudged after him.

She half-heartedly bent to pick up a few sticks that were dry enough in the damp soil, waiting for him to reach the real reason for this errand. Maybe he only wanted to resume their lessons on wielding—it had been days since the last one. She could hope.

Once they were well away from the group, Derik stopped pretending to search and turned to face her.

"Alright. What's going on? Is this about me not telling them the truth? For the record, I still think we shouldn't—but I thought that's what you wanted back there."

The direct question startled her. Since when did he care what *she* thought?

"No," she said quickly. "I'm glad you didn't tell them. I mean… not glad, exactly, but after everything Haverson said about the Syarans following us, it didn't feel like the right time. Just in case."

"Then why are you acting—" he gestured toward her, exasperated "—all strange?"

Amusement flickered across her face like a spark in dry grass. He was worried about her mood of all things? His open, unguarded expression stopped a sarcastic quip from rising to her tongue. She knew he had a right to know that Gerin had just found out about what happened and apparently Lian was in no hurry to tell him.

"Okay, first of all, I did not have anything to do with this. I just happened to be there," she said at last.

Derik's gaze hardened, and he crossed his arms, glancing toward the camp as if he could piece the story together before she spoke.

"Why do I get the feeling you *did* have something to do with this?" His tone chilled.

"Do you want to know or not?" she shot back.

His eyes flashed but he remained silent, so she took a deep breath and jumped into the retelling.

"So I saw Gerin on watch and thought I'd chat with him—nothing serious. We, uh, somehow started talking about the two of you growing up together."

Derik's eyes sharpened even further, if that was possible, but she pushed on wanting to get it all out and be done with it.

"Well one thing led to another and he mentioned your sister and then he told me what happened... from his perspective. And then Lian somehow just appeared and told us a...*different* version of events."

Her voice thinned at the end, and she wasn't sure Derik even heard it. His head jerked toward the clearing the moment she said Lian's name.

She followed his gaze and spotted Lian, that little snake, watching them now.

Derik locked eyes with him, shoulders stiffening, a muscle in his jaw flexing as the silence stretched between them.

Arine inched backward, half-hoping she could vanish before whatever this was fully exploded.

As soon as she moved Derik snapped his attention back to her. "Not so fast. Why were you asking Gerin about my childhood?"

Really, of course he'd make it about himself—as if she spent her days wandering around thinking of him. Just because she'd asked about *him and Gerin* didn't mean she went around constantly talking to people about him. What a typical egotistical absurd thing to think

"I wasn't," she said crisply. "I was asking about *his* childhood—you just happened to be some small dumb part of it, obviously."

She turned away so she didn't do something stupid like start to blush. Then she remembered how he had conveniently lied to her again about his sister and she whipped back around.

"And by the way, you neglected to mention that your sister is being kept under the King's care—just like my father." She jabbed a finger at his chest, then dropped it with a sharp breath. "So don't lecture me as if I have no right to ask questions when I'm clearly not going to get any answers from you, am I? Maybe next time try sharing information first."

Derik stood like a statue, simply staring at the finger she'd just lowered. Heat still buzzing in her veins, she forced her voice steady.

"Anyway, I understand why you couldn't share details about her, but you could have told me the situation. That's not even why I brought it up. I thought you'd want to know Gerin looked shaken—he stormed off that way when you woke." She nodded toward the trees. "You might want to find him."

Derik's gaze pinned her in place, heavy and unreadable. She resisted the urge to fidget, forcing herself to hold his stare. After a long beat he moved past her toward the woods. A few steps later he paused..

"I've got to go sort this out, but..." He glanced at her, a half-grin tugging at his mouth. "You owe me some stories from your childhood now."

Without waiting for her reply, he jogged into the trees.

She stared after him, the weight of his words catching her off guard. A laugh, soft and unsteady, slipped out before she could stop it.

But as quickly as the warmth bloomed, guilt clawed it away. She'd just been furious at him for keeping secrets, how could she brush that off so easily? Except... wasn't she doing the same thing with the others? No. Worse.

Her secrets weren't just inconvenient, they were dangerous. They were dragging people straight into the deadliest lands in Valasia, and still, she kept them. The thought knotted her stomach and pressed against her ribs until breathing felt tight. She didn't know if she was more frustrated with him—or with herself. The fleeting smile disappeared as the bleak road ahead reclaimed her attention.

Instead of going back to camp immediately, she found a dry seat on the ground. She needed a few moments to herself for once, and she hadn't tried to feel for any magic within herself in days. She steadied her breathing and closed her eyes. Once her mind was calm, she reached inward for even a flicker of magic. Chill air kissed her skin, and the acrid scent of the swamp drifted on the breeze. But no matter how much she tried, she didn't feel anything that could remotely be related to wielding. She opened her eyes with a sigh. The next time she saw Derik, she would need to demand some different training techniques from him.

When she finally rejoined the others, she sank beside Cilia. The charred lizards were little more than bones, and the group lounged by the fire in drowsy silence. Minutes slid past with no sign of Gerin or Derik. Arine welcomed the pause yet felt a slow unease tighten in her shoulders at how long they remained in one place.

The sun dipped lower, casting a hazy gold through the trees. Memories of past ambushes stirred her nerves, and she found herself checking on Lian so often her neck ached. He remained calm throughout, leaning against the same tree.

A flicker of movement finally broke the monotony and through the trunks came the two familiar figures. Tension drained from her as Derik and Gerin strolled into view, their pace infuriatingly casual, their conversation low and steady, as if they hadn't vanished into the woods for what felt like hours.

Gerin took his position on watch, relieving Lian. He paused a moment before nodding to the older man. Lian returned it with the briefest dip before moving on to find some food. Arine felt a wave of happiness at the exchange. She didn't know why, seeing as she hadn't been a part of any of their previous turmoil. But no matter how much they might annoy her at times, what they all had gone through on this trip made her feel a connection to them. She couldn't help but feel some joy at seeing such a deep rift between them start to mend. Plus, it was her meddling that sparked the truth to come out so she might have earned a little smugness at that thought.

Derik gave a ten-minute warning before they set out again. Arine groaned at the thought of forcing her aching muscles to march, though she'd only just fretted about their lack of progress. Reluctantly, she forced herself upright and began gathering her gear.

They managed only a few more hours before darkness made further travel impossible. With the swampland closing in, patches of firm ground were dwindling, and the best campsite they found offered barely ten square feet of stability before sloping into soggy bog. The air hung heavy with moisture, damp clothes clinging like a second skin. Fire was out of the question—there was neither space nor dry fuel—so they crowded together on the narrow patch of earth and slept as best they could.

Morning arrived damp and dreary, the earth slick with grime, but at least they were somewhat rested. The air no longer grew colder, a sign they were nearing the Decayed Lands. As they trudged deeper into the swampy landscape, it became a grueling process to cover even half as much distance as they had before. It was a maze of shallow and deep pockets of dirty, tepid water that were indistinguishable from each other until you stepped in the wrong spot. It also didn't help that the air smelled horrible. Arine half expected to see rotting fish floating in the water all around them from the stench, but the water was deceptively still.

No one trusted the dark, placid water and they tried to avoid anything that came up past their feet for fear of what might be lurking in its depths. Numerous times they had to backtrack to find alternate routes so that they didn't have to wade too deeply into it. Arine didn't know which was worse, the dark water or the twisted and bent trees looming overhead with their thick coats of rotting vine blocking out most of the sunlight.

Chapter 23

The swamp's gloomy state of brown and green was their life now. Each day began in shadow and haze, slogging through foul water while trying not to breathe the stench—or rouse the hidden wildlife. Everyone's heads seem to be on a constant swivel, eyes scanning for the swamp's many lethal mutations. No one spoke unless it was to whisper a change of direction.

The gnats and flies were large and incessant as they buzzed around their heads ensuring they were in complete misery. The only other sounds were the slopping of their steps as the mud sucked at their boots with each step and the smack of hands swatting at the different pests. Arine drifted into a dull rhythm, her mind hazing with heat and humidity, until—

"Argh, damn it!" Matthew's shout sliced through the drone.

Arine jerked around, hand on her sword, heart jolting for an unseen threat. But there was no attacker—only Matthew, cursing as he fought to free his leg from the muck. Derik lunged to steady him.

The group crowded closer once it was clear no beast was involved. A vine had coiled around Matthew's injured calf, its barbed needles clinging to his leg. When he tried to unwrap it, a handful of sharp needles remained in his leg. Removing it was agonizing work; half an hour passed before they pried it loose and picked out the tiny spines. The wounds oozed a pungent orange fluid, but most were shallow enough not to cripple him. Matthew's face was pale as they worked, but he didn't complain.

Arine examined the plant once it was hacked free. From above it looked harmless, a mottled blend of green and brown. Only the underside gave any indication of its predatory nature, glimmering faintly orange where the hidden needles waited to spring. When she prodded a similarly colored vine with a stick, it curled tight and fired its spines in an instant. She shuddered and resolved to watch every step.

By the third morning after the Outpost, the air had grown stifling. Arine woke up soaked with sweat and had to strip to her lightest tunic and trousers. The others did the same, except Ciran and Cilia who hadn't packed for warmer weather. They grimaced at each other, sweat beading on their brows, but didn't complain.

As the day dragged, progress slowed to a crawl. Detours to avoid the deeper pools forced constant backtracking. And by mid-morning they reached their greatest obstacle yet: a wide, black stretch of water. The group traded uneasy looks, each silently weighing whether to risk the crossing or lose more precious time skirting its edge.

Derik stood at the edge of the stagnant pool, scanning the surface for any sign of movement. The water lay glassy and still, broken only by the faint ripple of an insect skimming across it. He hefted a stout branch and tested the bottom ahead, searching for the shallowest path before shrugging back at Lian.

With no other route available, they stepped in one by one. The water crept higher, swirling around Arine's calves, and her throat tightened. Every step stirred up clouds of silt, blinding her to what might be brushing against her skin. Images of scaled bodies and sharp teeth flickered through her mind

She told herself that their noisy splashing would keep predators at bay, that the ripple of so many feet would confuse anything lurking. But her heart wouldn't let go of the fear. The water's warmth clung to her, strangely comforting and unnerving all at once. She almost wished it were ice-cold, maybe then, the beasts would find better places to hunt.

Jaw clenched, breath shallow, she pressed forward, each step a fight against both the dragging water and the thrum of panic in her chest.

Something slick grazed her calf—cold and unmistakably alive. A startled squeak escaped before she could stop it, and she lurched forward, nearly crashing into Ciran. Behind her, Cilia yelped and stumbled, panic rippling through the group. Boots splashed and water churned as everyone floundered for escape.

Only when the splashing ebbed and their ragged breaths filled the silence did they realize nothing was there. Arine's cheeks burned as she met the others' wary glances, shoulders tightening in silent apology.

When the stress of the unknown depths became almost overwhelming, the water finally started to get shallower. They quickened their pace until the water eventually gave way to higher ground. They continued forward across the brief stretch of dry ground, only to meet another dead end. They sank once more into the murky shallows and an anxious silence settled over them as they pressed on.

By midafternoon they finally found a narrow rise of land, barely wide enough for two abreast. Gratefully, they dropped cross-legged onto the damp earth, keeping their boots well back from the water's edge as they stole a brief, uneasy rest.

Arine chewed her dried meat without tasting it, willing herself to ignore the swamp water still slick on her legs while the others murmured in low voices.

Lian suddenly raised a fist, and the quiet conversation died at once. Arine and the others reached for their weapons as he pointed toward the water, thirty feet away, parallel to the path they had just crossed.

A long tentacle slid from the dark surface, slick and veined with delicate whisker-like threads that fanned outward, tapping lightly across the still water. The faint tapping sent ripples outward in an eerie rhythm. Then something leathery erupted from the depths, jaws snapping around a snake so well camouflaged it might have been part of the muck. In an instant both vanished, and the water smoothed over as if nothing had ever stirred.

Arine's heart thudded in her throat. She barely dared to breathe, eyes fixed on the deceptively calm surface.

"How long until we're out of the swamp?" she whispered to Ciran.

"One, maybe two more days," he murmured, gaze fixed on the spot where the creature had disappeared.

"Great." Arine replied, tightening her grip on a knife.

Jove muttered about hazard pay, earning a dry grunt from Matthew as he adjusted the bandage on his leg. "No amount of pay would get me back here," Matthew said. "But at least Yulia will have a nice dress for our wedding."

"You're engaged?" Arine asked, surprised.

She realized she'd learned almost nothing about Matthew or the others—maybe by choice. Since Theo's death, keeping her distance was easier.

Matthew's tired smile flickered. "Yulia started as a palace maid last year and decided I was worth keeping. We're marrying in the spring once I save enough for a small house. Nothing grand, just a place of our own."

Arine tilted her head toward Jove. "How about you, anyone waiting for you back home?"

He looked over at her before looking away quickly, red creeping up his neck. His black hair fell over his face as he tried to pretend to find the water at his feet particularly interesting all of a sudden.

"No ma'am," was his only reply and Arine suddenly felt rude for trying to pry.

Matthew nudged him with a friendly knee. "Jove's new to the unit—hasn't had time to meet anyone yet."

Arine offered a small, understanding smile and let the subject drop. Instead, she busied herself with testing her injured arm's range of motion. She slowly rolled her shoulder and found it was stiff but manageable. Only a dull soreness lingering near the stitches—pain she could fight through if it came to that.

The rest of the day passed blessedly uneventfully, though Arine's anxiety only sharpened with each step. The weight of not knowing what lay ahead, mixed with the strange, escalating attacks, was beginning to press in on her now that she had nothing to distract her from it all. What if they reached Mt. Farna and she couldn't do anything? The return trip would be just as dangerous, and far more humiliating.

Night fell as they reached a small island just before the darkness became dangerous. As they ate, Arine caught a flicker of light in the trees. She sucked in a breath, ready to call out to the others, before she realized it was only insects.

Tiny bodies glowed green and blue as they drifted toward the camp on an invisible current.

She watched warily at first, memories of the orange flower still fresh, but the gentle bobbing shapes seemed harmless.

Gradually she allowed herself to relax, following their lazy arcs through the dark.

They floated around their heads illuminating the darkness in a miniature light show as they weaved in and out of the vines that draped incessantly throughout the trees. Despite her unease with nearly everything in the swamp, she had to admit the sight was unexpectedly beautiful.

She wondered if these glowing creatures were a by-product of the Decayed Lands or if they had always lived here.

One of the green ones came close to her and she held out her hand as it looped around. It circled her hand a few times before landing tentatively on her finger and then zipped off when she moved slightly. A little green speck of residue lingered on her finger where it had landed.

"Now you guys will be able to find me in the dark if we get separated," she said, holding it up and smiling at the others.

Cilia laughed. "You're brave. I'd worry about turning green after everything we've seen."

Arine laughed in return before her gaze flicked down to the faint green smudges on her skin. She bent slightly, brushing her fingers against the dirt where no one was watching, trying to wipe the residue away. For the rest of the night, her hands stayed folded tightly in her lap.

To her surprise, Derik assigned her the first watch. A quiet flicker of satisfaction stirred within her at the thought of finally being trusted to pull her own weight.

She moved to the edge of the group and leaned back against a gnarled tree stump, bow within easy reach, and settled in for the long vigil.

The faint glow of the floating bugs cast soft light, enough for her to see more clearly than previous nights and sparing her the need to blindly search the dark for predator eyes. Around her, the swamp settled into a deep silence, broken only by the restless drone of insects weaving through the humid air and the occasional croak echoing from hidden frogs.

Her gaze swept the shadows, tracing every twisted vine and gnarled root. She stayed taut with vigilance, refusing to be caught off guard.

A couple of hours into her watch, a sudden splash jolted her heart. She clenched her fists, forcing her breath steady. *Just a frog,* she told herself when everything went quiet again. Nothing like the leathery, tentacled horror lurking beneath the water earlier. Still, the swamp was wide and wild, and just because they hadn't seen anything else didn't mean it wasn't there somewhere.

Another scraping sound came from just behind her. She twisted, heart hammering, only to find it was just Derik shifting at the end of the group as he adjusted his weapons.

"Sorry," he whispered.

"It's fine. I guess I need to work on my situational awareness," she murmured, settling back into place.

Her heart rate slowly eased as she returned to watching the treeline. She lifted the hand the glowing insect had landed on earlier; the faint green mark still shimmered but, thankfully, hadn't spread. Another rustle stirred nearby, but this time she barely flinched when Derik's familiar figure stepped beside her.

"Shouldn't you be getting your beauty sleep?" she asked as he sat down.

"I've got good looks to spare," he replied so seriously she almost tossed him in the water herself.

Arine snorted softly, not deigning to respond. They sat there for a few minutes in comfortable silence, listening to the soft sounds before Derik tensed beside her. Slowly he only grabbed her arm, turning her slightly toward a tangle of vine-draped trees twenty feet away.

"Look," he whispered.

At first she saw nothing. Then, squinting, she caught what she'd mistaken for one of the glowing insects—two bright green eyes gleaming in the darkness. The body behind them stayed hidden, but the eyes were small enough to promise it wasn't some hulking predator. A thin breath escaped her as tension eased from her chest.

The eyes disappeared, only to reappear moments later on a nearer branch. In the dim light she finally made out a shape: a sleek creature that looked part lizard, part cat. Smooth amphibian skin shimmered faintly as it crouched on feline haunches, a long tail raised in counterbalance. Along its back ran a narrow stripe of shifting color, glowing like the insects that floated lazily around them.

It peeked through the vines as though parting curtains and tilted its narrow head, studying them. One of the blue insects drifted too close and, with a sudden snap, a long tongue snaked out and plucked it from the air. The stripe along its back brightened as the bug vanished.

Effortlessly, it climbed closer, gripping the vines with quick precision until it perched just an arm's length away. Its large, luminous eyes blinked slowly, fixed on Arine. Tentatively, she lifted her hand, and the creature tilted its head in curiosity.

Before she could pull back, its long tongue flicked out, gently touching her skin. She froze, heart pounding, then realized she had held up the hand marked with the glowing green streak from earlier. The creature sniffed at the mark, then retracted its tongue, clearly deciding it wasn't edible.

A soft, melodic trill escaped its throat before it darted back into the shadows. Arine held her breath, waiting for it to return, but the swamp had swallowed it up.

"What do you think will happen to them if we fix things?" Arine whispered.

"When you fix things," Derik corrected softly. He hesitated, then added, "I don't know. If they adapted to this climate, maybe they can survive an easier one. But the land's changed so much, it might never return to what it was."

She nodded, relieved by the thought. "Good. I'd hate to think we were sentencing a whole species to extinction. When this is all over, maybe I will come back and see what's happened to all our favorite swamp creatures."

"I plan to avoid ever coming back," he muttered. "Constant dampness is not my favorite state."

"You're such a wet blanket."

He groaned. "How long have you been waiting to say that to someone?"

She laughed softly. "Pretty much the whole time we've been here."

But just as quickly, her worries returned causing her smile to fade and a heavy silence to settle over them. She cast one more look over at the sleeping bodies.

When she was sure no one was still awake, she cleared her throat and lowered her voice. "I still don't know enough. If I can't even figure out how to feel the magic that you say I have, how will I be able to unsever it? There has to be more you can tell me."

Derik paused, then let out a quiet sigh. "Everything I know is second hand. The Severing happened before I was old enough to manifest any real power, but when I was young, I knew I would be able to. It was like I could feel that part of me already, even if I wasn't strong enough to use it yet. That's why I wanted to start there. Since that doesn't work for you, we'll have to go over the basics and hope something unlocks when you're in the cave. Otherwise—"

"Otherwise it's all for nothing," she cut in. "Theo died for nothing. My father will die alone for no reason. The King will probably have my head cut off or something. I get it."

"Otherwise," he said firmly, "we'll figure it out when we get there."

Arine picked at the ties on her sleeves, studying his steady profile. "How are you so sure I can do it?"

"Because look at what you've already done," Derik said. "Finishing the trial, crossing half the country, fighting off slavers—those aren't things just anyone does, in case you were wondering. And you've done everything with no complaining and no ulterior motives but to help people other than yourself."

"Anyone would do the same in my position," she said dismissively.

"Not everyone would, and the fact that you think so only proves my point."

Arine's brow furrowed in disbelief. How could anyone, knowing they could save countless lives, choose not to? But then she thought of Syar and their relentless oppression was a reminder that some people were so brainwashed, they couldn't even tell right from wrong anymore.

Determined to focus on what she could control, Arine pressed, "Well, I'd feel better if you told me more about what to expect."

Derik didn't argue this time, instead he started reciting what he knew about wielding. As he spoke, they shifted closer until their shoulders touched, and Arine didn't pull away. He explained how wielders channeled energy into objects to create artifacts, and how the final effects varied from person to person. Two wielders might craft the same artifact, a healing charm, for example, but one might mend a wound from the inside out, while another heals the surface first.

"Do you think I need to be mindful of how I unsever magic then?" she asked, unease tightening her chest. Would she have to worry about *how* she did it as well now?

"I think no matter how you do it, it has to be better than what we have now," Derik replied firmly. "I also know you can't worry about everything. Let's take a break before you find something else to latch onto. Plus, you owe me a story from when you were young. Don't think I've forgotten."

She glanced over, expecting to catch a flicker of amusement or a teasing grin, but his face remained steady. The quiet glow in his gaze betrayed nothing but sincerity.

She huffed, crossing her arms, though a reluctant smile tugged at the edge of her mouth. "Fine, but you'll have to be more specific. What kind of story?"

Derik tapped his fingers against his knee as he thought.

"One with your dad. When he was teaching you to use a sword."

The weight pressing on her chest loosened, just a little as she thought about her childhood with her father. She sifted through memories, searching for something light and funny. Her thoughts kept circling back to the first time her dad had taken her out back to practice. Maybe it wasn't the funniest story, but it made her feel more at peace.

"I grew up in Toumre, not far from the Capital," she began.

Derik settled in closer as he listened.

"The people there are pretty similar to those in the Capital, especially when it comes to what they think women should and shouldn't do. Fortunately my father didn't care about any of that. He practiced his swordsmanship every night without fail, and when I was seven, he asked if I wanted to learn too. He said it was my choice, but warned it might mark me as an outcast."

She smiled at the memory. "He didn't try to convince me either way. He just waited."

"At first, I didn't know what to say. I'd never seen a woman carry a weapon in our village. I wondered if the other kids would make fun of me. And maybe you'd think I agreed because I wanted to be some legendary prodigy or prove something..." She shook her head softly. "But really, I just wanted to spend as much time with my father as I could. He was my favorite person. Saying no would have meant spending less time with him, learning other 'proper' things instead.

"So I said yes. We practiced almost every day after that. Some people whispered behind our backs, but most just left us alone. My father was respected enough that they probably chalked it up to one of his quirks."

The memory warmed her chest, but when she glanced at Derik, the warmth slipped away.

He was staring at her, his brows slightly drawn, his expression distant. Not because he wasn't paying attention. No, he was *too* focused, as if he was holding onto every word, like he was trying to imagine what it would have been like to have those moments himself. Her hand twitched in her lap, tempted to reach out, but something about the set of his shoulders made her pause. He wouldn't want her pity. She cleared her throat and searched for a lighter topic to chase away the silence.

"I have to admit, that first night I almost wished I'd said no. I was more bruised than from all my childhood scrapes put together." She forced a small laugh and after a beat, Derik's low chuckle joined hers. When she glanced back at him, the tightness in his expression had softened just a little.

"If you want to compare bruises, you have nothing on me. The swordmaster at the castle doesn't care who you are. Gerin made fun of me for months after I was so bad in practice one day that the next morning I woke up resembling an ugly quilt with all the brown and black bruises I had."

"Well I'll have to meet this swordmaster, anyone that doesn't give *his royal highness* special treatment is someone I think I'd be friends with."

"Yeah, actually, I think I'd probably keep the two of you far away from each other. Who knows what type of cruel training you would help him devise."

A faint smile curved his mouth, though the shadow in his eyes lingered. Acting on impulse, Arine reached out and took his hand. He glanced up, startled, but didn't pull away.

"I'm sorry you didn't get those moments with your parents," she said softly.

She gave a gentle squeeze and started to withdraw, but he held on, his thumb brushing over her knuckles before he finally looked away. "I'm fortunate in other ways," he murmured. His eyes shifted toward the dark trees, the quiet gesture of a man burying his pain too deep for words—something Arine knew all too well.

When his gaze returned to hers, his hand tightened.

"We'll get the father you remember back," he said, voice steady. "I promise."

He held her eyes until she gave a small nod, forcing back the sting of tears. The fear, the doubt, all the weight that had been pressing on her through the attacks and the constant danger, sat heavy in her chest, but for now she matched his resolve and buried them deep.

He let go of her hand, lifting his toward her cheek as if to brush away the moisture she tried to hide—then a soft cough shattered the quiet. Arine jerked back, and his hand faltered midair before dropping to his lap.

"I apologize," he murmured, his tone suddenly stiff. "I forgot myself."

The silence stretched, heavy with things unspoken. Her breath caught, unsure how to bridge the gap between this softer Derik and the Prince she once hated. Would he hold onto this kindness, or slip back into old roles once they returned? She wasn't sure if she was willing to risk putting herself out on a ledge for a fleeting glimpse at who he might be.

"I think my shift is over. I should wake Jove," she said at last, pushing to her feet.

His face could have been carved from stone. "Yes of course, you need to get your rest."

She moved away, heart still racing. Worries piled on top of each other, now not just about the Severing. What if he had just let the moment overtake him? Was she a fool?

She gently shook Jove awake and slid into her spot, careful not to disturb the others. Her eyes flicked toward where Derik had sat moments before, now swallowed by shadows. A tight knot formed in her stomach. Tomorrow, she'd act like the conversation never happened. She'd laugh, speak plainly, and make sure everything was normal. Even with that vow, her mind kept drifting back, replaying every word until sleep finally claimed her.

Chapter 24

Arine woke to the muted rustle of the group packing up. She rubbed her eyes, shaking off the last fog of sleep—only to find the world swallowed in a clinging gray haze. A thick mist lay across the swamp, blurring everything beyond arm's length, and turning familiar shapes into ghostly smudges.

Only Lian sat close enough to make out, and even he was no more than a shadow as he tightened the straps on his pack.

A curse drifted from somewhere down the line, followed by a quick, muffled apology as others fumbled through the dense fog. Boots scraped cautiously across the slick ground, every movement tense to avoid slipping into the shallow waters lurking just beyond the murky edge.

Derik's voice cut through the air, strong and commanding. Heat crept up Arine's neck as last night's awkward memory surfaced, but the fog at least hid her blush. She slid into place behind him as he ordered them to tie themselves to one another. Lian took the lead, Matthew brought up the rear, and the others filled the space between. Derik tied her rope with a brief, silent motion, his stoic expression betraying nothing. Relief washed over her—he was committed to pretending the past evening hadn't happened too.

They set off in single file, their progress slow and deliberate. The glowing bugs and curious creatures of last night had vanished, replaced by an oppressive quiet and the cold damp of fog. The swamp had transformed from a fairytale into a nightmare. The thick, damp air muted the world to shades of gray. The fog clung to their skin and clothes like a living thing, cold and unyielding. Each step was met with slick vines whipping her unexpectedly, like snakes slithering through the mist, or worse, the tentacles of that swamp beast lurking in her mind. Her heart tightened, breath shallow and quick, the weight of constant unease pressing heavy on her chest.

They pushed on through mid-morning, wading through calf-deep water that lapped just below the tops of Arine's boots. No matter how carefully she placed her feet, the swamp forced cold water inside, soaking her socks until every stride ended in a wet squish.

Halfway across another flooded stretch, Lian pulled them to a stop. Voices floated through the fog of Derik and Lian murmuring back and forth, but their words dissolved in the thick air. She felt the rope between her and Derik slacken as he moved back towards her, his bright blue eyes cutting through the haze.

"The water is continuing to get deeper and without being able to see, it's almost impossible to try to determine if going another way would get us to shallower water or just take us deeper. Lian has been trying to angle us in different directions, but the water line keeps increasing. All we can do is keep going straight and hope we can get through it quickly."

Her throat tightened, a knot of dread twisting deep inside. She nodded, though every instinct screamed to turn back. Derik kept his voice low as he ordered the group to stay alert, weapons drawn.

The fog swallowed the path ahead, and the water crept higher. Each step felt heavier, the uncertainty beneath her feet a silent threat as she moved forward. The water climbed past her knees, then her thighs, until it finally steadied just below her hips. Every step was full of anxiety, wanting to move forward to get out as fast as possible, but also not knowing what she could be stepping on or into.

Without warning, a violent tug on the rope yanked her backward. She tried to turn but Derik was still moving forward so she was caught between the two taut ropes for a moment.

A scream tore through the fog—Cilia's sharp, panicked cry—followed by a rapid, unnatural clicking that echoed through the gray air.

Directly behind her, Ciran lunged, dragging Arine backward as he fought to reach his sister. Arine tried to keep upright, but the swamp's mud clung to her boots, pulling her down until she lost footing and crashed face-first into the murky water. Instinctively, she clamped her mouth shut and squeezed her eyes tight, fighting the bitter taste of the filthy water.

Rough hands seized her, yanking her upright as shouts erupted through the mist. Derik's voice cut the chaos. "Arine, are you all right?"

She nodded, dripping and breathless. The rope that had linked her to Ciran now dangled loose, severed clean.

They splashed toward the commotion, silhouettes forming in the shifting gray. Jove and Ciran emerged first, wrestling to restrain a thrashing Cilia.

"Let me go! We have to go after it!" she screamed, eyes wild.

Gerin and Matthew were nowhere to be seen.

"What happened?" Derik demanded, scanning the fog for any sign of movement.

"Some giant beast with twisted limbs grabbed Matthew and dragged him under," Cilia gasped, her voice breaking. "Gerin and I tried to reach him, but the ropes held us back. It was so fast. Then the line snapped—I couldn't even try to pull him back." Tears streamed freely as she sagged against Ciran and Jove, no longer struggling.

Derik's jaw tightened. "Where is Gerin?" He demanded, but his tone made it clear he already feared the answer.

"He went after it," she replied numbly, her stare fixed on the swirling fog, searching in vain for any sign of them.

A splash cut through the silence. "Over here!" Lian called.

Gerin emerged from the mist, mud streaked and eyes hollow, clutching an extra sword—Matthew's.

"Matthew?" Derik asked, barely more than a breath.

Gerin shook his head. "I tracked it while Matthew fought, but by the time I reached them...the creature snapped his neck. It's some twisted hybrid of fish and alligator. Scales like armor. Claws like razors. I couldn't land a single blow before it vanished beneath the water, taking him with it."

Arine's chest constricted. How could Matthew be gone, just like that? They hadn't even had a chance to help him. It was like Theo all over again. Tears burned her eyes as the group stood frozen in the gray hush. She risked a glance at Derik. His face was from stone, eyes dark pools of grief. For a fleeting moment, she longed to comfort him but the memory of the previous night held her back.

Another splash echoed through the mist, shattering the stillness.

"We need to move," Gerin rasped, his voice rough with fear. "That thing looked me in the eyes. It felt...aware. I don't trust it not to come back for us."

His gaze held a raw terror that made Arine's skin crawl. The swamp seemed to tighten around them, every shadow now a threat.

"You're certain Matthew is gone?" Derik asked, voice flat but edged with steel.

"If I wasn't, I'd still be out there fighting it," Gerin said grimly.

Cilia's face blanched, lips pressed tight. "I was right there, it could have just as easily been me," she whispered, then whirled on Ciran. "I should have done something! You should have let me help!" "

Ciran held her gaze but said nothing. The unspoken truth hung heavy between them: any of them could be next.

Derik turned from the fog, sorrow flickering in his eyes. "We have to move, Matthew was a good man, but his death would be in vain if we let whatever that creature is get another one of us. We move—now."

He and Lian pushed forward through the dark water. The others fell in behind, their ropes trailing like pale lifelines. Arine noticed Cilia lagging, still staring into the mist where Matthew had vanished until Gerin took her hand and gently pulled her onward.

As Arine trudged on, the weight of Matthew's death settled deep in her chest. This mess, her mother's legacy, was claiming more than just lives. It was tearing at her soul.

Chapter 25

The water thinned around her legs within minutes, just shallow enough now to wade easily. The shore hadn't been far at all. If they'd moved faster, if they'd only hurried, Matthew would still be here.

A hollow ache settled in her ribs. She kept slogging forward, eyes unfocused, replaying the last desperate moments in a cruel loop. What could they have done differently for Matthew? Could they have saved Theo too?

Even if she restored magic, neither of them would see it. They had given everything for her cause, and their reward was an unmarked grave in a rotting world. How was that fair?

The thought rose in her throat like a stone. Should she send the others away—spare them before her mother's mistake claimed another life? The thought lodged in her throat, too heavy to swallow. She forced it down, focusing instead on the rhythm of movement: the slap of boots, the tug of mud, the hiss of water against her legs. Step by step, splash by splash, she pretended she was fine. If she kept pretending long enough, maybe she'd believe it.

The rest of the day slid by in a dull blur. By midafternoon the mist thinned, and the water stayed at calf level—a small mercy that did little to ease the heaviness in Arine's chest.

By nightfall they reached a patch of ground firm enough for camp. It was drier than anything they'd seen in days. Arine dared to hope the edge of the swamp was near, but the thought of those who would never see it smothered any relief.

She ate in silence and slipped away early, avoiding conversation. The rest of the camp was quiet too, subdued in the shadow of Matthew's loss. Cilia avoided Ciran, sitting stiffly beside Gerin instead, refusing to even look her brother's way. Cilia and Gerin whispered quietly to each other while the rest kept to their own thoughts. Arine drifted to sleep listening to the creaks and groans of the swamp she was growing to hate.

A piercing squeal ripped through the drone of insect noises, jerking her awake. Heart hammering, she scrambled upright and reached for her weapon, eyes sweeping the shoreline for the source. The air was still blessedly clear of fog and there was just enough light from the rising sun for her to be able to see. She hurriedly cast around for the origins with the others, eyes wild as they wondered what new horror was about to beset them.

Then she saw it.

Along the muddy bank, a barbed limb slid from the black water, hauling a struggling creature toward the depths. The victim—a small, dog-like beast with a scaled hide and razor sharp teeth—thrashed frantically, claws clawing at the mud. The limb's hooked tip pierced its hind leg and flared outward, locking it in place. The animal's frantic scrabbling only drove the barb deeper. It couldn't pull free without tearing its leg clean off.

In seconds, the dog was dragged under, the surface rippling once before going eerily still.

Arine's pulse hammered in her throat, cold sweat prickling at the back of her neck. There was no going back to sleep after that.

Forgoing breakfast, she pushed her bedroll back into her pack quickly as she tried not to jump at every new sound. Around her, the others packed in tense silence, movements brisk and efficient. No one needed to say it—they had to get out of this swamp of nightmares before it claimed another life.

They set out in tense silence, every one of them on edge, nerves frayed thinner with each step. There was something about not being able to see any of the predators that had so easily snatched their meals off dry land that made you realize how easily you could be prey yourself. It was starting to wear on even the strongest of their group.

By midafternoon the ground began to hold, the trees spreading apart as the water thinned. Arine loosened her grip on her sword and let her shoulders ease, a small relief after hours of wading. Still, her gaze swept the thinning trees and damp ground, alert for any last-minute threat.

An hour before sunset, the swamp ended. It was as if someone had drawn a hard line across the earth. The trees they had just passed sagged with rot but still clung to life, sparse patches of leaves trembling on skeletal branches. Beyond the invisible divide it was as if life itself had been stripped away. The trunks were nothing more than blackened husks, hollow and crumbling, reaching skyward like spectral fingers. The air was unnervingly still, carrying a faint, bitter tang that stung the back of her throat.

She pulled the collar of her shirt tighter around her neck, pressing forward as an unease settled in her bones. This was it, the Decayed Lands. The final stretch.

Arine's feet slid across the brittle ground, small clouds of dust puffing up with each step. It felt less like dirt and more like walking through the ashes of a land that had cremated itself. The air was thick with the swirling gray particles, submerging them into the gray palette of their new world. Only the faint bleed of amber from the setting sun broke the monotony, a weak glow against the lifeless plain.

Ahead, a few clumps of trees intertwined with each other as if they had tried to suck life from their neighbors to stay alive themselves. In the end they all had failed and were now withered black husks of themselves just waiting for a strong breeze to crumble them. She had been ready to escape the swamp at all costs but now that they were safe from the tangible horrors she wasn't so sure she was better off.

Ciran stepped beside her, his voice low. "We need to find a place to camp that isn't exposed. The Decayed who still wander here won't be kind if they find us."

Arine frowned at the barren horizon. "I thought people living here were just a myth. How could anyone survive this?"

"'Survive' might be the wrong word." Ciran kept his eyes on the dark stretch ahead. "Most of the people here were those that fell sick with the rotting sickness and were cast out from their villages and shunned for fear of it being contagious. Any that last long enough seem to migrate here, it's almost as if they are drawn to it. But nothing grows, and there's little to hunt. Starvation takes most of them before the sickness does. Once they realize they have no chance, none of them have any mercy to spare and knowing that we carry food will be the only trigger they need to attack us, even if droves of them would die before overwhelming us. They don't care about death."

"How do you know so much about them?" Arine asked.

Cilia cut in before Ciran could answer, her voice flat but edged with satisfaction. "This time it wasn't my recklessness, was it?"

She held his gaze just long enough to make him squirm. Ciran's scowl deepened, but he finally spoke.

"About a year ago, I thought I could help them. A group of us went in with medicine and supplies, hoping to guide anyone still capable back to a safe haven." His face tightened, the memory clearly one he'd rather forget. "But we never found anyone fully aware of themselves. On the second day, we were almost overrun by a large group who noticed us and were ravenous for our food. We ended up throwing it and escaping while they were distracted. We didn't want to hurt them, and they wouldn't listen to reason. We never tried again."

He paused, eyes distant. "They seemed to move in packs, though I never heard them speak. Maybe some buried instinct drives them to stay near others, even as their minds and bodies decay."

A cold shiver rippled through Arine. The thought of human beings reduced to such a fate twisted her stomach, bringing to mind her father and how close he'd come to a similar end if the King hadn't intervened.

More than one person shifted uncomfortably at Ciran's words as they scanned the horizon to see if they were mistaking the dust for potential Decayed.

If they were attacked by any and couldn't escape, would they have to kill the poor souls?

Derik, as always, broke the heavy silence. "We keep moving," he said, urging them onward. "Let's find some shelter before nightfall."

From what Ciran had said, night or day made no difference. The Decayed would come if they wished. Their only hope—dark as it was—was that the sickness had claimed most of them already, sparing the group from having to kill what remained. Except Arine. She could never be spared from the weight of what her mother had done...and all it had affected.

Gerin led them toward a larger than usual clump of withered tree fingers jutting from the earth like broken ribs. They approached cautiously, scanning for any signs that others had claimed the spot before settling in. There would be no more fires for the rest of the journey, not that they needed them. The air was brittle and dry, and there were no animals left to cook, even if they'd wanted to.

It was a stark difference from the oppressive trees and vine coverage from the swamp. The moonlight was bright in the sky providing enough light to see once the sun fully set. Yet Arine hated the place already. Ash swirled in the air and coated her eyes, her mouth, her skin—the dead land clung to her. She had to force herself to eat, each swallow a battle after imagining what became of the bodies when the sickness finally claimed them.

The group remained subdued, the silence hanging over them like the ash itself. Arine drifted away from the others, settling near the jagged ring of skeletal trees that no one else dared approach. Grief sat like a stone in her chest. No matter how many times she tried to push the memories away, faces crowded in. Not just Matthew or Theo, but everyone who had perished over the years...friends and neighbors—each one another shadow of her inheritance.

The quiet pressed closer until it seemed the only thing left. The others had already drifted off to sleep, except for Lian, who kept watch on the far side of the clearing. When the soft crunch of footsteps broke the stillness, she jolted, startled to find she wasn't as alone as she thought.

She turned to see Derik dropping his pack beside hers without a word.

"What are you doing?" she asked before she could stop herself.

"I didn't realize this spot was taken," he said.

"I didn't mean—" She cut herself off with a quick flick of her hand. "Never mind."

Derik sat without asking, settling close enough they could converse without the others hearing. She should have told him to leave—after the way they'd parted the other night, it would have made sense. But she didn't. Maybe because, despite herself, she was glad for the company. He was the only one here who truly understood their mission...and her.

She shot him a sideways glance. Honestly, she was a little surprised he'd shown up at all. She'd half expected him to sulk for another day or two after her last rejection.

"Well, you can stay as long as you don't snore. I was trying to escape from all the noises you lot make at night."

"A Prince would never snore," he said, mockingly affronted.

She rolled her eyes and dropped back onto her bedding, a small, reluctant smile tugging at the corner of her mouth.

Silence stretched between them—not quite comfortable but not entirely strained either. She thought about saying something, but the words dried up before they could form. Across the space, he shifted now and then, as if he too kept brushing against his own unspoken thoughts. She fiddled with a loose thread on her sleeve, focusing on the tiny movements just to avoid the weight of his presence.

When he finally cleared his throat, the sound cut through the stillness and she allowed herself a small, almost imperceptible sigh of relief.

He hesitated at first, the words slowly forming as if he hadn't even known what he was going to say. "I knew Matthew for years. He was closer to Gerin and I didn't speak to him as often after the incident with Helena." His voice caught as he mentioned his sister. "But I considered him a friend. Do you think it was heartless of me, that I should have had us go after the beast instead of continuing on so quickly?"

Arine blinked, startled by both the question and the vulnerability behind it.

She chose her words with care. "I think you had six other people that you would have risked if you had and from what Gerin said, there was nothing to go after." She felt him turn his head towards her as she spoke. "I can't say what decision I, or anyone else would have made, but I also don't see anyone else constantly keeping us moving forward, despite the obstacles."

Arine hesitated, then pressed her own question. "Why do you seem like two different people? One that pushes everyone away with cruelty, and another that acts like he cares, especially about his family and friends. Why are you being kind to me now? How do I know which is real?"

"This is not an act," he said quickly, frustration sharpening his voice before he caught himself.

He drew in a slow breath and ran a hand through his hair. When he spoke again, his voice was careful, each word deliberate—as if he were weighing them.

"I am different with you," he admitted.

Arine froze, a thrill darting up her spine. She held her breath as he went on.

"I could say it's because we're away from the King's watchful eye, but honestly, it's because you're the first person I've met who doesn't have an ulterior motive. You're here to save your father and the land. With you, I don't have to second-guess every word or glance. That—" He paused briefly, searching her face. "That feeling is... something I've come to like."

That this might be his first genuine connection with someone made her chest tighten with sadness, but at the same time, a quiet warmth blossomed in her chest knowing he trusted her. Still, a small, nagging voice told her it wasn't enough. She didn't want a man who had to be away from the King to not bend to his cruel whims—she wanted this version always.

"Why not just be the kind man all the time?" she asked softly. "I understand not everyone can be trusted, but how does pushing people away help? Doesn't it hurt to have them see you as a monster?"

"If I weren't seen that way, then the King would doubt my ability to enforce his policies on his behalf and then I wouldn't have the freedom to help those I can."

"By help, you mean taking punishments on yourself instead of changing the laws that demand them," Arine countered, her voice sharpening. "That's a bandage on a wound that only keeps getting deeper."

He sighed, weariness creeping into his voice. "Not everything can be done in a day."

She studied him in the dim light, wondering how many times he'd rehearsed the same justification in his own mind. He wasn't irrational, but she just couldn't understand why he chose this path instead of doing more.

"I would rather push for change as soon as a problem is known, especially when change is so clearly needed." Arine said, heat rising in her voice. "Not wait around and let good people die while I bide my time."

Derik's eyes darkened. "You think throwing up your hands and demanding change feels good. Maybe a small victory comes from it, but mostly you reveal your hand—and then you're powerless. The one who truly moves the needle? The one who works quietly, unnoticed, over time."

He shook his head. "Martyrdom is easier than the grind of slow, invisible progress. Public outbursts satisfy for a moment but rarely create lasting change. Real impact is patience, even when no one sees the work."

"So your point is you do more good hiding behind a mask than standing up for what's right?" she asked, disbelief coloring her voice.

He looked away. "Treason isn't a light sentence, Arine. I want to help...and keep my head attached. Must I choose one or the other without knowing if I even made a difference?"

"No," she whispered. "But it hurts knowing so many suffer right now."

"After you unsever magic, everything will be different," he said quietly. "You can stay in Draske if you want and maybe we can do something more, together."

She didn't answer. Anger burned at the system he defended, yet she wasn't ready to imagine life beyond this journey. She would return to heal her father—that much was certain—but after that? Could she stomach a palace that would echo with memories of Theo and Matthew, losses already heavy on her shoulders?

"How do you keep it all separated?" she asked, voice raw. "I think about Theo and Matthew, and I know logically it's two lives lost versus everyone we might save. I can't stop thinking it's my fault though. That I wasn't strong enough to fix this on my own."

"What?" She felt him sit up and move closer to her. "None of this is your fault, you were dragged here against your will, remember?"

"I know that," she said roughly, sitting up so he wasn't looming over her.

She hugged her knees, feeling the cool press of the night on her skin. "But...it doesn't change the fact that other people will die because of me, as if my life is worth more than theirs when they have families, lives, dreams, too. I watch you making decisions based on that, risking their lives instead of mine and I just have to allow it because in the end they can't fix this problem my mom..." her voice caught. "It just feels like I am somewhat complicit. It is my shared blood that caused this, after all."

Derik was silent for a beat, then his tone softened. "I think the opposite. Do you want me to be honest?"

She gave a bitter laugh. "You know how I feel about honesty."

"Before I met you, all I knew was that someone named Nadyia caused all of this. Not just the sickness and hunger, but the deaths of my own parents. They were strong wielders—the Severing tore the magic from their bodies, and they couldn't survive the emptiness."

Arine absorbed the heavy truth. When magic was cut off, powerful wielders often died outright; the weaker ones lingered, some lost to madness, a few surviving with lasting scars.

"I spent years blaming her, and by extension, her family left behind," Derik continued quietly. "That's why, when we first met, I couldn't control my anger. It felt like a cruel injustice that you'd lived without even knowing about it. I was jealous. The King made sure I knew exactly what happened, and who was responsible. But one thing I know for sure now is that the sins of our family are not our own. The fact that you're here—risking everything to make this right—means you're anything but selfish. You're extraordinary."

Derik's words hit her like a blow. Distantly she knew he had meant to reassure her, but instead the weight of his words settled heavily in her chest. They justified all of her worries of being hated for who she was...who her mother was. Cold sweat trickled down her spine. Was that why someone had attacked her in camp? Revenge for a long-lost grievance? Blood feuds had ignited over less, after all.

Fear pressed in, sharp and suffocating. How could anyone see her as anyone other than the daughter of a murderer—intentional or not. The world tilted beneath her, leaving her breathless.

Derik reached over and put a hand on her chin, lifting it up so that their eyes met in the moonlight. The movement caught her so off guard, her mind paused its turmoil to focus on him instead.

"For some reason, I think you skimmed right past the last thing I said and are only focusing on the worst," he said softly, his voice steady and kind.

Confusion knotted inside her. After the way she'd reacted the night before—and knowing that every time he looked at her he must see the daughter of the woman who destroyed his family—why was he being so kind?

"No matter what I do, I can't change what happened," she whispered, her defenses slipping. "How can you look at me and not remember that you lost your parents because of my mother?"

"Because I know you," Derik said simply. "I've spent every waking moment with you for days. You risk yourself for others without hesitation. And..." his voice softened, "...because I know what it's like to be hated for a relative's actions."

Arine's thoughts drifted back to their first meeting—the guarded, cutting Prince she'd mistaken for a heartless enforcer. Now, seeing how he took punishments for his men, how he protected Gerin and his sister, and how he was here sharing his pain, she felt a shift. His life, like hers, was shaped by a legacy not his own. He was admired or despised for the family name rather than the person. And somehow, he still carried hope. Maybe... she could trust him more than she'd allowed herself to believe.

Tentatively, she rested her head on his shoulder. Without hesitation, his arm curved around her waist, warm and steady, as if he'd been waiting for her to lean in.

"Do you think they will hate me when they find out who I am?"

"Who?" he asked.

"Everyone."

Derik's mouth curved faintly. "Are you sure you want the real answer?"

She elbowed him, earning a quiet grunt.

"Some will always hate you," he said after a beat, his voice low and steady. "And not always for the reasons you expect. Some will envy you—your strength, your bloodline—more than they hate what your mother did. But you will also be allowed a seat at tables only some can ever dream of because of it too. That will give you power to make changes you wouldn't get to make without the judgements and constant critiques you will have to suffer through. You can hide if you want, but you'd be giving up the authority that could let you change anything. Trust me. There is always a price to power, and only you can decide if it's worth paying."

Arine turned his words over, uneasy. The idea that strangers might care who she was—might love or despise her for it—felt unreal. At least the world didn't know yet. For now, she still had time to figure out what she wanted to become.

The silence stretched between them, and for once it wasn't uncomfortable. They both seemed content to simply exist in the quiet, side by side, steadying each other after the weight of everything they'd said.

Then a twinge of guilt crept in. Derik had sought her out, his own grief pressing on him, and she had pulled the conversation into her own spiraling thoughts.

"I'm sorry," she said softly. "I made this about me when you're the one grieving Matthew. I'm sorry we couldn't do more for him."

Instead of responding, Derik squeezed her arm, and she didn't push it. The day's events and the newest revelation seemed to crash over her all at once, pulling at her eyelids. A yawn slipped out before she could stop it.

He slowly withdrew his arm but caught her wrist when she shifted to move away. The light touch startled her, her heart skipping as he leaned in and pressed a soft kiss to her forehead.

"Don't concern yourself with what others will think of you because no matter what, they will never come close to you." He paused, then added with a faint grin. "When you aren't ignoring orders that is."

She snorted despite herself. "Just wait."

"I will," he said as he settled back onto his bedroll. "Goodnight."

"Goodnight," she whispered, a tired smile stealing across her face.

Sleep didn't come easily, not with the lingering hum of his words in her chest and the quiet weight of his presence a few feet away. Her body was exhausted, but her mind wouldn't settle. All of the terrible moments of the day seemed to pale in comparison to Derik thinking she was special. Because, despite what seemed to be his best attempts at making her hate him in the beginning, she realized she didn't. And that maybe she never did.

Chapter 26

When Arine woke, it took a moment to place herself in the gray haze. The air hung heavy with ash, coating her skin in a fine grit.

Across the clearing, Derik stood with Lian, both men scanning the lifeless horizon. When his gaze found hers, he offered a small, easy smile.

Before she could think, she returned it, a quiet warmth flickering in her chest.

She gathered her things and joined the others, dropping down beside Cilia for a quick breakfast. Cilia didn't say anything, but Arine squeezed her shoulder in silent solidarity, memories of the swamp still lingering.

Arine had to force down her pieces of dried fruit. The ever-present ash coated everything, scraping unpleasantly down her throat with each bite.

"What's the best way to keep the ash at bay?" she asked through a cough as Ciran approached

"Not much you can do," he said, grimacing at his own food. "Masks help a little. I can show you how to make one."

Together they tore a spare shirt into rough coverings for their mouths and noses. Arine worked quickly, grateful for even a small reprieve. When she finished, she held hers up for inspection.

Cilia gave an exaggerated nod of approval. "Stunning craftsmanship."

Arine laughed, a brief, welcome lift in her chest. It felt good to have her friend back.

The lightness vanished almost as soon as it appeared. Cilia's smile slipped, her eyes dark beneath the lingering joke.

"Okay," she said, clearing her throat, "if we can't know *what* we're doing out here, can we at least know *where* we're going? So I can daydream about the end of this ridiculous trip?"

Ciran paused mid-task and looked up, his gaze catching Arine's. In that moment, she didn't see the distant, guarded, outsider he had been painted out to be since he caught up to them—only the man who had saved her from the pit and carried Cilia's thrashing body through the forest without hesitation. After the ordeal in the swamp and the raw grief of Matthew's death, she couldn't believe either of them would ever willingly harm her or wish the world to suffer.

But the weight of her worries pressed hard against her chest. Trusting them meant risking everything. She couldn't bear the thought of them pulling away, of watching their friendship crumble under the truth of her family's sins. Not yet.

Ciran's steady green eyes held hers, patient, waiting. She knew a casual deflection would leave a wound she might never repair. At the last moment she offered a fragment of truth instead.

"We are going to the heart of the Decayed Lands," she said, forcing her voice to stay steady. "To a cave on Mt. Farna."

She glanced between them, bracing for their reaction.

Cilia's voice dropped to a harsh whisper, disbelief sharpening every word. "So this is a suicide mission? No one's crossed the center and lived in years. The land's gone mad—quicksand pits, crumbling ground. What reason could you possibly have to go there?"

Arine had always known the terrain was dangerous, but hearing it laid bare like this made her stomach twist. Derik's urgency to begin the journey in early winter suddenly felt justified. If the land decayed any further, reaching the cave—and reversing the Severing—might become impossible.

"I'm sorry," she said quietly, her voice tight with more than regret. "I can't tell you why...not yet. It isn't because I don't trust you. I'm just...not ready."

Arine glanced over at Ciran and caught the thoughtful look in his eyes. Before she could say anything, Cilia let out a long, exaggerated sigh, crossing her arms defiantly. "I still don't see why we have to go. It sounds like a death sentence. Maybe we should just turn back and live to fight another day."

Her gaze flicked toward the guards and settled on Gerin, her voice dropping into a teasing murmur. "But if we *are* doomed, at least I'll have something nice to look at on the way out."

Ciran's frown deepened instantly, clearly not appreciating her flippancy. Arine bit back a smile, grateful for the shift in mood.

"On your last trip," Arine asked quickly, before anyone could press her for more, "did you actually see these sinkholes? Is there any way to avoid them?"

"I mostly stayed on the fringes, so I only saw one sinkhole myself. It wasn't one of the large ones, just a few feet across. But when we tossed a big rock in, it disappeared within seconds. Some of these pits move slowly, but if we come across a faster one, we'll need to act immediately." Ciran replied as he tied on his own mask. "The worst part is they're nearly impossible to spot until you're right on top of them. Only the tiniest changes in the ash on the ground give them away, and you have to be incredibly sharp-eyed to notice. Our best advantage will be our numbers. If we stay alert and move fast, we should be able to pull anyone out before it's too late."

"Great," Cilia mumbled sarcastically. "At least there won't be any hidden creatures hiding in the ground this time I suppose though."

Ciran just shrugged, eyes fixed on the swirling gray horizon.

Without another word, Cilia rose and drifted toward Gerin, murmuring something Arine couldn't catch. Left alone with Ciran, Arine traced a small circle in the ash, the powder sifting through her fingers like dry sand.

"I wasn't lying when I said it isn't about trust," she whispered, barely lifting her eyes. "I hope you believe me—especially after everything."

Ciran said nothing at first, but his eyes softened slightly. "I think what you're really afraid of is that once we know the truth, we'll see you differently." He hesitated, shoulders tightening before he added, "Maybe you shouldn't think so little of us."

Arine's breath caught, and she looked down, fingers twisting nervously. "It's not that," she murmured. "It's just...I've learned so much, so quickly, that I don't even know what I believe anymore. How can I expect anyone else to understand?"

He reached out as if to touch her leg but stopped short, his gaze flicking to Derik for a brief second. Her breath caught, but she pretended not to notice as he let his hand settle on the ground instead.

"We can wait," he said quietly. "Just know you can trust us when you're ready. Even Cilia. She's reckless, but she cares."

His eyes darkened. "Until then, be careful about putting all your trust in the Prince. His uncle... he's more dangerous than most realize. Not just because of how he treats his subjects."

"You know I agree with you about his policies," Arine replied. "And we can all try to make a difference when we return. Everything will be different then."

Ciran glanced toward Derik again, who was bent over their trail, trying to erase their footprints while the fine ash clung stubbornly, refusing to be hidden.

"Be careful before then," Ciran urged, his voice low, but intense. "Ask questions. Make sure no one's keeping secrets. And promise me you won't do anything without me there."

Arine wasn't sure what fear drove him, but since they were all headed for the cave together, keeping that promise felt simple enough.

"I promise," she said softly, just as Derik straightened and looked their way.

"Time to move," Derik called.

Ciran gave her one last steady look, and she tried to return a reassuring smile before he turned away. His warning echoed in her mind. The King's cruelty wasn't in doubt, but once magic was restored, maybe real change would finally be possible.

They rose and moved out, the morning passing without incident as they trudged toward the distant mountain peaks. Remembering Ciran's earlier warnings, Arine kept a wary eye on the shifting ash beneath her boots, watching for any sign of the hidden sinkholes he had described. But with how the ash seemed to shift and move with each step, she wasn't sure what she should be looking for.

They saw no signs of others as they continued towards the mountains. Someone might have been hiding among the few dead but still-standing trees, but any movement would have stirred the ash and given them away.

The stale air forced them to drink more water than they'd planned, and Arine was already feeling the effects by midday. She hoped the lack of water wouldn't become a problem—if, by some miracle, they healed the land—but even then she had no idea what the aftermath might bring.

As the day stretched on, her unease only deepened. The shrinking water supply nagged at her, a dull pressure building behind her eyes. Lost in the haze of worry, she failed to notice the ground—or that Lian and Derik had stopped—until she stumbled into them. Startled, she muttered an apology and stepped back, her thoughts moving sluggishly.

She blinked against the glare and looked past them. Ahead lay a patch of stunted trunks no higher than her chest, nothing remarkable—until Cilia's sharp gasp cut through the silence.

"Oh my God," Cilia whispered, staring back the way they had come.

Arine squinted toward the horizon. The land was so flat they could see for leagues in any direction. A faint shift stirred the gray dust in the distance, and then she saw it: another group advancing along the edge of the swamplands, their steps kicking up a wide, rolling cloud. The plume was far larger than the thin trail left by her own party—and it was coming straight toward them, following the exact path they'd taken.

She could see the small black dots of the tree grouping they had camped at the night before between them, and dread tightened in her chest.

"They have to be following us. They are too far south to be a group of Decayed." Ciran said grimly, voicing the thought already churning in Arine's mind. "There's no other explanation."

And with how close they were already, they would keep pace or overtake them if they didn't quicken their pace. No one could have followed them through the swamp without guidance. Had a message been sent from the Outpost, or was someone leaving signs along the way?

"Why would anyone risk the swamp and this wasteland just to chase us?" Cilia said, her voice tight with frustration as she turned to Derik.

Derik didn't answer right away. He stood rigid, eyes fixed on the advancing cloud of ash behind them, anger radiating from his silence. When he finally spoke, his words were clipped and cold. "Keep moving."

Arine could only guess at his direction of thoughts for how they were still being followed.

Cilia darted in front of him, blocking his path. "No, we have come through that swamp only to be led here, to a land of death, to now find out we are being stalked by a group that was willing to attack a barricaded Outpost to get to us. You owe us an explanation. We have done nothing but follow you blindly and help at every turn."

"You speak as if we dragged you here," Derik said coldly. "You forced your-selves into our company. And given the situation, perhaps it's time we revisit the story of your arrival. Don't forget, even after Matthew's death, you're still outnumbered."

He stepped closer, eyes narrowing. "You were closest to Matthew when the beast took him, weren't you? Quite the performance—a perfect distraction."

Cilia recoiled as though struck.

"How dare you accuse us again," Ciran snapped, yanking his sword free. "I can think of a few reasons someone in *your* camp might want an alliance with another power."

Derik's smile sharpened, ice over steel, and a chill ran through Arine despite the dry heat. For the first time, she sensed how truly dangerous he could be.

"Why are you so sure it's one of us," Ciran shot back, jabbing a finger at Gerin, "when the person with the most to gain if you were gone is standing right there?"

Gerin's hand went to his hilt. "What's that supposed to mean?"

"I mean, blood always tells, doesn't it? And if Derik somehow didn't make it back, who is much more likely to be recognized as the heir?"

Arine looked at him sharply. *What was this really about?*

"It isn't him for the same reasons it's not us." Cilia said, stepping up to try to diffuse the situation. "He was tortured right beside me, if you recall."

"You've known him for days at most and you don't have the best track record in men, so I don't think your opinion on his character is valid," Ciran snapped at her before turning back to Derik.

Cilia's mouth clicked shut, color flooding her cheeks, but she held her tongue.

"You say our behavior is suspicious," Ciran went on, his voice rising, "yet you ignore the fact that he's spent years trying to have the King cast you out—and now you're suddenly allies? If anyone here is a traitor, it's him." He leveled his sword at Gerin. "The King's bastard."

Arine sucked in a breath, the revelation hitting like a punch to the chest—then chaos exploded.

Jove's blade hissed free behind her as Cilia screamed for Ciran to stop. Derik hesitated only a heartbeat before stepping forward, sword half-drawn, poised to strike if Ciran advanced

She couldn't let them tear each other apart.

Arine forced air into her lungs and raised her voice, sharp and commanding. "We're heading to the epicenter of the Decayed Lands—to the place where the Severing happened."

The words cut through the clamor. Swords stilled. Faces turned.

She stepped forward. No more secrets would be kept, even if it meant they might hate her. Better that than more lives lost because of her family's past. The rest could wait until everyone calmed down.

"And, since my mother was the one to sever magic in the first place, Derik believes I can undo it and reverse what is happening to the land and the people."

Silence followed, thick and brittle.

Cilia blinked, confusion knitting her brow. Ciran stared at Arine as though he'd missed a step in the conversation. Gerin's eyes stayed fixed on Ciran, wary but startled all the same.

Cilia let out a loud laugh and then immediately stopped when she realized no one else was laughing.

"Is that true?" Gerin asked Derik quietly.

"Yes," Derik said flatly.

"How?"

"That, we won't go into detail on," Derik replied, his eyes shifting between Gerin and Ciran to see if they were done trying to kill each other.

Or maybe he was assessing their reactions, still trying to determine if a traitor was in their midst. Whatever he saw, it was enough for him to sheath his sword and move past them.

"We can gossip later, right now we need to put as much distance between the group following us as possible while it's still easier to move around. Once we reach the sinkholes we won't be able to move as fast so this fighting we're doing only helps them. Especially since our tracks are almost impossible to remove with this terrain. They will know exactly what path is quickest while we will have to figure it out, inch by inch. So at this point, as far as I'm concerned, anyone delaying us is a suspect."

His voice was hard, his stare sweeping each of them in turn. Arine wondered if he could really suspect Gerin, after everything he'd already done to protect him. Ciran still clutched his sword, glaring at Derik, but the fire from moments ago was gone.

Arine, though, worried more about herself now that they weren't about to run each other through. Her friends had just learned the truth—that she was the daughter of the woman responsible for the world's ruin. How many of their families had suffered because of her mother's actions? Would they hate her now? Could she even blame them?

Derik started walking without another word. Arine cast one last glance at the others, searching their faces for a spark of trust, for some sign that they didn't despise her yet. The silence gave her nothing back. Heart heavy, she fell in line behind him. The rest followed, the tension pressing down heavier than the ash beneath their boots.

For the first time, Arine was grateful for the dry climate. The lack of water forced everyone to conserve their energy, making conversation nonexistent as they traveled. It would give her time to think of ways to convince them not to hate her before they were forced to stop for the night. She could only hope they would see that she was trying to make things right and believe that she hadn't known the truth until Derik found her.

As the day stretched on, however, the steady headache built behind her eyes, muddling her thoughts. The water rationing didn't help, nor did the anxiety gnawing at her whenever they stopped to rest. No one else seemed to struggle with the amount of water they were allocating each day, so she kept her head down and swallowed her discomfort. A headache wasn't worth drawing more attention to herself.

She trudged across the endless ash, so caught up in her worries that she almost missed the flicker of movement—a small lizard darting past her boots. For a heartbeat she thought it was a hallucination, the first sign of life she had seen since entering the Decayed Land. But when she gestured toward it, Jove's eyes widened too.

Its small body was the same muted gray as the ground, and its spindly legs propelled it across the ground without stirring the dust. The creature didn't shy from them; if anything, it seemed to follow, always keeping a few paces away. Its tongue flicked rapidly, and she soon realized what it was doing—snatching tiny flecks of ash that hung suspended in the air after the group disturbed the ground.

Half an hour later, Cilia murmured to Gerin that another lizard had appeared on their opposite flank. Sure enough, a second one scuttled along at the same pace. Together, the pair shadowed the travelers like strange escorts. They seemed harmless enough, so no one tried to chase them off. Arine only made sure not to dwell too much on what exactly the lizards were gulping down out of the ash.

They pressed on as the light faded, more concerned with their pursuers than the shifting terrain. The sun sank into the horizon, bleeding red and orange until only a dull glow remained.

"Stop," Lian called suddenly.

Derik froze, lowering his raised foot and stepping back without hesitation. He glanced at Lian, brows lifted in question. The others approached cautiously, keeping their distance.

Lian pointed to the ground five feet ahead, slightly to the right. At first Arine saw nothing, the dim light masking any differences, but then—there it was. A faint seam, a thin crack snaking across the ash before curving out of sight.

Lian dug into his pack, pulled out a wooden spoon, and tossed it beyond the line. For a heartbeat, nothing. Then the ash rippled—and the spoon vanished.

"It's a fast one," Lian said, gesturing to the line. "My guess is since those move quicker, they are more distinguishable versus the slower ones where the ash doesn't move enough to create the seam like this."

Arine had no idea how he had picked that out while moving, regardless of how fast it was. She glanced over at Cilia to exchange a look of incredulity, but Cilia didn't meet her gaze. The rejection stung, and Arine quickly looked back to the ground.

"We will have to skirt to the side to go around and keep a sharp eye out since we've seen one," Lian continued. "There will be many more now before we reach the mountains."

Lian motioned for Derik to move behind him instead of his customary position in the lead and Arine suppressed a laugh at his momentary expression of relief before he exchanged spots. She supposed she wasn't the only one envying Lian for his eyesight. Regardless, she continued to diligently scan the ground for any signs of a sinkhole, even if it was in vain.

They pushed on until the last of the light drained from the sky, finally stopping at the edge of another sinkhole, using it as a barrier since the trees had grown too sparse to offer cover. The two gray lizards still shadowed them, curling up together nearby. Cilia tried creeping closer once or twice, but the creatures always jumped up and skittered away, returning only after she rejoined the group.

As darkness fell, Arine studied the horizon. A haze of ash marked their pursuers, still distant but closing steadily. They were making good time. She could only hope they couldn't spot the sinkholes as quickly as Lian. Maybe they would get lucky finally and this cursed land would help them for once.

Arine turned back toward the mountains, fighting her pounding headache to lift her gaze to the looming mountains. She had to crane her neck to see the tops disappear into the clouds that never seemed to move from their position. They were close now—days away at most.

She examined the terrain between them and the mountains; it seemed so innocuous, but she knew they were entering the most hazardous part of the journey. Cave ins and sinkholes weren't exactly something they could fight off. And even if they could, their track record in the swamp didn't bode well.

They ate in brittle silence. The occasional clink of a spoon against a tin bowl was the only sound. No one spoke. No one looked at her. The quiet wasn't just awkward—it was deliberate, as though they were waiting for someone else to break it, or worse, pretending she didn't exist.

The silence pressed in on Arine from all sides, thick and suffocating, wrapping around her chest like a tightening band. Her head continued to throb with the strain of it no matter how many swigs of water she took. Her thoughts raced in circles. Was it anger? Blame? She didn't know. But the tension sat on her shoulders like lead. She picked at her food, unable to eat, each second dragging her closer to the edge until finally the pressure became unbearable.

She cleared her throat loudly.

"If anyone has something to say about who I am—who I'm related to—I'd rather know now," she said, her voice sharp, cracking despite her effort to steady it.

She knew she wasn't handling this how she'd meant to, but at this point, she didn't care. Her head throbbed, people were still trying to kill them, someone among them might be a traitor, and she was exhausted from constantly worrying...about everything and everyone.

The stillness grew heavier, her pulse roaring in her ears. Then Cilia let out a sharp exhale and shook her head.

"Don't take this the wrong way but don't you think you might be being a little self-centered?" she said dryly. "I've been accused of being a traitor or a spy—twice now, after everything I've been through. And clearly, you must have believed some of it, or you wouldn't have held back information from me. Not to mention, Gerin over there has been exposed as the King's bastard. So I hate to break it to you, but even though your family lineage is a bit of a surprise, it's hardly the biggest shock of the day, if you ask me."

Arine blinked, unsure if she was being insulted or comforted.

Cilia smiled faintly. "At least now I know you were acting weird because of that, and not because you regretted trusting us."

Arine let out a shaky breath, tension easing just slightly.

"Plus," Cilia added lightly, "My father and mother were wielders, so I think I might have a good chance of getting some power myself if you actually succeed in all of this."

"Good Lord," Ciran called over, "I think your head might explode if that happens."

"Yeah, because I will be so powerful," Cilia shot back.

Ciran snorted, and Arine dared to let herself relax.

"Thank you," she said sincerely to Cilia. "I'm sorry for not trusting you before and for being so distant today. I was caught up in my own thoughts about what people would think when they found out and I projected that on to all of you. Even so, I know some people might only see me as the daughter of the person responsible for their child or parent or friend dying." She dared to lift her gaze to the rest of the group. "I...I'd understand if some of you even thought that."

Cilia reached over and squeezed her arm. "Well, despite what my brother thinks, I'm a great judge of character." She shot Ciran a glare before turning back to Arine. "I know you. I know what you're risking to fix this. The fools that hate you will just be mad because deep down they know they couldn't have done it themselves, so they will try to blame you instead of admitting they are the weak ones. That goes for anyone here, too." Her sharp eyes swept the group, daring anyone to argue.

Arine swallowed hard, emotion tight in her throat. She didn't know how she'd gotten so lucky to find someone like Cilia, but in that moment, one thing was certain: she'd never question their friendship again.

After Cilia's bold declaration, and with the shared understanding that everyone was carrying wounds, visible or not, the tension that had strangled the group for hours finally loosened its grip. It wasn't perfect, but a fragile sense of normalcy settled over them. As normal as things could be, anyway, after nearly tearing each other apart.

Cilia was the first to break it, her grin returning. "Hey Gerin—if you want to spar and burn off some tension from earlier, I don't mind getting sweaty."

He didn't so much as blink at her bold question this time. "I think this is the one time Ciran and I would agree on not expending too much energy, unfortunately. But when this is over, I'll show you a few moves."

Cilia's eyes lit up. Ciran groaned. "Please spare me."

Jove snickered quietly before Lian elbowed him. If it wasn't for her lingering headache, Arine would have joined in.

They slowly dispersed to set up their bedrolls for the night, but not without Ciran telling Cilia and Gerin to keep at least one foot between them. He even went so far as to threaten to put himself between them until Cilia indignantly moved her things further back. Arine laid down on Cilia's other side to make sure no fighting would break up their group's newfound peace.

Chapter 27

Arine was among the first to stir, never having found real rest, only drifting in and out of shallow dozes. She sat up slowly, rubbing at her temple as the first streaks of sunrise painted the horizon. Around her, the others began to rouse one by one, sluggish and quiet. The endless monotony of the landscape was beginning to gnaw at her nerves. It was just shades of gray and ash, stretching in every direction. Even their clothes had taken on the lifeless hue, making them resemble weary, soot-covered specters.

As the light grew stronger, she glanced back over their trail—and her chest tightened. The shadowy figures that had followed them without pause were closer. Much closer than she had expected.

Jaw tight, she crossed to where Ciran and Jove spoke in low voices. She caught the tail end of Ciran asking about Jove's prior experience before joining the guard, but at her approach Jove excused himself, slipping away to help Lian pack. Ciran's eyes lingered briefly on him before turning to her.

"How soon will they catch up to us at this rate?" she asked, nodding toward the distant cloud.

Ciran studied the horizon. "They must be traveling part of the night. Either they're confident with our trail to follow...or they fear their master's wrath more than the dangers here."

"Any idea who that master is?" Derik asked as he stepped beside Arine, his arm brushing hers.

Ciran shook his head. "Even though Syar and Yuak are similar in how they govern, they are both ruled by tyrants who would never be able to honor a deal with another ruler, let alone one they already knew to be as ruthless as themselves."

"What about the rebel leader?" Arine pressed, surprised he hadn't raised the possibility. Her stomach twisted at the thought of anyone rallying beneath Vanin's symbol. His atrocities in the war still haunted every whispered story.

She noticed Derik's gaze sharpen on Ciran at her words. He hadn't missed the omission either. She could almost see him marking another silent tally to the 'Ciran is a traitor list' she was sure he was mentally tabbing.

If Ciran noticed, he didn't show it. His voice stayed calm, even mild. "I've heard rumors, yes. But what sway would a would-be rebel hold with the Yuakans or Syarans? They despise weakness, and no one has even heard of this man outside scattered whispers. Hardly the equal of a *king*, is he?"

He smiled innocently at Derik. So he had considered the rebel—he'd just been waiting to throw the thought back at Derik.

"An interesting suggestion," Derik said evenly. "We can ponder it on the road. For now, we need distance before they overtake us."

She bent to gather her things, casting one last glance at the craggy mountains looming in the distance. Their snowcapped peaks vanished into the unmoving clouds, so vast they looked close enough to touch. The flat, colorless expanse made the distance deceptive, but at least the end of the trek was in sight. Soon, they would reach the cave. What came after—that would require some imagination. She could only hope that restoring magic would cause enough distraction to slip past the group still hunting them.

Arine tilted her flask back and shook it, willing even a single drop to fall onto her tongue. Nothing. She turned it upside down, gave it one last hopeful shake, then sighed and tucked the empty container back at her side. At least their lizard friends reappeared as they started moving. They popped out of the ground near where they had laid down the previous night and scuttled after the group.

Derik pressed them as much as he could, but they soon found out there was no longer an easy path forward. The sinkholes were steadily growing closer together and larger in diameter. Not even Lian was able to spot some of the ones this close to the epicenter. Twice he stepped into soft ash before realizing too late. They had to throw him rope, and he clawed his way backward, dragging himself out with a desperate, clumsy crawl before the ground pulled him under too far and restricted his breathing.

By midday, the sinkholes gave way to something worse—their first crevice. At first it looked like a thin zigzag splitting the ground beside a vast sinkhole. But within yards it widened, until only a running jump might carry you across. Arine edged forward and looked down. The pit was so deep the bottom disappeared into shadow, its walls unnervingly smooth. If you slipped, there would be nothing to catch you. Her head seemed to spin and she quickly took a few cautious steps back, noticing the others did the same.

Thankfully this crevice ended up diverting more to the west and didn't block their path, so they were able to keep moving forward. Arine's lack of water, however, was becoming unbearable. As the day wore on, her head seemed to weigh twice its normal weight, and she was having a harder time concentrating on anything for longer than a few seconds.

They stopped for a quick break as the sun was starting its descent across the gray sky and Arine forced herself to stand tall, and out of the corner of her eye she caught Derik watching her, concern etched into his face. Before she could reassure him, something rippled across the ash behind him. She squinted, wondering if it was a hallucination brought on by thirst—but then Gerin swore, confirming it was real.

Arine fumbled for her bow, notching an arrow as the others scrambled into position. The ground ahead undulated, a wide shape tunneling just beneath the surface. Their lizards squealed and bolted, as if they already knew what approached. The moving mound stretched eight, maybe ten feet long, three feet wide—far too large for comfort. She tried to imagine what kind of creature could be moving the ground in this manner, but her clouded mind was unable to think of anything that made sense.

When it was a few feet away its underground path shifted to circle them in a slow, tightening arc. Somehow it knew where they were, despite not having shown itself. Instinctively, they formed a ring, weapons outward. Arine found herself between Lian and Ciran, keeping pace with her eyes as the unseen predator traced another pass, closer this time.

Ciran wasn't going to let it do its reconnaissance unmolested. As soon as it came around to his side he jabbed out with his sword at the approximate place where its head would be. Faster than it had previously been moving, it swerved to avoid the full force of his sword and Arine heard the sound of Ciran's sword scraping along something hard before he pulled it back. There was no blood on the sword—only grit. Scales, then.

She kept one eye on the creature's ash mound as it increased its speed and switched up its movements to evade future strikes. It darted to the far side. A bow twanged behind her—Cilia's shot—but it missed by mere inches.

"Everyone do what you can from a distance to see if we can injure it or drive it off," Derik called from Lian's other side. "Do your best not to break formation and don't let it get close to you; we still don't know what kind of punch it's packing yet."

Arine drew back her bow, aiming where she envisioned its eyes would be. Ciran tensed beside her, sword raised. She released and held her breath. Her arrow shot towards the ground, cutting through the top layers of ash the creature had already churned up but like Ciran's sword, it bounced off whatever its outer layer was made of.

Leery after the ambush with the white spiders, Arine swept the horizon for signs of more attackers. Nothing but the distant silhouettes of their human pursuers. When she looked back, the creature slowed its circling near Ciran. A heartbeat later, it erupted from the ground in a startling spray of speed and ash.

Her body froze between horror and confusion. It was wormlike in shape, a long muscular coil the color of the ash. Its face was angular, its jaw splitting open to reveal rows of jagged teeth snapping inches from Ciran's head. Arine's stomach lurched as she realized why none of their arrows had pierced it—dull overlapping scales armored its hide, and it didn't have any eyes that Arine could see.

The creature's tail tapered into a flat appendage that it moved constantly back and forth along the ground behind it as if testing for movement. When Ciran slashed, it veered aside and dove, its pointed skull driving effortlessly into the ash until the surface swallowed it whole.

It resumed its circling. Faster this time. Hungrier. With their state of dehydration, she knew it would be able to wear them down and cause one of them damage at some point. She heard Derik issuing orders to Jove and Cilia from the other side of their circle but she didn't dare turn to look at what they were doing for fear of being its next target.

Arine's bow wavered as she tracked its path, every muscle taut. Behind her, across the ring, she heard another of Cilia's arrows hiss into the dust, missing its mark. Gerin staggered back as the creature lunged for him on its next pass, its jaws gaping far wider than seemed possible. He barely kept his arm intact before Jove's blade drove it off.

She racked her brain for a way to hurt it. There had to be some way for them to penetrate its exterior. Her pulse hammered with urgency, the dryness in her throat burning like fire. Only one reckless plan came to her, and there was no time left for hesitation.

She leaned toward Ciran, whispering her idea as the worm swept wide again. His eyes flicked once in understanding. When it circled back, he struck, sword flashing. Just like the last time, the creature tunneled away.

Arine broke formation to get a shot that would be straight on the beast's head if it launched itself again and pretended to stumble, landing on her knee. As expected, the beast immediately pivoted back towards her, sensing her fall. Its monstrous head flew up through the ash, angled straight for her.

Arine rolled hard, momentum nearly spinning her dizzy as her headache spiked. She tumbled clear of the worm's lunge, but her escape carried her farther from the safety of the circle—straight into line with Ciran.

The beast tried to twist after her, mouth open and grasping, but it had initiated its lunge out of the ground so it wasn't able to turn as quickly. As planned, Ciran was waiting. He struck with blinding speed, blade angled for the unarmored flesh inside its gaping jaws.

Arine's breath caught, almost cheering—until the worm jerked its head at the last instant. Ciran's sword clipped only the edge of its mouth, shearing off a tooth. The creature undulated and dove back underground before the strike could land true.

Arine scrambled back into formation, pulse hammering. Out of the corner of her eye she noticed the lizards watching from a short distance away. They seemed to be waiting now, not anywhere near the same level of frightened as they had shown when the creature first came into view.

The worm surged again, feinting at Jove before whipping toward Gerin. He stumbled, backpedaling into their line as Derik and Jove slashed to hold the beast at bay. It didn't retreat far. With a sudden snap, it lunged at Gerin again, forcing him dangerously close to Arine and Lian. Their circle wavered, fraying under the relentless assault.

Panic clawed at Arine, her pulse hammering in her ears. None of their weapons were making an impact and worse, the thing seemed to know it.

Cilia's scream split the air. Arine spun, terror seizing her—then a rush of relief when she saw her friend still standing, blood streaking down her thigh but all limbs intact.

She had no time to breathe. The worm lurched towards her, too close for an arrow. She dropped her bow, ripping her sword free to try to deflect what she could. Its head burst from the ash, rows of teeth clashing as it lunged. She swung, steel scraping its jaw, and dove aside again. Rolling hard again, she forced herself upright and bolted back to the line before it could cut her off.

The creature dove back into the ground where Arine had left a gap, and the line fell apart. Chaos erupted. Everyone scattered, scrambling to keep their distance and avoid being the next target.

Arine, briefly safe behind it, edged sideways, trying to reconnect with Lian. He noticed and mirrored her, both of them moving with deliberate slowness, hoping the beast relied on speed to sense prey. For now, it seemed to be fixated on Cilia's group—maybe drawn to her injury.

A thought struck Arine. She whipped her head back to the two lizards. Why weren't they afraid anymore? They hadn't moved an inch as if glued to the spot. Maybe the creature did indeed rely on movement to stalk its prey and couldn't distinguish movement close to a sinkhole due to the constant motion?

She squinted her eyes at the ground near their crouched bodies searching for any sign of a sinkhole. Fortunately Lian was there as her eyesight failed to make out any indication of one near the lizards. She grabbed him, spinning him around to point at the lizards.

"Are they near a sinkhole?" she demanded.

He studied the ground, eyes narrowing, then nodded, understanding dawning. "Yes. At the very edge of a fast one."

"We have to get everyone over there immediately," she said, watching the creature miss Derik by mere inches as he tried to help cover Cilia with the others.

Lian hesitated though. "If we are wrong, we will lose most of our maneuverability. There's a chance it can navigate the sinkholes too."

Arine's jaw tightened. "Our maneuverability is already gone. It's the best chance we have, otherwise we are just hoping it leaves after it maims one of us enough for a good meal."

Lian still looked torn, but finally shouted to the others, waving them over. "To the sinkhole! Move!

They bolted toward the lizards. Arine watched them as they approached, holding her breath. If it was just chance the lizards had picked that spot, someone could die for it.

The lizards scuttled aside hugging the sinkhole's rim, as if confirming her hunch. Relief surged through her chest.

Arine and Lian took up a position as close as they dared to it, Arine knocking another arrow just in case. The rest of the group staggered toward them, the worm snapping at their heels. They struck at it as best they could, driving it back in short bursts, retreating step by step toward the only chance they had.

Arine kept her bow steady, eyes locked down the shaft of the arrow, unwilling to trust the sinkhole alone to save them. Gerin stooped to haul Cilia up when her leg buckled—and the beast lunged. Arine loosed her arrow. The shaft struck home, burying into the soft flesh of its open maw. Not a killing blow, but enough. The monster twisted away, diving back underground, her arrow splintering off as it went.

The brief reprieve gave the others time to reach the edge. They clustered together, every muscle taut with fear. Arine's heart pounded as she glanced at the lizards. They too were waiting and watching, unmoving. Ash rippled as the worm surged toward them again, tearing through the earth like a storm, before it veered aside. It zigzagged back and forth but remained several feet away from the sinkhole's edge. Panic slowly ebbed from her chest, replaced by a rush of wild, unexpected elation. It had worked.

She caught Lian's eye, his tension melting into stunned recognition, and a laugh tore from her throat. The others joined in, ragged cheers breaking the silence as the worm's path curved further and further away. Even so, they continued to stand there long after every trace of it disappeared before anyone dared take their first step away from the sinkhole, the lizards included.

When at last they dared step back, Gerin knelt to bind Cilia's leg. Arine moved to help—only to find Derik blocking her path, fury carved into his features.

"What was that?" he demanded.

She blinked, thrown. "What do you mean? I saw the lizards by the sinkhole and realized it must mess with the creature's senses—"

"Not that," he cut in, his voice sharper than usual, but not steady. His hand twitched at his side, betraying the nerves he was trying to hide. His glare swung to Ciran. "Her stunt with you. How could you let her risk herself like that?"

Ciran gave him a long look before replying. "The plan seemed like a good one, all things considered. Besides, she's not a child and she's held her own so far. Why would I not?"

"That's not the point!" Derik's voice cracked sharp against the ash-laden air. "If something happens to her, *everything* is for nothing." His gaze swept the others as if accusing them all of conspiring to get her hurt.

Anger flared in Arine's chest. "Ciran didn't 'let me' do anything. I make my own decisions. I'll take risks if it means protecting the people I care about, and no one—including you—gets to decide otherwise."

How dare he try to keep her from helping? That was why she was here—to keep people from dying. Arine snapped, "This conversation is a waste of time we don't have."

She stormed off without waiting for his reply. Still, guilt coiled in her stomach with every crunch of ash beneath her boots. His words had hit harder than she cared to admit, but she shoved the thought aside, narrowing her attention to spotting sinkholes now that her rashness had left her in the lead.

The fight with the worm had drained her. Before long, each step started to feel like a battle for her to remain upright. She staunchly refused to let her hand drift to her head, not wanting to give Derik any ammunition to say he was right. Nothing she did helped though—her vision swam, and the pain seemed to surge now that adrenaline wasn't blocking it out.

After a few minutes someone quickened their pace to come up next to her. She dragged her gaze over expecting it to be Derik, ready to apologize, but found Ciran instead. Disappointment pricked her chest before she smothered it with a grimace disguised as a smile.

"I figured you might want some company up here," he said. She nodded mutely, too weary to say more.

He hesitated, as if deciding what to say before finally making up his mind. "I know this is probably the last thing you want to hear, but... Derik might have had a point earlier."

Hurt flared in her chest at him taking Derik's side.

"When he called you and Cilia traitors?" she retorted before she could stop herself.

Shame burned hot on her face. She didn't want to stoke more discord—not after the fight. She was just angry, exhausted, and her head was splitting. Maybe she really wasn't making the best decisions right now.

"No," Ciran said carefully. "I meant when he said that if something happens to you, everything is for nothing. I don't agree with how he handles things—but he's not wrong about that. If what you shared is true and you succeed, you could save tens of thousands of lives. That has to matter more than any of us."

Arine glanced at him, torn. There was truth in both their words, and it had been gnawing at her since Theo's death. How was it not selfish to let the others die for her all because they were the lucky ones who got picked for something without knowing the risks ahead of time to make their own decision? But she also knew if she did something rash that cost her her life, then even more death, beyond Theo and Matthew, would be on her hands. But how could they expect her to be okay with trading their lives for hers?

"It's not right," she said, voicing her frustration. "You and the others, every-one besides Derik, had no idea what you were getting into when you came. Even though you volunteered to follow us blindly, I can't send others to their death while I do nothing."

She stumbled slightly, losing her footing from the pressure in her head as she tried to concentrate on the conversation. Ciran grabbed her arm and steadied her as they walked.

"Are you okay?"

Arine tipped her face up toward the ashen sky, fighting to keep her footing. "Honestly... I'm not sure—."

Chapter 28

Arine woke with a groan, her head pounding even more, if that was possible. She struggled to recall where they had camped, her thoughts slippery and hard to pin down. Muffled voices drifted around her, and as she blinked her eyes open, her friends' faces slowly swam into view. Evening had fallen, the sun sinking behind the skyline.

Derik's commanding voice rose above the others, ordering them to back up. A moment later, his warm hands steadied her shoulders as he eased her upright.

"Take your time. Sit up slowly," he said softly.

"Did the creature injure you? We didn't find any puncture wounds," he asked as she sat up.

Her skull still throbbed, but she forced herself to focus.

"What? No," she said slowly. "I didn't get hit...did I?" She had no idea why she was on the ground, so had she?

"Do you feel any injuries?" he pressed, concern flickering beneath his impatience. "You passed out a few hours ago."

"I don't think so, the only thing that's been bothering me is this pounding headache from the dehydration."

She racked her brain for any memory of injury. Could she have brushed against some plant like the poisonous ones in the swamp?

"You shouldn't be affected by dehydration yet, at least not to the point of collapse. How bad is your headache?"

"It started as soon as we began rationing water," she said, massaging her temple.

"So, a day or so after we reached the Decayed Lands," Derik said, and she could see the gears turning in his mind.

The others stayed quiet, worry tightening their features. Finally, Ciran spoke. "It's her connection to this place, isn't it? None of us show anywhere near the same symptoms, and we've all been rationing equally."

"It's possible," Derik said reluctantly. "We know this place affects those with the rotting sickness, so there's no reason it wouldn't affect the person whose blood is bound to it as well."

"What does that mean exactly?" Ciran asked, his voice low. "Do you know if it will get worse?"

"I don't know." Derik's voice was tight. He let Arine steady herself, his hand firm on her arm. She managed to sit up, fighting to clear her vision and master the throbbing in her skull.

"Perfect," Ciran said sharply. "You clearly thought all of this through before coming out here. If she is like this now, what is going to happen when she gets to the cave and tries to undo what her mother did? It could kill her!"

The words froze Arine in place. Fear pressed at her chest as she looked to Derik.

"We don't know that for sure," he said at last, eyes dropping away from hers.

And suddenly she understood—why her father had concealed the truth, why he had hidden them away. It had killed her mother to sever magic, so how could Arine hope to survive when she hadn't?

The realization almost made her faint all over again. But she looked at the concerned faces of her friends and a calmness came over here. If there was anything this group of people, who had willingly protected her at risk to themselves had taught her, it was that one life is not greater than the world's. And if it came to it, she would give hers to fix this.

She smiled weakly at each before she spoke. "Even if we did know for sure, my life for the world's...it's an easy trade. At the right time of course."

"We are not willingly sacrificing you," Ciran said, looking to Cilia and the others for support.

"But don't you see how you were making this argument just a few moments ago...or I guess hours for you." She grimaced at how much it must have cost them to carry her for the rest of the day. "If you can die for me, I would be a hypocrite not to die for all of you and everyone else. This is a wrong that has to be righted."

She looked over at Derik, whose face could have been carved from stone. "Plus, like Derik said, we don't know for sure that it will kill me."

She tried her best to convey her confidence, but her traitorous head flared, and she doubled over in pain. *Was* the land trying to kill her? The others didn't seem to have anywhere near the same problems she was having. What if she wasn't even able to make it to the cave, would all this be for nothing? No, she had to stay positive. There had to be a way for her to undo this, she wouldn't give up and waste the lives they had already sacrificed.

Even so, the dark possibility of her fate clung to her. She had accepted death in principle, yet it still unsettled her if she thought too long on it—her body's fear lagging behind her mind's resolve. She pushed it down, unwilling to let it show, but the chill of it lingered.

Cilia pushed forward, breaking the tension. She waved the others back.

"Let her rest. We know what's bothering you now. We still have herbs for headaches, and the caves are less than a day away. We can finish this—all of us." Her jaw set firmly, daring anyone, even Arine, to argue.

No one spoke, and the camp slowly drifted back to its normal tasks. True to her word, Cilia brought her kit and mixed a paste from the herbs she had left. Arine took a large bite, willing to try anything to ease the pounding in her head. As she swallowed, she watched the others. She expected them to settle into their bedrolls, but only Cilia laid down, nursing her injured leg, while the rest milled about and murmured in low tones she couldn't hear.

"What's going on?" she asked quietly. "Do you think that beast is still following us?"

A shiver passed through her at the thought of fighting the worm creature in the dark, and in her current state, though the herbs did seem to help a little. The pain had receded to a dull throb. Even the slight respite felt amazing.

Cilia looked at the others, pausing on Derik, before looking back. For a moment Arine thought she might refuse to answer. She had a few things she would need to talk to Derik about it seemed. She glared at the back of his head while he talked to Lian for good measure.

Thankfully Cilia chose not to follow whatever order of silence Derik had given, which made her appreciate their friendship even more.

"No, we camped near a sinkhole just to be safe. But, we lost a lot of time with that creature," she said quietly. "And when you passed out, it slowed us down even more. Plus, we had to skirt another crevice. Not as big as the first, but it still cost us a good hour. When we made camp, the group following us was much closer than before."

Arine's stomach tightened. "How much closer?" she asked, bracing herself..

"Just over half a day, as best we could tell. And they're traveling faster than we are. Tomorrow they'll likely be closer still."

Arine sat up to look, but the darkness swallowed everything beyond their own outlines. She would have to wait for the morning to see for herself. A shiver of worry crawled up her spine as she laid back down. How much closer would they be then?

Then Cilia's words truly sunk in—this would be their last real moment of rest before the cave. The weight of what lay ahead pressed on her chest, making it hard to breathe. Her limbs ached with exhaustion, but it was the uncertainty that gnawed at her most. The cave wasn't just a destination—it was the heart of everything she'd been running toward and away from all at once.

She couldn't hide any longer. If they managed to outpace their pursuers, the next step would be all on her. What if she couldn't figure out what to do? What if all of this was for nothing?

She needed to talk to Derik before it was too late. She could be mad at him later for being too protective, the important thing was surviving to give her that opportunity. She slowly stood up, testing herself to make sure no lances of pain drove through her brain, but the medicine was working, at least for now

Derik and Lian turned as she approached. Lian gave Derik a brief nod before moving off, leaving the two of them alone. A flicker of concern crossed Derik's face. He offered his arm, and she took it without hesitation—there was no point pretending strength tonight.

"We need to talk," she said, motioning toward a quieter spot.

"You should be resting," Derik countered as they walked.

"I should be doing whatever I want," she snapped.

Could he go one hour without telling her what to do? The retort was sharp, but she forced herself to swallow the rest of her anger. She hadn't come to argue—she needed answers.

"Look, I need to know what's going to happen tomorrow—tactically. This might be our last chance to prepare with how close our pursuers are," she said.

In the dim light, she thought she saw him flinch. "What is it?" she pressed. "Don't tell me you lost the dagger."

"No, I still have it." He studied the ground, silent so long she thought he wouldn't answer at all. When he finally spoke, his voice was raw with frustration. "There isn't much more to tell."

Her stomach dropped. He had to know what to expect, how else could she even hope to unsever magic?

A cold weight settled in her chest. "What do you mean?" she whispered.

Worry and exhaustion lined his face as he met her eyes. "I'm sorry. Very few beside your mother knew how to bind magic the way she did. It was a secret technique, not shared widely out of fear—fear of being forced to share it or defend it."

Her heart sank. If he didn't know what to expect, how could she possibly succeed? He must have read the fear on her face, because he leaned closer, catching her hands in his.

"You can do this. I know you can. At the very least, this illness the land is causing in you is proof that you have some sort of connection with it."

"Or I've contracted the rotting sickness myself," she said flatly.

He squeezed her hand, steady and warm.

"That isn't the case," he said firmly. "We haven't been here long enough for that to happen."

"You don't know that for sure though," she said dejectedly. "It could be whatever connection you think I have is just making the rotting sickness hit me faster. And what does it matter, even if it's not. We are just going to be killed or captured as slaves tomorrow when the groups catch up to us because I won't be able to figure out some way to reconnect magic to the land, after never witnessing or hearing how it works before in my life."

She knew she was whining but she didn't care. She needed to get it out or it was going to consume her.

"I do know it for sure," he said again, unshaken.

She almost scoffed at him, knowing his blind faith was not going to help when it came down to it, but instead she took a deep breath and tried to force the panic down. Worrying wouldn't change anything either. At the end of the day, she would succeed, or she wouldn't and then they would deal with whatever came after.

When she looked back at him, she caught the lines of fatigue on his face, the stubble shading his jaw, the ash smeared across his skin. He was as worn as she was, yet still meeting her with steady confidence. Against her will, a flicker of warmth stirred inside her.

It wasn't easy to push her anxiety away but in the end, she didn't want to waste her last night feeling sorry for herself or worrying over what might or might not happen.

She forced a wry smile.

"If you are so sure I will be fine then you owe me an apology for earlier. If I'm still going to be alive after tomorrow, you don't want me on your bad side."

A slow grin tugged at his mouth. "Hmm. That almost sounds intriguing."

She shoved him lightly, rolling her eyes. "I'm serious."

Somewhere along the way, she realized his arrogance had stopped grating on her. His face—once insufferable—looked less foolish and more...something else. Dangerous to think about. She gasped dramatically to cover the thought.

"Or maybe you were just jealous. I was the one with the secret, master plan this time."

He pressed a hand to his chest in mock offense, and she laughed despite herself.

The laughter faded, leaving a quieter moment between them. Derik's voice gentled. "As much as I enjoy this, you need sleep. We'll leave at first light, and you're distracting me from my watch."

"Uh, excuse me—you were fine distracting me in the swamp!" she exclaimed.

But, she could feel the weariness from her headache still lingering and it kept her from having too much real weight behind it. She stubbornly stayed put though, not wanting to waste what could be her last, peaceful moments sleeping.

Derik studied her, gaze lingering before he relented. "I'll make you another deal. You can keep me company—at great risk of distracting me from my duties—if you promise to at least *try* to get some sleep while you do."

"Done," she said, and moved to get her things. He put a hand on her shoulder and *tsk'd* at her.

"My rules and we need you to be in the best shape tomorrow morning so you will wait here while I get your things."

She grumbled a little but knew it wasn't a fight she was going to win. She let him fetch her pack and bedroll, settling down where he placed them, opposite his own. His leg rested against hers, a quiet anchor, and the unexpected closeness eased something in her chest.

She thought he might try to stay silent in hopes she would fall asleep but he surprised her. He was only able to give her part of his attention, but it was enough. He shared fragments of his childhood, tales of Gerin and Helena, small bits of mischief and memory.

He spent a lot of time talking about his sister and describing to Arine what she had been like. He used the past tense though as if she was not the same person anymore even though she was still alive, just broken. Arine supposed not being able to have control of your own body would make anyone a shadow of their previous self. It made her sad to think that Derik had lost most of his family aside from his cruel uncle.

She responded and asked questions but as the night wore on, she could feel her tiredness pulling her under no matter how much she fought. She was so relaxed listening to his random stories that she was lulled to sleep; the last thing she remembered was Derik regaling her with a particularly funny story about Gerin and Helena having a competition to see who could coax the most chickens into one of their rivals' bedrooms at the palace without anyone catching them.

A soft tapping pulled her back. Her eyes opened to see Derik's face directly over hers as he was trying to gently wake her. The sun hadn't yet risen, the red and orange rays just barely peeking over the horizon. It illuminated just enough to see the outline of his head in the grayish-red morning.

Their eyes met and she couldn't bring herself to look away. His mouth opened as if he was about to speak but he was frozen as their eyes stayed locked on each other. No one else stirred on the other side of camp yet.

Before she realized it, Derik's mouth was on hers. The kiss was fierce, desperate, as though he believed he'd lose the chance if he didn't take it now. Foolish or not, she kissed him back, clutching what little time they had left.

Then pain lanced her skull, brutal and sudden. She broke away with a gasp, clutching her head. Derik pulled back instantly, guilt flickering over his features. She reached for him, wanting him to know she wasn't angry—but he was already turning, moving toward the others, the fragile moment shattered.

He woke Cilia first and she quickly brought her over more medicine. Arine swallowed the paste quickly and waved the others off to pack. She needed a moment—not only to steady her throbbing head, but to make sense of what had happened. Derik had kissed her like it mattered, like there could be more waiting beyond all this. As the end drew near, that single moment rooted her in something real, something to hold on to.

After a few minutes crouched in the still morning, the pain dulled from a spike to a low throb. Her breathing evened out, her knees steadied, and she rose.

They marched on, Lian in the lead. The dark horizon gave no hint of how close their pursuers were, but Arine hoped that something had stalled them overnight. The worm creature was still out there, after all.

Eventually, the sun rose, casting a pale light over the horizon—and revealing their pursuers with stark clarity. No one spoke, but the silence was taut. Arine saw the glances over shoulders, the hushed exchanges between Derik and Gerin.

The enemy was closer than ever—so close the ash stirred up by their boots seemed ready to merge with their own. Every time Arine looked over her shoulder, her stomach twisted tighter. They picked up their pace as much as they dared, but they were closing in with terrifying certainty, and she had no idea how they would outrun them.

Worse, her own body was beginning to betray her. Though Cilia's herbs had kept the worst of her headache at bay, her limbs had started to feel like they were filled with sand. Each step became a battle. Cilia, still limping from her injury the day before, was also struggling to keep up. They were running out of time.

She looked up at the looming mountains and she could no longer see the white tops, no matter how much she craned her neck. A hollow ache settled in her chest. How unfair, she thought, that they could have come so far only to be stopped within sight of their goal.

Then their lizard companions shrieked—shrill, panicked cries that tore through the silence. The creatures bolted, spindly legs propelling them across the ashen plain faster than Arine had ever seen.

Too exhausted to question, too desperate to think, they lurched into motion after them. Ash sprayed beneath their boots as they ran, trusting the lizard's instincts more than sense. But the creatures were too quick—within moments they vanished ahead, their tiny movements leaving no clear path to follow.

They slowed, disoriented, scanning the barren horizon. Arine forced her bow up though her arms trembled with fatigue, her headache blurring her vision. The group still trailed them in the distance, closer than the morning, but not near enough to explain the lizards' panic. Around her, the others turned in restless circles, scanning the horizon as they tried to puzzle out what had sent their guides fleeing in such terror.

She was just about to lower her weapon when she felt it—a faint tremor beneath her boots. Her eyes shot to Derik, who was already frowning at the ground. The vibration was subtle at first, a steady hum rising through the ash. It grew, pulse by pulse, until dread settled over her.

A crevice was forming. Somewhere close.

The shaking intensified, rattling her bones. She just managed to resheath her sword before a violent jolt sent her sprawling along with the others. Cilia cried out as her injured leg struck the ground. The ash plumed up around them making it difficult to see as it coalesced, almost like fog. Arine struggled to rise, sluggish and dizzy, until she saw Ciran's eyes widen in alarm.

She looked down. The fracture wasn't forming nearby—it was opening directly beneath them.

Derik hauled her to her feet, shouting orders above the grinding roar of the rock deep below them starting to rip apart. Ciran fell down as he attempted to backtrack, the ground shaking so badly everyone was having difficulty standing. She and Derik had to help get Ciran's feet under him as they passed and together they moved towards where Jove was hurriedly scouting a path as quickly as he dared, conscious that sinkholes were still just as much a threat. When she glanced back, she saw Lian and Gerin supporting Cilia, all shuffling forward similarly behind them.

The trembling had grown into a deafening roar that rattled her skull and made it nearly impossible for them to stay on their feet. Twice, the violent jolts sent them sprawling into the ash, and behind her, she heard Cilia cry out again and again, each shout coming from a little farther back.

Then, with a sound like lightning striking stone, the earth tore open twenty feet away. Relief surged—they'd been spared—until another crack split across the ground, this time running straight between Arine and the trio still struggling behind.

Derik turned, taking in the new crevice with a single, assessing glance. Pain flickered across his face as he realized what had to happen. A heartbeat later, Ciran's expression mirrored the same dawning horror, and Arine's stomach lurched as Derik cupped his hands around his mouth and shouted over the roar.

"Turn back! You won't make it!"

He hauled her forward, iron grip clamped on her arm, half-dragging her toward Jove, who had already outpaced them and stood on a patch of seemingly stable ground. Every step jolted her battered body.

Ciran moved with them at first, mechanical and dazed, then suddenly, he broke away, sprinting back toward Cilia. Derik lunged to stop him, but Ciran ducked under his arm just as a final, deafening crack split the air. The ground heaved violently, throwing them all to the earth once more.

Arine slammed into the ash, breath knocked from her chest. Gasping, she lifted her head in time to see Ciran sprawled short of the new chasm, just on their side. Relief surged when she spotted Cilia, Gerin, and Lian safely across the divide, having heeded Derik's warning in time.

They were all pinned to the ground, the grinding of the stone underneath them almost deafening as it scraped apart to make a gap at least fifty feet across.

After several long minutes, the shaking started to die down. They tentatively got to their feet just as ash exploded along the newly formed crevice, billowing past sight. Even with their masks, the amount of particles in the air had them all coughing and choking.

When they could finally stand again, Derik steadied Arine by the arm, and together they joined Ciran at the edge. He stood staring through the haze at his sister and the others—trapped on the far side, injured, while the pursuers gained ground with every moment. Arine didn't need to see his face to feel the weight of the worry he felt for his sister.

No one spoke as Lian and Gerin helped Cilia to her feet. Everyone just stared at the gap knowing there was nothing they could do. Arine racked her mind for a solution, but none of their ropes would be long enough to span the distance.

Finally, Cilia called out to them, cutting through the stillness.

"Well, we can't stand around here all day. You guys have a lucky break, don't squander it. We will try to lead them away from you to buy you more time."

Arine saw Cilia motion for Lian and Gerin to help her rise so they could get moving, but Derik shook his head and turned to Gerin instead.

"Get to safety. Don't let her talk you into anything reckless. We'll find you when this is over. Hide in the forest—they'll likely pass you by and follow us. Without our tracks, we'll have the time we need."

Cilia bristled, ready to fire back at being called the instigator—though they all knew she was—when Ciran cut her off.

"Listen to him, Cilia. Get to the forest." He held her gaze for a long moment, then turned to Gerin, his expression still hard. "I expect her back in one piece. You'd better see to it."

Cilia rolled her eyes. "Please. I'll take care of them, thanks. Now, if any of us want to live through this, we'd better get moving." Her bravado faltered as she glanced nervously at the approaching shapes in the distance.

They were close now. With the flat land it was hard to gauge, but Arine guessed no more than half an hour until they were overtaken. A lump formed in her throat as she watched her friends hurry along the crevice's edge and wished she'd found the words to say goodbye before it was too late.

After a few paces, Gerin paused to heft Cilia over his shoulder, and he and Lian broke into a trot. From her precarious perch, Cilia turned back, waving grandly. The gesture drew a laugh from Arine—sharp and aching with the sting of missing her already.

They lingered even after their friends vanished into the ash cloud, waiting to see if the pursuers would break away to intercept them. Fortunately they clung to the safe path, unwilling to risk the sinkholes, and pressed on toward Arine's group.

As the enemy neared, their details sharpened. They were clothed in the same haphazard fashion as when they were at the Outpost and before. Some wore more expensive leather garments, while others had regular travel clothes and cloaks. A few bore the dark features of those from Yuak, while others were pale with red accents stitched into their attire, marking them as Syarans. All had weapons of some sort and looked absolutely terrible from their journey, giving Arine no small satisfaction.

There were at least twenty-five still left in the group. They didn't walk in any particular order so it was hard to get an exact count, especially with her headache starting to worsen. the most surprising detail was almost all of them bore some sort of injury. She saw some had clothes tied around wounds and some were limping as they kept up the pace their leader was setting.

She squinted, trying to pick out whoever led the group, but the figure stayed buried in the middle, their face obscured. What would have happened if the crevice hadn't separated them? The anger almost radiated off of them as they stared across the ravine, foiled from catching their prey after having been driven so hard.

None spoke but something seemed to root Arine to the spot, as if she needed some sort of sign or reason for why they were so intent on stopping them.

Movement rippled through their ranks as the leader barked guttural orders in Yuakan. As one, the slavers pivoted, following the trail Cilia and the others had left. Arine's heart clenched. All she could do now was pray her friends were fast enough.

She caught a glimpse of the leader as he lingered at the rear. His mask hid most of his face, but something about his presence prickled at her memory. He held her gaze a moment too long before turning away, and a chill threaded through her as she wondered what kind of person could command such merciless devotion.

Beside her, Ciran stared across the divide, face blank as he watched the slavers follow the path his sister had just taken. Arine reached out to squeeze his hand but he didn't seem to notice so she let it go, giving him some space. The herbs from the morning were starting to wear off and she realized Cilia had the rest of them with her, so there would be no relief now.

Derik's voice cut through the silence. "We can't do anything to help them, unless we get to the cave and finish what we started. After that...we'll find them." The last words were for Ciran, though he gave no sign of hearing. At Derik's signal, Jove moved to the front, and their diminished group pressed on into the ash.

•➺➺· ·◆· ·➻➻•

Chapter 29

Even with Jove spotting sinkholes almost as well as Lian, their progress was agonizingly slow as they made their way towards the base of the mountain. The sinkholes were so prominent and large now, Arine was starting to worry they would find their way entirely blocked by one before they could reach the safety of the cave.

Three times already they had to walk almost a half a mile westward before they could continue towards the mountains, and that was after either Ciran or Derik accidentally stepped into a sinkhole, requiring them to spend more time getting them out. Jove did his best to call out directions, but it seemed like it was getting harder to avoid them. They didn't dare go too far east, in case they ran into the Yuakans and Syarans coming around the crevice, so every detour pushed them west, farther off course.

Making things worse, Arine's headache was torturous again. Every step was a fight and more often than she liked, she had to lean on Derik or Ciran to keep moving. Nothing she did helped. She could only put one foot in front of the other and hope she didn't pass out again.

By mid-day her gaze was solidly on the ground as she continued forward, not daring to look elsewhere for fear of becoming too dizzy. She had no concept of how close they were to the base of the mountains, but she thought it seemed like the ground was getting less ashy in some patches.

The ash cloud from the earlier quake finally began to thin, but as they emerged from it, Derik swore under his breath.

"We're not done yet," he called, voice grim.

Her knees nearly buckled. She wasn't sure she could take more—another sinkhole, another beast.

He pointed west, and her stomach dropped. They had finally made it to the base of the mountains, but now she knew where the Decayed were.

A little ways ahead, clustered at the base of the mountains, a mass of bodies shifted restlessly. Most of the Decayed slumped against boulders or sprawled on the ground, but enough still wandered to make Arine's stomach knot. They didn't seem to be watching for intruders—just existing, broken and aimless—but their presence was far too close to the only path forward for comfort.

The four of them crouched low, though it was clear the ash would settle soon and leave them exposed. There was no time to find out why the Decayed had gathered here. Their only chance was to reach the pass before they were noticed. It didn't look like any of the Decayed would have the stamina to pursue them up the mountain side at least.

"We need to head there," Derik said, pointing toward a gap in the rocks. "The path to the cave will be in that area. It will probably be overgrown and hard to see, but it should branch right off the main trail to Falke. It won't take too long to identify it once we are in the pass. The climb will be the hard part. We'll be exposed the entire way."

"Of course. Nothing can be simple, can it?" Ciran muttered as he tightened the straps on his pack. Arine didn't even bother to voice her disappointment as she followed his lead, checking to make sure everything was secured.

Derik's gaze flicked to her. "How are you feeling?"

"Terrible, but I'm used to that at this point," she replied, not bothering to pretend otherwise when they could all see for themselves. "Maybe a little better. The pain's leveled off."

He gave a small nod, but his eyes searched hers. "Tell me the second you falter. If you need me to carry you, I will."

Before stepping away, he adjusted the strap of her pack—an unnecessary fix but an excuse to stay close a moment longer. Her pulse jumped as his fingers brushed her cheek and the tightness in her chest wasn't from the pain this time.

Then he turned to the others, motioning them forward. As one, they rose and sprinted toward the pass.

Arine risked one last glance at the Decayed. None seemed to notice them and as her group drew nearer the rocks, she had to keep her eyes on the uneven ground—jagged stones caught at her boots with every step.

They'd gained a small lead before the sharper-eyed among the horde caught on. The less-rotted ones raised their voices in broken cries—some hoarse and rasping, others bubbling with wet, guttural sounds where the rot had eaten their throats. The noise sent a shiver down her spine, but the sluggishness of their movements eased her dread. Even with her slowing the pace, the Decayed wouldn't be fast enough to cut them off. The possibility of having to cut them down had made her stomach twist.

They scrambled up into the pass, clambering over boulders that blocked the trail. Arine's breath came ragged, but something shifted inside her. The pounding in her head, the leaden weight in her limbs—gone. She almost stumbled from the sudden absence of pain. For the first time in days, she felt only her ordinary fatigue, sharp but bearable.

She wanted to weep with relief. Was this why the Decayed had gathered here? Drawn and trapped by the sickness? Whatever the reason, she didn't dare question it now. She was simply grateful to move under her own strength, especially with the climb ahead.

Derik was already scaling the slope, hunting for the safest line up. At the base, faint grooves in the rock hinted at an old path, but rockslides and drifting ash had erased most of it. The trail narrowed until only one could climb at a time. As Derik hauled himself higher, Arine and the others waited below, hearts hammering, praying no pursuers appeared before it was their turn.

Two massive boulders shielded them from sight—but also blocked their view of whatever might be closing in.

"I'm going to see how far behind they are," Jove said, then slipped to the edge of the boulder and crouched low, moving fast and silent around the corner.

Ciran scowled at his retreating back. Arine knew he probably thought it was a stupid risk, but he didn't say anything.

She forced herself to stay still, every muscle trembling with tension. When Derik finally made it high enough to create enough space for her, she didn't hesitate. She began climbing, palms scraping rough stone, while Ciran stayed behind her, eyes sharp for pursuit.

She had gone only a few feet when Jove's voice carried up.

"Three Decayed—faster than the rest. They're close. We might stay ahead...if they can't climb."

A shiver rippled down her spine. She gritted her teeth and pushed harder, arms aching, desperate to gain ground. Loose pebbles slid under her boots, each step tested before she dared shift her weight. Twice she slipped, skidding back before clawing upward again.

Minutes later, Ciran started after her. They just needed a little more time for Jove—but time was running out. Boots crunched below.

Jove spun to meet them, blade flashing as the first Decayed lunged.

She forced her attention upward, heart hammering in her throat. She wanted to glance back, to know if he was holding them off, but one slip would send her tumbling straight into the fight herself, probably with a broken bone or two.

Arine tried to close her mind off to the fact that they were poor souls who had just been overcome with the rotting sickness. Her father could have been one of them if he hadn't gotten the medicine from the King.

She pushed the thoughts away, she could only focus on reaching Derik. Above, he'd found a ledge wide enough to rest. She fixed her gaze there, climbing faster. At last the sound of fighting below faded, replaced by the scrape of boots as Jove started upward again. Relief burst from her in a ragged breath.

When she reached the ledge, Derik leaned down and hauled her the last few feet. She murmured her thanks and braced against the rock, waiting for the others.

Ciran and then Jove finally scraped over the edge behind her. She shifted to peer down into the pass—only for her stomach to drop at what she saw.

Most of the Decayed were still where they had first seen them, but a significant group had come after them and were clamoring towards the pass. But that wasn't what made Arine's stomach clench. The Yuakans and Syarans had caught up. They were still some distance out, but moving fast—too fast. In minutes they would be in the pass. It seemed the crevice hadn't extended far enough to the east to stop them.

She pointed over to them and Derik nodded grimly. They were trapped. Despite their own predicament, her heart ached for the Decayed still milling below. They weren't climbing, weren't fleeing, just waiting to be butchered. She shouted and pointed down, but none so much as looked up—except one. A man her father's age, gaunt in tattered clothes, a belt knife dangling uselessly at his side. He met her gaze for an instant, then turned away, rummaging absently at the mountain's base.

Derik drew her focus back, pointing toward the ledge where the cave entrance was said to be. It still lay some distance away, and the mountainside around it showed clear signs of collapse. It had large chunks torn away, forming the heaps of rubble scattered below.

The path up was mostly climbable, but the final stretch narrowed into a precarious ledge, dangerously exposed. If any skilled bowmen lurked among their pursuers below, that last section would be a deadly bottleneck.

They hurried upward, desperation lending speed. Sweat stung Arine's eyes, her palms slick and treacherous on the stone. More than once she had to wipe them against her tunic before reaching for the next hold, praying she didn't slip.

Remnants of what looked like old switch back marks helped guide them to the start of the narrow part without incident. Even so, Arine felt like her heart was beating out of her chest from the need to go fast, coupled with the fear of actually trying to move fast up the uneven slope.

When she dared glance back, her gut twisted. The pursuers had reached the bottom of the cliff—and behind them lay a trail of bodies. She spotted the older man, hacked down and discarded like refuse.

She tore her gaze away, stifling the bile that rose in the back of her throat, and focused on Ciran as he edged out first to give Derik a break. His pack created too much space for him to face outward, so he had to turn inwards towards the mountain as he creeped across. She took a deep breath, wiped her hands one more time, and followed. The ledge was just wide enough for her feet, but the shifting breeze and loose stone made every step feel like a gamble. She gritted her teeth, refusing to let the thought of one misstep send her spinning into the void.

Arine had barely crossed a quarter of the ledge when the sound she dreaded hissed past—an arrow, streaking for Ciran. She gasped, fingers scraping the rock as she flattened herself against the mountainside. Another shaft clanged off the stone where she would've stepped if she hadn't stopped.

Her pulse spiked. Should she go forward or retreat? Before she could decide, a bowstring snapped behind her—Derik and Jove were firing from their covered position. Her limbs felt heavy, stomach roiling with panic, but she forced herself to keep moving. Stopping meant dying. She varied her pace to throw off their aim, muttering a silent thanks to the men holding the shooters at bay as two more arrows skittered wide.

Ciran reached a stone shelf and ducked behind boulders. Relief flickered, but she had no time to savor it; her own survival balanced on each step. Her legs trembled, palms slick as she gripped the crumbling wall, the ledge narrowing beneath her boots. Her tongue stuck to the roof of her mouth as she crept forward, every breath harsh in her ears. As she approached the end, her anxiety spiked like a blade to the gut, fear of getting so close and failing at the very end almost overwhelming her.

She saw Ciran fumbling for his bow but he was too slow to cover her. A final arrow hissed toward her—she could somehow feel it coming before she heard it. With no other choice, she flung herself forward, pain stabbing through her thigh as she slammed onto the edge of the ledge hard.

The shaft skimmed past harmlessly, but she landed inches short of safety. Her left leg scrabbled for purchase while her pack dragged her sideways, pulling her toward open air. Fingers clawed at the crumbling rock, finding nothing. Panic surged as she twisted, fumbling at her straps—then a hand clamped beneath her arm.

Ciran hauled her up, steady and unyielding, until she tumbled onto solid ground. For a moment she could only lie there, muscles trembling, her body realizing just how close it had been. Breath ragged, she forced herself upright, grabbed her bow, and slid into cover beside him. A shaky laugh slipped out before she could stop it.

Ciran's brow rose at the sound, but he quickly went back to loosing arrows to cover Derik's crossing.

"Just remembering the day we met," she muttered, knocking her own arrow.

He huffed, half amused. "Different story if I hadn't saved you then too." His voice was a little breathless.

Arine let the moment steady her, then glanced across the pass. Derik was already halfway over, braving arrowfire. She spotted the archers hiding behind a large boulder. One of them lay dead already, but there were three more still shooting. She took aim and waited for an opening, but her arrow flew wide as they ducked.

"Feels like a lifetime ago, doesn't it?" she murmured when the archers vanished from view.

Silence answered. She turned and caught the pallor of Ciran's face, his breath ragged. Grabbing his shoulder, she spun him—his next arrow flying wild. "What are you doing?" he snapped.

She ignored his protests and saw his pack had hidden the wound: a deep graze scored across his right flank, blood seeping steadily.

"You're hurt. If you don't wrap that, you'll bleed out." She shoved him aside and took his spot at the front.

He didn't argue, which only confirmed how bad it was. Meanwhile, the enemy archers had regrouped, firing at Derik and Jove again. Derik was close enough that they still had one chance to hit him. She drew, aimed, and released—just as the enemy fired back.

She frantically tried to track their arrows. The first went wide, while the second flew right at Derik. She gasped. Somehow, he froze, eyes flicking to hers across the chaos. The arrow slammed into the cliff, shaft quivering almost against his face.

She was sure her mouth was hanging open in shock, too stunned to do anything before she remembered the danger they were in and aimed another arrow at the group on the ground. She dropped another archer with her shot, their body slumping from behind the boulder. Then Derik vaulted the last stretch, landing beside her. In one motion, he turned and drew his bow again, and together they drove the remaining bowmen back while Jove scrambled across to safety.

All four of them pulled back from the edge, finding relative cover from the bowmen on the ground. While Jove had had the easiest crossing, all things considered, his face was still pale as he surveyed the group now starting their own climb up the mountain. Arine quickly helped Ciran finish rebandaging his side. The bleeding hadn't stopped, and he likely needed stitches, but all she could do was cinch the cloth tight and hope it held. They were almost to the end; he would make it until then at least.

When they almost had Ciran ready to go, Jove began laying out his weapons—testing his bow string and setting his sword on the ground beside his loose arrows. Arine paused in her work, frowning.

"Are you leaving them here?" she asked.

"No. The group is still climbing up the first section. This ledge is the best place to hold them off. I know enough about these two to know neither one of them is leaving you so that leaves me to hold them off while you...do whatever it is you need to do in there." His tone was steady, almost matter-of-fact, as he positioned himself.

A knot of fear and gratitude twisted in her chest. She glanced at Derik, who gave Jove a solemn nod.

"Hold them and we will be back before you know it. I'm not sure what will happen when Arine makes the connection so try to stay back from the ledge just in case things get...rocky."

He threw a wry smile in her direction. She rolled her eyes at the attempt at humor, though she knew he meant it to ease her nerves. Still, fear whispered that she might not see Jove again. On impulse, she scooted over to him and gave him a quick, fierce hug. He stiffened, surprised by the show of emotion before waving her off as he muttered something about needing to get ready.

With Derik carrying a makeshift torch and Ciran able to stand now that he was rebandaged and not leaking blood quite as fast as before, the three of them gathered their weapons and turned toward the looming cave mouth. Ciran's gaze lingered on Jove one final time and Arine thought he might try to talk him out of staying behind, but in the end he kept his silence.

Together, they stepped forward—Derik leading, Arine in the middle, Ciran close behind. She felt as if the whole world was watching even though only a handful of people knew what was happening. They were finally here and if all went well, they would be able to heal the world and right the wrongs of the past.

They slipped inside, the cave mouth narrowing as it tunneled into the mountain. Derik's torch lit only a few feet ahead, leaving the depth of the passage a mystery. Small creatures scuttled in the dark, claws clicking against stone, and Arine prayed none were mutated. Her head throb had miraculously eased, but she doubted they could survive another fight in their state.

At first, they moved in silence, straining for any sound beyond the rasp of their boots and the scratching of vermin. When nothing stirred for some time, Arine let her shoulders relax a little.

As they squeezed through a narrow section, she noticed a sheen on the wall.

"What is this?" she asked, pointing.

Derik lifted the torch higher. Golden lines spiderwebbed across the rock, glittering faintly. Arine brushed the wall, the slick veins of metal mixed with the jagged stone.

"Gold used to be mined from these mountains. This must be a shaft from before the Severing," Derik said.

Ciran shifted impatiently, unimpressed.

"How far is it? I don't like leaving Jove out there for long."

"It can't be too much longer," Derik said. "He'll hold them. That ledge gives him the angle he needs—unless something unexpected happens."

"That's what I'm worried about," Ciran muttered.

Before Arine could answer, a faint glow drew her eye.

"Look!" she whispered, pointing ahead.

They quickened their pace, leaving the gold vein behind. Arine's nerves sparked as the tunnel opened into a cavern. A small stream ran through it, faint daylight filtering in from a crack in the ceiling. There didn't appear to be any paths that she could see. She looked over at Derik for confirmation and he gave her a brief, tight nod. They were here. The muscles in his jaw were clenched tightly—she didn't like that he was so obviously worried.

Arine, half from thirst and half to delay, hurried to the stream. Seeing that it looked as clear as any other she took several large gulps. She didn't even care if it was tainted with rot or anything unseen, she was so thirsty she would have drank from a mud puddle at this point. The others joined her, filling waterskins in case they had to flee quickly.

When she finally rose, her chest tightened. As she examined the room fully, a wave of unexpected emotion overcame her. This was where her mother had died. She could almost pretend she remembered it, though she knew it was only her mind trying to fill the void. She blinked hard, forcing the tears back. Derik gave her a moment before stepping close, his hands warm on her shoulders.

"Are you ready?" he asked quietly.

She squared her shoulders and nodded. "I'm ready."

Derik nodded and slowly pulled the knife out. He turned it over in his hands, staring at it for a long moment, as if weighing whether to give it to her. At last, he held it out.

Arine lifted her hand slowly, pulse quickening. What if simply touching it triggered something? She hesitated, then reached forward—

"Wait!" Ciran's voice cut through the cavern, sharp and urgent. Arine froze, her hand suspended in midair.

Chapter 30

Ciran lunged forward and smacked the knife from Derik's hand. It clattered across the stone, skittering to a stop near the stream.

"What are you doing?" Derik demanded, stepping after it. "She has to use the knife—I'm not trying to hurt her, you fool."

Arine glanced between them, her pulse spiking, confusion knotting her chest.

"I knew you couldn't be trusted," Ciran hissed. His blade was out in a blink, the point flashing toward Derik's chest. "Is Jove in league with you too?"

Derik froze, shocked, hands half-raised in surrender. Arine was still trying to understand when the sword tip pressed closer, halting him mid-step.

"Ciran, stop! You don't understand—the knife is how it works," Arine said, her voice strained.

His eyes stayed locked on Derik. "He was the one who told you that, wasn't he?"

"Well... yes, but it's not like he's going to stab me with it," she shot back, desperate to calm him.

Derik stood rigid, Ciran's blade at his throat. He didn't dare speak, but his eyes widened, and Arine's heart hammered in her ears. She didn't understand what was happening.

"Right, because bloodbound magic can only be released by the person whose blood bound it." Ciran said flatly. "I remember the story,"

Derik's gaze narrowed and Arine's breath caught. There was only one time that story had been told.

Her voice dropped to a whisper. "It was you. You were listening that night... the night of the attack."

The horror of it struck her like a blow. "You've been lying to us—to me—this whole time? Have you been leading the Syarans and Yuakans here too?" The questions tumbled out half-accusation, half-disbelief, because she couldn't bring herself to accept it—not from him.

"No! He and Jove are working with them," Ciran snapped, his glare fixed on Derik.

Arine wondered if her head wasn't as clear as she thought—none of this made sense. Her thoughts spun as she tried to follow.

"I admit I was listening that night, which is how I know no one else was. After they kept following us—even through the swamp—I knew someone had to be leaving signs. It couldn't have been Matthew, and Gerin grew less likely by the day. I had stupidly started to believe Derik meant well, stopped watching him as closely, and chased a different hunch. But clearly, he's just as good a con man as his uncle."

The sword at Derik's throat trembled, close enough to draw blood as Ciran shook with rage. A thin trickle slid down Derik's neck while he held still, eyes locked on his accuser.

Arine shook her head, unable to make sense of it. "Wait, what? If Derik wanted to hurt me—or hand me over—he could've done it at any point before trekking through the swamps and Decayed Lands, don't you think? He could've simply given me to them the first night at his camp."

She tore her gaze from the blade and caught Derik's furious glare fixed on Ciran. She recognized the look—he was already calculating whether Ciran's injury gave him an opening, seconds from doing something reckless that could doom them both. But Arine was still unsure of what had even set Ciran off in the first place.

Ciran nodded toward the fallen knife. "I'll show you what I mean. Grab it and bring it here. Don't try anything, or I'll incapacitate him."

Arine bristled at being ordered, but after only a beat she hurried to grab the knife. As her hand closed around the hilt, she felt nothing. A flicker of disappointment ran through her—she had hoped the unsevering might come naturally.

She held the blade up, just out of Ciran's reach.

"Turn it over," he demanded.

She flipped the knife over, examining the pommel. It was the same one from the night with the King—golden vines curling around a sapphire set in a gold setting.

"Did you know blood binding can be layered?" Ciran asked, his voice edged with accusation.

"No..." she admitted. She hadn't even known blood binding existed until Derik told her.

"I'm not shocked Derik didn't fill you in, but seeing as it was his uncle's favorite pastime before the Severing, I know he is aware of the practice."

Ciran pushed the sword a little deeper and it looked like Derik was almost having to hold his breath so as to not impale himself.

"Until I understand fully, do you mind not slitting his throat?" Arine asked, irritation sharpening her words as she fought for patience.

Ciran eased back slightly and Derik flicked his eyes toward her in brief thanks, but she ignored him. Whatever this was, Ciran clearly believed it mattered.

"The King kept his ability to wield a secret for the most part because he was so weak. But what he lacked in power, he made up for in deviousness. He was the one to discover that he could first blood bind objects to himself and then later bind the same object to another wielder. When he was near them, this allowed him full control over them. He spent most of his time creating a trove of artifacts that when activated by another's blood, unbeknownst to them, would also bind their magic. And since magic is part of who you are—so are you."

Arine took in the revelation slowly, her mind still not willing to accept what Ciran was saying. If that was true, the thought was horrifying. Losing control of your own body—it was unfathomable. Did the person even know they were controlled? Did other people know or did they just think you were the one making the decisions even though it was someone else. Though she had to admit the similarities were strikingly similar to how the King was controlling her and Derik by using their family as collateral.

But Ciran wasn't finished. "And you know what his favorite disguise for such objects was? A ring." He nodded toward the knife in her hand and, with his free hand, traced a circle around the golden setting of the sapphire.

Arine blinked. What she'd assumed was the stone's mount was in fact a band. And not just any band—it was the same design, minus the colored veins, as the ring Derik had once placed on Haverson's table. She remembered his reaction then, and a cold rush of betrayal knifed through her. For a heartbeat she almost hurled the blade away, but the knowledge that doing so would doom them all stopped her hand.

"If you wield to unsever magic," Ciran continued. "You will restore magic, but you will also be bound to the King forever."

It seemed like time stopped as she slowly looked up to meet Derik's eyes. The King had sliced her hand that night in front of Derik in the castle and then Derik had joined her on this trip to keep her in line. She had been so dumb thinking he might actually care about her, when all along he had just been trying to lull her into a false sense of security so she never questioned anything and allowed herself to be bound to the King. How could he?

Derik shook his head. The motion cut his skin on Ciran's blade, and Ciran pressed harder, forcing him to hold still. Arine's memories tumbled over one another—every moment with Derik suddenly poisoned with doubt. She looked down at the knife in her trembling hands. She had come this far, so many people had died and were dying right now, for what?

She looked back up just in time to see the arrow streaking from the cavern's mouth. She gasped. Derik saw her expression and lunged aside despite the sword at his throat. He wasn't quick enough. The shaft drove into his back, the tip punching through his chest.

Only his desperate sidestep spared his heart. He crashed to his knees, gasping, blood pooling fast. When he tried to rise, his movements were sluggish. Arine's stomach clenched as she spotted the tar-black sheen on the arrowhead. Paralyzing poison.

Ciran froze in shock, his blade wavering, as another figure emerged from the shadows. The man's bow was already drawn, another blackened arrow aimed straight at Ciran. Gone was the shy, quiet companion they had traveled with. Jove's face twisted with hatred, his voice hard.

"Not another step," he snapped.

"And here I thought it would be hard to fool the smart and cunning nephew of the King," he snarled as he kept his bow pointed at Ciran's chest. "One wrong move from either of you and you're dead too."

Arine tried to think but her mind felt like putty. All she had in her hand was the small knife. She wouldn't be able to do anything before he released the arrow so she stayed still, rooted to the spot, mind scrambling to catch up.

Jove moved toward Derik, who lay with dark blood seeping through his shirt at the ribs. "What will they think when I tell them you were so distracted by these fools that you never even noticed me?" he asked, nodding at Ciran. "Thanks, by the way, you and your sister made it easy."

He sneered at Derik as he curled into a ball on the ground, groaning. Arine wanted to move—to help him—but Ciran's life was tied to that bowstring. Arine almost wondered if she hadn't passed out and this was some odd hallucination. First Ciran, then Derik, now Jove? Was there anyone who hadn't been trying to lie, betray or kill her at this point?

"Why?" she croaked.

"You'll learn when the others arrive. I don't speak for Syere," Jove said. He glanced at her for weapons. Seeing only the knife, he refocused on Ciran and loosed an arrow.

"No!" Arine cried, yanking for her sword—too slow. The arrow clipped Ciran's blade and pinged away. Jove's surprise snapped into fury; he dumped the bow and drew his own sword.

"No matter what you do, you won't be able to leave here. The others will be here in moments and then you will wish you had let me kill you."

Ciran didn't respond as he feinted to the side and spun back to swing at Jove. Jove parried just in time and pivoted.

Ciran was a better swordsman on a regular day, but not with the arrow wound. She knew he wouldn't be able to hold Jove off for long. And she still had no idea why Jove—or the Syaran's would be allied with the slavers and following them. Clearly this was coordinated if they had slipped Jove into the group to lead them here—but why?

"Jove, please tell us what is going on," Arine called in desperation.

He ignored her, his face a mask of hatred as he continued to hack at Ciran's defenses. With no better options, Arine darted around Ciran, aiming to trap Jove in a two-on-one—but she was seconds too late. Jove parried at the last instant, pivoted, and sliced Ciran's sword arm. A scream burst from Ciran's throat.

Arine didn't think, she just lunged. Her blade drove into Jove's chest.

Her hand slipped from the hilt in shock as he staggered back; blood fountained from the wound. The man who had traveled with them, ate with them, laughed with them for weeks crumpled to the ground, dead.

It took her a moment to wrench her gaze away from Jove's motionless body, her heart hammering in her throat. The reality of what she'd done pressed down on her, but she forced herself to remember why she had done it. Ciran. Derik. She turned and scrambled to Ciran's side, nearly tripping over her own feet.

Dropping to her knees, she saw a deep gash carved across his chest as he lay sprawled on the ground, eyes closed. Panic surged through her as she pressed trembling fingers to his throat. A pulse fluttered weakly against her touch, he was still alive, but only just.

Blood was everywhere; the sword's poison had spread through his whole chest from the angle of the cut.

A scraping sound made her whip toward the cave mouth, braced for more attackers. But it was Derik, crawling toward her, the only movement the poison would allow him.

Arine hauled him up as best she could. Pulling the arrow would only speed the poison's spread — she knew that much. There was nothing she could do to stop what was already in him.

Derik's voice came thin, each word an effort. "I'm sorry," he rasped. "I swear I didn't know for sure but…I suspected when he gave me Haverson's ring the morning we left and told me Haverson would obey anything I said when it was presented to him. Even then it was only a guess though—he hid it from me too. On the way here I tried to get the band off, but nothing worked." A cough racked him, blood splattering with the phlegm.

Arine tried to shush him, but he shook his head as he continued, words barely above a whisper.

"I didn't tell you more about magic because I couldn't stomach leading you to it. And then I got to know you and I didn't want you to hate me. I told myself I'd tell you and then each night passed and I couldn't find the words; I was a coward. I thought maybe, if it truly was a binding ring, we could destroy it afterwards or find a way to undo it once magic was back."

Arine stared down at him, his words washing over her like cold rain. "My life for the world's, right?" she said softly. "It's an easy trade—for you."

He swallowed, pain making his face strain. "I didn't want—" His voice broke. "I don't want that for you, but I didn't know what else could be done to save everyone."

Her chest felt tight, too full of things she couldn't name…betrayal, disappointment, hurt that burned hotter because part of her still wanted to believe him. Part of her still cared.

She hated that even now, with his confession laid bare, her heart was fighting her mind. That she could feel both disgust and longing in the same breath.

Her hand trembled as she pressed it to the ground beside him, needing something solid to hold her steady. She searched his face, wishing she could hate him, wishing she didn't care whether he lived or died. But she did. And that hurt most of all.

"You should have told me," she said at last, tears spilling down her cheeks.

"I didn't know what to do," he wheezed. "I thought I could figure it out before it was too late. I'm sorry."

Her chest heaved with a ragged breath. She shook her head, unable to look at him for a moment because it hurt too much to see the regret in his eyes.

"How can I ever trust these words?" she whispered. "How am I supposed to believe anything you say when you kept this from me?"

"I know. I've never had someone I could trust before—and I was afraid to lose you, lose—us. I know I was a fool. Please, believe me, Arine." His voice cracked on her name, and she realized she was fully supporting his weight now.

Blood pooled around him and his face was drained of all color. She lowered him to the ground slowly as he closed his eyes, breath coming in and out in ragged bursts. Her hands hovered helplessly over the arrow, knowing pulling it free would only make things worse. She was angry and devastated at the different betrayals. Why couldn't he have just trusted her?

Arine rummaged through her bag, searching for bandages before hurling it aside, knowing how little they would help. How could this be happening? Derik and Ciran lay dying just as they were about to finish this. It wasn't fair. She had done everything asked of her—survived the swamp, crossed the Decayed Lands—and now her friends were bleeding out before her eyes. Was this payback for her mother's choices?

Her heart felt crushed beneath the weight of it. She looked down at the knife in her lap, hating what it had done to her mother and the choice it was now forcing on her. Did she even want to unsever magic anymore? She could face death—her friends already had—but could she face a life enslaved to someone else's will? Life without freedom was no life at all.

Her conversation with Derik rang in her ears—just words and posturing about which was the harder path. She almost laughed at the irony. Now here she was, staring at the knife, seconds slipping away while her friends bled. The group hunting them would arrive at any moment. If she delayed much longer, the chance would vanish forever.

She forced herself to look at her friends lying motionless nearby. They had been willing to die for her. She thought of the sick families across the kingdom, of a land starving and decaying. Deep down she knew: if she did nothing, she would never forgive herself. She would never rid herself of the guilt.

She drew a steadying breath. She would find a way to break the binding. She would never stop fighting. She understood what Derik had meant now when he said it was a harder path to live and continue to fight instead of flaring quickly as a martyr. A resolve hardened within her. This would not be the end—not after everything they had endured.

The King's words echoed in her mind. She had to cut her hand and draw blood. With trembling fingers, she gripped the blade and sliced her palm before she could change her mind. Blood welled up. She held her injured hand over the other, letting it drip onto the knife, willing with all her being—something.

The moment her blood touched the blade, the world erupted.

Chapter 31

Arine was certain she was exploding. Her body no longer felt like her own; fire raced through every atom of her being. Pain tore through her, timeless and unrelenting, as if she had been trapped there for hours—or days—while some essence ripped her apart from within. She couldn't move. The only sensation left was the unbearable pulling of her body into pieces.

For a heartbeat she longed to let go, to surrender and drift into peace, but something—some small, insistent tug—held her back. Back to where? She couldn't recall anything except the surge of energy rushing through her and spilling back into the world. It felt like suffocation, yet she hadn't been breathing to begin with.

She tried to force her body to respond, to claw back even a shred of control, but grasped at nothing. Irritation flared and she struck out with her mind against the force ravaging her. She pushed with every ounce of will, shoving it down.

Slowly, second by second, the pressure began to ebb. She didn't let up, knowing instinctively that if she faltered, it would consume her. She fought on in that void, clinging to herself, resisting the current of raw energy flowing through her. And in the midst of it all, one thought anchored her: she would never again be pushed around—by anyone, or anything, not even this. With one final flare, the essence was gone.

Arine's eyes shot open and she filled her lungs with a ragged breath of air. She was drenched in sweat, limbs shaking. Memories slammed back into her all at once, her body quivering with the echo of whatever she had just unleashed. She was alive. She ran her trembling hands over her arms and torso to confirm.

Exhausted but seemingly uninjured, she tried to sit up. Yet something had changed—she felt a new sensation inside her that she couldn't quite explain. It was like she had been missing a piece of herself her entire life and had never even known what being whole felt like until that moment.

She raised the arm that had held the knife, but before she could examine it, the mountain groaned. A deep rumble shuddered through the cavern as cracks raced across the stone at her feet, splitting open to reveal a jagged vein of gold. She reached down to brush the almost glittering surface—pain lanced through her body, sharp and pulsing. She gasped and stumbled back, tearing her hand away. The agony vanished as suddenly as it had come, leaving her breathless and trembling, her heart hammering against her ribs.

The ground still trembled faintly beneath her, and she blinked through the haze of pain just in time to see Derik's hand slip from her leg. His grip broke, his arm falling limp. A cold dread replaced the fading burn in her veins. She caught his wrist, finding his pulse thready and fading. Whatever she had done—it hadn't helped him or Ciran

Desperation clawed at her. She snatched an arrow, reaching for the strange power now humming inside her. Maybe she could imbue it—like the healing rods she had heard of—make it something that could save them.

Her hands shook as she clutched the arrow and tried to focus, willing it to become more than wood and feather. She should be able to do something. Anything. But nothing happened. The arrow remained lifeless, as if mocking her desperation.

Panic rose in her throat. She squeezed her eyes shut, every heartbeat screaming that she was running out of time. She knew she had restored the world's connection to magic; she could feel it, warm and alive, just beyond her reach.

So why couldn't she shape even the simplest artifact? She cursed herself for not pushing Derik for more training despite his avoidance of it. Her breath came shallow and fast. She tried again. And again. Still nothing.

With a strangled cry she hurled the arrow; it clattered across the rock. Tears blurred her vision. "Why?" she screamed into the depths of the cave. She gripped Derik's shoulders, urging him to stay awake—stay alive—until she could figure something out. How could the world be so cruel, when she had done everything she could to make this right?

She fell to her knees beside him, her body trembling with helpless frustration. The truth settled like a stone in her chest. She couldn't save him. No matter how desperately she tried, she couldn't do anything.

She lifted her gaze to the jagged gap in the cavern's ceiling, a perfect slice of blue sky above. The mountain shuddered again, dust raining down, as if the world itself taunted her. A strangled sob tore from her throat. She tipped her head back, her voice raw and ragged as she screamed up at the heavens, pouring out every ounce of rage, grief, and despair she had left.

Suddenly something inside her stirred like a dormant part of her had awakened. Power roused, answering her grief, her fury. Trembling, she tried to direct it into Derik and Ciran, willing it to heal them. It surged out of her, a current she could barely hold onto, and poured into them. For an instant, their bodies glowed with a soft, impossible light.

Her shock shattered her fragile grip, and the power burst outward in a blinding wave. The mountain rattled, walls quaking, grit raining down—then the light vanished as suddenly as it had come. Arine swayed, vision swimming, her limbs turning to lead. Exhaustion dragged at her bones. She nearly collapsed where she knelt.

She sat there, fighting to stay conscious, barely daring to breathe—much less hope she'd actually healed them. She closed her eyes, tears slipping down her cheeks as she waited in the suffocating silence.

Seconds crawled by before the mountain convulsing worsened, shaking loose a slab of rock that slammed into the far wall. Still, she stayed where she was, arms wrapped tight around her legs. If her friends couldn't leave, she wouldn't—not only because she might not have the strength, but because she couldn't bear to.

Only the sounds of the mountain rumbling around her echoed in her ears as tears streamed down her face.

Through the silence a familiar voice reached her ears. "I knew you could do it."

Sobs broke free, but she still couldn't open her eyes, afraid her mind was playing tricks on her. Only when she felt his hand on her shoulder did she open them—first meeting Derik's steady blue gaze, then past him to where Ciran was slowly sitting up.

"I thought you were dead," was all she managed to get out between gasps, not sure which she was addressing first.

Ciran stared down at himself in disbelief—the wound gone beneath the tatters of his shirt. She glanced at Derik's chest. The arrow lay in two splintered pieces in a pool of blood. It must've been forced out by whatever she'd done to heal him. Without thinking, she touched the healed skin, the dried blood still marking where the arrow and poison had been.

"I'm sorry," Derik whispered again, and those simple words dragged her back to herself. She clenched her jaw, refusing to look at him, afraid of what might spill out if she did.

She staggered to her feet as the mountain trembled, rock fragments pelting the ground around her while she searched for the knife she'd dropped. Her gaze found it lying among the rubble. With a shaky breath, she bent and picked it up, half expecting something to surge through her again. Nothing happened. Swallowing hard, she turned it over in her hands, almost afraid of what she might see.

The sapphire was still there, but the gold band was gone. Her stomach dropped. She searched the ground, careful not to brush the gold veins that now spidered out throughout, until Derik stooped and lifted something from the dust. He turned it over once, then held the ring out to her.

If she hadn't known what it represented, she might've thought it beautiful—veins of deep blue marbled through gray, the exact shade of her eyes. She reached for it slowly, dread tightening in her chest. The instant her fingers brushed the stone, another searing pain tore through her, so intense it felt as if her body had been set alight. With a strangled cry, she dropped it, clutching her hand against her chest as the aftershocks of agony pulsed up her arm.

She stood, panting, watching as Derik bent to retrieve it, her pulse still thundering. Then it hit her—why Haverson had recoiled from the purple-veined ring Derik had shown that night. She couldn't hold this one, just as he hadn't been able to hold his. Could she have it if it wasn't touching her?

Before she could find out, the mountain roared again. A deafening crack split the air as a slab of stone sheared free and crashed down only feet away, shards exploding outward in a storm of debris. Arine threw herself to the side, the impact rattling through her bones. The severing knife flew from her grasp, skittering across the stone before vanishing into a jagged fissure.

She scrambled toward it, peering into the darkness, but the crack dropped too deep to see. Derik appeared beside her, brushing dust from his arm as she shook her head, breath coming fast.

"Hold onto the ring for now," he said, voice grim but steady. "We'll talk about it—thoroughly—when we're not about to be buried alive."

Derik nodded and slipped the ring into his tunic pocket just as Ciran rejoined them, her pack and his weapons slung over his shoulder.

"I still think we should tie him up and leave him," Ciran said, without a hint of sarcasm as his gaze flicked to Derik, "but prudence says we'll need him to get past Jove's friends—unless the quake tossed them off the mountain."

"I haven't decided what we'll do with him," Arine replied curtly as they hurried toward the door.

Derik's eyebrow arched—curiosity and caution flickering in his expression—but she offered no explanation, and Ciran didn't press it. He grabbed the fallen torch and took point—the position Derik usually held.

As they moved through the tunnel, they finally caught a bit of luck. Several Yuakans and Syarans lay crushed beneath collapsed stone. They didn't bother to stop to check for survivors.

They tried to move as fast as possible, but it was much harder when it felt like the mountain itself was trying to shake them to death: Arine needed help whenever they had to climb over anything, still weakened from what she had done in the cave. They were knocked over, sprawling a few times, and when they were getting close to the end, they found a giant boulder had fallen in the middle of the passage, blocking the entire space. They had to climb over it to squeeze through a small gap between it and the ceiling to proceed.

As soon as they hit the ground on the other side, another quake ripped through the mountain, sealing the opening behind them with a deafening crash. Arine swallowed hard, realizing how close they'd come to being crushed—or trapped forever.

Without a word, they redoubled their pace to the mouth of the cave. When the first shaft of sunlight pierced the widening crack ahead, they bolted for it—Derik half supporting, half dragging her forward.

When they finally burst into daylight, Arine froze. More bodies littered the ledge. A handful of Syarans and Yuakans had made it outside, but the mountain hadn't spared them. Five broken forms lay scattered across the rocks, crushed beneath slabs of stone that had sheared from the slope.

Her gaze drifted to the jagged edge where part of the shelf had been. Judging by the missing figures, more had fallen into the abyss below.

She scooted closer to the edge, knowing there could still be able-bodied enemies below ready to shoot at them, and peered over. At first, she didn't understand what she was seeing. She'd expected to find the remaining Decayed along with any Yuakans or Syarans who hadn't made the climb—but the people barely registered, because the land around the mountain was in color.

She hadn't realized how much she had missed the colors of the world after traveling so many days in the gray ashy landscape until she saw the vibrant green grass and the multicolored hues of the flowers. As for the temperature, it was cold, very cold—a stark contrast to the warmth of the swamp and the tepid air of the Decayed lands. She had almost forgotten they had chosen to travel during the onset of winter. The oasis before her stretched only a league or so beyond the mountain and would soon succumb to the frost. Arine could only hope that the land would now be able to heal and come spring, there would be a rebirth of life across the scarred terrain.

She drew in a deep breath of cold air and smiled. Derik and Ciran mirrored her awe, sunlight catching on the sharp lines of their faces. She was still furious at them—sickened by the lies—but relief cut through the anger. They had done it. They had reversed the Severing and saved everyone, whether they deserved to or not.

They grinned at each other like fools. When she met Derik's eyes, she forgot—just for a heartbeat—the depth of his betrayal. His smile was bright, until it faltered and confusion crossed his face. He opened his mouth to speak, but shouting from below cut him off.

They turned toward the valley where a small battle was raging below. She squinted, trying to figure out who was fighting and immediately recognized the remaining Yuakans and Syarans. She could see a man, presumably the same leader from earlier, laying about with a massive sword that took two hands for even him to wield. At first she didn't recognize who was fighting them until she realized...it was the Decayed. Or rather, the formerly Decayed.

Her actions in the cave seemed to have healed them, similarly to Ciran and Derik. She wondered if reconnecting the link between magic and their world or the power she had used to heal her friends had brought them back to their former selves. Either way, they were definitely in better shape, and they greatly outnumbered the slavers.

From the ferociousness of their fighting, they did not seem to be pleased about their companions being mercilessly killed earlier. The Yuakans and Syarans fell quickly. Only the large man and a few others managed to retreat deeper into the pass before vanishing. It was over faster than she had expected since the Yuakans and Syarans were well trained, but she supposed the fervor of the newly healed Decayed would not be denied.

She sank back, resting as the mountain's quaking eased. For a moment, she let herself feel the joy of it all. They had succeeded. They were alive. It was more than she'd ever dared hope.

The narrow path back down the mountain still looked intact; once the tremors stopped, they'd be able to cross it. Without arrows flying, it might almost be easy.

As they waited, she reached inward for the new part of herself—the one that let her wield. She could still feel it there, like another layer of skin or muscle. No amount of focusing made anything like the healing that had happened in the cave take place again though.

She wanted to ask Ciran and Derik if they felt an ability to wield, but didn't know if that would be awkward if they hadn't inherited the ability. So she stayed quiet, eyes fixed on the valley below. She wasn't ready to speak to either of them anyway.

Even though she didn't want to face the many revelations in the cave, her thoughts turned back there no matter how hard she tried to avoid it. She didn't know if she would ever be able to trust either Ciran or Derik again after all the lies. She honestly didn't think she had ever met a group of people she cared so much about that had so many twisted secrets tangled up with them.

As she sifted through everything they'd said, a thought struck her—safer than the others she'd been avoiding.

She turned towards Ciran. "When did you know it was Jove?" she asked him.

"I suspected, but never had proof," he admitted. "He was smart—never said too much, kept to himself—but the explosion at the Outpost was strange. How else would he have been so close, unless he caused it himself to try to make an opening?"

"Why didn't you say anything?"

"I didn't want to risk alerting him until I had something concrete to prove to the group. With myself being the usual suspect if I didn't have facts to back up an accusation like that, well you remember how tense it was getting. I'm sure it wouldn't have ended peacefully."

"Next time, maybe just bring up your concerns," she said wryly. "It might save us some trouble."

In the sunlight, without ash clouding the air, he seemed different. She couldn't quite place it, but as she studied his face, it was clear something had changed. Had restoring magic given him the ability to wield—or was she just not used to what he looked like without any ash covering his face anymore?

Ciran grunted in reply, then nodded toward the former Decayed milling about below. "Why do you think they were all clustered here?"

She tore her gaze from him to look down. "I was thinking about that on the climb. Maybe it's tied to the pain I felt. Maybe they suffered something similar until they reached the epicenter."

He frowned in thought. "Would that mean they have a similar connection to the source—like you?"

"Maybe. I mean, why do some people get the rotting sickness and not others? There has to be a reason. Maybe it was mostly those who would have been wielders."

"That does make sense. They could be from families who no longer had enough status after the Severing to afford the medicine."

"What about you—do you feel anything different now?" she asked tentatively.

"Uh oh," Derik said, cutting in.

Arine shut her eyes briefly. *What now?*

"That looks like a fairly large group," Ciran muttered, his tone making clear how little he wanted another fight.

Arine opened her eyes and glanced past a group of former Decayed below who were trying to restore some order. A few cast wary glances upward but made no move toward the mountain—so that couldn't have been what Derik meant.

She lifted her gaze further, past them to the east, where the ashy lands of the Decayed lands still covered most of the terrain up to the edge of Killian Forest. The telltale ash cloud hovered over a large group coming their way—fast enough that they had to be on horseback. They were sticking to the edge of the mountain ranges so they didn't have to worry about sinkholes. At their pace, they'd reach the survivors below within the hour.

"We'd better move—get down and out of sight before they arrive," Derik said uneasily.

He didn't have to tell her twice. They gathered their things and hurried back across the ledge. As she'd predicted, everything was much easier without arrows raining down every few seconds.

The trail down proved trickier. Arine spent more time sliding on her backside than walking, somehow managing to avoid any major cuts or bruises. It wasn't graceful, but she'd take it.

Just before they reached the base, the thunder of hooves echoed up the slope. The former Decayed had wisely fled in the opposite direction as the well-armed riders approached, leaving the three of them alone—for now.

They ducked behind a large boulder, hoping the newcomers would chase the fleeing Syarans or Yuakans instead of poking around the deserted area.

They were wrong. The riders pushed through the pass, heading straight for them.

"What do we do?" she whispered. She didn't recognize any sigils on the men's clothes, so she had no idea who they were or what they wanted.

"Stay low—they might still pass us," Derik murmured. He peered around the boulder, and when he turned back, worry shadowed his eyes. His gaze flicked toward Ciran. There was an odd note which she couldn't quite place and she cocked her head at him to try to puzzle it out. Before she could speak, Ciran suddenly sprang up.

"Cilia!" he shouted, running toward the approaching riders.

Arine turned to Derik, whose agitation was unmistakable. "What's wrong?" she asked cautiously.

"Whatever happens, let them take me. Don't interfere," he said urgently. He gripped her hand before pushing her forward. She stumbled, moving before she even realized.

"Why, what do you mean? Who are they? If they are with Cilia, it will be okay," she said, turning back but he just looked at her with a pained expression.

The riders were nearly upon them now. Cilia's voice reached her, greeting Ciran with relief but she stayed focused on Derik.

"Gerin and Lian aren't with them," Derik said quietly.

A spike of fear ran up her spine. She couldn't think of any scenario where either of them would have left Cilia or refused to come with her, especially given her state.

She had no time to consider it before Ciran appeared around the boulder. He was flanked by two soldiers with swords drawn at their sides.

"Please step away from the Prince, ma'am," one of the soldiers—a woman—ordered.

Despite everything, Arine was struck by her presence. The woman wore full armor, her hair cropped short like a man's, and held her weapon with the confidence of a seasoned fighter. But it was her expression that made Arine's stomach twist—pure hatred, directed squarely at Derik.

Arine instinctively stepped between them, but the soldiers maneuvered her aside—firmly, though not cruelly. A man seized Derik, dragging him to his feet. He wrenched Derik's arms behind his back so roughly that Arine thought his shoulders might pop from their sockets.

She spun toward Ciran and Cilia. "What are you doing? Who are these people—and why are you letting them treat him like this?"

Cilia sat mounted on horseback, her leg bound but her bearing unshaken. She clearly held authority—neither she nor Ciran were restrained. They both had the decency to look ashamed, but neither moved.

"They won't hurt him too badly," Cilia said, though the assurance rang hollow. Blood trickled from Derik's split lip as the soldiers dragged him to a nearby horse and threw him across the saddle, bound like a common criminal.

Arine turned on her friends, outrage and confusion warring in her chest. "Who are they?" she demanded. "What are they doing with him?"

"They're taking him back to our father," Ciran said quietly.

"Who is your father?" Arine ground out.

Ciran met her gaze, "His name is Vanin."

Acknowledgements

Thank you to **Andie Smith at Sun & Spines Editorial** for your insight, care, and dedication to making this story stronger.

To my proofreaders—**Alex Deal and Camille Gupta**—thank you for catching what my eyes could no longer see and helping this book shine at its best.

To my **family**, who never let me forget why I started: thank you for your love, your patience, and your belief in me, even when I doubted myself. To my husband, for your unwavering support through long nights and endless rewrites, and to my children, for reminding me daily that adventure and imagination are worth holding onto.

And finally, to **the readers**—thank you for stepping into *The Withered Realm*. I hope you find a little courage, a little wonder, and a reminder that even in a broken world, there's always something worth fighting for.

About the author

Brittany M. York was born in 1988 in Iowa City, Iowa. She loved to read from an early age, memorizing the children's books that were read to her at bedtime before the words made sense on the page for her. Brittany grew up in Meredosia, Illinois, a small town where corn fields dominated most of the horizon and fantasy novels became an escape to another world. She graduated from Illinois State University with a degree in Communications. Eventually, she moved to Dallas, TX where she pursued a career in Auto Finance before she began writing in 2018.